AWRY

CONDUIT ONE

MEGHAN CIANA DOIDGE

AUTHOR'S NOTE: CONTENT

The Conduit series is set in a secondary world that shares many common traits with our own. The divergences in language, governing bodies and countries, technology, and geography are all intentional choices by the author.

Content of note: violence, language, attempted kidnapping of a minor, attempted sexual assault, teenage intoxication, death of a family member/grief, memory loss, mention of illegal human and shifter trafficking, and history of childhood abuse (not main character).

Overall series note: ***spoiler alert*** While the romance arc is a very slow burn, the love interests are half-brothers (no sword-crossing) and the main character doesn't have to chose between them (aka MFMM why choose).

Content warnings and a list of tropes/themes can be found on MCD's website: www.madebymeghan.ca/awry

AUTHOR'S NOTE: READING ORDER

Awry is the first book in the Conduit series, which is set in the same universe as the Mirth duology. While it's not necessary to read all the interconnected series, the ideal reading order is as follows

- Awry (Conduit 1)
- Grand Romantic Delusions and the Madness of Mirth, Part One
- Grand Romantic Delusions and the Madness of Mirth, Part Two
- Snag (Conduit 2)

More Conduit Series books to follow. Reading list doesn't include the shorter stories interspersed throughout all of the main series, but more information can be found at www.madebymeghan.ca.

FOR MICHAEL

Always ready for a new adventure as long as I'm with you, in this universe and beyond.

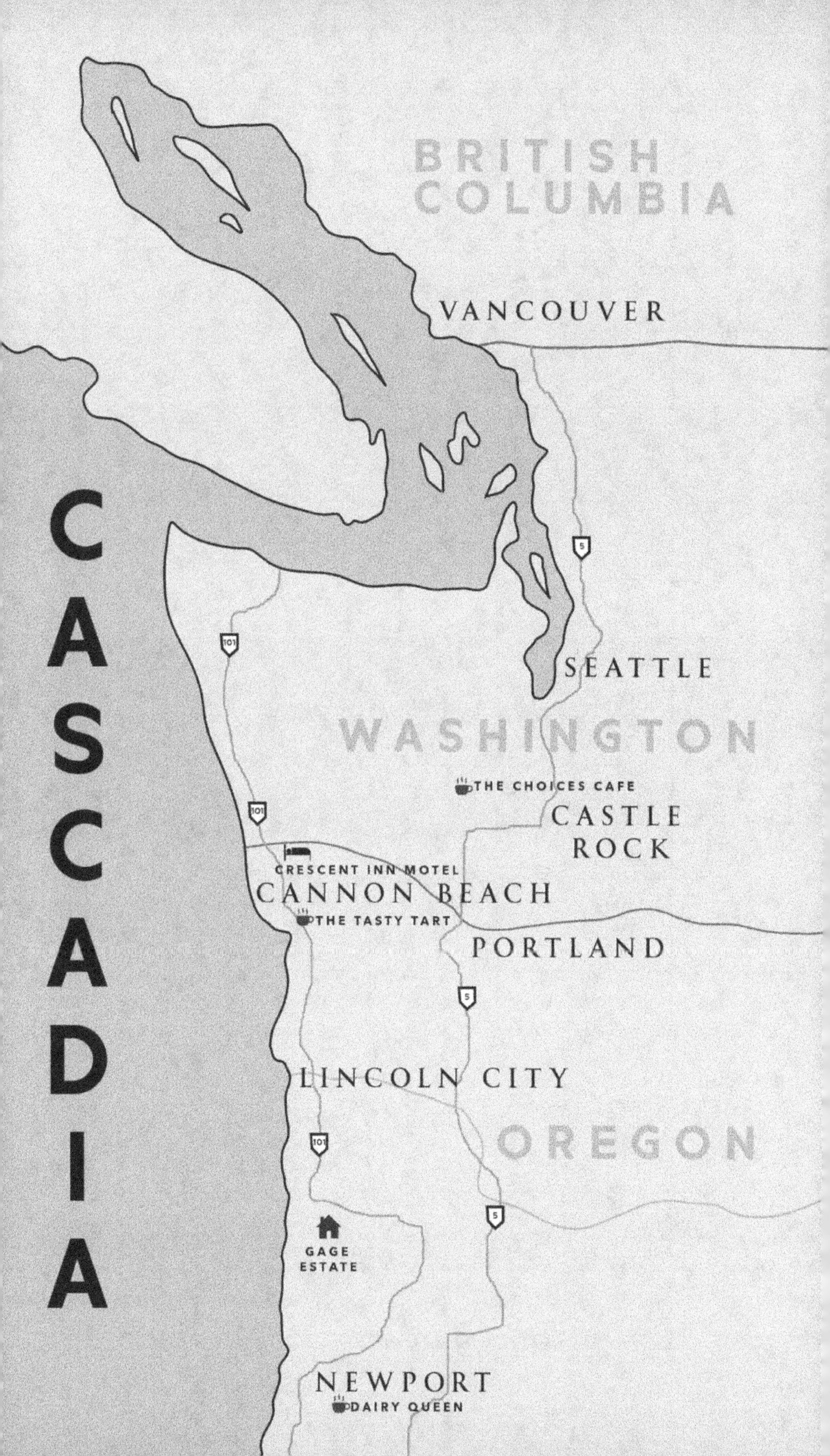

BRITISH COLUMBIA
VANCOUVER
CASCADIA
5
SEATTLE
101
WASHINGTON
THE CHOICES CAFE
CASTLE ROCK
101
CRESCENT INN MOTEL
CANNON BEACH
THE TASTY TART
PORTLAND
5
LINCOLN CITY
101
OREGON
GAGE ESTATE
5
NEWPORT
DAIRY QUEEN

INTRODUCTION

On my way to investigate my aunt's untimely death, I chance upon a teenager with purple eyes. Her destiny is so vibrant, so intertwined with the essence that fuels all our lives, that I cannot stand to see her caged and crushed.

What I don't know is that rescuing the teen isn't chance or happenstance at all. It isn't just another random bit of destiny I can *fix*. It's a snag in the weave of the universe that unravels ... everything.

I am exactly who I am meant to be. I belong to no one but the universe. My destiny was spun and measured before I was born. I never really had a choice. But the path that brought me to becoming the Conduit at least a century before my time has been manipulated. And along the way, I've somehow lost far more than I ever knew I had.

Friends.

Lovers.

Soul-bound mates.

More than just my life has been twisted, all our fates ripped away.

And I remember none of it.

ONE

ZAYA

THE GIRL AT THE COUNTER IS MAYBE FIFTEEN. Tiny but long limbed, her multicolored scraggly hair hiding her face as she bows her head over a greasy plate of fries. But I saw the deep blue of those eyes, verging on violet, as she cast her gaze around the cafe. Her two companions, who couldn't look more like stereotypical bikers if they tried — leather jackets, beards, club patches and all — are easily three times her size. As they'd entered, their grip on her upper arms was beyond proprietary.

The violet eyes are as rare as the power the girl has simmering in her veins. But it's the glimpse I catch of the raw skin on her wrists when she pushes up the sleeves of her overly large, ratty sweater that disturbs me more than the eyes or the power I can feel all the way from the other side of the cafe.

I touch the essence amulet I wear under my own

sweater. Unlike the girl's hand-me-down, my sweater is luxuriously soft, thin-knit black cashmere, intentionally oversized and tailored to slide artfully off one shoulder and be figure flattering. For spending the day in the car and the cooler weather, I paired it with merino wool-lined faux-leather pants and bespoke lace-up black leather boots.

It's early March. Which, on the West Coast of North America at least, means rain and early-morning fog and crocuses poking their way through the awakening earth. It also means I'm technically only three weeks away from my thirtieth birthday, despite still looking closer to my midtwenties. As I always would.

The girl's legs are bare. And dirty. If she's wearing shorts or a skirt, I can't see either. She isn't carrying a purse, nor does she appear to have a phone. Anyone else her age — essence-imbued or not — is usually glued to at least one device at all times, even this deep into the so-called wilds of Cascadia.

The cafe is filled mostly with nulls, aka those who can't wield essence in any form. They'd all gone silent when the trio entered, and the murmur of conversation is slow to pick up in the aftermath of their bombastically noisy arrival. An older woman had hustled out from the back kitchen area, smiling broadly — wearing the expression like it might be armor — and nudging the other younger female server aside to take the bikers' orders at the counter herself. The owner of the cafe, I assume. She ignores the violet-eyed teenager.

Everyone ignores the girl wedged between the bikers perched on the stools at the front counter. Their huge thighs press against hers, caging her between them as they mow through their burgers.

The younger server, her curly blond hair streaked pink and pulled up in a bun, sets my Caesar salad in front of me, cocking her hip against the edge of my table, effectively blocking my gaze of the girl and the bikers.

Deliberately?

"Thank you," I murmur.

"Eat, princess," one of the bikers snarls, not all that quietly. "I ain't got no problem forcing you." His accent is slanted in a Southern direction, and he chuckles darkly, pleased with himself.

"Anything else?" the server asks me stiffly, her order pad in hand and her expression guarded.

I glance at the salad, served in a large bowl. It's taken longer to make and serve than the burgers and fries the trio at the counter ordered. The creamy dressing is so thick that it's difficult to discern the green of the lettuce. I should have known better than to order a salad in a roadside diner.

But that's not why I already know I'm not going to sit here and eat it.

I open my mouth to ask for the bill. But then I say instead, "A chocolate milkshake and chicken strips ... to go, please."

And with those words — fed to me by a power both beyond myself yet flowing through me — I do something I almost never regret, no matter the personal cost.

I give the threads of fate just the tiniest of twists.

The server frowns.

Not completely aware of what I'm doing — my actions abruptly dictated by the innate *knowing* I triggered before I'd even thought things through — I feel the certain-to-be-stupid, utterly foolhardy plan unfold with each choice I make in the moment. I reach into the side pocket of my bag and pull out the fold of twenty-dollar bills I shoved in there before leaving Seattle, where I overnighted. The cafe is outfitted with a sleek tablet set to the side of the cash register on the far end of the counter, near the front door. But the wilds — aka the stretches of neutral and not-so-neutral territory between major cities or shifter-claimed territories — still prefer cash exchanges.

Peeling three green hologram-stamped bills from my short stack, I set them on the edge of the table. "I'm actually in a bit of a hurry."

The server's gaze flicks over me, then across the table to take in the brand-new, top-of-the-line phone and the designer sunglasses set next to my elbow. Both items are ridiculously expensive. But even though I could now rather suddenly afford many more such things, I didn't pay full price for either. I rarely paid full price for anything.

I trade in favors, not cash. Though owing me isn't a burden to be undertaken lightly.

Beyond the windows, the sky is gray, rain threatening. But I would wear the sunglasses in the bright interior of the cafe if I could get away with it. My eyes are perpetually sensitive to light. And for those who know what they're looking at, they firmly mark me as awry. The sensitive sight is one of the drawbacks of the type of power I wield as effortlessly as breathing.

The other not-so-effortless manipulations I can achieve? They occasionally come at a far steeper price.

The server is still checking me out, or rather trying to figure me out, shifting her gaze to the black vegan-leather designer bag on the bench seat beside me. The large bag might be more understated, but it's also worth more than the phone and sunglasses put together. I don't much go for labels, and the one typically found on this designer's work has been removed — or rather, never adhered — before it was gifted to me. A thank you for something I can barely remember doing.

That intermittently hazy memory isn't typical for an awry with my affinities. But nothing about me or my affinities is typical.

I add another twenty to the pile of bills on the edge of the table, though it's possible that doing so will make me even more memorable. My actions are being guided by that same flicker of *knowing*, and unless it comes with a miasma of death and destruction, I usually follow my own innate senses.

To be completely clear, if only to myself — I usually follow whichever way my essence and the universe itself leads, headlong into mayhem and potentially self-destructive deeds.

The server sniffs offishly, then picks up the eighty dollars and tucks it into her bra in a practiced, minimal move. A tattoo rings her wrist. At first, it appears to be a string of daisies, similar to those necklaces that kids make in movies and storybooks. A purely intentional choice, given that her name tag also reads 'Daisy.' But hovering at the beginning of what's starting to feel like a major *knowing*, even one deliberately triggered, my unintentional focus reveals a shimmer of numbers hidden underneath the flowers, etched into the delicate skin of the underside of her wrist.

The numbers are an illegal trafficking tattoo. The shimmer that only someone like me can detect is a nasty twist of fate manacled around her wrist. It's old and stretched, though she's in her early twenties at most, and she'll wear it — her entire fate anchored in it — until she embraces the After.

I look away quickly before she notices and understands what I've seen of her.

I shouldn't have stopped for lunch. I shouldn't have pulled so far off the highway. I should have driven straight through from Seattle to Portland, then cut out to the coast. Not because I'm vulnerable or memorable — I am, and nothing I do can make me otherwise. But because I shouldn't get involved. I'm a so-called *power* now. The comings and goings of servers in diners and bikers in neutral territories should not be my focus.

From when I pulled up, I remember the name on the sign outside — Choices Cafe. Epically ironic.

Because I only have responsibilities. To the universe. Literally. Whether or not I've taken those responsibilities on by choice. For the record, I haven't. None of it has ever been a choice. Not truly.

The server tucks her order pad in the pocket of her white apron, her gaze flicking to the window, to the parking lot. Two huge motorbikes — the massive noisemakers the bikers pulled up on — occupy the spots directly across from the front door. But the server instead curls her upper lip at the 1972 Silver BMW 3.0 CSi parked in the very last spot adjacent to the windows. Adjacent to the booth I'm currently occupying.

"Nice ride," she sneers, either pissed or jealous. Hard to tell.

"My uncle's," I say, only partly lying. Because he's dead, the car is part of the estate I inherited from him, and he was just a few more generations removed than 'uncle' implies.

She snorts, stepping away and crossing around the counter instead of in front of it — which would put her within arm's reach of the bikers — to input my new order on the tablet next to the cash register. She makes an obvious effort to keep her gaze on the kitchen through the pass-through window instead of looking ahead while walking. Beyond simply ignoring the bikers and the girl, she's actively trying to avoid drawing their attention.

I wonder how much market share the nearest biker club holds in the local, highly illegal human and shifter trafficking trade. I just as quickly shove the thought away. Not my business. Really, really not.

Then most contrarily, I set my gaze on the teenager with the violet-tinged blue eyes again, already knowing without actually formulating a plan that I'm about to do something really stupid. That I'm about to follow a prompt I've yanked forth from the universe, about to snag a thread of fate and twist it to achieve an outcome that isn't technically mine to direct. Likely more than one thread. And in hindsight, I already swayed onto this path rather thoughtlessly, from the moment I pulled off the highway and took the detour that brought me here.

But at least I'll have a milkshake and chicken strips, right? Yeah, I just went with the random requests that occasionally filtered through me from the universe. Or at least I did so most of the time.

I push the uneaten salad slightly across the table, lengthen the strap of my bag, secure the phone within its depths, then sling it across my body.

Then I wait. More often than not, the execution of a knowing — intentionally triggered or otherwise — is all about timing. Miss that timing, and the backlash isn't ... well, terribly nice. Most often for me.

While I wait, I pull the amulet out from the depths of my sweater. The gold-caged pink diamond is uncut but polished — and some 200 carats in size, so large that it fills my palm as I close my hand around it. The gemstone must be worth ... well, millions on the open market. But in the world conducted and controlled through the harnessing and wielding of essence? It's priceless. So it's a good thing only I can wear and wield it.

I blink down at my hand. My nails are painted in a pastel rainbow, hugely contrasting my normal black-on-black-on-gray wardrobe.

Damn.

I had thought that choice of color my own, whimsical but as a response to the unrelenting gray rain of the late-winter season. Except my nail color matches the unwashed hair of the teenager with the purple-hued eyes.

A *knowing* doesn't usually sneak up on me like that. Explode full force in the moment? Yes. Carefully, deliberately curated by myself to elicit the response I want? Yes. Sneaking through my subconscious days ahead? No.

Energy from the gold threads encasing the essence amulet thrums under my palm. My deliberate skin contact calls forth a welcoming pulse of power. Because it wants to be used, to be useful. And I'm the Conduit for that power.

Literally.

The Greeks would have called me one of the Moirai, the personifications of destiny. To Romans, I would have been one of the Parcae. For the Norse, the Norns, and to the Celts, the Matres. Except I have no sisters, I'm not actually a goddess wielding divine power, and I'm decades away from being able to control the power anchor and conductor currently hung around my neck.

My most recent inheritance, which includes the necklace, is only three weeks old, on paper and in my blood.

In this incarnation, I'm simply one of the awry — meaning I'm capable of harnessing and manipulating essence from any and all sources in a world where the awry are greatly outnumbered by the nulls, shifters, and mages. Any and all of whom occasionally hunt us en masse. Except in the pockets of the world in which our kind has claimed territory, we awry are mostly solitary, or part of small families whose living members span generations. If our essence is dim enough, we hide in plain sight because that's easier than trying to function in any mage or shifter community, where pure power and bloodlines determine privilege.

The biker nearest to me stiffens, glancing around, then tilting his head and inhaling deeply to sample the air.

I'd known he was a shifter. But apparently, his senses are acute enough to pick up subtle shifts in essence resonance.

I *know* both bikers the same way that I could know, would know, far too much about any of the people occupying the diner if I spent a few minutes studying each of them. Even though up to three weeks ago, that aspect of my abilities was little more than mental sleight of hand or a parlor trick.

The cook slides a white paper to-go container and a white plastic to-go cup through the pass-through window from the kitchen. The server is already waiting for them, fiddling with the coffee maker and keeping as far away from the bikers as she can.

I cinch my bag a bit tighter across my chest, then shove my sweater sleeve up my right arm, exposing a gold-scaled, dark-brown topaz bracelet that twines around my wrist and up my forearm. An almost imperceptible shiver runs through the flattened spiral of metal and carved gemstone — a reaction to the shift in temperature.

Unlike the necklace, the bracelet isn't a newly acquired inheritance. It passed to me from my mother moments before her death. Again, literally. I was nine years old. My mother was far too young to have her thread snipped. For one of us — the awry — at least.

The server snags the to-go containers and stuffs them both in a brown paper bag, along with some napkins and a paper-wrapped straw.

The threads woven around the purple-eyed teenager pretending to eat her fries condense under my regard. She's surrounded by a multitude of spirals and offshoots leading in all directions. She won't be embracing the After anytime soon. No, the bikers have different plans for her. Long-term plans.

I try to not shiver at the thought.

Unsuccessfully.

The biker shifter on the girl's right glances up from his phone, looking around with a scowl. He can feel me or scent me and the power that stirs through my steady focus on the teenager.

What do I smell like underneath the vanilla and cocoa-butter elixirs I slather myself in daily? Still the wild mint that grows along the beachfront of my aunt's West Coast property? Or has my inheritance sharpened my scent into something more robust?

And ... it's not my aunt's property anymore ...

The shifter biker glances at the door but doesn't turn around. Doesn't look my way. He's never come across the likes of me, never scented the level of essence I wield.

Because I exist only in the *Now*.

If the mythos threaded through our family history can be trusted, there is another of me — similar but not the same — in the *Before*, and yet another in the moment of the transition to the *After*. Beyond that? That's for mages with an affinity for the dead to glimpse. Though not, as far as I know, to understand.

The server drops the takeout bag on my table, barely pausing as she crosses by me. I'm up on my feet, the rolled paper at the top of the bag crumpled in my left hand as I shove my own bag behind me, so it hangs against the small of my back. The strap is tight enough across my chest that it stays in place, as I'd intended. Bumping into anything in the next couple of minutes could disrupt the flow.

How do I *know*?

I just do.

I ghost the server's footsteps past the next table, then the next, practically breathing down her neck — and momentarily cloaking my scent in the sweet lemon hand soap and barely discernible kitchen grease clinging to her. This close, I can also pick up a hint of musk that tells me she too is a shifter of some sort. A quiet undertone. So she transforms into a prey animal, unlike the heavily scented predators situated on either side of the teenager with violet-tinged eyes.

The server senses me in her next step. And in the following breath, the thread I've been waiting for, that I've been coaxing forward with pure intent, manifests between the teenager and me.

I step around the server and deliberately make eye contact with the nearest shifter biker right before I slip on my sunglasses.

Both bikers swivel in their seats to watch me pass.

Yeah, my eyes are pretty striking.

The name patch on the leather vest on the larger of the two, skin tanned and dark beard clipped along the edge of his jaw, reads 'Breaker.' 'Chains' is the other biker. Pale skinned with dirty-blond hair in a messy bun and a scraggly beard, he appears just slightly shorter than his biker brother, though nowhere near as burly. I don't have the time to study the emblem emblazoned on their club patch, or the context with which to decode it. I assume they're locals, but I really have no idea.

I flash a toothy, welcoming smile at both bikers, then completely and utterly dismiss them a moment later. Turning my back and deliberately triggering their prey drive as I step toward the door.

My hand presses against the crossbar handle, and the door swings outward to my touch. The bikers' regard feels hot, verging on stifling, against my back. I don't try to entice them further. I need them distracted, not charging after me. I've gotten out of worse situations, but that was before my power was such an obvious snare.

I step over the threshold, and the already tenuously thin connection I've made with the purple-eyed teenager grows taut. Before it frays, I *press* an intent — *bathroom* — along that thread.

I feel the girl shift on her stool behind me. And for a moment, I worry that she is too powerful for me to *push*, that I'll need more time, more focus, to even get the attention of the thickest, clearest of the threads within the tangle of destiny that surrounds her.

Breaker stands, his phone held loose in his hand. His essence is sharply tainted — contaminated somehow? — to my senses. Almost nauseatingly so. He swivels in place, canting toward me. Still unpracticed at focusing with quite so much power to anchor me — aka the amulet that's currently dangling between my breasts — I'm inadvertently towing him in my wake.

I might like to pretend I'm clever, but subtlety has never been my strong suit.

The door begins to swing shut behind me.

My *push* hasn't worked.

It was stupid and rushed, and now I'm going to have to shake off the —

"Bathroom," the teen says. "I need to pee." Her accent is Southern as well. But pure and sweet, though her tone is meek, scared.

Chains, the still-seated biker, grunts, hauling her up by the upper arm as if she can't walk on her own. As if she can't be trusted to take three steps down the short hall that bisects the cafe.

As I'd guessed, Chains isn't that much shorter than Breaker, but his potent essence is less … malicious. Not that I'm usually able to sense the fine stitching of an individual's essence … except when it's pertinent to executing a knowing. Though it's possible I've inherited a new level of awareness. Or it's simply information I'm going to need.

If Chains follows the teen into the bathroom …

I shove the possibility away, thought unfinished.

I might manifest an event into being just by thinking about it. If it's already set, I can't do anything about it. Except react in the moment. Which is how I'm accustomed to moving through the world anyway, so no big deal.

I keep walking, aware that the other biker, Breaker, is still watching me as he leans against the front counter with his phone partially raised.

Shooting video?

He's going to be really surprised when he tries to watch it. A still photo of my vehicle might be more reliably captured. But since it came with my inheritance — well, one of my inheritances, one of over a half-dozen classic cars I now own — I doubt it. When I'm skimming a knowing, my path is usually obscured from pure tech. Usually.

Occasionally, though, the universe has different plans, which is why I also have backup systems in place. Again, usually. This particular path hasn't been … well thought out. So my backup systems will be more about cleaning up in the aftermath, rather than the usual process of fogging the edges of my present.

I cross to the classic BMW, hoping the car might draw some of the bikers' focus off me. Bikers like cars as well as motorcycles, right? I unlock the passenger side, placing the to-go bag in the front seat after pulling the milkshake out of it and tucking it into the aftermarket cupholder. Then I step around the car, keeping my pace casual.

I'm moving along a quiet eddy of *intention* now. It stirs around my booted ankles. I unlock the driver's-side door, sliding my bag behind the seat.

Breaker's interest in me is an ever-thickening thread between us. Normally, I would endeavor to thwart such a connection — because with it, I can feel that he is a *power* or a subset of a power. Part of a pack, no doubt, but also something I've not encountered before.

I don't ever deliberately draw the attention of power.

At least I didn't up till three weeks ago, when my own mostly clandestine existence took an abrupt turn.

Instead of ignoring Breaker's regard, I look up, fortifying the connection between us as I slip into the driver's seat. I can't see Chains from the corner of the building. But the older woman, the owner, has stepped out from the kitchen and appears to be talking to someone at the mouth of the hallway. Hopefully Chains.

Breaker sneers at me through the cafe window. He reaches down and cups his genitals … so apparently he's flirting, not contemplating kidnapping me?

Or maybe both are one and the same for him.

Nausea flutters in my belly, and I whisper a quiet prayer to a god who doesn't have any reason to listen to me that the purple-eyed teenager is too young to have caught Breaker's or Chains's attention. That they haven't raped her or forced her to service them.

Then I deliberately ignore the utterly unhelpful focus of my own thoughts. Instead, still smiling broadly, I send a flicker of *intent* through the temporary connection I've fortified between Breaker and me as I start the car.

At least I'm hoping the connection is temporary. Again, the tenor of his essence concerns me.

I add a thought, a suggestion, along the thread stretching between us. *Something important needs your attention.*

I turn the key in the ignition, and the car's engine awakens with a smooth growl.

Breaker glances back over his shoulder toward the cafe owner and whoever she's flirting with — the cocked hip and her reaching out to lightly brush her hand across a broad, leather-clad shoulder tells me everything I need to know. Then he's looking beyond to the door to the cafe bathroom. Breaker's mouth moves, head tilted in a question. Is he asking after the teen?

I need to keep moving.

I *push* harder, weaving more specifics along the thread of his life force that I've got in my grasp. I'm not actually capable of manifesting nothing out of nothing, and I'm definitely not a telepath in the traditional sense, but I can push forward something that was already about to occur ...

A phone call.

A problem only you and your club brother can solve.

Breaker frowns. Then he finally settles his gaze on his phone. A moment after, he beckons to Chains with a sharp impatient jerk of his head. The cafe owner steps forward as the other biker also crosses into my line of sight.

The owner looks up and over the bikers' heads. And in the briefest of glances, she meets my gaze through the window, then instantly starts calling to the server, Daisy, pulling her into an animated conversation.

All the while, she continues to obstruct the entrance to the short hall that holds the bathrooms.

Are they ... helping me?

I release the clutch and allow the car to roll out of the parking spot. Not for the first time, I wish that I could influence inanimate objects, such as the two huge motorcycles parked right by the front door. A couple of blown tires would be really helpful right now — but without me being caught in the act of slashing them.

I shift into gear and tap the accelerator. Then I carefully drive around the side of the building, parking before the kitchen entrance at the back. The weathered metal door is conveniently propped open with a brick. Such conveniences often pop into existence when I'm guided by a knowing.

Thinking about the daisy-chain tattoo around the server's wrist, and the cafe owner who employs a woman who was once sold through an illegal shifter-trafficking market — and therefore might not have legitimately secured her freedom — I leave the car running.

TUCKED WITHIN A GENTLE EDDY OF *INTENT* — MY own — I step through into the back hall. It opens to the kitchen on my right, specifically into the dishwashing station.

The cafe owner and Daisy stand at the other end of the short hall, their bodies canted toward each other, laughing and smiling. A show, I'm sure now, as they all but block the way to the front door as well as the view of the bathroom door. At least from the bikers, who are now dealing with whatever minor crisis I've sent their way via Breaker's phone.

To my right, the young dishwasher spins, startled at my abrupt appearance and opening his mouth to address me. I simply smile with all the charm I can evoke in the moment, waving toward the door to the ladies' room. The dishwasher nods, grinning back at me.

His inherent essence is a gentle whisper, barely stirring the threads of pure energy that encircle him. He's another shifter of some sort. I wonder if he hides a trafficking tattoo under his rubber gloves.

I had presumed that the cafe had gone silent when the bikers entered, dragging the girl between them, because the two were well known. And maybe they were, but they weren't local. They don't provide protection to this area. The Southern accents have told me as much.

Was a call in to the local club already? Or the police, if they could be trusted in this area?

Both options are more reasons to keep moving.

As I press open the bathroom door, I whisper a bit of luck into the cobweb-thin thread that has sprung forth between the dishwasher and myself, letting it go as soon as the good intent is sent. It will settle as it wills. Maybe into nothing. Or maybe it will be the edge the boy needs in the moment he most needs it.

I step through into the bathroom, carefully shutting the door as silently as possible behind me. Light-blue square tile grouted in white runs across the floor and halfway up the walls. Two toilets are encased in two stalls, and the air smells of more of that lemon hand soap.

The teenager is hunched over the middle of three rounded white ceramic sinks. A stream of cold water runs freely over her raw wrists. Her violet-tinted eyes are red-rimmed and puffy when she looks over at me, but she's not currently crying.

I push my sunglasses up onto my head, wrapping my left hand around the amulet that helps both to focus and to constrain my use of my powers — in theory, at least — letting the teen take in my own eye color. Her irises hold more blue. Mine, when not subtly masked by a lick of intent that is seldom reliable when I try to actually use it, are more purple.

My lack of melatonin — the scientific explanation behind the exceedingly rare violet-eye phenomenon — is more striking than hers. My skin is paler as well, and my hair is currently light brown streaked with copper, red, and gold. Though no matter what color I try to add — red, blond, or anything else — the highlights all wash out to a copper hue within a few weeks.

"Do you need a way out?" I ask, hushed.

The teen's mouth drops open, and hope blooms across her face and through her entire body on her next breath. It's gone an instant later, and her shoulders slump. She shakes her head. "I can't ... I don't want —"

"Me to get hurt?"

She bites her lip, shaking her head. Not in denial, just in ... despair. "You don't know me."

"What if I told you I could survive anything they can do to me? Anything just about anyone can do to me? But that coming with me might put you in more danger? Temporarily, at least."

I'm getting more hints from the *knowing* now that I'm standing so close to her. So I already *know* that things are going to get worse before they get better. But since that's one of the ultimate truths of the universe, it isn't news to me.

I'm also playing a bit fast and loose with my own power, so it's a given that it's all going to eventually bite me in the ass. Possibly literally, given the presence of shifters.

The teen's brow furrows.

I release my hold on my amulet, drawing her gaze to it. I wonder if her awry senses are awakened enough to feel its energy. Her gaze flicks to my bracelet next, brown topaz and gold still twisted around my wrist and forearm. So perhaps she can sense essence-infused artifacts. Not that the bracelet is actually an artifact.

Even though I'm distinctly aware of the threads I've forged between me and the bikers, and Breaker specifically, shifting and thinning, I just stand quietly under the teen's regard.

"I can't push you," I say gently. "Some choices have to be your own. Not everything is determined by fate alone."

Startled, her eyes flick up to meet mine. "Can you get me home?"

"I'll die trying," I say, aware that I've uttered my own destiny — a single, short thread of it, at least — as the words fall from my lips.

I've never been great at keeping my mouth shut, even when I'm trying. Or ignoring a knowing even when doing so was in my best interest.

I reach for her.

She steps closer to accept my hand.

The thin threads already connecting us solidify so suddenly and sharply that it's like a punch to the gut. I lose my breath within the momentary onslaught of sensation. It settles into an unadulterated rightness. More than a simple thread of destiny.

I've never felt the like before. Even accepting my inheritance was less ... steady, less resolved. But most essence-wielding is like that. Most essence, most power, grows slowly, and not necessarily steadily.

"What ... what was that?" she asks in a whisper.

I meet her gaze, blinking and still feeling a little out of body. "Fate," I whisper back. "It seems ... we are meant to be here, in this moment and beyond."

She smiles. It's tentative, shaky. Her grip on my hand is almost punishing.

"What's your name, sweetness?"

"Presh ..." She exhales hope along with the gift of her name, fortifying the connection between us further. Then she inhales strength — I can see it flooding through her — and gives me more. "Precious Guerra."

I lean into her, taller by a half-dozen inches. My necklace swings forward, drawing her attention again. "Zaya Gage," I say. Then I add, teasingly, "Granddaughter of Necessity, Daughter of Darkness and Night." Even though I'm speaking the utter truth. As I always must when I'm about to walk the path of my own destiny.

To my death, I had no doubt.

Presh giggles quietly, as I'd hoped she would. Though depending on how much of the family history I'm willing to accept as pure truth, I'm not lying.

Without another word, I tuck her under my arm. Head held high, gait steady and sure, I traverse the *knowing*, simply walking her out of the bathroom, down the hall, out of the back of the cafe, and into my car.

She belts in and manually locks her door.

I place the to-go bag in her lap. Before we've even skirted the side of the cafe, she's already eating ravenously.

We don't even make it out of the parking lot before the two bikes roar to life behind us.

I hit the accelerator and head back to the highway.

Because whether we're riding the threads of fate or not, the highway is going to be the fastest route to wherever we're going.

TWO

THE BIKERS HANG BACK ENOUGH THAT THERE'S A moment after I round a long curve — still steadily heading back toward the highway — that I think they might just never appear in my rearview again. They do. And there is something seriously nefarious about their languid response to my stealing Presh. It unnerves me, even more than them pushing to catch up to us and trying to run us off the road would.

The teenager strapped into the passenger seat beside me is shoving greasy chicken strips into her mouth like she hasn't eaten in days. Despite the fries the bikers bought for her at the cafe, maybe she hasn't. Maybe she hasn't wanted to eat, to make herself vulnerable in that way.

Maybe the hunger strike was the only part of her life she could control.

I could ask a lot of questions.

And Presh could be, should be, questioning me right now. But instead, she viciously rips the paper off the straw, stabs the straw into the milkshake, and takes a long slurp.

Then she slams the heel of her hand against her forehead, stifling a squawk of pain.

I put the heat on, full blast. The car is not as vintage on the inside as it appears on the exterior, though the locks and windows are still manual. The engine hasn't been retrofitted as electric, but it does have a fossil fuel converter. When needed, heat or air conditioning instantly spills out of the vents, taking no real time to warm up. I have hazy memories of driving down the coast in this car with my mother, back when it ran on gas. After spending hours on the beach, I spent what felt like the next hour wrapped in as many towels as I could commandeer, waiting for the heat to actually start warming the car.

I glance in the mirror, shoving the unhelpful thought away. It isn't like me to linger in the past. All that is set in stone, unchanging. All my focus should be on navigating the immediate present. For me, there is never any point to trying to live in any moment other than the breath I'm currently taking. Unlike the girl slurping up the dregs of her milkshake beside me, my future is as unchangeable as my past.

Now, at least. Three weeks and a day ago, I still had some sense of ... choice, even if it was a false sense.

"My phone is in my bag," I say. "Behind my seat, side pocket."

Presh carefully wipes her hands on the paper napkins, bundles the now-empty takeout containers back into the brown bag, then tucks the crumpled bag under her seat — so it isn't a tripping hazard. She loosens the seatbelt just enough to swivel around, her gaze riveted out the back window for a moment.

"Are they going to kill us now?" she asks calmly.

"No," I say, completely confident in my assessment.

"But ..." She chews her bottom lip. "You don't know."

She hits the word *know* hard, so she has some inkling of what my violet eyes mean. I am awry, like she is awry, but our power levels aren't remotely the same. She could eventually be the most powerful seer or telepath or curse weaver in the world, and she still couldn't harness the essence that I wield just by breathing, just by existing.

Without me, there is no existence, no future or fate, for anyone else.

Or so I've been told.

It's possible my ancestors were just seriously full of shit.

"Zaya?" Presh prompts quietly.

"We're too valuable to kill," I say, steady and sure. I don't mention all the things worse than death. I have no doubt the bikers have a club-approved list of personally bent atrocities ready to unleash, tailored to the moment.

Presh nods shallowly, reaching around my seat to unzip and dig into my bag. She pulls out my phone, and the wad of twenties falls all over the place between our seats. She sets the phone on my thigh, scrambling to gather the money. Her shoulders are slumped like she's anticipating a beating.

I tighten my grip on the steering wheel, keeping my focus riveted to the road and waiting for the next section of the *knowing* to reveal itself. Of course, that doesn't mean I can't prompt it along as planned.

"Put the money in your pocket," I say, my tone harder than I want it to be.

"I ... I ..." She inhales shakily, navigating a spike of anxiety that I can practically feel. "I don't have any pockets."

Yeah, that doesn't help with my anger situation. "Your bra?"

I catch the shake of her head from the corner of my eye.

Her head is still bowed over the money she's clutching. "I'm not going to hurt you," I say.

"I know."

"I'm going to get you where you need to go."

She blinks at me for a moment, once again weighing my sincerity — and maybe my ability to follow through. "You just walked us out of the cafe," she says, seemingly changing the subject, except it's all the same conversation.

"I did."

"How ..."

"Because I knew I could."

She nods, chewing on her lower lip again. "I can't take all your money."

"I don't need it. I never really do."

She mulls that over for a bit. Then she scoots her pelvis forward, yanks up her oversized hole-ridden sweater, and tucks the wad of twenties into her white cotton panties.

For one of the very first times in my life, I think about pulling the car over, getting out, and simply killing the bikers. Except I suspect they're simply one thread of a greater issue. Also, my so-called offensive capabilities are somewhat ... unconventional. And unpredictable.

I am clever, though. I can come up with things in the moment. If the universe is willing.

A large green road sign appears up ahead, announcing the upcoming exit onto the highway.

"I need a direction," I say. "Are we going north or south?"

"Um ... which way are you heading?"

"I'm taking you where you need to go. Your accent says you aren't from around here. Not originally."

"No. I'm not. I ran away."

I don't push her because that's not the info I need in

the *Now*. I don't want to slow down, because the transition onto the highway will give the bikers slowly and casually closing the distance behind us a great opportunity to run us off the road. "North or south?"

"I don't know where we are."

Right. And there's that hot, sticky anger brewing in my chest again, churning my stomach. "The cafe was on the edge of Castle Rock, about two hours south of the city of Seattle."

"But still in Washington, then?"

"Yes."

"Near Portland," she whispers. "I was trying to get to my ... my brother."

Fuck. That's at least another hour away, even at highway speeds. And the bikers aren't going to let us get anywhere near a city. "South," I say, speeding up, even though there's no tricky way of getting onto the highway that the bikers won't notice.

We're going to need a haven before Portland. And my contacts are ... capricious in this part of the world. Anywhere near Vancouver, where I reside when I'm not traveling, and I would have just called in a favor from the local police. In California, I have multiple crime bosses and politicians owing me favors.

"I could ... my brother ... just about any of my brothers would come for me."

"You should call one of them," I say, loosening my grip on the steering wheel just long enough to hand her my phone.

Presh hums quietly to herself, her gaze on the phone now cradled in her hand. A quiet attempt to calm herself a little, perhaps. "They, um, they aren't going to be happy about ..."

"You being kidnapped?"

"Well, they might not know. I was supposed to wait. But I ..." Her breathing tightens, becoming ragged around the edges. "I thought ... I saw the cage ... he had it delivered and ... then there was a ..." I barely catch the next words. "A dire mage. You know ... with the black-rimmed eyes. And hers were so pale that ... that ... she looked ... like ..." Presh swallows harshly, shaking her head.

Yeah, I've looked a dire mage in their black-edged eyes before. Thankfully, though, they were usually more scared of the color of my own orbs. But the more pale-skinned and pale-haired a dire mage is? That loss of pigmentation seems to directly equate to the amount of life force they've stolen, leeched — consumed — for their own nefarious purposes.

And though I have no idea who the 'he' in Presh's recounting is, I do know exactly what purpose a dire mage would have for keeping an awakening awry in a cage. As a long-term power source. Assuming the mage has enough control to not just drain someone like Presh down in a single sickening slurp.

"You don't have to tell me," I say, urging a little more speed out of the car as I merge onto the highway. Thankfully, though the traffic is dense, it's still moving. One road trip, I crawled from Seattle to Portland, taking five hours for a three-hour trip, all the while going out of my mind to 'stay in the moment' and vowing to fly the next time I needed to make the journey.

Except this time, Portland isn't my final destination. Though it is the nearest commercial airport to that destination. Not that I flew commercial if I could help it.

"Okay ..."

"You can if you want, but you don't have to."

"Breaker and Chains didn't rape me," she blurts. "I'm ... like you said, I'm ... well, my father is their boss."

"He's the president of their motorcycle club?"

"The Cataclysm."

Oh, that is cheerful. The Cataclysm Motorcycle Club — mostly composed of Bear Clan shifters, if I remember correctly — are infamous enough that I've heard of them even though I've very deliberately never set foot within the Federation. The country that occupies the most southern strip of what was once the so-called United States. I would have thought that bears wouldn't enjoy the south, but territories are created for many complex reasons, including ideological beliefs.

The cage and the presence of a dire mage in a biker club now make perfect sense, corresponding neatly with the purple hue slowly overtaking the blue of Presh's eyes. If she were a shapeshifter, her beast would have asserted itself around the time that her body decided it was mature enough. The power she manifests instead — the power I can feel from her — might still be practically unscentable by most. But shifters didn't become presidents of infamous motorcycle clubs without being especially powerful, even among their own kind.

Her father likely took a whiff of Presh one day and suddenly discovered that she is unique. Invaluable. Even within his world of guns, drugs, prostitution, and most likely some aspect of the even-more-lucrative shifter trafficking or flesh markets.

Presh is still staring at the phone.

The bikers move through the highway traffic far more smoothly than I can. Weaving almost playfully around cars and running along the shoulder of the highway, they're suddenly right behind us, hemming us in. I've never tried to manipulate strands of fate while driving. I'm not certain I can do so without also risking a four-lane pileup.

Presh glances behind us. Then, staring straight at our pursuers, her shoulders roll back, and she lifts her chin defiantly.

I grin.

She swivels back. "I don't know the number. Any number. I had it all programmed in my phone."

"I'll help," I say.

"You … their numbers won't be listed."

"That's fine." I shift the car into the right-hand lane, hitting the accelerator to dart around five cars before slipping back into the next open lane. I can feel it now. The eddy we're riding has solidified again. I let it direct the steering wheel … just a little bit.

"Open the phone app," I say, noting the bikers making an effort to catch up to us. The highway is a bit clearer for a stretch ahead, so I press all the way down on the accelerator. The engine responds eagerly.

"Done."

"Look at the numbers." I can't figure out if drawing the attention of any authority figures by seriously speeding is a bad idea or not. Would I just get any cops who tried to stop us killed? Would they simply hand us over to the bikers even though this isn't Cataclysm territory?

I push the thought away, to be explored after I connect Presh to her brother. She needs the grounding while I find us a way out. "Look at the numbers," I repeat. "And think of your brother."

"Um, which one?"

"Whoever you want to talk to."

"Well … I don't know them all that …" She huffs, interrupting herself. "I know. Focus." She inhales deeply, all but glaring at the phone now. "I want to speak with my brother Rath."

Something shivers through me at the odd name. "Wrath? As in anger?"

"Rath," Presh repeats, pronouncing it sweetly but determinedly. "No *W*. It's his biker handle. Will that work?"

I nod, suddenly more distracted than I want to be during a high-speed chase. Maybe the shiver means nothing. But maybe it means that Rath is the right choice, and all of what that entails.

"I want to speak with my brother Rath," Presh repeats, talking deliberately to the phone. "Like that?"

"Yes." I really only need her intent, if this is even going to work, but words will help her focus. I allow myself to slip a little further into the eddy of *knowing* we're riding, just enough to split my focus a smidge, not enough to lose control of the car. "Again."

"I'm going to call Rath," she says.

I reach for the whisper of *intent* that curls around her hand, around the phone. "You know the number."

Her shoulders stiffen slightly, but before she can refute my assertion, I add, "You've seen it come up on the screen numerous times. As the call connects. It's there ... it's right under your fingers. See the numbers."

I *push*, trying to not draw from the necklace. This is a parlor trick. I can do this sort of thing without even thinking about it. Well, when I'm not hurtling along a crowded highway near the top speed of a performance sports car while being chased by bikers.

"The numbers ..." Presh murmurs. Then her fingers fly over the keypad, and the phone starts connecting the call.

I'm forced to slow as the traffic tightens up ahead, probably in response to an on-ramp. The bikers smoothly slip back into our wake. Drivers on either side of them visibly blanch, then involuntarily hit their brakes before correcting themselves.

Even two shifter bikers can create a lot of havoc. Few individuals — essence-wielders or not — can take them on one-on-one.

Presh stares down at the screen, waiting. The phone is still trying to connect. "What if ... he won't recognize the number. What if he doesn't ... ?"

"He will," I say, making it the truth just by speaking it.

Yeah, there's a whole lot of arrogance connected to what I do. Some of it passed down to me, some of it taught. Even more of it is lived experience.

The call connects.

"What?!" a deep voice snarls over the phone speakers.

"Rath!" Presh all but screams, then she dissolves into sobs. Her hand bounces on her thigh, and she nearly loses hold of the phone as her limbs go limp with relief.

"Where the fuck are you?" Rath demands.

The word 'fuck' sends a delicious and completely inappropriate shiver down my spine. Damn. That is quite a connection. And we aren't even sharing the same space.

"I'm ... I'm ..." Presh gulps air, trying to quiet her sobs and speak at the same time. "Highway ... Washington."

"Nearing the Oregon border now," I add cheerfully, raising my voice a little to be heard. "Being chased by two of the Cataclysm."

"Who the fuck is that?!"

"Zaya Gage," I say. "And you?"

Silence answers me.

A long beat of it.

Then, "Zaya ... Gage."

Another heavy pause.

Then, "Fuck you."

This abrupt rage-filled 'fuck' isn't as nice as his first.

Presh squeaks in surprise. Her eyes round and her shoulders hunch, instantly shifting back into a wariness that the rapid consumption of food and conversation had eased.

"Why, Rath ..." I purr. "We don't even know each other yet. How could you possibly know you'd even be interested in fucking me?"

My protective instincts are all riled up, sharpening my tone until I'm promising him all the death and destruction I can call forth. Which I'm guessing is a lot, because no one adopts the name 'Rath' without being into a lot of shit that I could twist to my own intent.

The destruction — or conversely, the luck — I can wield always extends from another's fate.

A weighted silence hangs at the other end of the line.

Presh whimpers.

"It's okay, Precious," I say, keeping my eyes glued to the highway and my foot as heavy on the accelerator as I can safely manage. "I'll find us somewhere safe. You can have a nap, get cleaned up. Then hopefully one of your other siblings isn't such a vicious asshole."

I get I'm not helping by tagging on that last bit. But though I still have only an inkling of what this girl has gone through in the last few days, I'm not handing her over to some raging alpha. And yeah, I can tell his shifter proclivity just based on the few words that have tumbled out of his mouth.

"Okay ..." Presh murmurs.

"Presh! What the fuck?!" Rath snarls over the phone.

"I meant, it's okay," Presh says in a rush. "That you ...

Rath is okay, Zaya. I promise. I ran. I should have called … but then I got off the train in the wrong place. They weren't on the train, I don't think … like, not following me … but I didn't know where I was, just a train yard or like a port, or I don't know what that's called when there isn't any water. I should have dumped my phone. I know I should have. I just … I didn't know where I was." Her voice breaks.

"Keep going," Rath says. He's calmer now, moving around. It's subtle, but I can hear it in the background.

"I've never been very good at school," Presh says, speaking to me. "Geography, I mean. But I'm really good with —"

"Presh …" Rath is back to snarling now.

I wonder if he's a wolf shifter. Or maybe a canine of some other sort.

"Breaker and Chains," I say promptingly, with my eye on both bikers in my rearview.

A series of blistering curses emanate from the speaker, not all of them in English. I don't take the time to work out the other languages involved, but I have to ignore another delicious spine-tingling reaction. Because apparently, Breaker and Chains have a reputation, and I need to stay focused on them.

"How did they find you?" Rath says, then immediately interrupts his own question. "Where are you now?"

Yep, that's the pertinent info. "Open the map app," I say to Presh. "Take a screenshot and —"

"Make sure it's zoomed in enough," Rath interrupts.

Presh pokes around on the phone. I can still hear Rath moving around in the background, bits of conversation — hushed like he has his hand over the phone mic instead of muting it. Like he doesn't want to risk breaking the connection.

I move into another opening between cars even before it's fully clear. My foot heavy on the accelerator, I jump us ahead of the bikers, weaving through traffic again. The BMW is older and likely not as souped up as the motorcycles, but it has to be faster. Right? Except I'm not much of a driver, and most bikers live and breathe riding at high speeds from a young age.

"I'm on my way to you," Rath says. "I'm going to send you somewhere safe. I'll text the address and the route you should take to this number, okay?"

"Okay ..." Presh swallows. "How far away are you?"

"I'll be there," Rath says, not actually answering her.

Too far away. I know it even though he doesn't say it. I know because there is no way I can manipulate a knowing and bend Presh's fated path without having payment come due. Being able to simply deposit Presh into her brother's arms would be way too easy.

Rath is talking to someone in the background, lots of muffled shouts and orders. Presh leans right over the phone, trying to hear. Bowed over like that, she meets my gaze and swallows.

I keep my foot on the accelerator.

Rath is going to direct us off the highway. There's a slight chance that if I get far enough ahead, I can exit without Breaker and Chains noticing. A slight chance that I endeavor to give a little *push*.

The problem is, I can't affect my own fate, only the thread that is tied to Presh. And Breaker and Chains. Even my ability to tweak other threads still has limits — or it did before the amulet I now wear was involuntarily slung around my neck. And those limits are randomly enforced by an occasionally capricious universe.

Alternatively, what I perceive as a tiny twist of fate

might be amplified far beyond my intent and control. For example, if I weren't already riding a *knowing* and trying to keep Presh focused while driving a car, I could try to reach out and coax Breaker to crash into the highway guardrail. But even if that actually worked? I might murder a dozen or more innocent bystanders at the same time. While Breaker, presumably a bear shifter, would likely walk away.

"Sent," Rath says over the phone. His tone becomes edged, hard and forbidding. "Zaya Gage, get my sister to me and I'll give you anything —"

"I'm set," I say glibly.

"I mean it," he snarls. "The Cataclysm —"

"Are bad guys. I get it."

I can practically hear his jaw clench as he bites off his next words. "Breaker is a berserker."

My stomach sours. Everything glib and sure slides away from me as my connection to the *Now* goes a little fuzzy. "Oh," I breathe.

"Yeah, oh," he says mockingly. "Are you strong enough, fast enough?"

"Strength and speed aren't going to have anything to do with it," I say hollowly. I glance at the rearview mirror. I've put some distance between us and the bikers. But I do wonder — before I can stop myself — how awful it's going to be to die under the teeth and claws of an unhinged berserker.

Wondering isn't going to stop it from happening, though.

"Most packs ... put berserkers down."

"Yeah," Rath says. "Most do."

"Zaya?" Presh whispers. "It's okay. We just ... have to not provoke him."

"That ship has definitely sailed, Precious," I say, mostly

feigning my glib tone. "But I promised you. My word is binding. Literally."

Presh nods.

"Good to hear it," Rath says. "Your exit is coming up. Pay attention to the road."

I stifle a snarky response to that command. I haven't taken my full attention off the road once.

"Check in every ten minutes by text," the bossy asshole continues. "Call me if you need me. I'm coming to you. I'll find you. Do you have the link? I've sent you a specific route, don't deviate. Don't get out of the car."

Presh pokes around on the phone. "Got it." She clicks the link in a text from Rath, and the map app opens again. "We're still an hour and fifteen minutes away," she says, renewed fear whispering through her words.

"Check in every ten minutes," Rath reiterates. "Don't stop. Don't get out of the car."

He can't do anything about it either way. No matter what sort of safe house he's sending us to, we're on our own until we get there. And possibly even after if I can't shake the bikers.

"Presh?" Rath asks.

"Yeah ..." She glances at me, squaring her shoulders again. "We're on our way."

"I have to hang up now," Rath says. "There are some calls I have to be the one to make."

"I know."

"I love you, sis. I'm coming for you."

"Okay," she breathes.

There's a moment of quiet. Then Rath says, "I'm trusting you, Zaya Gage."

"You don't have much choice."

"No, I don't." His teeth snap around that admittance grimly. "But I will hunt you to the ends of the earth."

"I won't run," I say, not all that angry now. Just resigned and focused. Still, I can't have him threaten me and also get in the last word. "You aren't my end, Rath. It's not you who will snip my thread."

The silence that falls in the car is heavier after that pronouncement. But I've never been one to take stupid threats lightly.

"I'm coming for you," Rath growls.

The line goes dead.

The thrill once again triggered by his rough tone, shivering through my system, lingers.

"Show me," I say, ignoring the sensation instead of dissecting it. There is no point, there is never any point, in thinking beyond the *Now*.

Presh angles the phone into my line of sight, displaying the map. I absorb it in a glance. Apparently, Rath is sending us out to the coast.

The *knowing* rises, grabbing hold of me instead of just lingering on the edges.

I hit the accelerator hard. The BMW shoots forward, weaving dangerously through traffic toward the next exit.

Dangerously for anyone not capable of riding a *knowing*, that is.

WE SEEMINGLY LOSE BREAKER AND CHAINS FOR all of forty minutes as I speed toward the coast, following the directions Presh has pulled up on my phone. Long enough that it starts to rain in earnest, and some of the tension leaks out of Presh's stiff shoulders.

The *knowing* doesn't fade, though — the price hasn't been paid yet — so I can't relax.

The route is unfamiliar to me. Definitely back roads, which I presume is why we lose the bikers on our tail for so long. Rath's route kept us on Highway 30 for ten minutes. Then, in a slight weaving pattern, we've been cutting on an angle toward Highway 26 since. The map shows us meeting up with the coastal 101, then cutting down toward Cannon Beach. The route has obviously been carefully designed to keep us off the main thoroughfares, but I completely understand Rath's caution about us stopping or getting out of the car.

We're deep in the wilds of Cascadia. Neutral territory doesn't necessarily mean unclaimed territory, and more often than not, some *power* — possibly a shifter or mage exile, or even an awry with purple eyes like mine — controls these little fiefdoms. Not necessarily nefariously, though. Given the fact that the roads are properly paved, though not all that recently, and the homes we pass are still mostly standing, this cluster of residences and the surrounding territory has someone overseeing it. And rules that are enforced as that overseer decrees.

The bikers finally come at us from the side, as if they've got a tracker on us — or on Presh specifically. Alternatively, they simply had to take a farther exit off the highway, then cut up from there. But that's something to worry about after this moment passes.

Because an instant after I register the ear-numbing roar of their motorcycles, they blow through a stop sign, forcing me to swerve right.

Presh screams.

At the speed I've been pushing on the rain-slick roads, I'm not an experienced enough driver to regain control of the car.

With Breaker and Chains right up our ass, the vehicle careens wildly. Then, tires skidding and slipping, we swing around in a half spin, and the passenger side slams into something solid.

Metal crunches.

Presh hits the side of her head against the window, losing hold of my phone.

Before I even recover from the bone-jarring stop and reach for her, my door is ripped open, and I'm grabbed by my neck and hauled sideways.

My seatbelt hinders my attacker for long enough that Presh screams again — this time in anger and concern — and latches onto my other arm. A knife flashes before my face, and I instinctively sheer back from it, giving Breaker room to slice through the shoulder and lap belt. His dark hair, beard, and tanned skin make it easy to distinguish him even in the gloom.

As he's withdrawing, his hand on my neck shifting to firm his grip on me, I grab his wrist with both hands. I twist and somehow — miraculously even — manage to stab him in the thigh with his own knife.

He grunts.

Grunts.

As if I've merely scratched him.

Then he yanks the knife back out of his thigh and head-butts me.

My sunglasses snap, falling off as my vision blackens around the edges. Presh, practically wrapped around my other arm, snarls and spits in panicked anger.

Breaker hauls me out of the vehicle, managing to

wrench me free of Presh's hold, presumably because she's still belted into her seat.

Her angry panting sobs keep me focused, though.

Breaker spins me around. I catch a glimpse of Chains hovering behind us and grinning manically. Using the momentum of Breaker throwing me around, I punch Chains solidly in the throat. I'm not strong, and the shifters aren't even remotely weak, not even in their human forms. But a punch to the throat is still nasty.

Chains stumbles back, gasping for breath, then choking.

Breaker howls with laughter, dragging me to the back of the car as I kick and flail. His hold on my neck doesn't falter, and I can barely breathe. The other side of the car is crumpled against what appears to be a shoulder-high stone wall. At a glance, the wall has taken more damage than the car. Likely due to some healthy application of extremely expensive essence weaving by a mage with a fabricator affinity — one with the ability to meld essence with metal and other materials. That essence might even hold a glimpse into the future, what with my mother and one of my so-called uncles both seers. Of sorts.

The car has slid all the way off the road. An open beach and pounding surf spread out from the other side of the wall. We aren't even remotely south enough to have reached the dunes of the Oregon Coast, but on a clear day, I might be able to see a particular curve of the coastline from the right vantage point off this beach. A curve on which spreads an expansive estate that I need to ... claim.

Not something to be thinking about while being strangled.

Breaker takes each blow, shin kick, and foot stomp that I manage to land with barely a reaction. He slams me back over the trunk of the car, pressing over me. I score a vicious scratch down his cheek — evoking a minimal flinch from him — before he captures both my hands in one of his and presses them over my head, against the back window. My arms aren't long enough for that stretch, and my shoulders protest.

"Stay in the fucking car," Chains growls. To Presh.

I twist and buck, but Breaker pins me against the trunk, pressing his huge body over me to do so. He loosens his grip on my neck, but not on my hands. I gasp, gulping as much oxygen as possible because I already know it's only a brief reprieve.

The asshole then slams my head back with his free hand, his thumb under my right eye, forefinger over top.

For a panicked moment, I think he's going to gouge my eye out.

Instead, he leans close, gazing at me and grinning manically. "I was right," he crows.

He means my eye color, identifying me as an awry. And seriously? Only an utter moron would need a closer look to confirm the fucking vibrant violet color of my eyes.

Then Chains is leaning over me as well, smirking. "The boss is going to be extra happy."

Breaker grunts.

Then, as I expected, he starts yanking and pulling at my clothing. One-handed, because he's still got my hands pinned over my head, plus my legs and torso pinned by his body.

"What the fuck are you doing?" Chains snarls.

"This cunt ain't protected," Breaker grunts, trying to get my skintight faux-leather pants off me while still firmly pinning the bulk of my body against the car. Every time he gives me a bit of space, I twist and buck.

"You don't take from one of the awry," Chains says in a warning tone. "Not without —"

"I'm fucking her." Breaker's spittle sprays over my face and neck. He smells like old, wet leather, spiced aftershave, and the heavy musk of a predator. "She wanted a chase, I gave it. Now I get my reward."

"It's broad daylight," I say. "You fucking morons."

They blink down at me, pausing, as if they haven't noticed we're only a few feet off a residential street. Heavily tree lined, yes, and no streetlights or cars or pedestrians as far as I can see. But despite the steady rain, the gray-skied afternoon offers no real cover or shelter. The few houses I glimpsed before being literally run down are large, on large lots, but a bit shabby. This far off the highway and away from a city center, this is definitely neutral territory.

People are either crazy powerful, or crazy unlucky, to live in neutral territory. Both of those possibilities work better for Presh and me, though, than they do for clearly affiliated asshole rapist bikers. Of course, being 'rescued' from the rabid bikers just to be kidnapped by a local wouldn't be an improvement.

"I'll be quick," Breaker says, actually fucking bargaining.

"You'll lose your shit," Chains says. "I'm not explaining to the boss why I had to put you down."

Breaker's nostrils flare angrily. Maybe Chains's stupid club moniker actually means something? Is he Breaker's keeper?

"I've got her under control," Breaker sneers. "She's weak. But she'll wet my dick just fine."

Chains eyes him assessingly. Then he snaps, "Behind the wall." He crosses back around the car without looking at me again.

Precious.

I squeeze my eyes shut.

I'll make it through this. I always do. But Presh ...

Breaker hauls me up, shoving my upper body over his shoulder. I land at least one kick to his groin before getting the wind knocked out of me. He stumbles.

Finally. Fuck.

Even walking stiffly, he manages to make it to a short path that cuts through the stone wall, then hauls me around the wall itself. He grabs my hips, yanking me off his shoulder and slamming me onto the ground. The impact, not all that softened by the wet sand, is jarring.

I roll over onto my stomach, managing to make it onto all fours. "Behind the wall is going to have to do," I say, panting through the pain and not even remotely addressing my would-be rapist.

"You going to run for me, cunt?" Breaker taunts. "I like that."

I can hear him loosening his clothing. Zippers being opened. Jacket, vest. Then his belt buckle clinking.

Presh is screaming at Chains on the other side of the wall, begging. Her shouts are cut off by the sound of flesh meeting flesh and a body staggering back against a car. The other shifter has gotten pissed enough to hit her.

Getting a bit more space between myself and Breaker, I roll over instead of trying to get to my feet. No running for me. I never get to run when I'm this deep into a *knowing*. I just suffer it — and remember the goal.

I remember Presh's raw, red wrists and her bowed head while being held between the assholes in the cafe. I don't have to know all the details of why she ran away in the first place to understand that she needed to run.

She needs to keep running.

So I don't. I don't run.

I sit on my ass in the sand, catching my breath. I ignore how much I hurt already, because it's going to get worse. Sparks of energy twine around my wrist and up my forearm — my bracelet responding to my prompting, to the situation.

More specifically, the sulky creature that masquerades as a gold-and-brown-topaz bracelet is responding to my current needs. Sullenly, though, because he's not a fan of damp, chilly conditions.

Huffing in anticipation, Breaker gives up on getting his belt all the way off, simply unzipping and yanking his dick out of his leather pants. He doesn't even bother with the top button, just tugging his fleshy length through the open zipper. No need to get naked to enjoy raping me. Though he's taken off his jacket and slung it over the stone wall — so as to not get it dirty or scratched up, I presume.

His dick is soft. A couple of kicks to the groin will do that. He jerks on it — none too gently — and takes a menacing step toward me.

I curl forward onto my feet in a low crouch. Then, grinning up at him, I plant my knees in the sand, rising into a kneeling position with my hands clasped behind me and my head tilted back — as if offering to blow him.

He hesitates, just for a moment. So he isn't a complete idiot. But then lust overrides his functional reasoning, and his angry-red dick hardens in the three lumbering steps it takes to reach me.

"I'm going to fuck your face until your throat bleeds," he says, close enough now that I can see he's already smearing precum around his tip as he gives it a harsh twist at the end of an upstroke.

Presh's sobs renew. But quieter, muffled, as if maybe

she's gagged. Chains has dragged her closer. Tucked just behind the wall, best guess, but Breaker is so huge that he blocks any sight of them. Apparently, Chains wants to take in the show. Or maybe it's a lesson for Presh. Maybe the sick fuck is going to jerk off. Maybe he's lining up for his own go.

I grin widely, flashing my teeth.

Another hint of hesitation has Breaker stilling with his hand on his dick. He narrows his eyes. "You better not bite me, bitch."

My mind has finally cleared. Getting head-butted by a shifter, then severely strangled is a bit to get over. I finally catch sight of the thin tendril of Breaker's life energy twisting around him. His fate, as some prefer to call it.

It's wispy, blackened at the edges, and it has only a single branch.

Leading to me.

"Promise, cunt. Or I'll fuck the princess and make you watch," Breaker continues, blissfully unaware that death stalks him. Both literally and figuratively.

Figuratively, the essence that imbues all of us with life — again, the energy that some would refer to as fate or destiny — is about to be snipped.

I can see that, clearly.

And literally? Well, the actual death stalking the rapist shifter is now curled heavily around my lower right arm. Tucked behind my back, ready to strike.

My silence or my stillness or my unwavering focus is making Breaker uneasy. He grips his dick, which is softening again — presumably because he gets off on fear, and I'm just not being helpful — and spews more nonsense.

"I'll make her scream," he pants, jerking off viciously.

"Make you watch how I make her bleed. I'll take her ass first. I bet —"

"It's not me you have to worry about biting you." I interrupt because Presh doesn't need to hear this shit, and I need him to come a step closer.

Then I wink.

He takes the last step, near enough now to shove his dick in my face.

Finally.

I sway back even as a massive bushmaster snake slides up my arm, up my back, and over my shoulder — growing larger and larger as he moves.

The snake strikes, latching inch-long fangs dripping with venom onto Breaker's puffy, near-purple dick.

Muta.

In his actual form.

Although he looks like a snake — a long gold body with dorsal blotches of dark brown that form inverted triangles, ending in a horny spined tail — Muta is actually an aspect of the divine who was trapped in the body of a snake. As a punishment, perhaps. At least according to family legend.

So kind of like me, but not really. I have opposable thumbs and a more well-rounded diet. But Muta has the wicked fangs and venom, among other otherworldly tricks.

It's also possible he's one of my ancestors. Again, depending on how much of the family mythos can be wholly believed.

Breaker screams, stumbling back and pulling nearly ten feet and fifteen pounds of venomous snake over my shoulder. By his dick.

"What the fuck!" Chains shouts. With Breaker moving, I can see him shoving Presh to the side, harshly. She falls against the stone wall, smacking her shoulder, then tumbling into the sand with a cry. Her hands are bound behind her back, and she's gagged with some sort of dirty rag.

"I'm sorry, Precious," I say, making eye contact with her. "It's going to get a little bit worse before it gets better."

Her eyes widen, but she manages a nod.

Then I surge to my feet and barrel toward Chains. The other shifter biker has pulled a pistol from a shoulder holster hidden by his leather jacket, and rushes closer to the shrieking Breaker. The gun looks and feels mundane in origin, not an essence-wrought fabrication. And it's maybe an automatic? I'm certainly no expert.

Chains hesitates, just for a moment, instead of shooting the gigantic snake off his buddy's dick.

I get the hesitation over potentially castrating a friend. Not that a bullet would hurt Muta anyway.

I make a grab for the gun. But although he's not quite as big as Breaker, Chains is still easily twice my size. He sees me coming before I get a good hold on the gun. We grapple, slipping and scrambling in loose sand, which is wet only through the top layer from the rain.

I take a hit to the side of my face that leaves me reeling, almost losing my hold on the gun.

Breaker is still shrieking.

Then Chains suddenly trips, stumbling backward.

While he's trying to break his fall, and with my feet only barely anchored in the sand, I slam my shoulder into his chest.

We fall in a tangle of limbs.

Presh shrieks in pain behind her gag.

My weight is enough to drive Chains all the way down, head first into the stone wall. He goes still.

I perch on his chest, panting and clutching at the gun still in his hand.

Presh has her legs wrapped around Chains's ankle, tears streaming down her face and soaking into the gag. She crawled close enough to trip him.

With a roar, Breaker finally screws up the courage to slam a meaty fist into Muta's broad, flat head.

The bushmaster releases his hold on Breaker's dick, falling into the sand, momentarily stunned.

I'm shocked that Breaker has managed to hurt Muta at all. Then, as the shifter turns his red-eyed gaze on me, I see his face. His furred face. Slightly elongated snout. Flattened brow. Sharp canine teeth puncturing his bottom lip.

He's taller and wider than before. Arms longer and viciously clawed.

Seemingly half-transformed, Breaker lowers his head and bellows at me and Presh. Energy blasts over me, though it's the sound itself that freezes me in place.

As it's supposed to do.

My right eye has swollen shut.

There is something really wrong with my left arm.

And ultimately, I'm only human.

Even whole and healthy, I'm no match for an enraged shifter, let alone the creature Breaker is transforming into.

"Run, Presh!" I cry.

And she tries. Gagged, with her hands behind her back, and something clearly wrong with the leg she used to trip Chains, she tries to run.

She isn't even going to make it off the beach before Breaker reaches us. She'll never get to the other side of the stone wall and back to the car.

I wrench the gun out of Chains's grip, snapping his

finger as I do so. Praying the weapon doesn't have a safety and that it's loaded, I fire it at Breaker.

The half-transformed shifter doesn't even bother trying to avoid the shots, taking three to his chest. And since he gets close enough that I can't miss, two more to the head.

Because he isn't just a bear shifter.

He's a berserker. A meld of man and beast created by the consumption of human flesh — usually that of an essence-wielder.

Fire and steel have no effect on him.

But my blood will.

If he drinks me down, if he eats my innards, he will slaughter ... everyone. For miles.

Starting with Presh.

I won't die. Or, more specifically, I won't stay dead. But everyone else will.

Berserker Breaker gets a hand around my neck, lifting me off my feet. I shoot him in the eye with the last bullet. The gun is either empty or it jams. Being shot point-blank in the eye finally makes Breaker stumble. But he just grabs my hand and the gun in one massive clawed paw, snarling and spitting all over my face. Then he crushes my hand around the gun, breaking every bone and mangling the weapon at the same time.

I scream.

I can't help it.

I can hear Presh screaming too, though she's still gagged.

Breaker tightens his grip on my throat, holding me at eye level. The eye I shot out is already healing. My kicks are weak, ineffectual. I can't breathe. He presses his face to my neck, inhaling deeply.

"I'm going to eat you," he says, words mangled by a jaw

that no longer aligns and vocal cords that aren't wholly human.

He can talk in his berserker form. Shape sentences. But I'd always been taught —

"Fuck you," he says. "And eat you. At the same time. Steal your essence. Become ... more."

He's already 'become more.' The idea that his club has allowed a berserker to fully manifest, to continually exist — that they've maybe even nurtured and condoned that existence — is unbelievable. Chilling.

Still dangling me by the neck, he swipes viciously clawed fingers across my belly. Shredding flesh and internal organs. I nearly black out from the pain. Then he tosses me on the ground.

I can still hear Presh. She's ... trying to crawl closer? Trying to reach me?

It draws his attention. "You next, princess."

He leans over me, one hand braced beside my head, the other poised to ... do whatever he wants to do. Whatever I can't stop him from doing. Luxuriating in his kill, he inhales harshly to pull my scent deep within his lungs.

I'm bleeding everywhere. But somehow, pathetically, I still manage to pull myself away from him on one arm while holding my guts in with the other. Though that arm isn't quite working.

Even this wounded, I can still see the snub of the single line of his essence, his life force, his fate. And even dying, I can still feel the tug of the *knowing* coaxing me backward, just a few more inches.

Breaker's dick is limp, long, and blackening. It's covered in pustules and sores that I have no doubt are also spreading up his stomach and down his legs. The parts of him that aren't fur covered, that haven't transformed.

Muta's poison is spreading. But that poison might take fifteen to thirty minutes to take down a shifter like Breaker — and who knows how much longer to quell a half-transformed berserker.

Presh doesn't have that long.

I don't have that long.

I'm dying.

I have maybe two minutes.

And after I'm dead?

Breaker will slaughter Presh. No matter what his original orders were. He'll eat us both.

And then he'll slaughter everyone in the area, up and down the coast until someone powerful enough comes along to put him down.

It's my hazy understanding of those orders — the guidelines around Presh's kidnapping — the faint tug of the *knowing*, and Chains trying to lightly dissuade Breaker from raping me, that have me dragging myself back over Chains's still-prone body as Breaker pauses to tear the rest of his clothing off.

I assume the spreading pustules are hurting him. He's only immune to fire and iron, not Muta's amped-up venom.

I collapse over Chains. And I reach ... I reach through the eddy of the *knowing* ...

Breaker comes down on me hard. His claws burrow into my torn-open guts.

Fuck. I scream.

The sight and sound of the beach, the rainy gray sky, and Presh's ragged sobs get even hazier, dimmer.

Then awareness comes rushing back with a snap, as if I've been forcibly shoved forward into a moment of clarity. By the universe.

Breaker ruts against me, though there's no way his dick is working anymore, nor has he bothered to get my clothing off.

Guided by the *knowing*, I keep reaching, up and then around Chains's leather-clad leg.

Breaker's jaw widens as he hunches over me — at least two feet taller than me in his berserker form — and tries to rip out my throat.

Muta strikes from the side, slamming into Breaker's face and sinking his fangs into his uninjured eye. It's enough to momentarily stop the berserker from finishing me. And just long enough for my hand to close around the hilt of a single-edged, rune-marked, six-inch blade hidden in a narrow side pocket of Chains's pants.

The blade the *knowing* coaxed me toward.

I know, because that coaxing falls away as soon as my hand closes around the hilt. Though it's also possible that death has encroached enough to muddle my sense of knowing.

"Please don't be steel or iron," I murmur. Then I swing the blade up and back, slashing across with my last remaining strength.

I slit Breaker's throat.

Not steel. Nor iron. Maybe silver? Or even titanium. And it's definitely essence wrought.

Because Cataclysm Motorcycle Club brothers or not, Chains keeps himself armed against a berserker.

Blood gushes from Breaker's slit throat.

I close my mouth and eyes, but a bunch gets up my nose. And for more than a moment, I'm drowning on top of already not-so-slowly dying.

Impossible to kill when fully transformed or not, the berserker gasps, gurgles, and then collapses on top of me.

Something snaps in my upper back. My spine, no doubt.

It doesn't hurt.

But then, I'd already known I wasn't getting out of this alive.

I knew it from the moment I forced the *knowing*, from the moment it had truly hit me in the cafe. The moment I'd seen Presh's purple-tinged eyes and the rope burns on her wrists.

"Worth it," I mumble, trying to not get too much of Breaker's blood in my mouth. "Precious ... worth it."

I didn't even need the soul-deep connection that had snapped into place between us in the bathroom to know the value of Presh's safety, of her life.

Despite the pain, despite the repercussions, Precious is worth dying for.

I LOSE SOME TIME. MAYBE THIRTY SECONDS OR A minute, becoming aware that Presh, sobbing against the dirty gag, is trying to roll Breaker off me. Her hands are still tied behind her back, shoulder braced against his side. But her knees just keep digging deeper into the sand. I can't help because my legs and one arm don't work anymore. The pain is harsh, all encompassing. More so than I've ever experienced.

Presh finally manages to shift Breaker mostly off me. But right as she does, I feel the other asshole, Chains, take a breath. The back of my head is resting against his belly.

He's not dead.

Presh needs to run. Leave me and run.

"Stop, stop," I gasp.

Presh pauses. Still on her knees, she hunches over my head and shoulders, blinking down at me. I make my free arm work. I still have the blade in my hand. I get it under her gag and slice it off, scoring a red line across the side of her face that isn't swollen. Chains slapped her hard. Maybe multiple times.

"Turn." The word is garbled around a mouthful of blood. My blood now, I suspect, not Breaker's.

Presh turns, her movements slow and pained. I somehow manage to slice through the zip ties on her wrists, though not without cutting her again. Her hands are practically purple.

I let go of the blade then. It tumbles into the blood-soaked sand.

"Take the car," I say, closing my eyes, because even clouded over, the sky is too bright. The rain has picked up. I'm soaked in it, which is a bit of a blessing, I suppose, because it's got to be washing some of the blood off.

I'm going to be pissed about my broken sunglasses.

After I get the dying part over with.

I lose a bit more time, becoming aware of Presh chanting, "No, no, no!" over and over again. She sobs between the words as she presses something against my guts.

Her sweater.

Without it, she's wearing only a thin tank top and underwear. I turn my head just enough that I can see she's still got the wad of twenties tucked into her panties.

Good.

"You need to go," I say, forcing the words out of my mouth. "Two possibilities and one certainty are about to happen." I can't move my legs or arms, but I can still feel that I'm stirring the essences of fate with my words. I don't want to be doing that. But what was the point of dragging Presh out of the cafe if I don't get her to safety?

"I ... I don't think I should move you," Presh says.

It's not totally clear to me, but I guess I stop talking for a bit, because suddenly Presh is sobbing again and asking, "What possibilities, Zaya? What possibilities?" over and over.

"It's never taken me so long to die before." I choke on blood, then spit up a mouthful.

"What?!" Presh cries.

"Never mind, take the car."

"It crashed."

"It will work."

"I can't drive stick!"

"You'll sort it out."

"How do you know?"

"Because I say so."

"That's not an actual reason!" Presh is either screaming or my hearing has become overly sensitive.

Why is this death unlike any others I've experienced? Is it my inheritance?

Or ... is this death ... final?

Is something bigger and greater than me screwing with my own fate?

I've only been the Conduit for three weeks, and I slept for most of the first week just to absorb the onslaught. Maybe my connection, that connection, is still too weak, too tenuous yet, to pull me back from this level of trauma?

Presh bends over me. I think she's trying to shield my face from the rain with her body, but she presses too hard on my torn-asunder guts, and I can't hold back a strangled scream.

"Sorry, sorry," she whispers.

"Listen to me."

"I'm listening."

"You really aren't."

"Please, Zaya. You ... you promised."

"Oh, Precious," I murmur. "This isn't the end, but you need to go. This is going to draw attention. The blood will call to creatures you don't want to face. There's a reason those assholes stopped for lunch on the edge of neutral territory, then ran us off the road here before we got ..." I don't manage to finish that sentence clearly, choking on blood that has suddenly accumulated at the back of my throat.

Presh turns my head gently, opens my mouth, and clears my airway as if she knows what she's doing. I get the tiniest hint, more a whiff of a sense than a full *knowing*, into the future that awaits her as we're skin to skin. The gentle power simmering within the teen that will grow and spread. That will heal. And not just flesh and bone.

"So worth it ..." I say, closing my eyes and savoring that sense like it's a gift from the universe, offered up to help me get through this ... next transition.

"Or ... what, Zaya?" Presh asks gently, trying to keep me talking.

I huff at her managing me, but say, "Or the noise disturbance will eventually bring what passes for law enforcement. And you don't want to have to talk your way out of this scene."

Her tone firms a bit, as if I've given her something to hang onto with that bit of info. "The two possibilities, right. Okay. And the certainty?"

I meet her purple-hued gaze. It's easily been a year or more since I've seen even a hint of my own eyes on a stranger's face, as opposed to reflected in a mirror. The last time I'd been in the same room as Coda, maybe. My ... tech. For lack of a better word.

And the next reflection I see? Will my eyes be a shade lighter? Again?

"The certainty is that I'm going to die. I really should be dead already."

"No," she says firmly. "Your bleeding has slowed —"

"Because I've bled it all out. There is no more blood to bleed." My inappropriate attempt to be playful about blood loss and dying falls seriously flat, but I don't hear it myself until after the words are out of my mouth. "It's going to be a bitch on the other side ... of this ..."

"What do you mean? Other side?"

I grimace. My mouth is running too much. I'm not thinking straight. I mean, dying does that to a person, but I need Presh to move forward because I can't help her while I'm dead.

I make another attempt to say the words that will make her go. I try to open my mouth. Nothing comes out.

Then finally, the pain fades away.

And with it goes the sound of Presh's renewed sobbing and begging.

Then the gray sky blackens.

I can't even close my eyes.

The darkness takes me.

I feel, see, taste nothing at all.

THREE

I BREATHE, MY CHEST HURTING, WEIRDLY compressed as if it's the first time my lungs have ever been inflated.

Which it is, I suppose. In this particular reincarnation.

After getting some oxygen recirculating through my system, my hearing filters back, and I pick up Presh gasping, saying, "She's breathing! She's breathing!"

I think my eyes are open, but I see only darkness. Then Presh leans over me, my phone pressed to her ear and tears streaming down her face. And I realize that instead of running, like I told her, she's managed to rig some sort of shelter over my head and shoulders ... with hunks of driftwood and ... Breaker's remarkably intact leather jacket.

Right. He removed it before attempting to rape me.

"Presh," I moan, rolling to my side in a move that takes way too much effort. Not enough time has passed.

"How ... how ..." Presh hiccups, then she practically screams, "You died!"

"Yeah," I mumble, not remotely in control of my limbs yet. "I do that. Occasionally."

Someone snarls over the phone still pressed to Presh's ear, loud enough that I can hear the command but not the exact words. Presh winces and almost drops the device into the blood-and-rain-sodden sand as she gets the phone switched to speaker mode.

"Get in the fucking car and get out of there," a deep voice says over the phone, clearer now.

"On the same page," I say, making it up onto all fours. Well, kind of slumped on my knees and elbows, really. I doubt the snarling asshole on the other end of the phone can hear me, though.

"I went to the car ..." Presh stammers. "I promise ... but ... I couldn't ... I couldn't get it started." She continues explaining, but I'm either missing chunks of sentences — my brain not quite firing properly yet — or she's speaking very erratically. "... my arm ... saw the phone ... Rath."

Rath.

That's whose voice is coming through the phone, all snarling and demanding.

For a moment, he had sounded so familiar — in an aching, lost, other-life sort of way. Which didn't make any sense. Doesn't make sense.

Someone else groans nearby. I realize that while I was dead, Presh has managed to drag me only a couple of feet away from Chains. And Breaker. Hence all the blood soaked into the sand under my hands and knees. I turn my head the little I can control it and keep it steady at the same time. I look up at the sky. Does it look the same?

"How much ... how long?" I try to ask, completely confused.

Presh gets what I mean, thankfully. "About fifteen minutes."

Fifteen minutes?

How am I fucking awake, let alone trying to move, after only fifteen minutes?

The last time I died, I didn't truly wake for a week. Though that wasn't quite the same thing as all the times before, because I had simply dropped dead where I stood when my inheritance transferred to me without warning. When I became the Conduit.

But the last time, the time before that, eighteen months ago, I lost three days and woke up in a fucking morgue —

Then I feel the *knowing*.

The eddy of energy runs under my hands and knees, covered in blood and sand. It's trying to tug me back to the car. Me and Presh.

We need to go.

Now.

I start crawling, leaving the makeshift shelter, the unconscious biker, and the dead berserker behind. I'm not capable of doing anything about what happened before I died right now. I'm only capable of falling into the *knowing* and hoping it keeps me moving. Ramifications, repercussions, will have to wait.

Because I wouldn't have woken if staying on the beach was an option.

Presh is with me, tugging at my shoulder and trying to help me up. But she's hurt. In a bunch of places that I don't stop, can't stop, to assess.

She's also talking again. Into the phone, I think. "The car won't start, and the ... the motorcycles are ... too heavy."

I don't hear Rath's response. Presumably because he's not shouting anymore. Or not shouting on speaker, at least.

Behind us, Chains groans again. Louder this time. He's waking up.

I hesitate, pushing up onto my knees until I'm sitting back

on my heels. My clothing is shredded and soaked in a mixture of congealing blood, rainwater, and gray sand. My hair is heavy with that combo too, draped over my shoulders. Otherwise, as far as I can see, I don't have a scar or a wound on me.

I'm weak, lightheaded, and I'm so thin that my bones are jutting through my pale skin. But that's all as expected, including losing the bulk of my muscle mass to fuel the transference from death to life.

Even if I was dead for only fifteen minutes this time.

I glance back at Chains. He's sprawled where he fell, still partially up against the stone wall.

Presh crouches beside me, huddling into me. She cups the phone against her chest and shivers, her tank top and panties soaked through. "Yeah, he's still alive. Should ... we ... kill him?"

I take a moment, trying to see the threads of life surrounding the shifter biker, but that part of my bag of tricks isn't back online yet. Which confirms that I'm only on my feet because I need to get Presh out of here.

Well, partly on my feet.

Okay, mostly still on my knees and hands.

"His death is not mine or yours to take," I say.

She blinks at me, then tries to smile. "Because you say so."

I manage a soft laugh at her throwing my words back at me. "Yeah, something like that."

A voice — no doubt still Rath — muffled against Presh's chest comes through from the phone. It sounds demanding.

Both of us ignore him, slowly getting to our feet and walking the short distance around the stone wall and to the back of the car. Presh is limping. I'm unsteady, not completely back to the land of the living and in command of my body yet.

"See?" Presh says, pointing to the side of the car crumpled up against the wall. Trying to confirm its not-operational state.

"It will run," I say, ignoring the stupid pinch in my heart over the destruction of a thing as pretty as the classic car. It's just an object. It can either be fixed or not.

Presh huffs. At what she perceives as obstinacy on my part. But I'm not stubborn ... well, I'm not currently being stubborn. I do just *know*. Because a quick glance around is enough to tell me that the car is our only obvious option for escape. And a full-blown *knowing* generally smooths the way for me.

How?

No idea. I just go with it.

The trunk opens under my hands, even though I should have needed the key. Again, I usually ignore little things like that, because I can't actually control such things, even if they're otherworldly in nature to begin with. It's simpler to assume that the original crash jarred something loose in the locking mechanism.

I note that one of the massive motorbikes has fallen over. Perhaps that's why Presh is limping? Or maybe that injury is from when she tripped Chains?

I open my suitcase, yanking out the first items of clothing I come across — a tank top, underwear, sweater, and some leggings. All way too large for Presh, but dry.

"Strip," I say, pulling out a similar set of clothing for myself and setting both to the side.

Rath's voice emanates over my phone. Apparently, Presh has put it on speaker again. Or my hearing is coming and going. "I can see you're not moving." The snarling asshole's tone is cool now, but clearly frustrated.

"He's tracking the phone," Presh says, setting the device down in the trunk, tugging the wet wad of cash out of her underwear, then struggling to strip off her tank top and panties.

I gather her multicolored hair in my hands, giving it a twist and squeeze. Then, as she stands there naked and shivering, I use her wet tank top to try to wipe off the diluted blood still staining her tanned skin.

Presh starts to dress her lower half as I cross around her to clean off her back. She's got welts all over her that are going to bloom into nasty bruises in the next few hours. On her hip, shoulder, and the entire right side of her face. Plus a nasty cut on her right temple — from the car crash, presumably — that I'm careful to not prod too much so it doesn't start bleeding again.

Nothing life threatening, so I can wait until we feel a little safer to address her wounds.

"Still not moving," Rath snaps over the phone's speaker.

We ignore him.

I help Presh get the new tank top and sweater on. She winces, but doesn't cry out. Then I strip myself. I'm not wounded, but I'm also not fully in control of my limbs, my body, my thoughts.

The *knowing* tugs at me. Insistently.

"Toss the clothing over the wall." I lean over to wring out my own hair, inadvertently getting more watery blood all over my bare feet, before I dress in clean clothing. "Raining or not, our DNA and essence signatures are all over the beach already. But it's better to limit how much of Breaker and Chains we drag back into the car."

"I'm sending a cleanup crew," Rath says over the phone.

"I'm pissed about my boots," I say, somewhat randomly. I have someone, usually coordinated through Coda, that I can call to help clean up my messes as well. But I'm not that functional at the moment. "I got them custom made. In Italy."

Rath huffs over the speakers, but doesn't bother answering me. I haven't asked what club he belongs to, but apparently he's high ranking enough that he can call in favors. Like the safe house he's trying to get us moving towards, and the aforementioned cleanup crew.

Presh bundles all the bloodied clothing together, limps back a couple of steps, and awkwardly heaves the pile over the wall.

I hand her an elastic hair tie when she returns, pulling my own hair up in a wet mess of a bun with a second one. Normally, I carry only a single tie when I travel, utilized when washing my face before bed. I ignore the implications of having two in my travel kit for this particular journey. Just like I ignored that my pastel rainbow nail polish matches Presh's hair color. That kind of thinking is a trap of endless, mind-smothering loops of what-ifs.

My nail polish matched Presh's hair. Past tense. As with my wounds, the color on my fingers and toes is gone. My hair cut and color, my lash tint, the birth control that I really only use so I don't menstruate, have all been ... reset. For lack of a better way to put it. Reset with my death.

And yeah, I don't really know how it works. Just that it happens. Same with the slow aging. I have some sort of default setting that kicked in around age twenty-five or so — and the universe just ... reboots me.

Presh grabs the phone and the still-wet cash. I try to

close the trunk, but it doesn't want to firmly latch. I'll have to avoid another high-speed chase or big bumps.

"Muta!" I call sharply.

A moment of silence follows my command, reinforcing the stillness of the entire area, other than the pounding surf on the far edge of the expansive beach. Then a massive snake slithers out from under a crumpled portion of the stone wall. Muta hates being wet almost as much as being cold.

Presh meeps like she's forgotten there was a ten-foot-long, extremely venomous snake hanging around on the beach.

I crouch down, slightly worried that I won't be able to straighten back up, offering my right arm to Muta.

"I ... I thought maybe I'd just hit my head really hard," Presh whispers.

"You did," I say. "But Muta is real."

Muta sets his broad head in my hand, covering my entire palm. He flicks his tongue over my wrist, smelling me. He's not a fan of me dying, and I like to think that aversion is grounded in more than just my body going cold and uninhabitable. But even after twenty years — since my mother died on my ninth birthday and he transferred his protection to me — I'm not quite certain he gives a shit about anything at all. Not with actual empathy or the like.

Being an aspect of the divine trapped in the body of a snake and tied to a human bloodline doesn't mean that Muta is capable of ... well, feeling. Opinions regarding his status? Yes. True affection? Big nope.

Muta slithers over my hand and up my arm, shrinking, condensing, and then hardening into a spiraled bracelet of gold and topaz once more.

"Oh, my goddess," Presh breathes, making me wonder

if that's just an expression or whether or not she worships a particular entity. If she does subscribe to a faith, I need to be careful what I say and do around her. For a while, at least. I can be a bit gentle as the unassailable truths of the universe, and all the fundamental energy that actually propels it, start slapping her in the face.

"He's pretty, but he's a total asshole," I say instead of delving into a subject I don't have the fortitude to navigate at the moment. I actually manage to straighten up and stand steady on my feet. "Just like most males."

Presh laughs quietly. "I'm not a fan myself." Then seeming to remember the phone she's carrying and who might still be listening to our conversation, she adds, "Other than my brothers. But you meant ... like you meant ... as, like, lovers, right?"

"Males are good for lots of things ..." I wink as I guide her to crawl across the driver's seat into the passenger seat. I'm more than aware of the eavesdropper lurking on the edge of our chat. I'm also aware that Presh needs to fill this space between us, this moment in general, with something slightly more normal than being kidnapped, threatened with bodily harm and rape, then watching a woman she's just met die and come back to life. "But I generally prefer their mouths shut, unless otherwise occupied."

A snort emanates over the phone's speaker. It's drowned out by Presh's quiet giggle as I climb inside the car and shut the door. Both of us are still barefoot. Presh because my shoes probably won't fit her, and me because I'm still only about twenty percent functional. At most. And that minimal functionality needs to be applied to driving for the next thirty minutes at least, so I'm not bothering with socks and shoes.

I'm not sure I have five minutes in me, let alone twenty-five more on top of that.

I reach for the keys.

The car starts, purring gently after the initial roar of the powerful engine. Heat blasts out of the vents, though I don't remember having the fan running so high at the time of the crash.

I leave that thought unexplored, along with all the other recent thoughts about nail polish and hair ties. Oh, and a car whose trunk opened by itself, and that wouldn't start for Presh but easily starts for me.

"What the fuck?" Presh pretty much snarls.

"About time," Rath snaps over the phone.

The clutch gives me a bit of trouble — likely my problem rather than the car being difficult — but I get us moving, inching around the abandoned motorcycles.

"Sunglasses," I say. "Glove box. Please."

Still shivering, Presh finds my second set of black-framed designer sunglasses and passes them to me. I put them on, feeling instantly relieved. Though that might have more to do with settling into the flow of the *knowing* rather than any mitigating of my sensitive sight.

As we continue along it, the beachside road is still empty. As before, the houses, most of them still larger, older dwellings set back from the road behind ancient-looking trees, appear likewise empty. But I have no doubt we've been seen, noted. Someone might just be waiting to take a jaunt down to the beach — before Rath's cleanup crew arrives — to take care of Chains for us.

Presh gets the map app open and the directions to the safe house on screen. According to the app, we've still got twenty-seven minutes before we reach our destination.

"I'm on my way," Rath says unprompted. Though he

still doesn't give any hint of a timeline. Presh slumps back in the passenger seat and doesn't question him.

I glance in the rearview mirror, just once. Just in time to see Chains stagger out into the middle of the road, watching us drive away.

I shift gears, gaining a bit more speed, briefly thinking that disabling the bikes might have been a good idea. But I don't mention it to Presh. The *knowing* pushed me to the car, not the bikes.

"I've ... I've got to make a few calls, Precious," Rath says. "But Rought is tracking you, and Reck is on his way as well. Just ... coming from another direction."

More interesting names. A little heavy on the obvious, perhaps, making the assumption that it's 'Rought' and not 'Rot,' and that both have dropped the *W*'s as Rath has. Presh doesn't respond to her brother, not that there's much information in anything he's said. But I glance over to see that she's actually fallen asleep. An exhausted, involuntary sleep.

"She's sleeping," I murmur. An ache lodges in my chest, even though a moment before, I was feeling slightly easier. And I honestly don't know if it's the *knowing* readying a twist or a turn, or if it was Rath's mention of two more of his club members. More brothers?

Why would those nicknames mean anything to me?

Rath, Rought, and Reck.

I've never heard of any of them.

Rath still hasn't hung up. I pick up his breathing over the line — or more like an inhalation before saying something — but then no words follow. I'm not wholly inhabiting my body yet, so there's no way I'm taking my hands off the steering wheel to disconnect the call myself.

"Call me back if you need me," he finally says.

I don't bother answering, because not only don't I know him, I rarely have occasion to actually need ... anyone or anything.

That *something* lodged in my chest aches. An empty ache, like a hollowed-out wound.

It's just from dying, I tell myself. I should be sleeping, not trying to operate a fucking car. But it hurts worse after Rath ends the call and the line between us literally disconnects.

THE CAR DIES ABOUT A MILE FROM OUR destination. The engine just cuts out, but I have more than enough time to roll us to a gentle stop partway off the road. Then I turn on the hazard lights.

Just a few minutes earlier, the seaside vista opened up to the west, and the road suddenly smoothed, recently paved. I blink through my exhausted haze and spot actual street-lights ahead through the rain-splattered windshield.

Rath's route has kept us near the ocean, but as we headed farther south, we seemingly left claimed territory behind. The houses became more sporadic and run-down, the road overgrown and marred by potholes. Those derelict residences then gave way to seemingly abandoned businesses and warehouses, with faded For Sale signs propped up in broken front windows.

Presh jerks awake, blinking and gasping for her next two ragged breaths. Then she locks her gaze on me, and she instantly settles.

"The car?" she murmurs.

We both ignore whatever nightmare was running in her head while she slept. Only time eases that sort of thing. I already know that I'm going to relive the events of the beach in my waking hours for years. In the long dark of night, they will haunt me enough to make sleep only a dream. But we have to keep moving to achieve that delightful future, anticipated nightmares or not.

I've never killed a person before. Berserker or otherwise. Well ...

I've never personally slit the throat of a sentient being before. Even though when a knowing moves me, people often die in my way or in my wake. But I didn't typically bathe in their blood as I'd inadvertently done with Breaker.

"We're close enough to walk," I say, but I don't make a move to open my door yet. Rain continues to accumulate on the windshield as I wait. I'm exhausted, yes. But I'm also giving Presh the moment she needs to ask me the questions that have to be flooding her mind now that she's slept for a bit.

She grabs my phone, but then just rolls it over and over in her hands without dialing. "Do ... do all awry have that ability? To die and then just come back? Do I?"

"No. No, Presh. I am the only awry with that ability, as dubious as it is."

Still slightly bowed over the phone, she tilts her head just enough to look at me out of the corner of her eye. I can't tell, now that the panic and the adrenaline have ebbed, if she finds me terrifying or if she's just naturally reserved and thoughtful about discussing the nature of my power.

"I ... missed you healing."

I nod, looking back out the front window. I don't fill any of the dead air between us. I'm not sure I have a conversation in me. Though I do know I can't sit still for much longer.

"But you actually died."

"Yes."

"I went to the car. It wouldn't start. I tried the bike, and it fell over on me. Then I remembered the phone. I was going to start walking. I ... I ... was just going to leave you."

"I told you to leave, Presh," I say gently.

She lowers her voice in a whisper. "It was Rath who made me go back."

"What? Why?"

She shakes her head, not offering any further insight into whatever conversation took place with her brother — who should have demanded that his little sister race toward safety while I was being rebooted on the beach. "You were still dead, I thought. But you had ... healed?"

I nod, not offering any clarification. Mostly because even though I know my aunt also had the ability, I've never seen anyone else do what I can do.

"How long ... that wasn't the first time that had happened to you. You said ... you said it was taking too long ... and then you didn't expect for it to happen so quickly? I mean, for you to wake up so quickly?"

I think about that for a while, but the memories surrounding my deaths are indistinct. More than hazy. Especially the first time it supposedly happened, thirteen years ago now. Of that I have no memory, only my aunt's recounting. Even she hadn't known I would revive, hadn't known I was Everlasting like she was. She thought I was actually dead.

I could pontificate about why the universe brought me back, but I don't. Because it just is.

"The ... healing ... of my physical body happens quickly." I'm not actually certain that using the term healing is correct. When it happens, I'm just suddenly whole again, but that process drains me in other ways. Normally, I would sleep for three days at minimum, but gaining back the weight and the energy drain could take weeks. Will take weeks. "But we need to keep moving, okay? I'm semifunctional now, but might not be for much longer."

Presh swallows, possibly stifling her next follow-up question. But then she dials the phone and switches it over to speaker.

Rath answers on the fifth ring. "You're there?"

"We're walking the last bit," Presh says. "The car died."

"Send me a screenshot of your current location on the map, then keep moving. I'll have someone pick up the car."

"How much longer, Rath?" Presh asks, practically pressing her lips against the phone even though she has it on speaker.

"I'm ... I'm sorry, Presh, I'm at least an hour out," he says, sounding like a caring brother for a moment. "I ... we ran into a bit of interference."

Presh's hand shakes. "Dad?"

"No," he says gruffly. It's instantly obvious that there are things he doesn't want to discuss within my hearing. And that's fine by me. It's not my business. I'm in this moment for Presh, and Presh only. "You know he can't cross the border."

She huffs at him, annoyed. "You know what I mean."

"Room five," he says instead of answering her. Again. "The door will be unlocked. Get in. Lock the door behind you. There's a gun taped under the side table. Then text me."

"Yeah, yeah," she says almost playfully.

I've never had a sibling or even a cousin close to me in

age, so maybe this is just typical relationship dynamics between an older brother and a younger sister. Of course, that younger sister has just been through some major shit, so maybe Rath's reaction has been mild. So far.

Or maybe he's barely hanging on, and I should expect him to explode all over me when he finally shows up.

"Reck might get to you first, and ..."

Presh waits for Rath to finish the sentence. But when he doesn't, she says, "He's seriously pissed?"

"Yeah ... but not at you."

Something is hidden in the pause between 'yeah' and 'but.' It tickles my awry senses, as if I should *know* what is going on. With this situation? Or with this family?

I don't.

"Okay."

"Just ... keep the gun near."

She huffs again. "I know."

"Go." He disconnects the call.

I get out of the car, really not certain how I'm actually still on my feet. I grab my suitcase out of the broken trunk, because we're going to have to change again, and Presh needs some focused healing.

I realize that I haven't fully answered Presh's questions — and also that I might have downplayed the most important part. "Precious," I say, "you were listening, right? When I said that no one has the ability to come back from full death like I do?"

She chews on her lower lip, nodding. "I've never met anyone with purple eyes."

"You will learn what you can do, what your own purple eyes mean, in time. But being an awry doesn't mean that you can throw yourself toward death and expect to survive it."

She crinkles her nose. Then, reminding me that she's only a teenager, she says, "It looked seriously nasty. I don't think anyone would actually want to be able to do that, Zaya."

"Okay. Good."

I've really fucked with Presh's fate today. My death hopefully evens out that balance, but ... I didn't think about the ramifications of a burgeoning awry, with no understanding of what her powers might be, using me as any sort of measuring stick.

Both of us are exhausted again just by the effort of getting out of the car. So we walk in slow silence along the side of the road, shoulders brushing, but not speaking. Huge raindrops pelt us, pelt the pavement so hard they bounce off, causing pretty flares of backsplash.

THE DAY IS GETTING GRAYER AND WETTER AS WE approach our destination — a cute, two-tier motel with white siding and light-blue doors perched on a low cliff overhanging a sandy beach. The Crescent Moon Inn. It's the first building on the ocean side of the road that we've come across since leaving the car. What appears to be a mostly residential area spreads out beyond the inn. Even in the brief glance I get of it, it's obvious that this entire township has been completely revitalized by someone, or an organization, with deep pockets.

The No Vacancy sign is lit, but the parking lot isn't even a third full. Best guess? Rath — which is to say, his biker club — has enough pull to rent out the entire place for the afternoon, excepting any already occupied rooms.

Presh and I are soaked through. Again. But thankfully, my wheeled suitcase and bag protect most of what we're dragging along with us. Or that I'm dragging, because Presh's limp is getting worse and worse.

A few cars going in the same direction have slipped past us while we walked, slowing and politely giving us a wide berth but not taking a second or third look. I'm not surprised. Even if they can't see my eyes through my sunglasses, we're strangers walking through neutral territory. Well, limping through. But still upright.

The clerk behind the reception desk in the motel office doesn't look up as we pass, rather pointedly turning their back and cranking up the volume of the overhead TV.

I'm not quite certain how I'm still managing to put one foot in front of the other as we cut straight through the parking lot and up to unit five on the ground floor. No one steps out of any of the other rooms. Unit five is literally in the center of the building, which feels like an odd choice. I would have picked a corner. Because if we have to run, anyone could be hiding in any of the other ground-floor units.

It's not my call, though. And I'm too spent, beyond tired and into the realm of utterly numb, to fuss.

The *knowing* releases me the moment I lay my hand on the door latch, and I pause for a moment. Waiting. Allowing my barely functional senses to stretch out around us — an awareness more than anything actionable, really.

The gutters on the corner overhanging the front reception area and office are clogged, overflowing. Just beyond that corner of the building, a few seagulls circle, likely directly above the composter tucked around the side of the motel. A few cars speed past on the main road. No one else abruptly appears or looks out a window.

My awry senses — usually attuned to the essence of life — aren't functioning at the moment. Even Presh with her spiral of branched, multi-tiered threads is just a quiet, shivering presence tucked at my side.

"Zaya?" she asks in a whisper.

"We're okay here," I say, turning the latch and opening the door.

Inside the room, the far bedside table lamp is on. The overhead lights are off. Fresh towels — presumably in addition to those already in the bathroom — and a large first-aid kit are set on the nearer of the two double beds. The walls are painted a soft beige, and the machine-quilted comforters are light blue. The gauzier of the two front curtains is drawn, but the darker-blue blackout drapes are still open.

I pause again, dripping on the threshold. Nothing moves or shifts in the plain but clean motel room. It smells like unscented air freshener.

"Zaya?" Presh asks again gently, touching my elbow as if she expects me to tip over at any moment.

And she's not wrong.

"I'm not totally functional," I say.

It doesn't completely explain my freezing in place twice in a row, but Presh nods, firms her grip on my elbow, and practically shoves me a couple of steps into the room, just enough to close the door behind us.

Straining up on her toes and panting through pain while doing so, she runs her hand along the top and then along the unhinged side of the door, activating a pressure-triggered locking mechanism. Unseen bolts clank into place on the door one by one, three at the top and bottom and five along the edge, judging by the sound.

The door will be fortified against shifters or any mage with the strength to simply bust through it. If I had any brainpower to spare, I could check the front window and would likely find essence-fortified glass as well. The walls are no doubt similarly constructed.

So unit five was actually a very deliberate choice, given what Rath knows of who was chasing us.

"Whose territory?" I ask, because I should at least know that much.

"The Outcast Motorcycle Club," Presh says, puffing out her chest a bit, proudly. "My uncle's pack." She holds up the phone, which still displays the map app. The icon that indicates our position is just a smidge over a slightly shaded border.

I've heard of the Outcast MC. A mixed clan — not exclusively bear, wolf, boar, or cat — they hold a huge territory. A large section of Oregon, presumably with continual plans for expansion. The Outcast territory actually encircles and protects my aunt's estate, which is at least two hours from here by car ...

No.

Fuck.

The Outcast Motorcycle Club protects the borders of *my* West Coast estate. Once I get that tangle of shit sorted, I need to set up a meeting with Presh's uncle, or one of the Outcast lieutenants, to renegotiate the contract that dictates those protections.

Even the idea is exhausting.

Only vaguely aware that I've abruptly dropped the conversation, I loosen my hold on the suitcase and drop my bag off my shoulder. Then, careful not to touch anything else, I take the two necessary steps to the bed and grab all the towels. Presh stays by the door. Because as has become too obvious, she is way more versed in this … clandestine shit than she should be at her age.

I step back and offer the pile of towels to Presh. She takes the top one, still favoring one arm, and lays it lengthwise before my feet. I step on it, and she steps on the other end. Thankfully it's huge, presumably sized for shifters.

I drop all but one of the towels to the side, wrapping the last one around Presh and giving in to the impulse to pull her into a hug. It's intimate considering we barely know each other. Yet her arms latch low around my waist, and I rock her gently nonetheless.

Even though the tug of the knowing is no longer guiding me, I have a hard time letting her go. Until she starts shivering again.

We wipe our bare feet on the towel. Thankfully, the pavement was smooth enough on our way to the motel that neither of us appears to have cut our feet. We towel dry our hair, then strip out of our clothing by the front door, leaving everything in a pile on the floor towel and dragging the suitcase to the bathroom. I pull all my soaps, shampoos, conditioners, lotions, and face creams out of my travel kit, lining them up on the side of the tub and the counter.

Presh tries to swallow a smirk. Unsuccessfully.

"What?" I snap playfully, so tired I can't believe I can form the words, let alone the teasing tone. "I like to feel and smell pretty." The creams and such are actually fairly quietly scented — a custom Madagascar vanilla-and-cocoa-butter blend made for me based on my skin type, among other attributes, by a potion mage in Vancouver.

The mage's wares are rather ... well, famous. She's also a former paramour of my uncles. Her word, not mine. And yes, more than one so-called uncle — a designation my family uses for any older-than-me, male-identifying person who shares even a hint of my bloodline. I have a lot of cousins with even thinner blood connections as well. Either way, I'm glad the branding on the mage's bottles and jars is subtle. Otherwise, Presh might freak about how much money we're about to slather all over our bodies.

Not that I've paid a cent for any of it.

I don't think about how it might be odd for Presh to smell exactly like me when her shifter brothers show up. Because her doing so is actually an extra precaution, an extra bit of protection that I can give her in the immediate now. Once I'm done, it will smell as though there was only ever one person in this motel room. Me.

And I can't be tracked by scent. Not for long, at least. I might not be bequeathed with strength or speed, or any overtly offensive magic, but my inherent essence protects me in a multitude of minor ways. Admittedly, those ways are completely unpredictable, so I try to augment them when possible — hence the custom creams.

Presh and I shower. Then, with both of us cocooned in all the dry towels remaining, I carefully apply most of the emergency healing patches I have on hand to her bruised shoulder, hip, and ankle. I don't even bother looking in the first-aid kit the motel provided. I know what I've brought is better, more potent. I add another patch to the side of her face, carefully cutting out a section so it fits around her eye, then apply the leftover piece to the reopened cut on her temple.

The patches are pricey, heavy-duty, essence-imbued

emollients. For which I've actually paid full price, from a different potion mage contact in Vancouver — one with a healing affinity. I'm hoping Presh isn't naturally resistant to magecraft as some essence-wielders are — and many of the awry specifically. As I occasionally am.

I don't usually carry so many patches with me, or even have so many on hand at one time, because they come with short expiration dates. And yes, my packing extra healing patches for this trip is yet another of those pre-knowing things that I'm actively ignoring. My abilities have never previously ... stretched so far from the before through an actual knowing, so this is all new to me.

Not to mention that I'm just too tired to dissect it.

"It tingles," Presh whispers as I fit the last patch. She's been watching my every move as if she's committing them to memory — and maybe she is. Maybe her slowly awakening power is guiding her as well.

"Too much?"

She shakes her head, biting her lip. "Don't ... don't you need some?"

"Do I look like I do?" I don't have a mark on me, though I need to eat my weight in dark-chocolate-coconut or salted-caramel ice cream. And poutine, if I can find a place that uses turkey or chicken gravy, not beef. But that's not going to happen any time soon.

"No," she whispers.

I wait for more questions as I dig through my suitcase to put together a cozy outfit for Presh. She must have at least a half-dozen more stored up by now. She doesn't ask them, though.

She's just as exhausted as I am.

We get dressed. A light-gray cashmere sweatshirt and

drawstring sweatpants for Presh, over a too-large sports bra and panties. An ankle-length drawstring cashmere skirt and merino-and-silk tank top for me. Drawstring items don't usually make up so much of my wardrobe, but they're certainly coming in handy for this particular trip, what with Presh being tiny and me dropping twenty pounds or so after dying.

I'm seriously testing the coziest offerings among the limited items I stuffed into my suitcase for this trip. The silk robe and anything that isn't size adaptive is pretty much useless. Presh is able to cinch the waist of the sweatpants enough that they don't fall down, but she still has to roll up the cuffs. My only pair of hand-knit merino-and-cashmere-wool socks are too large, but she just pulls them on and hums contentedly. I go barefoot.

Had I had any inkling that I was about to be caught up in a knowing involving shifters, I might have packed more oversized sweaters. Or a gun and some silver shot. Not that I own any sort of weapon, and not that the pistol I took off Chains even worked on Breaker in berserker mode. But I had followed the impulse to drive down the coast without thinking much about it.

Ironically, if I had planned it out, I would have booked a flight instead. I could blame it on my inheritance still settling in. Except that abruptly fleeing the city, or the country for that matter, isn't all that out of the ordinary for me.

I once wandered into the airport and randomly caught the next international flight to depart, finding myself flying to New Zealand, then living there for over six months with only my backpack, passport, and the clothing I was wearing. There had ultimately been *reasons* for that trip — a milder version of the knowings that grab hold of me far more strongly now. But I wasn't one to dwell on the past. Or even luxuriate in the present, really. So when I needed to leave New Zealand, I did, almost as abruptly as I'd arrived.

Presh curls her warm fingers around my wrist, and I realize I've been standing in the middle of the bathroom for so long that all the steam has faded from the air and cleared from the mirror.

"Do you want ... to sit down?" She tugs on my arm a little.

I shake my head. "Not yet." Once I sit, I know I'm not getting back up.

I not-so-carefully repack the suitcase with everything I've pulled out except the rest of the healing patches. I wipe the drain and pull out any loose hair I can find, using a washcloth that I'll add to the pile of wet clothing at the front door. I'm hoping we've both washed off the last of the blood, but the tub is going to need to be bleached.

"Rath will look after it," Presh says, her tone gentle as if she knows I'm barely holding the newly gathered pieces of myself together.

"Did you ..." I frown. I might have lost time between the door and the shower. "Text him?"

"Yes. Right away."

She tugs at my hand again, and this time I allow her to pull me to the bed nearest the door. But I don't sit down until I've bundled all the discarded clothing and used towels in one larger towel, knotting it at the corners. It will need to be burned to be really safe. Fire destroys essence residual, along with blood and DNA.

"Can we sit?" Presh asks, utterly exhausted.

"Yes. I'm just going to check your patches. Are they still working?"

"Still tingly?"

"Yes."

She nods, letting me check the patch on her hip, then perching on the edge of the bed. I can reach the others while she's sitting.

"Healing," I say, pleased to confirm that she isn't resistant to magecraft. At least not beneficial craft. A good thing, in this case. An issue to tackle in the near future, for all other cases. The patches are the work of a powerful healer, though, and Presh in her current unawakened state wouldn't draw the attention of a mage of that caliber even if placed directly in her path.

I'm adept at steering people's paths. Usually.

"Thank you."

"Do you want to lie down?" I ask.

"Will you?"

"No."

"Then I'll stay up with you."

I sit, finally, on the edge of the bed facing the door. I tuck Presh on the side next to the wall, which makes it easier to shield her with my body but not as easy for her to run. "You roll back," I say. "If someone comes through that door you don't recognize, you roll back and drop between the beds."

She nods.

Remembering Rath's final directive, I reach around her and pass my hand under the side table. I find the gun — a lightweight energy weapon of some sort, not projectile. Wrapping my fingers firmly around the grip and keeping it pointed away from Presh, I yank it free from the tape. It's black, snub-nosed, and essence-fueled at best guess. Likely requiring little to no accuracy when wielded by a novice, but good for only three or four full-powered shots.

"Right," Presh murmurs. "I'm just so tired."

"It's the adrenaline. And the healing patches."

I set the gun beside me on the bed, pressed under my hand and pointed toward the door. Other than instinctively using what weapons come to me — when guided by a knowing — I've never trained to handle guns of any sort. I have a feeling I should pass the weapon to Presh. A feeling that despite being easily fourteen years younger than me, she has the experience I lack. Except she snuggles into me, tucks her arm around my bicep, threads her fingers through mine, and sets her head on my shoulder.

I let her drift. But I hold on.

Just for a bit longer.

I keep my gaze on the door, and I try to hold myself awake and aware and pinned in the moment. I can't fall asleep until I know Presh is safe. As safe as she can be. Though the quiet, unsettled ache in my chest still hasn't really faded. And that, along with what little info I've pieced together about her family, tells me that Presh's safety might not be as simple a thing as getting her to her brothers.

"Thank you, Zaya."

"Anytime, Precious," I say. And I mean it.

I'm not certain, despite the countless knowings I've experienced, that I've ever loved anyone as quickly as I've fallen for Presh. It's as if ...

Maybe we're essence bound? Maybe she somehow belongs to me, with me?

But that's an utterly idiotic thought.

Because no individual belongs to me.

Just as I belong to no one, yet belong to everyone at the same time.

I'm not really a person, not with hopes and dreams, stumbling on and off a destined path. I'm Everlasting, yet I don't actually exist. Not solely for myself, at least. My mark on this universe is fundamental, yet not in any way individual. At least not since three weeks ago, when my inheritance abruptly and suddenly transferred to me without warning. Stopping not only my heart but ending my life — and my immediate future — as I'd known it.

FOUR

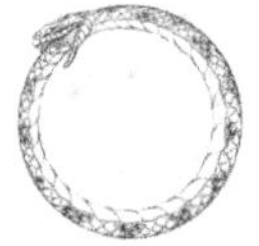

RATH

The interior light filtering through the thin curtains of unit five of the Crescent Moon Inn is muted, dim. I'm an hour and a half later than I want to be, but I managed to get enforcers on site from about ten minutes after Presh arrived.

And the woman claiming to be Zaya Gage.

We got jumped by some unaffiliated bikers on the way to the motel, and I'm nursing a fucking silver bullet wound that I could heal just by transforming. But I don't have the time — or the space — to let my beast out right now. My uncle is already going to have questions when he notices how many Outcast I've pulled in for protection duty. He adores Presh. All of us do. But along with the ongoing surveillance and cleanup, the bribes and favors that I've called in and promised in the last three hours mean he's going to have questions. Pointed questions.

And I don't yet have answers.

Thankfully, he's currently distracted. And has been for just over three weeks. The circumstances of that distraction aren't something I'd normally be thankful for, but even I know I've invested too much in this operation, financially and resource-wise. Presh would have been okay meeting up with any club member, rather than having me racing across the fucking country to collect her. And Reck, because there was no way to keep him out of it.

But I also know that Zaya Gage is dead.

She died right in front of me. Thirteen years ago.

And the repercussions of that ... that utter ... soul-deep loss have been ... life changing. And not just for Reck, Rought, and me.

So whatever the fuck is going on, from the moment I heard that name, that stranger's voice over the phone, I knew I wasn't going to leave Presh to be escorted home with a minimal guard. With just whoever was nearest.

Likewise, I know I'm not going into that motel room less than fully armed, fully armored. For any and all essence-wielding. And with a shit-ton of backup.

I won't, however, be waiting for Reck.

Reck, I know already, is going to be an explosive fucking problem.

My phone buzzes before I get all the way off my bike. I've parked on the far side of the lot. On either side of me, Grinder and Doc Z remove their helmets but stay perched on their bikes, waiting on my next orders. All three of us are wearing our Outcast leathers, patches clearly on display. As are the half-dozen enforcers arrayed around the property.

Doc is particularly pissed that I've been riding for the last hour with just a healing patch on the bullet wound, but it is what it is. Someone claiming the name of my long-dead first love has rescued my sister. I hadn't even known Precious needed rescuing —

The phone buzzes again, reminding me not for the first time that I'm all up in my head, not thinking clearly. I haven't been since that first phone call. And it isn't just adrenaline …

It's this sickening hope that I'm not going to be able to quash until I lay eyes on her. The fake Zaya.

I glance at my phone. Rought's name flashes on the screen. I need to answer the call because I've sent him farther up the coast, farther away from the impostor. Because he can't be here. Because he's still all in.

He's never wavered, not once in almost thirteen fucking years.

My younger brother is perfectly rational, maybe even too much so, in all other aspects of his life. But he's completely unhinged about the girl we three loved and saw murdered in front of us.

I answer the call, barking, "Report!" like a complete fucking asshole.

Rought's Southern-tinted drawl comes over the line. He retains it because of his mother's side of the family mostly, because neither of us has lived anywhere near our sperm donor since … then. "Someone fucking slit the throat of a fucking berserker up here, then just left the corpse on the fucking beach."

I scrub a hand across my forehead. "We already knew that."

He scoffs. "Yeah, but knowing it is different than seeing it. It's Breaker."

I squeeze my eyes shut, a surge of misplaced adrenaline competing with my pounding headache. "We already knew that too," I say, though Presh hadn't exactly spelled it out through her terror. I swear I can feel my heartbeat in my fucking jaw, in the aching roots of my teeth. "What we don't know is what the fuck was he doing kidnapping Presh?"

"No idea. Except there's no way he was even adjacent to our territory all on his lonesome."

"Chains was with him. He's not on the beach?" Berserkers, even if they are capable of acting remotely human, never travel alone. And trusting one within a mile of Presh? Un-fucking-believable. Even for our shared sperm donor.

"Nope," Rought says. "The Cataclysm is going to be livid."

The Cataclysm. He doesn't mean the entire club or pack. He means the man, the president of the club. The evil fucking asshole who also happens to have spread his seed so liberally that none of us sired by him know how many half-siblings we actually have.

"Wars have been started for less," Rought says, not sounding the least bit concerned about it.

"Not when it's self-defense."

"There's no way Presh did this. And there's way more blood soaked into the sand than even this bastard could bleed out. So whoever else bled here, no doubt died here, has been taken, along with whatever weapon was used, and the second bike."

"Chains," I say. Repeating myself like a stupid asshole because I can't mention Zaya. Can't mention that Presh was sure that the woman who'd rescued her had died, then came back.

I can't deal with that. With the possible ramifications of that. Not right now.

"Yep. You don't get one without the other. But a dead

man couldn't have gotten back on his bike and driven away."

In addition to being Breaker's babysitter, Chains is a lieutenant for the Cataclysm. I've lost count of how many times he beat down Rought, Reck, and me during one of his 'teaching' moments. All of us under eighteen years old at the time, and without our beasts to fortify us. Breaker joined Chains's training sessions on more than one occasion. Before Reck fucking destroyed both of them in a day that's still etched into my memory.

My older brother might have saved Rought's life that day. Maybe even mine.

We hadn't been patched yet, so despite our bloodline, we didn't have the protection of club status. And our sperm donor firmly believed in survival of the fittest, so our deaths would have been a mere footnote for the Cataclysm. That brawl was two against one, and neither bear shifter walked away easily. It wasn't long afterward that the three of us permanently left our father's custody, and Breaker went berserker. With Chains assigned as his permanent keeper.

At the time, our sperm donor seemed to let us go easily. But even though I haven't been able to confirm the suspicion or share it with anyone, I'm pretty certain he still has his claws deep into Reck. So there might have been more at play with our apparent ease at walking away from the Cataclysm — the man and the club — and coming into our uncle's care permanently than I'd thought at the time.

Zaya Gage — a fake Zaya Gage — popping back into our lives is going to fuck up everything we've struggled to build. Every relationship and —

"Right, well, Pinky and her crew are here," Rought says over the phone, pulling me out of my thoughts. "They'll get the body melted and the site scoured."

Pinky is an Outcast mage. She runs the crew that keeps all the club's more … physical businesses as clean as possible. Rought keeps our digital footprint just as squeaky. I keep our reputation stellar within the community and with our partners, managing those businesses and always looking for expansion opportunities.

"Based on what I can see," Rought is saying, "there are four sets of footprints to the beach and three out, if drag marks count. You've got eyes on Presh and her friend?"

'Friend' is how I've explained the identity thief tagging along with Presh during her escape — to everyone but Reck, at least. She-who-is-yet-to-be-named-within-Rought's-hearing-range. The fake Zaya needs to be gone before Rought even gets a whiff of her. I would have stonewalled Reck as well, except he picked up on what was happening and called me.

And yeah, I will deal with whatever surveillance — traditional or essence-wrought — Reck has on me, or in my office, or in the clubhouse, after this shit gets dealt with. I've let that asshole's actions slide, given him the benefit of the doubt, for too many years already.

"I'm about to have eyes on them," I say, hoping Rought puts the pauses in the conversation down to a bad connection.

"I hear there's a sweet ride that needs my attention," Rought says. It's a statement, not a question.

"Yeah," I say. "Grinder tell you? We gave it a look before we hit the motel. It's scratched up bad, wouldn't start. Hurt my heart just a little." Then I add without thinking, "A silver-glossed beauty, 1972 or 1973 BMW 3.0 CSi."

The line goes really quiet.

I'm starting to feel stupid, hanging out in the parking lot as if I'm avoiding what is yet to come. Getting antsy about it like some toddler, and I don't put two and two together until the words are already out of my mouth.

The fucking car.

"A silver 1972 BMW," Rought says, his voice sounding thin, stretched, over the line.

Fuck. Fuck. I open my mouth to answer, to say something.

The line goes all the way dead.

The emotional asshole has hung up on me.

The thing is, we're evenly ranked in the Outcast MC. We've got the same claim on Presh as well. I can't just order him to stay the fuck away.

"Problems?" Grinder asks. He's dark-haired with medium-brown tattoo-covered skin, and a beard going gray, mostly around his chin. Another Outcast lieutenant, he's actually higher ranked than me. But Grinder rarely bothers about that, content to let me lead when the situation dictates it.

"Not if you had kept your mouth shut," I snap, shoving my phone into my inner jacket pocket as I finally step away from my bike.

Grinder doesn't rise to my tone. "What did I do or say that wasn't mine to delegate?"

Yeah, he heard the entire conversation with Rought. Doc would have too. Because all three of us are shifters, with all the heightened senses that come with that, no matter that we three don't share the same beast under our skin. I don't know a single other shifter with my beast counterpart. It's been delegated to mythic status, really, even in Asia. I know because I spent a year in Shanghai while completing my second master's degree on the mythos of essence, with a rare-breed shifter focus.

"Nothing," I growl, vaguely answering Grinder's question. Rought oversees all the Outcast mech, including our bikes and other vehicles. Grinder messaging to let him know that a car needed transport and aftercare is completely appropriate.

I head for unit five, noting the motel manager scurrying alongside the lower level of rooms, aiming to intercept me. He's been hovering by the front window in the office, watching us since we pulled up.

"We need to get eyes on Chains," I say, "starting at the beach location. Apparently, he walked away. Or rode away. I want him found and detained."

"On it," Grinder says, tugging out his phone.

Doc is a still, silent presence on my right. Being quiet really isn't her thing. At least not when we're alone. But I know she's picking up shit from me, as we arrive at unit five — and I just stand there. Staring at the stupid door, and not rushing in to grab my sister.

Doc Z — Zephyr — and I are friends, I suppose, and fuck buddies when we get an itch. Or when she gets the itch. But I haven't told her about that summer with Zaya thirteen years ago, or all the summers stretching back the eight years before that when we were all just kids playing on the beach together. Until we all became something much more.

I don't talk about it with anyone, not even my brothers.

Someone needs to die tonight. Under my claws. Or I need to find an anonymous fuck that won't mind me being rough. And not just for what happened to Presh. Because everything else feels like it's unraveling, completely beyond my control.

Zaya Gage.

We three — her three — are already broken. Cobbled together and barely functioning. But I didn't know how cracked and eroded I still am, not until I heard her name and that raspy, sardonic, pissy tone over the line. None of the sweet or playful girl I ...

No. Someone is trying to fracture us, using rescuing Presh as a way in. It's too much of a coincidence otherwise. And the timing is ridiculously suspect, what with the heart attack that took down our uncle three weeks ago.

A cold resolution settles over me as I reach for the keycard the manager is holding aloft in my direction from the other side of the door. The window is set to the left. I've avoided crossing by it, as has everyone else. The window and door are both graded to repel essence of any kind, from both sides. But only the stupid rely on other people's dedication to their work, or the quality of the materials they use.

I pluck the card from the manager's hand, ignoring how badly he wants to shit his pants. The Outcast work hard for our rep so that we don't have to enforce it very often. The manager — a null — has probably never set eyes on a ranked member before. But the motel owner is a low-level mage and was more than accommodating when I called.

Operating any establishment on the border with the so-called neutral territory is a bloody business. But the property is lucrative, and we've used it as a safe house more than once. Plus, I have ongoing plans to expand that border, reclaiming more of the coast, and giving the motel more of a buffer to the north. As a result, unit five is always held vacant for an Outcast, no reservation needed.

"Go." I warn off the manager, swiping the master key card across all the locks. Numerous bolts release with a resounding clunk.

Grinder steps to the side with Doc, filling the spot the manager was hovering in before scurrying back to the office.

He reaches for the handle, turning it so I can keep my hands free. I'm pretty damn essence-proof and big enough even in my human form to completely fill the doorway, functioning like a bulwark in these sorts of situations.

I give the door a harder kick than I intend, and it slams back beside the window, startling Presh awake just across from me.

My youngest sibling, my only sister as far as I know, almost falls off the bed. The light-brown-haired, pale-skinned, painfully thin woman perched next to her manages to get her free arm in front of her, holding Presh upright. The woman's other hand is wrapped around the grip of the pulse gun she has pointed directly at my chest.

I'm staring. Going from coldly enraged to numb ...

Because the gun I expected. It's a lightweight, untrace-able piece I slipped into the room myself ages ago.

But ... Zaya Gage — a slightly older version of Zaya, and looking like death warmed over — is sitting on a motel bed in Outcast territory.

Alive.

And glaring fucking daggers at me.

Glaring at me as if she doesn't know me at all.

As if she's seriously considering shooting me.

The numbness holding me in place cracks, splintering like a skiff of ice over a dark well of vicious despair.

Her eyes, vibrant and utterly beguiling, are the wrong color.

Bright, soul-fucking-searing violet.

Not the warm, deep purplish-blue I gazed into summer after summer. Not the deadened, darkened purple that stared up into the storm-blackened sky, unseeing. The eyes that still haunt my nightmares, for almost thirteen years now.

My Zaya would be a month away from her thirtieth birthday. This woman, with her slight frame, her dusky pink lips, and her cheekbones and collarbone looking like carved white stone or the age-bleached fucking bones of some prehistoric creature, is too young.

Rage threads through me, and I have to fight against the actual prehistoric creature raging inside me, threatening to tear through my skin.

Because my beast can smell her.

Because despite the eyes being wrong, she smells the same ... muted vanilla tones, with that under-layer of wild

—

It's a fucking spell.

I know it.

Just like whatever dire allure or glamour she's using to mask her true appearance.

"Rath!" Presh cries, up on her feet and running toward me.

Fuck. Less than a second has passed. How could I feel so much in such a short period of time? It's as if I'm the one who's been dead for thirteen years, and suddenly ... suddenly ... everything is different. Again.

Presh flings her arms around me, and I hug her to me automatically without taking my eyes off the impostor. The fake Zaya sighs, leaning way over to set the gun down on the side table, putting it out of reach. Her hand is shaking. It hadn't been a moment ago.

I squeeze Presh tight.

The impostor — I refuse to even refer to her as Zaya — closes her eyes, swaying slightly like she's exhausted.

Presh peels back from my embrace, blinking up at me and smiling. Her eyes are reddened. She's got an expensive-as-fuck healing patch on her face. A patch I know wasn't in the first-aid kit that the motel had on hand. I inhale, and I can smell more of that emollient under the vanilla tones that have smoothed over Presh's natural scent.

As if she's cloaked in it. That has to be intentional. Does the impostor think that'll confuse me, if she masks my sister's scent along with her own?

The impostor is watching us.

No. She's watching Presh. Her gaze is far softer than it was when she was looking at me.

My little sister peels away from me, tugging at my hand and pulling me farther into the room. "This is Zaya, she ... she's like me." Presh looks up at me, chewing her lower lip.

Frowning, I look at my sister. Really look at her. I can't sense what she means until she tilts her head, and I catch the purple undertone in her dark-blue eyes.

"Zaya," she says, "this is my half-brother Rath."

And suddenly my heart is in my throat. I get that it's just my pulse thrumming through the veins in my neck, but it literally chokes me for a moment.

Presh hasn't manifested as a shifter.

She's ... awry.

The running away and subsequent kidnapping make so much more sense now.

"Pleased to meet you, Rath," the impostor says. Her sweet rasp is thinner, almost reedy now. No hint of the playfulness or that sudden scathing anger she sent my way on the phone.

She reaches for Presh.

I jerk forward, not sure if I mean to yank my sister away ... or to crush the fake Zaya to my chest and beg her to stop looking at me as if I'm a fucking stranger.

They both frown at me for a moment. Then Zaya shakes her head a little and turns her attention back to

Presh. "We should check these," she says, indicating the healing patch that practically covers one side of Presh's face. "Still tingling?"

Presh shakes her head in response, moving back to the bed.

The impostor gently peels the patch off, narrowing her eyes at the dark bruise across Presh's cheekbone as if she could murder it with a single thought.

And maybe she can kill like that. I have no idea what sort of awry she is ... unless the eye color is just part of her disguise —

Of course it's part of her fucking disguise! What the fuck else could any of this be?

Fake Zaya peels the smaller patch from Presh's temple. The wound there is puckered, partially healed but still raw looking.

"Ribs," the impostor says.

Presh lifts up the sweatshirt-sweater thing she's wearing that looks like it costs the price of a used car. Zaya peels the healing patch on Presh's lower ribs away, nodding once as if slightly more satisfied. What I can see of that bruise looks days old.

That doesn't help with the anger, though.

"Hip?"

"Motherfucker," I mutter under my breath.

They both ignore me.

Someone beat the hell out of my little sister. I hope it's the dead fucker on the beach.

No. I hope it's fucking Chains. Because I am going to slit his throat myself, no claws needed.

The impostor peels the patch off Presh's hip and nods again, somewhat satisfied. She reaches for a fresh patch. I hadn't noticed the short stack on the bed beside her.

Between those and the four pieces she's already peeled off my sister, she's casually tossed at least ten thousand dollars away on healing a stranger.

An awry like her.

Which makes a bit more sense.

Except the awry connection muddies the idea that the impostor is involved in this kidnapping scheme as some kind of attempt to worm her way back into our lives. So ignoring the fact that I wouldn't think it possible to replicate the tumultuous energy underpinning her gaze, the eyes have got to be fake, along with the resemblance and the scent. That makes more sense.

And there is no 'back into our lives.'

There is no going back.

Zaya Gage is dead.

While I just stand there like a seething chump — I don't miss the confused looks Presh is darting my way — the impostor rips one of the new patches in half, then applies one half to Presh's deeply bruised cheekbone. My sister sighs, then giggles quietly as the essence in the patch triggers.

I can smell it, and I know what she's feeling. I've needed healing above and beyond my own shifter capabilities more than once.

Including the night I watched the real Zaya get murdered.

I'm so angry now that my nostrils feel wet. And too hot. A bad sign. I don't want to be scalding anything in this room, not with Presh ...

Presh isn't a shifter.

I can't wrap my head around it.

Awry are rare.

The Outcast MC has some contacts who would fit

within the awry subcategory of essence-wielders, but no awry members. While the power they wield is usually rare and valuable, actually dealing with an awry is tricky business. Most clubs avoid doing so.

"I'm afraid this is ... was broken," Zaya murmurs to Presh. She means my little sister's cheekbone.

Presh chews on her lip again. "And my forehead? Will it scar?"

Zaya rips the second half of the new patch in half and applies a quarter to the wound on Presh's right temple. "It will heal cleanly," she says. "Take the rest of the patches —"

"I can't take more," Presh protests. "What if you need them?"

Zaya sighs, lips curling into a slight smile. "I'll avoid violent confrontations for the next couple of days."

Presh snorts doubtfully, even playfully. As if she knows this woman, as if they're friends.

Zaya grins at her wearily, bundling the remaining patches together with a thick stack of twenty-dollar bills, then tucking them into the pocket of Presh's sweatpants. "Don't get them too hot or cold," she says. "Body temperature is fine, obviously ..."

Her head is bowed, and something ... something in her tone is tinged with sadness.

I literally loathe the fact that I can read her like that. That it even matters enough to me to see it, sense it, and that I need to fight an impulse to do something about it.

I tell myself that I need to know her in order to understand what's going on here, and that's the only reason I'm watching so closely.

"That's ... that's it, then?" Presh whispers. "We're ... you —"

"Your brother is here," Zaya says.

I'm livid again. In an instant. I didn't realize that the smoldering fury had eased until it sparks again. She can't even say my fucking name ...

And then I realize I've been fucking calling her Zaya in my head.

Fuck me. I can't get sucked into this, whatever this is.

"But ..." Presh shuffles a little. "Maybe you would be safer with us?"

The impostor smiles at her. Then she reaches up and smooths a strand of light-blue hair that's fallen free of Presh's messy, multicolored bun, tucking it back behind her ear.

She touches my sister as if she actually cares for her.

My chest aches. Because that could have been real. If the real Zaya hadn't died, then —

I shut the thought down.

Again.

The impostor stands up, swaying almost imperceptibly on her feet. Her own clothing looks two sizes too big on her. I understand the clothes not fitting Presh, but on her it doesn't make any sense.

I haven't even glanced around the room yet. I note the suitcase and bag by the door, along with the towel-wrapped bundle. The rest of the place looks spotless.

I briefly meet Grinder's gaze — he's stepped up to cover the open door at my back — and nod toward the bundle.

He nods back, reaching for it without stepping over the threshold.

The impostor watches the entire exchange. Intently. I get the sense she always looks focused like that, but I wonder — because I'm a fucking idiot — what it takes to hold her attention, to make her see nothing but me —

"You need anything back from in here?" Grinder asks

her. Referring to the bundle of towels and what I assume is more clothing. "Or can I take care of it all?"

She shakes her head, offering him a slight smile in thanks.

He grunts, pleased.

It's easier to burn everything, or to have Pinky melt it, than clean and return it. Scrubbing blood and DNA is bad enough, but removing all traces of essence residual is near impossible. And if they dragged Breaker's DNA into the car, then into the motel, it'll connect them to the scene on the beach. Assuming anyone bothers to look for the asshole.

The fact that Chains is still unaccounted for bothers me. I resist the urge to pull out my phone and check into it.

"This too, I guess?" Presh says, passing fake Zaya a phone.

It's a newer model than my own. Not available yet as far as I know. And even though I'm not typically a tech guy, I'm instantly jealous.

Yes, apparently I'm all over the fucking place today.

The impostor accepts the phone, tucking it in the pocket of her long skirt. The device isn't remotely heavy, but even cinched with a drawstring, the skirt is way too big on her, so it sags at the side, revealing her sharp-edged hipbone.

There is no fucking way my cock should twitch at the sight. At that sliver of skin.

She's too skinny. Sickly, even. She's not remotely my type. Though admittedly, that's a deliberate choice — a revulsion — after losing my soul-bound mate thirteen years ago.

The impostor is playing some long con with me, with Presh, and my brothers.

But my cock fucking twitches at a tiny glimpse of fucking skin.

I look away.

"Rath has your phone number," Presh is saying. "As soon as I get a new phone, I'll text you."

I'm pretty sure I've missed some of the conversation.

"I'd like that," Zaya murmurs. She's got those amazing violet eyes trained on my sister. Again. As if she adores her or something.

I rub my chest, dropping my hand quickly when I catch myself doing so.

"Come. Let Doc check you," I say gruffly, realizing I've lost the fucking thread.

Zephyr slips into the room past me, carrying her smaller med kit, as if she's been hanging on my every word. She's already smiling at Presh. They've met a couple of times, I think. Her reddish-gold hair is tied back in a low ponytail, and her leathers are as skintight as they can be while still staying flexible. Like my own.

Doc Z's been the Outcast medic for five or so years, and she's two or three years older than me. I should probably know that for certain. I seethe internally as she turns her dark topaz eyes and slight smile to take in the impostor. Doc is the taller, though not by much. And she's got all the curves. Lush, even.

I can't remember the last time she crawled into my bed, but for one aching moment, I hope Zaya can't smell me on her.

No. Not smell. Zaya isn't a shifter. She senses *other* things.

But the impostor isn't Zaya.

So none of that shit matters.

I look away again, only to find Presh watching me, her

brow all crinkled in a frown. I pull out my phone, checking it for messages that I would have already felt come in.

Doc corrals Presh back to the bed, setting her kit to the side and opening it. It's some sort of mage brew or elixir that she pulls out first, all wax-and-cork stoppered and glowing deep pink. I know how expensive it is the moment she breaks the seal and I scent it.

Then she passes the fucking brew to Zaya, who's still hovering. Standing upright, but looking as if maybe she doesn't have another step in her.

I crush the impulse to sweep her into my arms.

Zaya looks genuinely surprised. Not that every emotion — as fake as they all must be — doesn't look genuine on her expressive face. She takes the brew with a smile, murmuring, "Thank you, Doc."

Right. Not even properly introduced and she can remember Doc's fucking name. Well, her club name.

Now I crush the impulse to stomp out of the room and start destroying shit. I haven't felt this sort of rage in years. Since I gave up hope, really. But what had I actually been hoping for? A fucking miracle? That it was all some shared nightmare?

Zaya uncorks the bottle and tips it into her mouth without even questioning it. Doc could have handed her poison or something to knock her out.

I watch her drink it. Swallow it. I fucking feel her relieved sigh.

"Tasty," she says.

Tasty. The word and its light, teasing tone — an echo of the past — sears through me, burning worse than the festering bullet wound in my shoulder. I nearly crush my phone in my hand.

Doc is talking. She's in a middle of a sentence, and I've

missed the beginning while I struggle to recover from a single fucking word as if it's a mortal wound.

I need to get out of here before I do something stupid.

"... should kick in quickly," Doc says. She's got her diagnostic scanner in hand now, running it over Presh. It's tech, but mage crafted. "Though I've never treated an awry."

"We're all different, I suppose," Zaya murmurs, settling her gaze on Presh again.

My sister smiles back at her, then says quietly, "I was ... wondering ..."

"Yes." Zaya answers as if she already knows the question.

Presh's face lights up. "Really? Are you ... I mean, do you live around here?"

"For the next while, at least. The property ... ah, my place, is just a few minutes past Lincoln City, so about two hours down the coast. The grounds would be the best place for any testing or training."

Presh is grinning so hard now that she radiates energy I can feel. That feel is a lot like how the real Zaya felt when she was around my sister's age. It's impossible to forget the feeling of her essence gently tingling against my skin. No matter how young we were, no matter how much time has passed.

No matter how hard I try.

"That isn't very far from the Outcast clubhouse and my uncle's property. The pack house," Presh says, taking another stoppered pink brew from Doc and cradling it in her hands for a moment.

"I, ah, wasn't planning on staying ..." Zaya touches something under her tank top. A necklace? Or pendant? Worrying at it unconsciously. But also with a touch of anxiety? I can't smell anything of her emotional state, though.

Not under that vanilla scent she doused herself and my sister in. "I ... just ... I have something to look into ... and I need to deal with ... an estate. My aunt's estate."

I'm feeling disembodied now, and no matter that I'm trying to tell myself this is a con, it feels way too fucking real, too *now*.

"You'll ... we can set up a time?"

"Something regular would be best," Zaya says.

Nope. I'm going to lose my shit all over the place, because this can't be a regular thing. I can't be driving Presh to and from Zaya's aunt's estate. And not just because I can't physically set foot on it myself. I've been barred from entry since that fucking night.

I won't do it.

"Presh!" I snap.

My sister nearly leaps out of her skin.

Still crouched by the bed, Doc pivots on her toes and throws me a look over her shoulder so scathing that I'm momentarily taken aback. The impostor narrows her eyes on me as well.

I soften my tone, hating that I feel as though I have to justify my reactions. That I feel like screaming like a confused and overwhelmed toddler when I need to be cool-headed. "Time to go."

I need Presh off-site before I can grill the impostor.

Doc straightens, holding her hand out to Presh. My sister takes it, standing and looking as if she does actually need Doc's help to stay steady on her feet.

I finally allow myself one moment of indulgence, stepping over and scooping Presh up in my arms, then carrying her out of the room without looking back.

I can feel Presh waving at the impostor over my shoulder.

Then I hear Doc murmur, "Do you need anything else?"

"Sleep," Zaya says. "But I'm not going to get it yet."

I miss the rest of their conversation, realizing even as I'm stepping away that I probably shouldn't be leaving Doc alone with an unknown awry.

Grinder shifts from where he's leaning back against the exterior wall to cover the door, guarding us all.

Then fucking Reck rolls up into the motel parking lot, tires squealing as if he didn't anticipate the turn off the main road soon enough. I swear his monster of an SUV nearly rolls itself. But then he's slamming on the brakes and launching himself out of the vehicle without shutting it off.

Behind me, Grinder stiffens involuntarily at my half-brother's overly aggressive arrival.

Reck is dressed in one of his stupid official suits, which I hate because it covers practically every inch of him like some kind of neutralizing armor. So he's not displaying his allegiances, even though everyone knows the Outcast are his for the taking. He's the favored to step up and take our uncle's place as president.

Except he walked away.

Now Reck hunts down our kind — under the guise of being an official agent of the Authority, aka the Purge, aka the assholes who think they can police how essence is used and how essence-wielders are treated. Some of their favorite tactics include collecting illegal essence-imbued artifacts, hunting so-called criminals too powerful for the null-run police forces to capture and detain, and arrogantly crossing international borders and encroaching on claimed territories while doing so.

My half-brother is a deadly bureaucrat. A glorified bounty hunter with an extermination license. He's got some sort of designs on being the head honcho of the Cascadian branch of the Authority within the next couple of years. Along with nebulous plans to take out Cataclysm MC — and specifically the Cataclysm, our sperm donor — when he's finally got that sort of firepower behind him.

It's all garbage, though. Just his way of dealing with the aftermath of losing Zaya by discarding all the plans we four formed. All those summers that we revolved around her — our center, our crux.

Shorter and a fair bit trimmer than me, but two years the elder, Reck reaches for Presh — and she for him — the moment he sets his dark-eyed gaze on us. He needs a shave, assuming he doesn't want to get written up by his superiors. Dress code and all that. He's a detective, or maybe a sergeant now, for the Major Crimes Unit.

I couldn't give two shits.

And I don't want to hand Presh over to him. Normally, I would trust Reck to get her to our uncle's place, no problem. But I'm not too sure how he's going to react to the change in her eye color.

The awry are equally revered, loathed, and feared. The asshole Authority are a mix of the loathing and fear. And I know they lock up essence-wielders like Presh preemptively. Or even outright kill them. I've heard Reck say so.

Preemptive elimination of a potentially dangerous creature.

As well, Reck has personal reasons to loathe and fear purple eyes.

"Little sis," he growls playfully, pulling Presh into a hug that leaves her legs dangling. "I don't see you for six months, and this is how you saunter back into my life?"

Presh wraps her arms around his neck and grins at him. "I'm okay. Now."

"You could have called me." He gently sets her on her feet.

"Chains took my phone."

"Before you ran away," he says, trying to force eye contact with her. "I would have come for you."

Presh keeps her gaze dropped to the pavement, not calling Reck on the obvious lie. None of us could have walked into Cataclysm territory and come back out alive. Not with Presh intact and in tow, at least. Not without involving the Outcast and starting a war with a club separated from us, as the crow flies, by another entire fucking country.

"We could have negotiated," I say softly, trying to smooth it all over because that's my fucking role, no matter that it chafes badly right now.

"He ordered ... this special cage ..." she murmurs.

I feel the moment the impostor moves closer. Grinder actually shifts to the side so the fake Zaya can lean in the doorway, as if he doesn't view her as the massive threat she is. She's still blocked from Reck's sight by my bulk, and with Presh coated in her vanilla-based scent, she's somewhat hidden from his senses. For the moment.

"A cage? What the fuck for?" Reck massages his right hand. That hand was all but crushed thirteen years ago, when he saved my life and Rought's. But lost Zaya. I'm not sure it actually hurts him anymore, but it's always a clear tell that he's agitated.

Presh looks up at him, steady and true. Daring him to really look at her, to look her in the eyes.

My chest aches, but I don't interfere. Even our baby sister knows the choices Reck has made, and how those choices keep him on the outside of the club, and the pack.

Not that Presh has been officially inducted, but the blood tie is an automatic admission.

Reck, still rubbing his hand, frowns at me, then at Grinder, then back at Presh. Still missing the fake Zaya in the doorway behind me.

Then he lurches forward suddenly, both hands reaching for Presh, and I have to stop myself from yanking her away from him. Reck cups her face gently, then gazes down at her. His eyes lock to hers. He leans closer and inhales deeply, trying to scent her newly awoken power under all the vanilla.

Vanilla and cocoa butter and wild, spiced mint.

Though it's my sense memory that it clings to, not my sister, I can't forget the seaside mint.

No matter how hard I try.

"Fuck," Reck murmurs. Then he tugs Presh into his arms and holds her, allowing himself to just be a big brother for a moment. He looks more shaken than I've seen him in a long time — given that he keeps most complex emotions locked down under a thick veneer of seething rancor.

He meets my gaze, grimacing.

And yeah, I know. Protecting Presh has now shifted to top priority.

We hoped she'd manifest as a bear. Then, being vaguely beneath his notice, that she'd get the fuck away from our sperm donor once she was legally an adult.

But none of the Cataclysm's bastards manifest as anything so mundane as one of the four main clans of shifters: bear, wolf, boar, or cat. And even within our mixed clan, our beasts — Reck, Rought, and me — are so rare we'd be classified as mythic if we didn't avoid official contact with any bureaucratic entity. Including the Authority. Though I assumed long ago that Reck would have had to disclose his own beast to them.

There is one place that our father's long reach shouldn't be able to touch Presh, though. No matter what happened there thirteen years ago. A coastal mansion and hectares of land allowed to grow wild. And an elder awry who might welcome —

I shove the thought away before I fully form it.

That isn't an option.

And our Zaya wasn't actually safe there herself.

Reck's shoulders suddenly stiffen. A flash of fury flickers over his face, instantly replaced by his typical arrogant facade.

He's seen the impostor behind me.

Zaya shifts in the doorway as Doc steps through and crosses to stand beside Grinder, med kit in hand. I don't have to look back at her to know the impostor is checking on Presh.

What would she do if Reck was a danger to Precious?

My head is aching every time I try to put any of this — all the impostor's actions — into a tidy order. If this is a long con, to what end?

"Grinder." Reck, keeping a hand on Presh's shoulder as he steps back, reaches through the open door of the SUV to lay his hand on the steering wheel. The vehicle is still running. "Get Presh to the Outcast. Come back for your bike."

Grinder looks to me for confirmation, even though he outranks Reck and me both. I nod.

"Pinky can stop by to grab the bike," Grinder says. "She'll be coming to clean the room, right?"

Pinky isn't a Coalition type, or even a member of the West Coast Coterie. Not answering to any of the organizations that oversee mages and teach or cooperatively cast magecraft. Even just hanging with other mages in general never was her thing — but she does enjoy riding Grinder. Mages and shifters don't usually mix, mostly because they're not really genetically compatible. Offspring from mixed bloodlines are rare. Grinder and Pinky don't seem to give a shit.

Neither of us answers him, but he just touches Presh on the shoulder to steer her around the other side of the SUV. "I assume you've disabled the protections?"

Reck nods. All Authority vehicles are keyed to a main user and designed to dissuade people from borrowing them. Those protections feature rather nasty side effects, such as dismemberment and death. Just another flashy application of the Authority's overkill policy. And a reminder of why they're called the Purge.

My half-brother's eyes are narrowed on the fake Zaya, though I haven't stepped to the side, and he hasn't moved closer. Doc leans against the exterior wall, all casual with one foot up on it. But she's set her bag down, keeping her hands free.

Presh is glancing between Reck and me, frowning again.

Zaya steps forward. She's got one arm folded across her ribs while dragging her suitcase beside her. Her gaze is on Presh. Seeing her off? She's pulled a long charcoal sweater over the tank top and skirt, and wears laced ankle boots on her previously bare feet.

No socks.

I shouldn't be noticing inconsequential things like fucking socks.

Reck doesn't take his eyes off the impostor. To anyone else, he might look arrogantly detached. Even professional.

But I can smell the rancor simmering just under his skin. He needs to be rational now. Sly and even tricky, as is his nature, but coolly rational. Otherwise, the fake Zaya Gage is going to shred him.

I've spent barely thirty minutes total in her presence — this time around at least — and I already know how she'll react to even a hint of aggression.

Grinder gets Presh in the passenger side of the SUV, then crosses back around to the driver's-side door. His gaze — far too knowing for my liking — slides over Reck, then me, settling on Zaya.

"It was good to see you," he says, "after all these years."

Zaya pulls her gaze off Presh, who is grinning at her out the open car door, frowning slightly at Grinder. Confused.

"Ah, well ..." He dips his head, smiling charmingly.

Charming? Grinder?

"You were young the last time we met," he says. "Maybe twelve or thirteen? I had come by to call on your aunt."

Zaya blinks, then she smiles tentatively. "You were ... you knew my aunt?"

Grinder grins. The expression is suggestive and sharp. "As well as anyone can know her, I suppose."

Now Reck and I are the ones who are blinking and confused. I don't remember Grinder and Disa being all that close, but then as kids we ran wild, avoiding as much adult supervision as possible.

Zaya laughs quietly.

That soft sound of joy squeezes around my heart, and for a moment, I think it will never beat again. An idiotic idea, because of course it keeps beating, maybe even a little faster than before.

Grinder just bobs his head, turning away. "Send your

aunt my good tidings, then, Zaya. I'm Grinder, but she might know me better as Timothy. Timothy Millard."

Zaya grimaces. "She's dead, I'm afraid."

He pauses and just looks at her, completely shocked.

As am I.

"Dead?" Grinder echoes.

She bows her head, whispering, "She'd have to be."

I'm fucking lost. I need answers, but I have too many questions to ask all at once. And I already know that each answer is going to bring more questions, and it will all just keep splintering and multiplying.

"Yes." Grinder sighs quietly. I've never thought about who he might have loved before Pinky. They've been together for eight or nine years. "I suppose so ... that is how *the thread is woven*."

Zaya tilts her head, exposing the long, delectable line of her throat.

I swallow harshly, and not because Grinder is obviously, suddenly, and randomly espousing some sort of arcane religious doctrine.

"Yes." Zaya lets go of the suitcase to wrap her other arm around herself. She sways slightly on her feet. Where is her fucking coat? It's too cold to only be wearing a thin sweater. "*Even the weaver isn't immune*."

They're speaking in tongues. Well, speaking in litany, more accurately. Words from when the old gods supposedly still walked the earth. The kind of shit that Zaya's aunt and her companions occasionally espoused, for people who believe in any of that. But as long as I steadfastly ignored my possibly mystical connection to the real Zaya, and the implications of the beast that resided uneasily under my own skin, I wasn't a believer.

I'm very good at ignoring the unquantifiable.

I take a deep breath, utterly pissed and about to start blasting them with questions. Then I catch the scent of an achingly familiar power. It's gone so quickly that I instantly decide I'm imagining it. But it staggers me just enough that I let the questions slide. Again.

Grinder nods, all solemn.

"A safe journey tonight," Zaya says, pronouncing it like it's a fucking benediction. I catch a tendril of that same effervescent minty scent again. "For you, Presh, and your loved ones, Timothy."

Grinder, suddenly looking like he's holding back a fuck-load of emotion, taps his chest three times with the first three fingers of his left hand over his heart. It's a reverent gesture, full of meaning, and I'm shocked at his directing it toward the impostor.

Zaya all but dismisses Grinder, deliberately shifting her attention to Presh. She and my sister exchange soft smiles. Grinder gets in the SUV, driving away even as he's pulling on his seat belt. I'm fairly certain Presh is waving at us, but the windows are all tinted.

All three of us watch as the SUV hits the main road and speeds off into the night, heading south. Well, Doc, Zaya and I watch. Reck hasn't taken his attention off the impostor.

The moment Presh is out of sight, Zaya shakes her head, inhaling deeply. Then she grabs her suitcase and pivots as if she's going to head to the motel office.

Reck instantly blocks her path, towering over her.

I shift to the side, not certain if I'm going to intercede or if I'm backing up my brother. I should be backing up my brother. Clearly, I should be. That shouldn't even be a question. But ...

Zaya tilts her head, raking her gaze over Reck, head to toe and back up again.

He smirks, fucking full of himself. As if she's going to drop her panties at the sight of him.

She's never been easy to impress —

No. The actual Zaya had never been easy to impress, never predictable. Fake Zaya just stares at Reck, all dispassionate and hard to read.

He stands under her regard for all of ten seconds. Then irritation flickers over his face, and he shoves his suit jacket to the side, drawing her attention to the badge clipped to his belt.

She shifts her gaze back up to capture his, staring him down.

His jaw clenches. He breaks the silence first. "I have questions."

"Your type usually does." Her tone is cold, as if he's a stranger. As if he's beneath her notice.

He bristles. "You fucking kidnapped a minor today!"

I stiffen, not liking the accusation when we already know the truth. Now is not the time to play Reck's games —

He keeps going. "You murdered a member of —"

"Oh?" she says mockingly "I didn't realize that berserkers and rapists are a protected class these days."

Reck's eye twitches. He glares at me, as if I've held back vital information. I haven't. He knew about Breaker already. He has a shit-ton of loyal informants among the Outcast. He also apparently has me under surveillance, and I haven't forgotten how pissed I am about that. But I also had no idea about any rape. And suddenly, my beast is clawing inside me again, because if Presh ... if Zaya has been —

Zaya shakes her head, sighing affectedly. "ID," she demands.

Reck narrows his eyes at her, remembering she's his primary target. "You? You need me to identify myself?" he asks mockingly.

His point being that if she were really Zaya Gage, she'd know him. She would know us.

"ID," she repeats, bored and flicking her free hand offishly. "Or is not following that protocol also a new policy with the Authority?"

She knows it's not. The requirement for Authority agents to identify themselves is a fundamental right, enforced by every level of government, no matter how independent. Enforced by the World Council, even — the organization that oversees all other recognized ruling entities, backed by the most powerful figures in the world. Countries and individuals alike.

Reck tugs his wallet out of his inner suit pocket with a snort. His arrogant, knowing smirk is back in place, as if he has the upper hand.

I can see that he's about to be blindsided. Even not knowing exactly how.

Or maybe he already has been. Because I've been in that barely functioning state myself for the last few hours.

He flips open the wallet, all cocky and sure, displaying his Authority ID. Zaya barely glances at it. Probably not even long enough to note his nonclub name — Carlos Guerra — emblazoned across it. She simply reaches over and presses her thumb to the iridescent medallion embedded in one corner of the ID card.

It glows platinum under her touch.

She's got diplomatic immunity. And not just within the country of Cascadia.

Even I know that platinum status is rare. Maybe a few dozen people in the world have it, and most of them are national leaders or connected to the World Council. She's untouchable. Reck can't even ask her name, let alone question her. Not without a shit-ton of paperwork and Authority lawyers involved. And even then, she can just outright refuse.

Reck yanks the ID away from her, staring down at the medallion as the bright platinum fades out of it. He covers his shock quickly, sneering, "Nice allure."

She snorts softly. Then she starts walking toward him. One step, two steps, until she's right up against his chest, and then ... he moves. He steps to the fucking side and just allows her to pass. As if he's afraid of touching her, which is valid given her immunity.

But given the rancor seething from him, it's more that he's afraid of her touching him.

We stand there like fucking chumps, watching Zaya. Me, Reck, and even Doc. But while we're staring like idiots, Doc has her eyes narrowed in concern.

What is she seeing that I don't?

Zaya moves steadily, smoothly away. Then she just ... stops. A couple of steps beyond the door to unit four. She stops.

Then she drops as if someone has bludgeoned her from directly overhead.

Doc is moving before I do, but Zaya still hits the ground hard, pulling her suitcase, which is thankfully small, over on her. Her head bounces once on the pavement, then she goes terribly still.

Sheer panic streaks through me. And for only the second time in my life, I'm frozen in place by it. I don't black out or hallucinate, but for too many moments, I can't move as I stare down at my recurring nightmare made real.

No. Not a nightmare. A memory that will haunt me beyond death.

Doc is checking Zaya's pulse, then touching her cheek lightly to roll her head and check for blood. At least I think that's what she's doing. Zaya is bleeding from the side of her head, profusely. Her skin is pale enough to see the blood clearly despite the low light.

"Perfect," Reck says, grinning like a smug asshole. "Hard to enforce immunity when she's passed out cold." He fishes zip ties out of his suit pocket.

"What the fuck, Reck?"

He ignores me. "Move!" he barks at Doc.

She's still crouched beside the impostor, checking her wrists and hands, though I didn't see Zaya even attempt to break her fall. Doc glances up at me. I nod stiffly, and she grimaces, not liking it one bit even as she straightens and takes a step back.

"She's hurt." Doc crosses her arms, glowering. "On top of being exhausted."

"She's a fucking pro is what she is," Reck says. "She could make millions on the big screen."

He grabs for Zaya's shoulder, as if to shove her over onto her stomach to bind her hands.

Then a big fucking snake is suddenly up in his face.

Reck shouts and falls back on his ass.

The massive brown-and-gold bushmaster rears up, occupying all the space between Reck and Zaya. Painfully familiar.

Reck scrambles back, dropping the zip ties and holding his hands up as if the snake is intelligent. As if he thinks he can convince the creature that he's not a threat.

My heart is hammering in my chest, and not because I'm scared of the fucking snake. Because I know it.

"Muta," I whisper.

"Fuck off," Reck sneers out of the corner of his mouth. "Stop seeing what you want to see."

The snake lowers its broad head and flicks its forked tongue at Reck. My idiot brother is still within striking distance. Muta is partly twined around Zaya's wrist, which he yanked across her unconscious body when he lunged at Reck. He's as big as I remember, maybe more so. He'll easily latch onto Reck's neck if my brother doesn't put at least six more feet between them.

"You were going to hurt her," I say without thinking. My mind is thrumming, overloaded but oddly blank at the same time. I don't want to believe it of Reck. But the snake *is* fucking intelligent. And more importantly, he's Zaya's protector. Since her ninth birthday.

"What?" Reck doesn't take his eyes off the reptile. "I'm just doing my job."

"The only reason Muta manifests without prompting is when —"

"This cunt isn't Zaya!" he shouts.

Muta's tail starts vibrating. He doesn't have a rattle, but the thrumming quiver of the horny spine that tips his tail is the last warning Reck is going to get. My brother might survive one bite, depending on what kind of antitoxin Doc's got on hand. But because Muta knows that — because he *knows* us — it's a safe bet that he'll deliver large amounts of potent venom, maybe even essence imbued, over multiple bites.

Reck finally gets his head on straight and eases farther back. Then he gets to his feet. "Rath, figure your shit out.

There's more than one fucking bushmaster in the fucking world."

I open my mouth to point out all sorts of things — all the connections I don't want to have already made. But the sound of a motorcycle pushed way past its limits pulls my attention away.

Rought. The other mechs that round out his team of three are presumably back with Zaya's abandoned car.

"Fuck me." Reck groans. "You called him in? So he can what? Slobber all over her?"

Rought is off his bike and storming our way before I manage an answer. He hasn't seen Zaya sprawled on the pavement yet. Or the big fucking snake.

Reck steps up to him, hand raised as if he's going to clap Rought on the shoulder and actually attempt to defuse the situation.

Except our younger brother slams him up against the side of the motel. The cedar siding splinters under Reck's back.

Rought isn't as big as me, but it's possible he could beat me — if I were ever stupid enough to come between him and the woman he believes to be his essence-gifted, soul-bonded mate. Not just the potential of a bond, or even the growing, slowly solidifying bond that I once shared with Zaya. But full-on bonded.

The two of them are — were — chosen mates. Rought still has a mating bite on his hand, which should have faded within a year of Zaya's death. Not that he should ever have bitten one of the awry in the first place.

The impostor's hand, and the rest of her skin in general, doesn't bear a single scar.

Rought might be able to take me on, given the circum- stances. But it's Reck I don't really trust. I should trust my elder brother, but I haven't for some time. Reck might be slightly shorter and trimmer than Rought, but he's deadlier, as if something twisted inside him then festered until only darkness fills every crevasse, every fissure in his soul.

All the places Zaya previously filled.

I mean, all three of us are fucked in the head, but Reck just might be a serial killer with a badge.

I get into it, managing to separate them. Then I'm forced to slam my open hand against Reck's chest when he lunges forward even as I'm holding Rought back around the neck. I've called on my beast, just a bit, and something cracks in Reck's chest under my blow.

He stumbles away, clearly in pain.

Rought has gone still. Then a low moan escapes him. I take my gaze off Reck, who looks like he's considering murdering us both, because Rought has finally seen Zaya.

He breaks my hold easily. Then he crosses to Zaya, completely ignoring Muta.

I open my mouth to shout a warning at him. Doc even darts forward, reaching like she might try to grab the snake from behind.

But Muta just shifts slightly to the side, his black eyes still riveted to Reck.

Rought crouches down, his gaze glued to Zaya's face. Then, as if she's made of glass, of hand-blown fine crystal, he lifts her gently in his arms, cradling her head and neck against his shoulder, and with her knees across his other arm.

Muta slithers to coil on Zaya's belly, so that he's guarding her even as Rought turns, walks past us, and crosses through the open door into unit five.

Doc follows, glaring at me and Reck as she passes. She snatches up her med kit and disappears into the room.

I turn my attention to Reck. "What the fuck was that?!"

"Me?!" He gestures toward the room, though his other hand is still pressed across his upper chest. I've hurt him. Badly. "Why the fuck did you involve him? He can't be rational about this! We had to watch him for two fucking years the last time she destroyed our lives —"

"The last time she destroyed our lives?" I ask quietly, interested in his revisionist take on our history. "She murdered herself? Then beat the shit out of us, putting me and Rought in the hospital?"

He snarls, his beast actually rising, edging his eyes in bright green and rattling in his chest. "You're on fucking suicide watch, then."

"It always was me," I say coolly. I know it's the situation that's making me livid. But I can't seem to separate the components, so I choose to be fucking irate at everything. Mostly Reck. "You were at the Authority Academy within six months."

He curls his lip at me, stepping into my space and lowering his voice. "Either she's a fake, an impostor, or she faked her death thirteen years ago to get away from us and is pretending she doesn't know us. Which would you prefer it be?"

I blink at him for a moment, almost feeling sorry for him. "Alive, Reck. I'd rather she be alive."

He jerks away from me, scowling like I've deliberately misheard him or misunderstood him. I haven't.

"You'd rather she be dead," I say. It isn't a question. It's a realization. "Those are her two choices, either with you or dead."

"I was never her first fucking choice," he says, as if that's some sort of counterpoint.

It isn't.

Because it was never about firsts between us four. It was only and always about forevers, beyond death. We were woven from the fabric of the universe, our essences, our souls, entwined around hers, around her. Only truly whole when together.

I can only stare at him, stupidly dumbfounded.

Reck scoffs at me. Then he spins and strides into the motel room.

I have to follow. A part of me wants to walk away.

A part of me already knows I'm not going to like the truth that's about to be torn free from a moment in our lives I thought long buried.

I TAKE A LONG BREAK FROM THE FUCKING tangled situation, contemplating the ramifications of just walking away with at least a section of my soul still intact. The part that survived losing Zaya only because I had other obligations to my family, my siblings specifically, and to the Outcast.

I focused on being the best brother and the best enforcer, then lieutenant, that I could be. I traveled then, and fleshed out my education. Rought is mostly self-taught in his tech skills — school never was his thing, or working with anyone other than family for that matter. But I actually have a fucking MBA and speak three languages — English, Spanish, and Cantonese. And at the same time I was studying abroad, I reinforced relationships with other allied shifter clubs. Then I came back to help run the club and the pack. Just the chance that Zaya Gage is actually alive changes —

Nothing, I tell myself. It changes nothing.

I check my phone, fielding updates and answering a few more messages, including a text from my uncle demanding a phone call. I text Presh's ETA to him instead.

Then, unable to avoid it any longer, I step into the room, interrupting a conversation in progress. Rought is seated on the edge of the bed, facing the door with Zaya unconscious and cradled in his arms. His currently gold-rimmed eyes are riveted to her face. Her breathing is shallow but steady.

Reck is pacing, doing a lot of gesturing. Doc has cleaned the wound on Zaya's head and placed a healing patch on the cut. She's setting out more of those revitalizing brews on the far bedside table. Muta is curled up on Zaya's stomach — all nearly ten feet of him now — but his wide, flat head is raised, following Reck's pacing motions.

"Think you can take me, little brother?" Reck says mockingly.

"I was literally born to be her guardian." Rought doesn't bother to look away from Zaya, so the insult is clear without even needing the words to back it. "So yeah, I can take you."

Reck takes a threatening step forward. But before I can intercede, before I can get between my brothers, Rought laughs harshly.

Muta's tail vibrates.

Rought finally looks up at our older brother. They really couldn't be any more different. Reck, I'm constantly informed by many of his admirers when they're drunk or stoned, is deliciously dark. Specifically, his hair, eyes, and olive skin. He's saved from being too pretty only by his sheer assholeness. Rought's hair is currently dark blond, but it lightens under the summer sun. His skin is naturally tanned, and when not edged by the gold of his beast, his eyes are a bright blue-green. Rought was, literally, a sun-kissed golden child while we'd been growing up.

I fall right in the middle, looking more like Presh. At least when her hair isn't dyed in a pastel rainbow and her eyes aren't transforming into the purple hue that marks her as awry. Also, I'm some part Asian. How much or what region my blood ancestors hailed from, I don't know.

I've got brown hair, hazel eyes, and lighter skin than either of my brothers. And though I'm bigger than both — taller and wider through the shoulders — if it came to it, Reck really could wipe the floor with both of us. Probably at the same time.

Because it's been a long time since Reck has cared who he hurts to get what he wants. He spent too many years in our father's dubious care and was heading in that direction even before falling for Zaya the first time.

The first time?

Fuck.

That thought implies there'll be a second time. But there is no second time when the other party is dead.

Rought holds Reck's gaze, fierce, forthright, and more … alive than I've seen him in almost thirteen years. Reck wasn't exaggerating about the two years of suicide watch. He just wasn't the one doing the watching.

It was Presh, I suddenly remember. Presh's first summer visit that finally pulled Rought back from that brink.

"I know, you fucking asshole," Rought says. "I know what you did." He articulates each word like he's setting the fuse on some complicated explosive device. The sort of device he's more than capable of building. Unlike Reck and me, Rought knows his maternal family, and the Southern lilt to his accent comes from spending most of his life with them, not our sperm donor.

I glance at Reck, expecting to see the sneering expression he levels on Rought when our little brother is in one of these shit moods. Instead, my elder brother looks a little thrown, a bit shaken by that statement.

"What does it matter?" Reck snaps back. "She's dead. And this impostor is wearing some sort of replicating allure, or —"

Rought scoffs. "What person could replicate an awry?"

"Another awry," Reck snaps.

"What other awry is powerful enough to take Zaya's form?"

Reck is the one to scoff now.

But I can feel my own internal arguments splintering more and more as Rought holds her, the supposedly fake Zaya, and Muta doesn't intercede, doesn't question my brother's right to hold her, to protect her.

From us.

Could be a different snake, right?

But ... the bushmaster's power signature, its *presence*, is as otherworldly and unique as it's always smelled to me — like well-composted soil and the aftermath of thunderstorms. And yeah, otherworldly. According to the little I know of Zaya's ancestral history, Muta might be trapped in the form of a snake, but he might also once have been an aspect of an all-powerful being.

A death god. If you believe in that sort of thing.

I used to believe.

"And Muta?" I hear myself ask. My voice is weirdly

thin. "How do you explain an identical piece of gold-and-topaz jewelry transforming into —"

Reck throws me a quelling look. "Like I said, lots of bushmasters in the —"

"The snake's power is unmistakable," I say.

Reck snorts. "Fine. But allegiances can change. After her death, the snake needed a new owner ..." He shrugs and doesn't finish his thought.

I try to stay calm and focused, pretending that my entire life isn't hinging on this moment. Not voicing any counter to Reck's new take on the snake's origins. My elder brother is changing his argument, his so-called talking points, moment by moment. And he never, ever does that.

Maybe Reck is just as rattled as I am. Maybe there is something else, some other dynamic, happening here? Something in what Rought alluded to?

Rought shakes his head at Reck, resolute but also pityingly. Then he gently touches Zaya's shoulder, right where it meets her neck. "And this?"

He slips two fingers under the edge of her collar, careful to not touch her skin. He tugs the necklace she's wearing free from the confines of her sweater. He gently lays it on her chest, nestled in the hollow between her small but fucking perfect breasts.

And I know. I know now. I know that I used to settle my hand there, in that exact spot, over clothing when we were too young for more, and pressing skin-to-skin as we grew bold enough to take what we wanted from each other. I would delight in just the feeling of her heart —

I'm losing my shit again. Because what if she isn't an impostor? What if she's just been hiding from us for thirteen years? Pretending to not know us now?

"Another replica," Reck snaps. But his voice is hollow,

and he's staring at the necklace, at the pendant specifically, as if it's even more terrifying than the massive snake still watching his every move.

And you know what?

It is.

Ignoring Reck, Rought runs his fingers down the chain. It's composed of thin threads of woven gold — yellow, white, and rose. The slumbering power embedded in the necklace awakens. And suddenly the air around us is crackling with licks of that energy, brushing against my arms, tugging at my hands. As if it's trying to pull me to Zaya, even while she's unconscious. Then to force me to my knees and make me bow, make me beg, make me weep, make me —

I shake my head, then my hands, shoving the feeling aside.

Doc backs away from the bed, also rubbing her arms.

"Go," I say.

She darts past me without another look. Which is good, because Reck isn't totally wrong about Zaya being dangerous.

She always was ... unpredictable. But the necklace she now wears is an uber-powerful essence artifact masquerading as a piece of art. Its golden threads stream down from around her neck to twist around a massive raw diamond. Even rough-cut, the pinkish stone must be worth ... what? Ten million? Twenty million?

But it's not the diamond that makes the artifact ultimately priceless.

None of us have laid eyes on the necklace for thirteen years. Not since that night. And it wasn't hanging around Zaya's neck then.

"Her aunt's dead," Rought murmurs.

Zaya said as much to Grinder.

I'm not functioning. Not going to be able to function.

"She's come into her inheritance." Rought touches Zaya's cheek reverently.

"No." I manage to make my brain, my mouth work. "That wasn't supposed to happen for at least another century. Her aunt told her —"

"You aren't fucking believing this shit?" Reck howls. "Him, I understand. He's been fucked in the head since she died! Living like some monk, like she was a fucking saint to worship in the afterlife. Like she was worth —"

"Enough," I say quietly. The undertone of violence in the air is solidifying, mostly around Reck. "The three of us fighting isn't going to sort it out."

"I have a team coming," Reck says, pulling out his phone. "I needed to call in a specialist to contain her."

Rought bares his teeth. "You believe what you want, Reck. You've always made up shit to suit your needs, to justify your actions. But your team will have to go through me to get to her."

"Don't be a fucking idiot."

"You don't have any grounds to detain her, Reck," I say, trying to keep calm. The Authority's presence is barely tolerated in Outcast territory. I don't want to get into yet another pissing contest. We don't need our uncle intervening. Dealing with the sperm donor regarding Presh and the very dead Breaker is going to be charged enough. Especially if Chains doesn't surface soon, hopefully in my custody.

"I'll label it a preemptive collection. We can sort out her diplomatic immunity ..." — he sneers that last part with utter disdain and disbelief — "... in a containment cell."

Rought laughs again.

But it's not really a laugh. It's more of a declaration of

pending destruction. I haven't heard anything that biting and forthright from him since the last time he stood between Zaya and —

"I'd like to see you try to hold her, asshole," Rought snarls.

"Then watch me." Reck doesn't bother looking up from the text he's sending.

Rought shakes his head, just once, utterly dismissive. Then he settles his gaze on Zaya's face again.

The violence I can taste thickening in the small room instantly fades by fifty percent.

"Never again," Rought says, quietly but firmly. "I'll never give her any reason to doubt me, or my ability to protect her, again."

"You're fucking deluded," Reck huffs. "Just as much as you were back then."

"Leave it," I say, rubbing my face. I'm ridiculously weary, even though it's barely past sunset, and it's still going to take days to sort all this shit out.

Reck abruptly lunges, as if he's actually going to make a grab for Zaya. And this time, he's pulled a handheld weapon.

Muta reacts. The snake uncoils, rising four feet straight up off Zaya's lap with his wickedly sharp fangs bared.

Reck's hand slashes toward Muta — the weapon is some sort of Taser, sparking with ignited essence-fueled energy. Rought, still holding Zaya in his lap, is going to get caught in the backlash.

I lunge too, grabbing for Reck's shoulder.

But though we're all fast on our feet, Reck started moving before I noticed. So I already know I'm not going to get hold of him in time.

Muta strikes, easily twisting around the path of the

weapon, just that much quicker. Or as if he's already gotten a glimpse of the next few seconds of the events unfolding before him.

That's not some kind of whimsical reckoning of the scene. The death-god bushmaster is *more*, like Zaya is *more*, like her aunt before her was *more*. Even *more* than Reck is, and he transforms into a fucking terrifying creature of myth and legend.

At the last possible moment, moving faster than I've ever seen anyone move out of a dead sleep, Zaya lunges forward from Rought's lap. She wraps her outstretched hand around Muta's neck.

Reck's weapon jams. Or misfires internally.

My hand clamps down on Reck's shoulder.

And we all just hang there, in that moment of violence unleashed but momentarily thwarted.

Zaya is somehow holding the massive snake at bay midstrike, though her hold looks loose, light. Muta's venom-weeping fangs are less than a thumb's-width away from Reck's wrist.

Reck is frozen midlunge, with his arm still outstretched. He's locked his gaze to Zaya's. Her eyes are vibrant, starlit nebulae of purple, with no hint of the whites or the black of her pupil.

Oh … fuck.

A suffocating energy swamps the room.

I struggle to not fight against it, to not slash at it with tooth and claw. To not tear through my skin and lash out with suffocating fog and icy rain.

I win that struggle. But then I continue to fight to take even a single breath against the pure, pungent essence that Zaya radiates.

Under my firm grasp on his shoulder, Reck is shaking, chest heaving.

"Fuck. Off." Zaya's voice is heavy, infused with that otherworldly power. As if the universe has spoken through her.

Reck's body jerks, instantly snapping fully upright. He turns, tears free from my hold, and just walks out of the motel room, then out of sight.

The suffocating energy collapses in on itself, as if it's being sucked back ... into the diamond pendant swinging forward from Zaya's chest?

"We've killed enough people for today," she murmurs, speaking to the gigantic snake and still sounding otherworldly even in a whisper. As if once more, it's not her speaking but the universe speaking through her.

Muta swivels his head just enough to flick his tongue at her. Then with a complicated twist and another swirl of unseen energy, he's once again a bracelet of brown topaz edged with gold, twined around and up her forearm.

Rought runs a gentle hand down Zaya's back. She sways into his touch, still frowning at the empty doorway behind me, frowning after Reck.

Then she passes out, collapsing back. Again.

Rought catches her, then stands and crosses around to lay her gently on the second bed, farthest from the door. Beside where Doc has set the revitalizing potions.

"I suggest getting him under control," Rought says without looking at me.

"And how do you suggest I do that?" I ask, just to say something. Because not only do I still have no fucking idea what's going on, I'm now shaken to my core, disturbed on a fundamental level.

Did Zaya's essence just rise to the surface and manipulate her unconscious body to stop Muta from biting Reck?

If yes, was it done to save the snake?

Or to save my brother?

And ... were all our futures somehow ... spinning off that moment? Would it, could it have become more than just a face-off between snake and shifter?

I've never seen or felt Zaya's power manifest like that, but her aunt scared the shit out of us when we were younger. Multiple times. Even more so on that night ... that night we lost our futures to the cracking sound of Zaya's neck breaking.

Rought hasn't answered me. He removes Zaya's boots, then gently tucks her under the covers. She rolls to her side, eyes closed but facing him as she tucks her knees up to her chest. I can see him actually restraining himself from touching her further, maybe even from crawling onto the bed and holding her. Rought has always been the best of us when it comes to boundaries and knowing his function. His ... place ... in the greater scheme of things? In the universe?

I always thought my younger brother underestimated himself. His strength, his abilities. I thought he'd allowed himself to fall completely apart, then only partially rebuild. But I understand now that he was just waiting. Waiting for what he was supposed to be doing, biding time overseeing the Outcast mech and tech.

Waiting for *her* to return.

He never faltered. He did shut up about it. About believing that she was somehow still alive, despite what we three had witnessed. Not that any of us actually talked about Zaya or that night. Internalizing despair is easier than facing it. We never even told our uncle the full story. Just enough of it to firmly pit brother against brother, to have a restraining order issued against our sperm donor in Reck's name and mine. And because Rought was still underage, only seventeen, rushed proceedings to obtain full legal custody for his mother.

I'm going to lose Rought to ... whatever this is.

Or I'm going to lose Reck.

I don't need to have any awry powers to see that pending future. It's right in front of me. And that incenses me all over again. If I ever paused to think about it, I would know that I choose anger because it's easier. But I don't pause.

I don't want to feel so much.

So I'll just feel this one thing and shut down everything else.

"She's going to destroy us," I say harshly. "Or, at least, finish the job Zaya Gage started thirteen years ago. Hell, even twenty fucking years ago."

Rought scoffs. "When she was nine? That's some long con, brother."

I snarl, "Either she's an impostor, or she is who she says she is and she's been toying with us this entire time, faking her death, lying to us. Is that the kind of soul-fucking-bonded you want? Is that someone worthy of sharing the three of us? Someone worthy of tying our lives to?"

Rought looks at me then, still crouched by her bedside. He looks ... sad, pitying. For me.

I walk away.

From that look, but also from *her*. I need to breathe. I need to think. I need to finish cleaning up the mess Zaya fucking Gage has dumped in my lap.

And yeah, I need to remind Reck that getting the Authority involved is going to fuck things up even more.

FIVE

ZAYA

A SLIVER OF SALTY SEA BREEZE AND SUNLIGHT filtering through gauzy curtains pulls me from a light sleep. I've been surfacing on and off for a couple of hours, but the fact that I can now sense someone with robust essence just beyond the exterior door informs me that my awry senses have at least somewhat reasserted themselves. Also, that I'm alone in the room — for now.

Delaying navigating the certain-to-be-complicated aftermath of the last couple of days a moment longer, I roll to my side and blearily note the items set on the bedside table. My phone, which I know without question I wouldn't have placed beside me while I slept, and three squat bottles of potion mage healing brew. Two of the stoppered bottles are uncorked and empty, only remnants of the elixirs they'd contained clinging to their interiors. But liquid filling the third bottle glows an evanescent pink.

Curling my knees into my chest, I try to relax into the

too-soft bed, tucking the lumpy pillow more firmly under my head and neck. But now that I'm awake, I'm aware of all the aches in my body. Deep joint aches that can be resolved only through movement. Also, I feel icky. And sticky. I'm swaddled in multiple layers of bedding, fully clothed in a tank top under a cashmere sweater, with my cashmere skirt now bundled up around my hips. It's uncomfortably hot. I'm actually sweating a little, and I rarely sweat — mostly by choice if I can help it.

I shove the covers back, noting that someone has pulled the duvet off the second bed and piled it on top of me for some strange reason. Have I actually died again? I tend to lose time around traumatic deaths, then need to sleep heavily. And what death isn't traumatic, really? It seriously screws with my body, my system. Even my recent memories, sometimes.

I sit up, huffing out a groan. Popping the stopper on the last mage brew — a revitalization elixir of some sort — I down it. It tastes like sweetened lemonade, which reminds me that all I want to be consuming is something thick, creamy, and chilled. Bonus points if it comes in chocolate or caramel, or even plain, delectable vanilla.

Yes, I want a milkshake.

Though ice cream will do.

But since that's not a new craving or easily assuaged at the moment, I shove the thought away so I can deal with the problem perched right in front of me.

My phone.

And whoever has screwed around with it while I was recovering from my most recent death.

Instead of pressing my thumb to the built-in scanner or raising the phone to read my face — two things that can be, and no doubt were, done while I'm unconscious — I press my entire hand over the screen, then wait. If I were a mage or even a shifter, I could trigger the extra security measures built into the phone by triggering my power in some fashion. But since I can't manipulate my own inherent essence in such a way, I need to wait until the phone picks up on ... well, me. Just me. And everything I carry.

Though I have only the barest of understandings of how to tap into it, or even of what my new role in the world, in the universe, means for my daily life, I know I am *more* than I was even three weeks ago.

The phone vibrates with a slight acknowledgment. Then a small box for a passcode appears on the otherwise dark screen. I enter my newest one-time-use code. I'll get another issued via a text message that will be wiped from existence after I read it.

Three red warnings pop up on the screen. The boxes are full of coded text that I don't bother deciphering. I have no idea why Coda bothers providing that much detail, because it means nothing to me except that the phone's security has been compromised. What little personal information was to be found on it has likely been downloaded, and tracking has been enabled.

I huff, seriously peeved.

But since I already know that Presh is worth the hassle of the hazy memory I have of her intense, overbearing brothers, I just triple-tap each warning message, dismissing it and alerting Coda at the same time.

Taking the phone with me, I shuffle into the bathroom. My suitcase is by the door, and as I pull out my neatly packed toiletries bag — quite certain that it was the opposite of neat when I repacked it — I don't doubt that every inch of every one of my belongings has been inspected as well.

I've already showered and am brushing my teeth when the phone screen flickers, displaying an intricate moving pattern of gray lines on the black background with the occasional slash of purple. It's not a phone call, at least not in the traditional sense, because it doesn't require me to answer it.

A beat later, the phone speaker is triggered remotely. A voice sounding like it hasn't spoken out loud in days mumbles, "What exactly have you gotten yourself into now?"

Coda.

"Initiating a voice-to-voice conversation?" I drawl. "Should I feel blessed?"

Coda doesn't answer, but I can hear background noise filtering in from the other end of the call. Rapid finger taps on multiple keyboards. I can visualize the banks of screens arrayed before the pale-skinned, hollow-eyed hacker, along with the energy drinks and caramel-short-bread-chocolate-bar wrappers littering all available surfaces. Coda will be wearing blue-tinted glasses, for light-sensitive purple eyes that are a few shades darker than my own. Well, my own before. I don't bother to glance in the mirror to confirm the verging-on-violet hue of my dry, red-rimmed orbs.

Hacker isn't the proper term for someone like Coda, who, despite their purple eyes, defies classification even among the awry. Coda does what I do — or at least what I used to do — except they interpret the threads of essence that surround us all on a microscopic, digital level. The life force, or fate as some call it.

I break the silence first. I always do. Coda might actually have forgotten they initiated a call with me at all. "Do I need to give you a detailed report, or are you in the process of backtracking my phone and pulling up every vid feed you can find?"

The pause after that question is long enough that I slather cream over every inch of my body, emptying the last of my travel stash in the process. I'm going to have to order more and get it shipped.

"Someone has tidied up after you," Coda mutters. "But either they missed this or couldn't thread it ..."

The sound of keys clicking over the speakers increases in frequency, as it often does when Coda is doggedly following a digital thread. It's punctuated by quiet grunts and mutters.

I tug on the last of my clean clothing. Stretchy charcoal jeans that are now annoyingly loose, a form-fitting black T-shirt, and the oversized cashmere sweater I slept in. The sweater is fragrant, and not in a good way. But I'll be ditching the bag — and the other tracking devices that have no doubt been hidden on and in it — and I love the light-weight charcoal sweater too much to leave it.

"Impressive work, your new tech," Coda mutters. "Oh, and this ... this little bit was pure artistry ..."

A moment later, it's a shouted, "What the fuck!" that lets me know Coda has found footage of the incident on the beach. From some private security system on one of the houses edging the shoreline?

"Your new tech," Coda sneers over the speakers, "isn't as good as me."

"The tech isn't mine," I say easily. "And no one is as good as you."

Coda huffs, still pouting. "I've cleaned up the residual, but what the fuck was that on the beach? I couldn't get a good angle and can't zoom in enough — yet — to get a clean image."

"A berserker."

"What?!" More sounds of keys being clicked are heard over the phone speaker.

I comb my wet hair and pull it into two long pigtails. I don't have a hair dryer, and I've got too much hair and not enough skill to twist it into anything prettier or smoother. Though I was too out of it to fully notice yesterday, I had indeed lost the expensive multilayered haircut and all my pretty streaks in the transition between life and death, then back again.

There's never been any point in me getting a piercing or a tattoo, because every time I die, I awake as a severely underweight blank slate. It's a shame, because I love the idea of wearing diamond studs, or even brown topaz to match Muta.

"A shifter man-eater?" Coda asks.

"That's usually the way they manifest."

"I thought packs took care of that sort of thing."

"That's the generally accepted decree."

Coda grunts. "Your tech has a trace on the other biker who was dogging you. But also ... it looks like they cleaned up after him for a bit ... then the trail goes cold, best I can tell at first glance. The second shifter goes by Chains, Cataclysm MC."

"Yeah," I say wryly. "We met."

Coda snorts. "Who is this dude tech? He's got great fingers and a sexy amount of reach ... you want me to put a pin in him?"

Now I'm confused. I mean, following Coda's thought pattern is never easy, sometimes to the point of me begging to be put out of my misery. And I know exactly what that entails, but ...

"You mean Chains?" I ask.

"No, your tech. I've already got recognition software running on the second shifter. I know you probably don't give a shit because you've got no sense of self-preservation, but I'm going to charge you for it either way. The tech's signature is familiar ... nice, clean work. His reach isn't as deep as mine, but you really can't blame him for that ..."

"There is only one of you." Because literally, Coda is the only awry tech I've ever even heard of — extremely pricey and extremely off the grid. Awry with exceptional powers are usually commodities, and traded between or hoarded by power players as such. But no one owns Coda. No one beats or blocks Coda in the digital realm either.

If it's been built, Coda can crumble it. If it needs to be wiped, Coda leaves no traces. But though I'm sure they have more than a few tricks up their sleeves, Coda in person is practically defenseless. Which is fine, because they're also a ghost. A digital ghost. Not the kind that can be summoned or influenced by a mage with a death affinity.

Coda has been off grid since we crossed paths in Belize in our early twenties and ended up rescuing each other from some never-identified black-ops mage squad hunting the hacker. Or, more specifically, hunting all unprotected awry throughout Central America.

Only one other person that I know of has ever tracked down Coda on the physical plane. And the result of that ... convergence ... is an ever-intriguing twist of fate that I had absolutely nothing to do with.

"I'm not completely without self-preservation skills," I say belatedly.

Coda scoffs. "All evidence to the contrary. Including just the last twenty-four hours of your existence. I assume the girl is worth it."

That last part is a statement, not a question. So I let it lie as such. Coda will get distracted in the next second or —

"Huh. Your tech isn't as circumspect as they think, even with cycling through a half-dozen code names." More tapping on keyboards. "This ident he tried to bury, like, ten years ago, leads to an actual person ... what kind of name is Rought?" But before I can respond, Coda adds gleefully, "Well, hello, gorgeous!" Like they've found a picture to match the great fingers and sexy reach.

Coda groans playfully. "If your dude didn't come with a dick, I'd be into him. Well, nineteen-year-old him, at least. Now that I have his face, I'll keep looking ..."

I huff. Again. "I have no idea who you're talking about."

"Not your type. You like them ... scrawny, urbane, and with built-in attachment disorder."

I open my mouth to protest that assessment, but I'm not sure I can offer up a counter to it.

"But he'll make you wish he were," Coda adds with a purr.

A perky voice in the background shouts, "What dick? I want to see dick that makes me wish for things."

Gigi. Aka the ever-intriguing twist of fate.

"Haven't uncovered a dick pic yet," Coda says. "But here he is shirtless."

"Oh, my, my," Gigi gushes, sounding closer in the phone speakers now. "He can pull my hair, spank me, and call me 'good girl' anytime."

"Slut." Coda giggles.

Muffled noises that sound a little ... mouthy? ... emanate from the speakers. Between those noises, Gigi lapses into French.

Coda responds in English. "You like him? I'll keep

looking for his dick for you. I'll 3D print it and watch while
—"

"Do I need to be here for this part?" I ask caustically.
I'm still nowhere near having a milkshake in hand, let alone
in my painfully empty belly.

"Is that Zaya?" Gigi asks.

"Hi, Gigi." I pick up my phone.

Abandoning the suitcase and the last of its contents in
the bathroom, I cross into the main room to pull on my
second-favorite pair of laced boots. These are brown leather
and also custom made, but come up to just over my ankle-
bone. I refuse to mourn the beloved boots I ruined on the
beach as I give the less-favored boots a cursory examination,
not finding any obvious tracking device. I can't go barefoot,
but I'll have to ditch them sooner than later.

"What the fuck is that!" Gigi shrieks through the phone
speakers.

I'm guessing not the pretty dick pic they were searching
for.

"Berserker," Coda grunts.

"It's grainy ... can you sharpen up the footage?" Gigi
whispers excitedly. Her voice now sounds even nearer, like
maybe she's leaning over Coda's shoulder.

"Camera was too far away," Coda snaps. "You're lucky
you can see this much over that wall."

Gigi ignores Coda's abrupt pissiness. I've never totally
figured out if the two of them are actually lovers or just
business partners. The interest in the hacker's dick pic, but
not necessarily the dick itself, just confuses that further —
despite the owner of said dick being deemed 'gorgeous,' a
term I've never heard Coda use to identify a male in all the
years we've been working together.

"My phone?" I ask pointedly.

"Clean," Coda pronounces. "Digital Adonis tried to sneak in a secondary and tertiary protocol. He really wants to know you, where you've been, and where you're going."

"Well, he's going to be disappointed."

"You know who he reminds me of ..."

A long pause ensues. Then more typing.

I eye my gorgeous designer leather bag, getting really pissy about having to leave it behind as well. I retrieve my favorite vanilla-mint and cocoa-butter lip balm and a pair of sunglasses, leaving my e-reader and current sock knitting project. All my money and passport and everything else important is tied to my phone, and I can access my current reading with it as well, but I'm pissed about the cashmere-blend yarn and the walnut knitting needles. Both are limited edition, not the kind of thing I can just go online and reorder.

Though Coda might be able to —

"Yep," the awry hacker gloats over the phone speaker. "Perfect match. Same fingerprints intersecting with some cleanup I did for you at least once before. Japan. 2022. A retrieval you ... *fixed*."

Now that is a weird connection. But it didn't necessarily mean anything. Talented techs got around.

"You pulled me into that job. Maybe AD is ghosting your trail." I find some paper embossed with the motel logo and a cheap pen in the bedside drawer, dashing off a thank-you note for the mage brews to the healer who'd helped me. Doc, who is somehow clearer in my exhausted memory than Presh's brothers. I have no doubt that between Presh and me, we've seriously dented the pack medic's supply.

Coda snorts, then cackles. "AD. Get it?"

Gigi responds in the background, "I get —"

"Adonis dick!" Coda explains unnecessarily.

"Right," Gigi huffs. "My IQ matches yours, you know."

"Stupid online tests," Coda mumbles belligerently.

I can't get caught up listening to another round of their charged banter. "I'm heading out."

"I'm always watching," Coda says, trying to be creepy and definitely pulling it off. The awry hacker hangs up.

I don't bother analyzing the postscript I add at the bottom of my note to Doc — or the whisper of power that flows through the pen, embedding into the paper as I write it. Because those words and whatever they portend are not meant for me to understand. But the universe apparently wants to give the medic a heads-up about something.

Choice, not fate, not love or devotion, twists the path.
And not always in the way intended.

That aspect of being the Conduit — random messages being filtered through my consciousness — isn't new to me. I've learned to ignore it. Mostly.

I fold and tuck the note in between two of the empty potion bottles. I glance around the room once more, realizing that the second bed has been slept in.

While I was unconscious.

I step around and closer, just enough to examine the dent in the pillow. And I don't even have to lay hands on the bed or bedding to pick up ... essence. A *presence*.

It takes a truly powerful person or entity to leave such a residual — and I'm not even usually attuned to such things. Well, the me from before three weeks ago wasn't particularly attuned. The necklace that swings forward from my neck is evidence that things might be different in the Now. Either way, though, I've only ever felt that connection with an awry before. And almost exclusively within my own bloodline.

The fading essence, the *presence*, on the second bed, isn't awry in tenor, though. It's ... it's more like the slipstream trails that Muta leaves when he's particularly riled up. Or hungry.

Muta is an aspect of a god or a divine power fused into flesh. But divinity runs in the bloodlines of all the essence-imbued creatures in this world. Just more intensely in some.

Did one of Presh's brothers sleep here? Or a guard they brought in? But ... I can tell it wasn't Doc or the guard I can still sense beyond the exterior door ...

I step away from that riddle. It'll show up again if it's something I need to pay attention to.

The motel door isn't locked. I step out into sunshine, which is a lovely change from the endless rain that drowns coastal Cascadia at this time of year.

I slip on my sunglasses, tilting my face up for a moment to enjoy the kiss of warmth on my cheeks, neck, and collarbone.

"Hungry?" I ask Grinder without looking at him.

The huge, medium-brown-skinned tattooed biker shrugs, leaning back against the exterior wall to the side of the door. With burly arms folded across his leather-swathed chest, he hasn't taken his gaze off me. But he's smiling, just a little. Taller than me by a lot, his hair is grayed at the temples, with more silver speckled through his beard, accumulating in a white patch on his chin.

My other senses aren't fully functioning yet, but I can't see or feel anyone other than the clerk in the office in the immediate vicinity.

A *knowing* tugs at me lightly.

"I need fries and a great milkshake. Possibly two."

"And some protein," he grumbles. His voice is deep and full of gravel. And oddly comforting.

I hadn't realized I was feeling ... discomforted. I'm not totally back in my body yet, with some part of what makes me *me* — separate from being the Conduit — still hovering in the aether. Tethered to my mortal form, but not fully inhabiting it.

It might take weeks to settle.

Unless I just ... lose that chunk. Because I have a sense, though no concrete proof, that I've lost chunks of myself before. Not just losing some of my life force, which is an obvious side effect of dying. But losing part of ... my soul, my essence?

Grinder unfolds his arms, continuing the conversation as if I haven't just been staring at nothing for a few moments. "There's a diner you might like in town."

He steps by me toward his massive motorcycle, reaching for a smaller second helmet that's already set on the back seat. Maybe Grinder catches hints of the future as well. Or maybe he's just smart about things such as his chance of keeping me in the motel room if I don't want to stay.

But then a gentle thread of a *knowing* tugs me to the side, not toward the bike.

"Let's walk," I say. "You can store your bike around back, along with your jacket and cut."

I'm fairly certain his leather vest with all its patches of allegiance is called a cut. He doesn't correct me. He does raise an eyebrow questioningly, though.

I smile at him as I quash the urge to ask him what sort of shifter he is. Mixed-clan shifters are always harder to read. And being mixed clan doesn't actually mean his beast isn't broadly classified as a bear, wolf, cat, or boar. Just that he chooses to identify as mixed clan.

He nods a little stiffly, then grabs his bike and pushes it, keeping pace alongside me as we traverse the shortest length of the building — passing the office — and circle around the back. He moves the heavy bike effortlessly. But then, he is a shifter, and inherent strength even in human form comes with the internal essence all shifters wield.

After parking the bike, hiding it from view of the main road, he tucks his jacket and vest in his saddlebags, leaving him clad only in a tight black T-shirt and leather pants. From there, I allow the *knowing* to tug us down a side road and along a parallel street that runs between the water's edge and the main thoroughfare.

A few cars, also heading south, pass along the main street, and I catch sight of a few people walking along the beach with their dogs. Locals, I presume, given that it's late winter. The one- and two-storey houses that line the streets beyond the Crescent Moon Inn are small, but on large lots. Well-kept in hues of white, blue, and gray. Just like the motel we've left behind, the surrounding area is obviously prosperous but not flashy.

Grinder doesn't offer directions, so I assume we're heading toward the diner he's mentioned. The milkshakes had better be worth the walk, because I'm pretty certain we're not all that near the commercial center of town.

WE'RE A NUMBER OF STREETS FARTHER ALONG, and still heading steadily south, based on the glimpses of the ocean to my right. And just as we're about to cross yet another perpendicular street running up from the water, the ear-blistering sound of more souped-up motorcycles draws Grinder's attention toward the main street, still one block up to our left.

His steps falter, just for a moment.

A trio of bikers speeds past, not slowing. Not even glancing our way. If they're displaying their club allegiance, I don't catch it. But Grinder grunts, perturbed. He tugs his phone out of his pocket, texting as we meander along the next two blocks.

He tucks the phone away, and we walk in silence for a while longer. No other cars or pedestrians pass us. A community mailbox is situated on the next corner, yet more evidence that the township of Cannon Beach is prosperous and well maintained.

"What did you see?" Grinder finally asks.

"I don't see," I say, not offering any other clarification. Mostly because the *knowing* hasn't tugged at me again.

"But you knew ... you asked me to remove my cut."

I shrug. "How many flavors of milkshake does this diner serve?"

He huffs as if he's not going to answer me. But after a moment, he says, "Five or six." Then his attention is pulled back to his phone.

That part of the *knowing* isn't for me to bother with. The aftermath, who those bikers were, and what or who they wanted.

It took me years to understand that messing with a *knowing*, even as gentle as the one that had pulled me and Grinder away from the motel, comes with even bigger ramifications than following one.

"Rath got waylaid on his way to ... Presh and you," Grinder mutters quietly. Not like it's a secret, but as though he's not sure I'd be interested.

My interest, however, is oddly piqued at the mention of Presh's overbearing brother. A genuinely out-of-character reaction, because Coda wasn't wrong. I don't go for that type. At all.

Granted, I don't really get riled up — sexually or emotionally — by many people. Maybe even by any people. I don't think about that too hard, examine it too closely, because there are all sorts of reasons I might have held myself back from genuine connection ...

Starting with the fact that everyone I love will eventually die, even while I am meant — some fundamental aspect of me, at least — to be Everlasting.

"Waylaid by other bikers?" I ask.

"With silver bullets locked and loaded."

"There was another biker at the ... with the berserker," I say, feeling my way around what Grinder is trying to tell me.

"Chains. We're tracking him. And yeah, could be he called in reinforcements when he lost Presh and you."

"But that would mean ... we're in Outcast territory."

"Yep. So was Rath last night."

So it could be unrelated club business — because I have absolutely no doubt that the Outcast MC gets into violent disputes all the time. Or Chains might not be willing to go home to his boss empty-handed.

"Don't worry," Grinder says. "Presh is with the Outcast. A small army couldn't get through the security on the main pack property."

The Outcast — aka Presh's and Rath's uncle, president of the club.

Grinder glances sideways at me, gauging my reaction maybe? "And you'll be under guard at all —"

"I really don't need a babysitter."

"I know," Grinder says, completely obligingly. "But you'll have one."

I don't bother to even shrug him off. I don't really fight or argue. With anyone. I just do what I want to do, and the only influence dictating those choices — more often than not — is the destiny handed down to me by the fucking universe.

Hard to argue with the universe.

Or destiny for that matter.

THE MAIN SECTION OF THE TOWN OF CANNON Beach is spread along the seaside. A long row of white-, blue-, and gray-painted buildings filled with restaurants and cute shops line a boardwalk that edges the open ocean. A large hotel is set over the beach on pilings — currently closed for the season, according to the sign. The white-capped surf is a muted thunderstorm lashing the beach, the relentless noise somehow comforting, grounding.

The opposite side of the street is geared more toward the locals, or summer residents perhaps. People, seemingly cheerful but focused on their own business, come and go from a quaint pharmacy, an even more adorable post office, a grocer literally overflowing with fruit and greens, plus a barber and hair salon. I can see signs for a gas station and a mechanic farther along.

No one does more than glance in our direction — which isn't unusual for me. Occasionally, the universe all but masks my presence, most often when I'm not fully functional, like now. But also completely randomly and unreliably. But I would have thought that Grinder, even without his bike and cut, would draw more attention.

The entire town feels very ... curated. Not false or fake, but definitely a well-loved business enterprise. And I have no doubt whatsoever that it's overseen closely by the biker pack that claims this territory. I also don't have to be able to decipher the patches on his jacket to know that the grizzled biker at my side is high up in that club. Which makes my next leap of logic an easy jump.

"An entire town to launder money through," I say teasingly. "Nice."

Grinder snorts and laughs. We've been quiet during our walk. He's modified his stride twice since we started out. I'm not winded or anything, but it's a longer distance than I anticipated — and I was dead, like, less than twenty-four hours ago. Though I might be a bit off on the timeline.

"The prez started pushing the club legitimate when he took it over almost thirty-two years ago and we became the Outcast. Well, more legit. We keep our hands in less savory biz because that's always going to exist, and needs to be regulated. For safety."

He's not wrong. Of-age prostitution and most recreational drugs might be legal in Cascadia, but the darker aspects of both will always be out there. "The prez?" I ask. "Presh's uncle?"

He nods. "The boys' uncle too."

Presh's brothers, I presume he means. I grin at him, not quite certain why I feel comfortable in his presence. I've lived my life among casual acquaintances and useful contacts. Friendships have always felt ... too indulgent, even for me. And a true friendship would require that the other person value me for more than ... well, my abilities.

This degree of comfort can't just be about Grinder

having known my aunt. In any other scenario involving my recent death, I would have put as much distance between me and anyone else remotely connected to that death as soon as possible. But I didn't even think about slipping out of the motel room, didn't bother plotting an escape route or giving Grinder a little bit of a *push* to slip by him.

"And you? Are you all legitimate?" I say, teasing. "Every day, every hour?"

He chuckles, tucking the phone away. "Well, a biker has to be a biker."

"Shifters need to be shifters," I counter.

He flashes me a wide grin, then he touches my elbow lightly.

I wait a moment to see if my essence reacts to his touch, to see if there's something I'm supposed to know about him — something that might explain this comfort I feel. But there's nothing. And I'm relieved that it's nothing more, nothing that requires something of me, some piece of me. Which is an odd reaction, so I write it off to my exhaustion.

"Do you want a tour?" he asks gently.

"Milkshake," I say. Firmly.

He snorts again, touching the small of my back and gently guiding me toward a corner diner a couple of buildings away.

In my next blink, the threads of all the people just going about their regular lives around us are woven through and around the streets and buildings, superimposed across my entire field of vision.

I stumble.

Grinder's hand shifts to my elbow, his grip firmer this time. "Just a few more steps," he murmurs. His big body curves toward me as if he's protecting me, as if he'll pick me up if I fall. Or even try to stop me from falling.

I'm not sure anyone has ever actually done that before. Not while I've been conscious, at least. And I'm not sure the gesture counts when it was just moving me out of ... necessity.

I'm not sure of anything right now. Which means I really shouldn't be on my feet yet.

I pause for a moment, blinking rapidly and looking up at Grinder instead of trying to take in the entire town. His threads aren't numerous or overly tangled, not like Presh's multilayered, multi-tiered destiny. But they are vibrant, balanced.

"Just tired," I say, inhaling deeply.

Under his predator musk, Grinder smells of evergreens and bonfires. More pure comfort. Though why those scents would be comforting to me, I have no idea.

"Aren't you a little high up to be assigned babysitting duty?" I ask.

He grins easily, though his gaze is sharp and concerned. "I'm high up enough that even the boys can't deny my ... requests."

It's obvious he means orders. "But it wasn't you sleeping in the other bed."

"No. It wasn't."

I wait.

He doesn't elaborate. Not even when I level a glare on him.

My stomach rumbles.

Loudly.

Keeping hold of my elbow, he picks up the pace until he's practically dragging me the last few steps to the diner. The contact doesn't bother me, though, because I have my own sight back. I usually have to look closely to see some-one's threaded path — but I've only been the Conduit for three weeks, and I've already died twice in that time. So 'usually' is really off the loom.

Not many people — even if they are powerful, highly ranked shifters — touch one of the awry willingly. Our powers are potentially invasive, manipulative. Uncontrol-lable, even. And more often than not, touch triggered. Telepaths, telekinetics, clairvoyants, harbingers, luck weavers, and curse breakers are a scary lot. And those are only the more well known of the subset of essence-wielders classified as the awry. We're known as 'twists' to some. Or 'the twisted.' We're everything that's wrong, amiss, skewed — the derogatory list goes on and on — within the world of essence.

I've been able to do a bit of weaving, both luck and curse, and a bit of mental manipulation for most of my life. But with the amulet now slung around my neck, I'm some-thing much, much more terrifying. More so because I haven't been wholly trained to wield what I now hold.

I just am.

A conduit for all life. The measuring stick of fate, some would say.

But Grinder knew my aunt, so his willingness to touch me isn't born out of ignorance or arrogance.

I survey the diner as we cross by the front windows. The signage etched into the glass door and emblazoned across the striped awning declares the place to be 'The Tasty Tart.' So of course, I instantly fall in love. The interior decor is mid-last-century-modern inspired, with royal-blue vinyl booths and stools, silver-speckled white laminate tables and counters, all edged in shiny aluminum. It's currently full of late-lunching customers, and obviously a spot the locals enjoy even when dining by the beach isn't in season.

"How many times did you bring my aunt to this diner?" I ask, narrowing my eyes, playfully distrustful.

"More than a few."

"You aren't going to fall in love with me too, are you?"

He barks out a laugh, hard enough to shake his shoulders and rumble through his chest. "Besides the fact that you're young enough to be my granddaughter?! Pinky would have my balls!"

Granddaughter, not just daughter.

Grinder is decades older than he looks.

He pushes through the glass door, drawing the attention of every patron and all the waitstaff in the seating area. They look at us for a brief moment, then return to their conversations and duties. It helps, I'm sure, that I'm still wearing my sunglasses and Grinder isn't in his cut. Though my senses are obviously misfiring a bit, most of the customers appear to be nulls. Not essence-wielders.

Still guided by Grinder's broad, warm hand on my back, I slide into the only empty booth with relief, sitting partway along the window and facing away from the door.

Grinder leans over to murmur in my ear, "Just a moment." Then he steps away and around the counter, pushing halfway into the kitchen through a set of swing doors. He keeps his gaze on me, the window, and the front door as he speaks to someone inside the kitchen.

A woman in her midforties, with deeply tanned skin and dark-auburn hair pinned against her head in tight coils, sets two glasses of water on the table, along with paper-napkin-wrapped utensils. She's wearing denim dungarees with a name — Tasmin — embroidered over top of the diner logo on the pocket of the bib. Despite the smile she offers, she looks like she could snap me in two with her bare hands. Another predator shifter. Not a wolf at best guess, but maybe some other kind of canine?

I could look closer and *know* for certain, but I'm seriously exhausted already. And deliberate use of my sight — for lack of a more specific way to qualify it — expends too much energy when I'm this close to the other side of a traumatic death.

Tasmin leans over as if to straighten the utensil rolls she's already placed on the table before me. "Are you okay?" she asks in a whisper.

I gaze up at her, oddly warmed by her obvious concern. Then, because I can't reward such selfless generosity with a half-truth — not to mention the implication that if I wasn't okay being escorted in here by Grinder, she would try to help me — I slowly remove my sunglasses.

Tasmin inhales sharply at the sight of my eyes, but doesn't otherwise react. She nods once, stiffly — acknowledging that I'm more than capable of helping myself if I'm not 'okay.' But then she says pointedly, "That don't make no difference to me, girl."

I haven't been a girl in way over a decade, but I find myself grinning at her.

She blinks again. Her brow furrows. Then she exclaims, "You're Disa's child! Zaya."

The name is like a knife through my heart. A shocking, visceral, and completely unanticipated reaction. Bedisa, aka Disa, who I only ever really called my aunt.

Bedisa Gage. The Conduit. The former Conduit. My mentor, my occasional caregiver ... my ... never a friend, never really a mother figure, but ...

Tasmin's nostrils flare wide, scenting me, no doubt sensing my sudden emotional reaction even through my scent-masking vanilla creams and salves. Then, inexplicably, she reaches over and pats my shoulder. "That old bruiser is ordering all wrong for you. Let me take care of it."

She hustles off, interjecting herself into the conversation Grinder is having with someone in the kitchen. The cook, presumably.

I'm shaky, hollowed out. Again. It's been hitting me in waves since I woke from the heart attack that had come with my becoming the Conduit, feeling the weight of the massive pink diamond hanging suddenly around my neck.

The manipulation of the divine always comes with ramifications.

I wasn't Disa's child. I wasn't even technically her niece, not first generation at least.

And I hadn't been this far down the coast since my midteens. I had vague memories of road trips with my mother before I was nine. Then after her death, year after year, with one or more of my so-called uncles. I remember staying on my aunt's estate. I remember training, honing the awry tricks that were unique to me, to my particular capabilities, or my capacity to manipulate the threads. Logically, I knew I'd spent months on my aunt's estate, through the summers and into the fall from ages nine to seventeen.

And then, seemingly abruptly, my aunt decided to start coming to me instead. Sometimes we trained together in Vancouver, where I was homeschooled and overseen by an always rotating number of distant blood relatives. But more often, we traveled from country to country.

Even with all that understanding of what those years of my life must have looked like, must have been like, I don't actually remember this town, the diner, or Tasmin.

Grinder's hand settles on my shoulder. "Zaya?"

I have a feeling he's been standing beside the table for a

while, waiting for me to acknowledge him or answer a question I haven't heard. "I'm fine."

"Clearly not," he murmurs. "I doubt anyone would expect you to be, either."

I don't bother answering that. No one ever expects things of me. I either had no one who cared enough to do so, or the few who might have cared that much if I'd been ... if I'd had a different destiny ... held me at a distance. Because I wasn't just Zaya to them. I was always, eventually, going to be the Conduit.

My aunt had *known* the moment she laid eyes on me cradled in my mother's arms. My mother told me the same story for the first nine years of my life, and my aunt recounted her version of the events for the next twenty.

After my mother died, Aunt Disa and I always spent our birthdays together. I had seen Disa two months ago in Seattle, to celebrate her two-hundred-and-forty-seventh birthday.

She would now miss my thirtieth.

We were both too young — for her to move into the *After* and for me to *Become*.

Grinder settles into the seat across from me, reaching across the table and nestling my limp hand in between both of his. He doesn't question me. He just sets his gaze on me and holds me in the moment.

I could cry. I'm so tired and overwhelmed. "I'd like to meet Pinky," I say instead. Because not only is being in the present my specialty, it is now my only choice.

He smiles, not questioning how I know that the mage is important to him, rather than just a casual relationship. So neither do I. "Yes. The moment you're ready." Then he nods toward me encouragingly. "Presh would love it if you answered her texts."

Yeah, I'm ignoring my messages. Continuing to ignore them. Because I usually don't stick around much after a *knowing* leads to my death. I withdraw my hand from Grinder's slowly. He watches me settle it back on my lap. I don't reach for my phone.

"I have to set out. Got some ... follow-up to do." Grinder grimaces unhappily. "But Cayley is going to make sure you get back to the motel."

"I'm not going back," I say, holding his gaze steadily so he can see my resolve even through my certain-to-be obvious exhaustion.

He nods like this isn't news to him, but doesn't offer an opinion.

Under the weight of his gaze, I cave and pull my phone out of my pocket. Three text messages are waiting for me. Two of them are from Presh. One from Rath. But ... I'm not quite ready to move forward yet, to keep moving. So I place the phone face down on the table. Just for another totally indulgent moment. Wallowing in whatever this is ... grief? Being overwhelmed? Some sort of anxiety?

I'm on the verge of something, perhaps a major *knowing* — one forced upon me, rather than stirred up by my intent, like with rescuing Presh. And for the first time in my life, I don't want to be hovering on that precipice. The thrill ... the high ... doesn't seem worth the fall.

I'll snap out of it.

I am both constantly changeable yet never changing.

"Is there anything you want to tell me?" Grinder asks gently, ducking his head reverently. He's huge, filling the opposite side of the booth, but he treats me like ... like he understands the divine power that runs through my veins.

"It's passed," I say, meaning the reason, the *knowing*, that had me tell him to hide his bike and take off his cut.

"I thought so. Unfortunately, I still have to deal with it."

I nod. He means the bikers we saw on the road, heading toward the motel. But that, happily, is none of my business.

He sets his phone on the table, fingers pressed to the edge nearest him. "Will you let me check in on you as well?"

I nod, and he slides his phone across the table, screen unlocked and a contact form already open with my name and nothing else filled in. I type in my phone number. "I doubt you need the address," I say wryly.

He grins. "I'll probably need a new invitation, though."

Yeah. The property will be keyed only to me now ... though I'm suddenly not sure about that. I might have to claim it ... somehow.

Grinder's smile falters, maybe even as mine does. Then he closes his eyes for a moment, as if navigating the same cresting wave of grief I'm riding.

I press his phone into his loose grip and touch the back of his hand lightly. I don't have the words for any sort of whisper of luck or longevity blessing, so I just let my latent essence skim across his skin. And hope that's enough of a thank you for his kindness and comfort.

He sighs and stands. Then, inexplicably, he leans over and presses a gentle kiss to my temple. "Find your way home, little one."

I nod. My throat clogs with grief as I fight through an almost overwhelming urge to either break, shattering completely — or to run, far and fast.

Neither is an option.

Running never really has been, though I've given it a shot a time or two. But the amulet around my neck means even that's gone now. There is no place to hide. I carry it all with me wherever I go — the power, the destiny, the *being*.

Grinder steps away, heading for the door as a pristinely maintained older-model green pick-up truck pulls up out front, parallel to the curb clearly marked as a no-parking zone. A dark-haired woman is at the wheel. Her gaze fixes on Grinder as she leaves the truck running and gets out. Though one motorcycle looks much like every other one to me, I'm fairly certain that Grinder's bike is strapped into the bed of the truck.

Tasmin sets a chocolate milkshake topped with real whipped cream and sprinkled with dark-chocolate shavings on the table before me, pulling my attention away from the window. A swirl of caramel decorates the entire length of the interior of the tall goblet.

"Thank you," I murmur, already pulling it toward me and fitting the straw in my mouth.

She pats my shoulder, her attention out the window, watching the newcomer and Grinder. "The halibut burger will be just a moment."

I'm not sure I've been touched this much in one day for years, and definitely not by strangers. Shifters are naturally tactile, though. I like it more than I ever would have thought ... as if maybe I've been starved of casual affection. Touch starved.

The Conduit isn't a person. Not a person to be gently caressed or coddled with milkshakes and fish burgers. She is a power. She is *the* power. The reason everyone else moves through the world. Without the Conduit, there is no fate, no destiny, no life force or essence threading the universe together.

My shoulder feels cold and empty when Tasmin drops her hand and moves away to exuberantly greet the newcomer at the door. I catch the name 'Cayley' and some polite inquiries after her family, then tune out. Outside,

Grinder climbs in the truck and pulls away. His gaze rests on me until he's forced to look at the road.

I slurp up a third of the milkshake, then all of the whipped cream, intentionally weathering the spike of headache that comes from drinking the supremely cold, supremely tasty beverage too quickly.

Worth it.

A striking woman with waves of near-black hair spilling down over her shoulders slides into the bench seat across from me. Her features are broad, with thick, dark brows and long lashes edging rich brown eyes. She's taller than me. And seriously ripped. She's wearing a slim-fitting black leather jacket over a tank top and black jeans, but I catch a flash of color as she steps around the table. Her laced boots, which are dark plum.

The leather jacket is covered in a multitude of fabric patches, as well as a prominent Outcast Motorcycle Club patch. The designs are heavy on calligraphy and of all sizes and shapes, including what appear to be tongue-in-cheek, occasionally naughty merit badges. The three that immediately catch my eye are: *It's Only Kinky the First Time*, *Good Girl*, and *I Don't Like to be Told What to do Unless I'm Naked*.

I'm a bit jealous — just for a moment — of the sex appeal and charisma she oozes effortlessly. Okay, also of the ridiculously cool jacket.

"I'm Cayley," she says. "And you've created quite the stir." She leans slightly forward, elbows on the table and chin resting on her folded hands. Her makeup is understated, her lightly tanned complexion flawless. She has her fingernails painted in a dark-plum-to-black gradient.

Ignoring that I feel like a malnourished, grubby, aimless child in her presence, I remind myself that appearance isn't everything. Then I take another sip of my milkshake, giving her space to elaborate — because I honestly can't remember much after slitting the berserker's throat, dying, and somehow still getting Presh to the motel safely.

I lost my car in there somewhere — I've forgotten to follow up on that — and drew way more ongoing attention than I'm usually comfortable with. Also, I have a vague sense that Muta might have made multiple appearances, and that's never great to deal with in the aftermath.

As Coda pieces together my last twenty-four hours, I hope the awry hacker isn't going to find more bodies that need to be dealt with.

Cayley tilts her head. It could just be a thoughtful gesture, except ... it's slightly more animalistic. She's a shifter, no doubt. Another canine of some sort? She smells like cherry blossoms on a rainy day — a scent I'm familiar with because it's one of my favorites. I'm going to miss early spring in Vancouver, and all the pink snow decorating the sidewalks.

It's a delicate, subtle perfume, maybe? Though I didn't think shifters wore scents because of their general sensitivity to such things.

"I thought maybe you could fill me in?" she finally outright asks.

I've almost emptied my milkshake, but I still feel utterly empty.

Clearly, I need another.

"No?" Cayley's tone is still all gentle, playfully beguiling.

I meet her eye to eye. I haven't put my glasses back on.

She doesn't flinch away. Inexplicably, she just nods, as if she expected nothing less.

Tasmin appears, sliding a halibut burger and fries onto

the table before me. The burger is huge. A half-inch-thick fish fillet, lettuce, tomato, fried mushrooms and onions, with some sort of tartar sauce melting over it all. Whole-wheat bun, lightly buttered and grilled. The fries are thickly sliced and golden brown. And I'm pretty sure the small ramekin is filled with garlic mayo. I'm salivating just looking at it.

Then Tasmin exchanges my empty milkshake glass for a whipped-cream-topped, thick and creamy caramel wet dream. A thick twist of chocolate syrup curls up the inside of the goblet.

I might groan out loud.

Cayley and Tasmin laugh. Robustly.

Then Tasmin settles her hands on her hips and looks at me expectantly. I somehow manage to wrap my hands fully around the massive halibut burger and take a huge bite. Various sauces and juices drip down all over my plate and fries. I chew, epically happy.

Cayley reaches for one of my fries, and Tasmin slaps her hand away. "I've got yours coming."

"Look at the size of her!" Cayley exclaims. "She's not going to be able to manage even a third of that plate."

Tasmin throws me a fierce look, as if I'm the one refusing to eat. I quickly take another bite, even though I haven't quite finished swallowing the first one.

Cayley chuckles quietly, watching me steadily.

"I don't want the two of you having any problems of the male persuasion," Tasmin says.

Cayley's shoulders stiffen, and her watchful gaze narrows slightly. "Why would we?"

Tasmin casts me a look, as if I'm supposed to under-stand and explain her odd statement.

I eat three fries at once, the burger still held firmly in my other hand. I have no idea what she's talking about. Grinder? He's self-reportedly old enough to be my grandfather. Any other males in my life are usually repeat one-offs. As in, I have five or so occasional bedmates kind of scattered around the globe that I don't actually take to my bed. To be honest, sex is ... fine. Skin contact is nice. But I'm not big on the transferring of fluids. And really, I can climax by my own hand, or the shower wand, a hell of a lot easier.

Cayley transfers her gaze to Tasmin. "Why would we?" she repeats, no playfulness in her tone now.

Tasmin just shrugs, as if she's not taking any responsibility for whatever she thinks is going to be a 'problem' between us. Then she waves over one of the waitstaff exiting the kitchen with a large bowl.

In her midteens, with dirty-blond hair, and a shifter as far as I can tell at a glance, the server passes the bowl to Tasmin, smiling at Cayley tentatively. "Hey, Cay."

Cayley barely acknowledges her. "Yo, Kris."

Tasmin slides the bowl over to Cayley — a delectable grilled-chicken Caesar salad, replete with crusty croutons, a hunk of cheesy garlic bread, and a parmesan tuile. I'm pretty certain the half-head of romaine has been grilled. And sprinkled with what might be candied lemon.

A world-class chef appears to be slumming at the Tasty Tart diner for the offseason. Not that I would ever say so out loud. I'll be outed as a food snob quickly enough.

If I'm sticking around.

Tasmin casts a narrow-eyed gaze over both of us again, as if we're unruly children. Then she heads off to check on the other tables with a huff, though I get the sense that she's not actually serving anyone but us. More managing or overseeing, perhaps.

The server, Kris, lingers for a moment, way more interested in Cayley than me, but then gets called away when the next order is ready.

I eye the gorgeous shifter across from me as she curates her first bite of salad. I'm pretty certain Cayley will trade a few of my fries for a few bites of her salad, but I might actually have to be friendly to pull off the transaction.

And it's not that I can't be friendly. It's just that I'm not wholly inhabiting my mortal coil yet, so even casual conversation, let alone the monumental intimacy of sharing food, is way beyond me.

We eat in silence for a while. I'm halfway through my second milkshake. It's just sweet enough to be soul satisfying without being achingly so.

Feeling a bit more grounded, I slide my plate slightly closer to Cayley, fries piled on her side. She takes one, then another, nibbling them between slow bites of her salad, a bit of lettuce, crouton, and chicken stacked on her fork each time.

She's reaching for a third fry when I finally feel it. The tug of a thin thread between us. I don't immediately sense what that connection means, but I'm not interested in disturbing the peace I'm currently luxuriating in to look closely enough to *know*.

That *something* shifts between us, though. Thickening as Cayley pushes her half-eaten salad slightly to the side, reaching across to steal another of my fries.

She savors the fry. Her gaze on me is weighty, even though I'm avoiding acknowledging it in favor of my milkshake. It's ... it's as if she's anchoring herself to me somehow ...

I really am too drained to take on whatever that means.

Of course, my state of mind and body means nothing in the grand scheme of the universe. I am Everlasting. And there's no point in fighting it. I'll just be forced to act either way. Until the moment comes that I'm allowed to embrace the *After*, and the mantle of the Conduit falls to my successor.

Though I've only been the Conduit for three weeks, I've already experienced the practical application of that lesson — a lesson first drilled into me by my Aunt Disa. I have, on multiple occasions, seen it forced upon my aunt's will as well.

I've watched her walk across a field riddled with death, ignoring multiple stab wounds and carrying me across her back as she righted whatever imbalance the *knowing* had pressed her to smooth. I followed her into a city ravaged by a dire-wrought plague, suffering infection and death just to shift the threads of one specialist, leading to a cure. I've faltered in jungles and rainforests, forcing my aunt to drag me along while she retrieved ancient artifacts of power that were never meant to be hidden away.

Two years ago, a *knowing*-prompted collection ended up being an utterly unique, exceedingly rare genus of flower. To this day, I have no idea of the significance of it.

Cayley suddenly sighs and slumps back in the bench seat, gazing beyond the window. She frowns, calling forth something she's been trying to avoid remembering. And yes, I can read that on her without trying.

"I know you." Her tone is low. She doesn't look at me.

"That appears to be the theme of the day." I keep the caramel milkshake close, taking tiny sips to savor it, but also so I can have the straw permanently fixed in my mouth during this conversation. A conversation I really don't want to have, but which I obviously must endure before I can move on. Before I can fall into bed with a full belly and sleep for days.

"No ... I don't know what Tasmin is on about ... but I *know* you." Cayley stresses the word 'know,' enough that she completely snags my attention. But there isn't even a hint of purple in her eyes as she shifts in her seat, half-turning back toward me. She doesn't mean *know* in the awry sense.

Cayley keeps her gaze on my hands curled around the milkshake, rather than looking at me. So maybe my eyes do disconcert her, at least for this part of our interaction.

"Eighteen months ago ... almost eighteen months ..." She's practically whispering, but there's an intensity to the words. As if she's forcing herself not only to speak to me, but also to acknowledge what she's saying to herself, for herself.

The thread between us is no longer only a glimmer. It's thickened but wavy, as if it might be in the process of branching or twisting tighter. But it's definitely firmly anchored now. She feels she owes me something. I realize that in the way that I just *know* things, and despite continually sipping the caramel shake, I feel heavy again.

This is why I generally walk away following a knowing. Unless I'm correcting an imbalance in the first place, I take on the imbalance that my actions often create. I deal with the consequences, the aftermath. Sometimes by dying — perhaps in place of those who were supposed to die before I *fixed* things.

It's also why ... why I maybe ... shouldn't answer Presh's text messages.

She can find another mentor and be better protected if

—

"I watched you walk into a mage-fortified warehouse full of heavily armed yakuza, then walk back out with six young mixed-clan shifters."

Cayley lifts her gaze to me, unblinking. She looks angry, then on the edge of despair for a moment. Then she closes her eyes and whispers, "I'd been on site for three days. On the third day ... well, let's just say I'd left the club without explicit permission, and I called in some favors from a chapter in my life that ... that ... hadn't panned out. I had a last-ditch plan. I hadn't slept more than a couple of hours since she'd been taken, and I was soaked and starving. Because I was afraid that if I looked away, I'd lose track of Kiki."

She takes a steadying breath and eats another fry. Her gaze is on the table between us, but not looking outward.

I wait. I could interject, maybe even *push* her recollection through to its end. But she needs to say it out loud, acknowledge it, so we can move on from this moment.

I think we're supposed to move on, together, for some reason. But again, I've never felt that sort of personal connection before. Had I felt something similar with Grinder?

What is going on? I'm not built for, meant for, friends or friendships ...

I shake my head and focus on Cayley. She hasn't continued, like maybe the memories are getting away from her.

"Kiki is your ... sibling?" I remember the teenagers involved, if not the fine details of the days following. And I can hazard a guess that Cayley is a better age to be a sister to a teen than a mother.

She nods stiffly. "Sister. We're ... kitsune."

Kitsune. An exceedingly rare creature — so rare as to be verging on mythical. Cayley might be allied with the Outcast, but she's more than just a shifter. Possibly more than she knows.

Her sister, Kiki, would have sold for millions on the

black market. A young kitsune is a prize for a collector and definitely sought after as a potential breeder for a pack desperate for an influx of new blood and genes.

"I didn't know," I say.

Cayley looks at me then, something like awe edging her expression. I want to look away, but I don't. We need to move past this ...

But why? For once in my life, I really don't know.

"You just walked right in."

I nod. "Yes."

"You came out covered in blood. The building on fire behind you."

Did I? That part is definitely a bit hazy. I hum, not disagreeing. "I don't think I killed anyone ... not directly."

Cayley laughs, sounding a little unhinged. "Those six teenagers you rescued wouldn't ... won't say a word about it, even under extreme questioning."

I narrow my eyes at that. I don't like the idea of extreme questioning in the best of circumstances, and certainly not after how much those teens were put through in a short period of time.

Cayley doesn't notice my pissiness. Or maybe she just ignores it. "One of my ... contacts ... checked in with me about a week after ..."

This is the part I really don't want to hear. Her hesitation to say it out loud tells me that without even a hint of knowing needed.

Cayley clears her throat, gaze downcast. Again. "That entire yakuza chapter was just ... gone. The building burned hot and fast despite it being wet monsoon season. Not a trace of evidence left behind. Dozens of operatives, millions of dollars in stolen goods and contraband just ... never recovered."

I don't say anything.

Although the three days after the extraction are hazy, I distinctly remember the frightened faces of the six teens. I remember that there were too many of them for me to hold onto at once. So after I ... coaxed ... the guards to open the cages, I tied us together with a mage-wrought spool of platinum thread — a brilliant and expensive bit of fabrication that could only be untied by the wielder, me.

I had simply *known* that I would need the imbued thread after getting Coda's emergency message. I'd been bumming around Tokyo aimlessly for three months before that call, picking up boring collection jobs and generally making a nuisance of myself by randomly fixing things better left unfixed.

I burned every favor I'd previously collected during my three months in the city getting to the teens, then getting them out.

The backlash from that kind of quick and dirty extraction is always severe. And Tokyo was no exception. Arguably even worse than dying under the claws of a berserker in front of Presh, mostly because of how I woke up.

Three days later. In a morgue.

In the process of being autopsied.

Muta ... reacted badly, then got loose. I wasn't in enough control of myself to rein him in.

Leaving everything behind — pretty much as I did this morning, except I had more things to abandon after three months of living in Tokyo — I somehow got to the airport and onto a flight to Vancouver.

I still had the spool of thread. I'd found it in a plastic bag along with my blood-soaked clothing, and needed to utilize its more ... malignant properties ... to get Muta under control. It took the death-god bushmaster months to forgive me for that little lure-and-lassoing trick.

As of right now, the Outcast MC — including Cayley — were just one of many packs who owed me a massive favor. Not that I bothered keeping track of which clubs and packs were specifically indebted to me. Coda kept a record of those sorts of connections, which I called on only when needed.

"How did you know to contact me? Or ask for me?" I finally ask. Because of all the people claiming to know my aunt and remember me over the last twenty-four hours, this more recent connection is even more disconcerting.

"I didn't. I called home. Finally. The Outcast knew that Kiki was taken, along with five of her classmates. The school ... all the kids were scholarship track at the same prep school ... contacted me right away. But they'd been gone for at least twelve hours before anyone figured out they hadn't checked in or been seen. They were kidnapped on a night off from school, and the school isn't in Outcast territory. So there were ..."

Cayley grimaces, still pissed about it all eighteen months later. "There were legal ramifications. Anyway, I tracked them on my own, as a ... private citizen, using my ... contacts. But I couldn't get to them. I couldn't ..."

She swallows, shaking her head. "I was ... I knew I was going to walk into that warehouse and probably make my sister watch them kill me or cage me as well. So I called home, to the club, just to ... check-in? Say goodbye? Let someone who cared know where the fuck I was and what the fuck I was about to do?"

She looks at me finally, her gaze steady, but still with that mixture of anger and awe edged in her expression. "Rought picked up. He asked me to wait, just a little longer.

And I guess ... he found you, somehow? Or at least knew that you or someone like you existed. He texted that he'd called in a few favors, but he didn't know if you'd get the message. If you'd come."

"Apparently I did."

This is the second time the name Rought — he of the imagined Adonis dick — has been mentioned in the last two hours. To Cayley, he's an actual person, a member of Outcast MC. To Coda, he's a skilled hacker — even if not as brilliant as Coda is.

"I ... I don't have the kind of resources needed to contact someone like you. And I ... I'm pretty sure the club would be pissed at Rought for the level of favor he took on just to get a message to you."

I don't really have any answer for that. Favors are traded in equal value, and I might never collect on the one that the Outcast now owe me.

Cayley squares her shoulders. "I did try the Authority first. That's their job. Their supposed ... mandate. To protect us, our kind."

My disbelief must show on my face, because Cayley laughs harshly and shakes her head.

"I had ... I thought I had someone ... a connection who would pull some strings. And he did. But ... it wasn't going to be quick enough."

"He's the one who gave you the after-report?"

She nods. "How is it that your reach was ... that you could do, solo, what the Authority couldn't even arrange in three days?"

I don't have an easy answer for that either, so I just stay silent.

She shakes her head again. "And just like the kids, I kept my mouth shut about you. Why? Why did I not ... say anything? The fucking Authority pulled me in for questioning, put me in a containment cell, the moment I got off the plane with those kids."

"I'm sorry. I guess … I must have thought you could take care of that part." I'd been well into the process of dying at the time. If someone — such as Cayley, who I really didn't remember — hadn't stepped up to take custody of the kids, I would have dragged them back to a safe house. Unless Coda had connected us with another trusted source, the teens would have had to wait a few more terrified days as I died, then recovered enough to get them out of the country.

I might not have wound up in a morgue if that had been the case.

Cayley huffs. "Well, yeah. I could take care of it. I did. But … you … you just walked those kids right up to me. My sister stumbling behind you, then trying to run the moment she saw me. She was, they all were, drugged out of their minds. The medic I had on call said they had enough fucking essence-twisted ketamine in their systems to knock out a fucking herd of elephants."

I nod.

She laughs, in disbelief now. "But you had them on their feet."

"They needed to be on their feet."

"How are you so calm about this?"

"What other choice did I have? Do I have?"

"You already had transport on site."

Not me. Coda. Coda would have had eyes on me the entire time — but not enough contacts in the city to save me from the fucking visit to the morgue. Though it probably wouldn't have mattered.

I owed the universe for taking the kids when their destiny lay elsewhere. It was my balance to pay.

I don't offer up any of that as clarification, though.

"We got the kids in the van, but I turned around, and you were just gone."

"Yeah, I do that."

She snorts. "And then there's the scholarships to the fucking Phron-fucking-tistery."

Right. The kids needed a little extra help, and some very specific trauma counseling and training. The Phrontistery, an elite global academy for essence-wielders overseen at the World Council level, was happy to provide both. I shrug. "That was a favor."

"A favor ... one for each kid? And with that specific campus? You have to have verified bloodlines stretching back six generations to even qualify."

"Six generations?" I frown playfully. "Sounds far-fetched. And I meant the other way around. The Phrontistery is now lucky enough to be training teenagers, who will soon be powerful alumni, who the yakuza deemed unique enough that they went to great lengths to kidnap them. To own them. The Phrontistery now owes me."

In truth, I'm probably even with the Phrontistery at the moment. They have access to an almost unfathomable network of exceedingly powerful players in our world. The bill between us is almost always evenly balanced.

Cayley laughs hollowly. "I'm sitting here across from you, and you are melting my brain while sipping a milkshake and mowing through fries. I thought the experience itself was surreal, but ..."

I finish the aforementioned milkshake with a noisy, definitive slurp. Then I pat my now-rounded belly happily.

"Because that's what you do, right?" Cayley asks. "That's the way you get paid for what you do. Favors."

"Occasionally, yes." Mostly, actually. Other than precious metals, cash is merely a series of zeroes and ones. And there are always more of those to be added together when Coda, or more specifically Gigi, manages financial transactions. Granted, most people can't afford an unspecified favor.

A true *knowing* — one I can't ignore or trigger myself — doesn't care about getting paid, though.

"You're a *fixer*."

A generic term for one of the revered — or more often reviled — awry who take on impossible jobs with impossible odds. Coda and Gigi, who is actually a mage, are also technically fixers. My aunt was as well. Just on another level.

"On occasion."

Cayley just blinks at me. I let her look, eating a few more fries. She yanks her salad back toward herself, stuffing a few no-longer-curated forkfuls into her mouth and chewing angrily. I wait for her to speak again. Because seeing me in this context has riled her up, causing some sort of internal conflict I haven't figured out yet.

She grabs a handful of my fries, dropping them beside the remains of her salad. They're lukewarm now, but still tasty. Also, I have half a plate left, so she can have as many as she wants.

"Fuck, fuck," she mutters to herself, still outright stuffing her mouth and speaking around half-chewed food. The so-called ill manners don't make her any less naturally compelling, though. "You're not going to let me escort you back to the motel."

There it is. She's on orders to guard me, maybe even assure my compliance. I've pissed someone off while yanking Presh off her destined path, hence my waking up to the tracking software embedded into my phone and the blatant search of my personal property. But I can't remember much of what transpired at the motel. I remember Doc, Grinder, and at least one ridiculously huge, stupidly pretty, and completely pissy brother. A biker — roaring motorcycle, patched leather jacket, tattoos, and all.

The brother I definitely communicated with, if you can call it that, was the one called Rath. I think? He was the voice on the line during the earlier phone calls. He'd been pissy with me then too. Aggressively so.

And Muta? Maybe Muta bit someone?

That's usually enough to seriously piss people off.

"I'm not going back to the motel."

"Well ..." she huffs. "I don't have a car, so ..."

I shrug. Then, confirming that I really, actually like her — highly unusual for me — I offer her a grin. "The universe will provide."

Cayley snorts doubtfully, shaking her head.

We eat the rest of our meals in silence, though I can still feel the connection between us. It's settled, but every now and then, she gives it a tug. I doubt she knows she's doing so. More likely, she's building up a series of questions, and every time she thinks of articulating one or more of them, she doesn't actually do so? It could also have something to do with the extra abilities that come with her kitsune nature.

Outside the diner, a brown-haired woman driving a gorgeous 1976 Chevrolet Corvette, custom-painted a high-gloss teal blue but with the original buckskin tan interiors, pulls up to the curb, illegally parking.

A For Sale sign is tucked in the side window of the car.

"Ask and you shall receive," I say, smiling. And just a little bit cocky.

Cayley glances outside — then swears viciously under her breath. "You, maybe. Me? Not so much."

With Cayley tracking her every move, the newcomer pops out of the vehicle — literally. Pertly bobbing, she practically skips across the sidewalk and into the diner. She's holding a printout of some sort, with tear-off tabs along the edge. She's curvy and seriously perky.

I can't figure out without taking a closer look whether Cayley hates her or wants to fuck her. Or maybe both? The kitsune shifter moves uncomfortably in her seat, then places both hands flat on the tabletop as if trying to hold herself still.

I slide out of my own seat while Cayley is distracted. Then I'm within a step of the new arrival, who is surveying the bulletin board beside the diner's front door, before the kitsune shifter can catch up to me.

The newcomer rearranges a few items on the corkboard, stealing some space for the sale flyer she's printed out, along with some pushpins.

I save her the trouble.

"Has it been converted?"

The perky woman flinches as though she hasn't heard me approach. But when she whirls around, her gaze goes straight to Cayley over my shoulder, so I know it's partly an act.

"Harls," Cayley all but snarls in greeting. "This is Zaya. That car isn't yours to sell."

Harls squares her shoulders and lifts her chin. "My name is Harlee Kimberly Larson, not Harls, and it's on the ownership papers."

"For insurance purposes."

Naturally, I've gotten myself tangled in something that's more than it seems. I'm not certain why I insist on being surprised when it happens, even without being guided by a knowing.

I tug the flyer out of Harlee's hand, scanning it for pertinent details while she and Cayley have a short but intense staring contest. The asking price for the car seems a bit low as best I can tell, but the classic has been fuel converted.

"I'll take it."

"What!?" Cayley cries.

"Really?" Harlee blinks as if she's seeing me for the first time. Then she glances between me and Cayley, slowly narrowing her eyes.

"You just said we needed a ride," I remind Cayley.

"So you're just going to buy one?" The kitsune shifter huffs, shaking her head admonishingly.

Harlee sets her hands on her ridiculously perfect hips and curls her lip. At us both. She's a mage, not a shapeshifter. With a strong affinity that I can't suss unless I look closer. But I'm not looking closer right now, not wanting to trigger another knowing — or even the weird overlay of threads that swamped my actual vision outside the diner. Not if I can help it.

Harlee is wearing a lot of bright colors, layers of fabric. I scan down to see completely out-of-season, flat-heeled sandals. Her toenails are painted teal blue, matching the car — that has to be deliberate — and she has multiple multi-colored bracelets encircling her left ankle. A mage with an affinity for charms? Or maybe potions? Though not a healer. At least not with a specific focus on healing.

"I thought you were in one of your riding-dick phases?"

Harlee sneers at Cayley. Then she juts her chin in my direction. "This one is a little skinny and pale for your —"

Cayley's hand shoots out, lightly snags my chin, and angles my head toward the miffed mage.

Again with the random contact. I've never been so eagerly, so casually touched in my entire life.

Cayley drops her hand an instant later, as if only just realizing that she's touching one of the awry. Or maybe just me specifically.

Completely stymied, Harlee shuts up, frowns, then actually looks at me.

She goes pale. Pink blooms across her cheeks.

Ah. The mage hadn't noticed my eyes.

Her own eyes are a gorgeous sky blue, ringed in a darker blue. Striking against her golden skin.

"Who is Dick?" I ask, trying to cut the tension. Because I do really want the car.

The shifter rubs her hand — the one she touched me with — on her thigh. "Harls means all dick, like in general."

Ah, I see. They're ex-lovers. "Which I don't have ..." I wink at Harlee. "But how can you tell without a closer look, mage?"

The cowed mage casts her gaze somewhere around my knees, swallowing.

Purple eyes really do freak most people out. But even more so when they've had some experience with an awry. The awry, in general, wield too much power to be considered ... well, harmless. As in, we are seriously not friend or lover material. Unless danger turns someone on. That does happen on occasion, and probably accounts for more of my own hookups than any sort of actual attraction.

I sigh internally, raising my phone into the mage's field

of vision. "The car? I can transfer the cash right now." I've already opened a payment app.

"I ... ah ..." Harlee flicks her gaze to the kitsune shifter, then away. "I'd be willing to trade ... a favor ..."

"No!" Cayley snarls. "Absolutely fucking not." After our conversation about her sister, Kiki, I'm not certain if the shifter is protecting me or Harlee. Though Harlee is more likely.

The mage flinches.

Cayley softens her tone. Well, she tries, at least. "You want to sell it? Fine. I'll buy it."

Harlee stiffens as if she's remembering herself — or rather, her goal of coming into the diner in the first place. A calculated move, it seems. To post the flyer about the car, yes. But also because Cayley is here to witness it?

"No. I won't sell it to you. Not to you and not to your ... newest ... sugar pussy."

Sugar pussy? Like sugar daddy? Why wouldn't it just be sugar mama? I'm not certain whether to be insulted or not.

"Don't worry, Harls," Cayley says nastily. "I'm still riding the same dick. On occasion."

"Why would I care?" she snaps back.

"Am I buying the car or not?" I ask, really tired suddenly. Both in general, but also of the conversation. There are too many layers to navigate, and none of it is my business. Though Tasmin had mentioned that issue of the 'male persuasion' that she thought Cayley and I might have. Related to the dick she's apparently riding, perhaps? But I can't imagine how that connects to me either.

"No," Cayley says. "You aren't buying that car, Zaya."

Harlee grabs my phone, inputs her info into the payment app, then shoves it back at me. She doesn't take her eyes off the kitsune shifter the entire time.

I hit a few buttons on the screen, transferring the cash.

Harlee carefully folds the flyer and tucks it in her woven tote bag, then retrieves her phone and a set of keys from within it. She's smug. And still staring at Cayley with her chin tilted up defiantly. "I'll need a name for the transfer of ownership papers."

"The name I paid with will be fine," I say.

Her phone buzzes, and Harlee finally breaks the second — or maybe third — staring contest with the quietly seething Cayley to look down at the screen and confirm that my payment has gone through. Her smugness evaporates. "Gage? Zaya Gage. You are ... you're a Gage ..."

"Yep." Cayley snatches the keys from the mage's hand, glaring at me. "I'll drive. Wherever you want to go."

"I need to pay for lunch."

"It's been covered."

I glance back over my shoulder, noting that Tasmin has been watching the little drama by her bulletin board with amusement. "Thank you."

"Don't be a stranger." Tasmin smiles back at me kindly, as if she knows me. Again.

That reaction, that weird familiarity coming at me from multiple directions is getting a little ... off putting. Not wrong exactly. Just ... uncomfortable? No. That isn't what I'm feeling. It aches, yes, but it's more that ...

I feel like my soul is aching ... even missing ... something ...

I shove the sensation away, pretending — even if only to myself — that it's all wrapped up in being recently dead. Even if I already know it isn't. I'm not a fan of lying to myself, but occasionally I need to just keep moving, and feigning ignorance is the easiest way to do so right now.

I nod at Tasmin, hopefully making it clear I'm not making any promises with the simple gesture.

Cayley holds the diner door open for me, now completely ignoring her ex-lover.

Harlee's face is flushed, and not just with anger. Something more has transpired between her and Cayley while I've been internally bemoaning the aching of my soul.

The mage trails us out onto the sidewalk. "I have things in the car."

"I'll get one of the boys to drop anything that doesn't belong to the car back to you," Cayley says, opening the passenger door for me.

"One of the boys?" Harlee snarks back. She's not perky at all now.

Cayley ignores her ex's jab, waiting until I climb into the car to shut the door behind me. The tan leather seats are soft and just worn enough to be comfortable but not overly damaged.

Thankfully, the window is already open a smidge, so I don't miss the final exchange between the ex-lovers. Not that I would ever actively eavesdrop otherwise. Never. Ahem.

"Cay," I hear the mage murmur as the kitsune shifter crosses around the front of the vehicle.

"No," Cayley says. "You wanted to hurt me, Harls? Good attempt."

"You're the one who —"

"You're the one who tossed me aside like a piece of shit." Cayley opens the driver's-side door and slides in. She starts and shifts the vehicle into gear before she even gets her seatbelt on.

"Destination?" she snarls at me.

"About two hours down the coast," I say. "At least I think it's that far. It's been a while since I've visited."

And I'm not actually visiting this time. I live there. If I want to stay.

Though I'm not actually certain I have a choice about that anymore.

The property is *more*, contains more, than simply a house, outbuildings, forest, fields, and sprawling beach-front. As the Conduit, any choice ... any and all personal choices ... might very much be a thing of the past for me.

"I know it," Cayley says.

And with the way everyone here seems to recognize my last name, if not me personally, I believe her.

The kitsune shifter hits the accelerator. "Check your fucking text messages."

I don't.

SIX

THE SKY IS CLOUDING OVER, INTERMITTENTLY blocking the late-winter sun, as Cayley pulls the Corvette to a stop at the turn into the long drive leading up to the main house of the estate. Following the highway as it shifted inland from the coast, we left the last seaside town, Lincoln City, in our rearview mirror about ten minutes ago. We've been traveling along the mostly forested eastern border of the expansive property since. The main house is set near the middle of that property.

A gate blocks our entry. A gate I've never actually seen closed before, and which is now apparently locked.

I slide out of the car, moving hesitantly now that I've arrived. For the last three weeks, I've been moving toward this moment.

For the last three weeks, I've been avoiding it in every way I can.

Finding myself in a diner I had no intention of stopping at, I practically welcomed the distraction with Presh and the clash with the Cataclysm bikers. I forced the knowing.

And I did so with the understanding that it would have consequences.

Namely, my death. Like that seemed preferable to my standing here now.

Coda isn't wrong about my lack of self-preservation skills. The hacker just might not know me well enough to know how willfully I ... disregard ... myself. Deliberately.

I know what's happened to bring me here. My aunt's death, and my inheritance. I just don't know the why or the how. But my being here is now tied up with so much that I don't understand — starting with the number of people who seem to know me, or younger me, at least. And even the connection to Cayley through her sister.

If I'm walking a path already measured for me — perhaps by my aunt herself — why does it feel so disjointed? So disconcerting?

"Open the gate?" Cayley leans over the passenger seat to call after me.

I shut the car door without responding to the shifter and slowly cross to the gate. I just stare down at the latch. I don't bother trying to unlock it.

My Aunt Disa and I never discussed this part — the actual transition — because it should have been decades away. Even a century or more.

I was supposed to ... live, to have a life —

I shove the thought away. Whinging and whining aren't my thing, so I'm not going to start now. Or I'm not going to get caught up in it, at least.

Even without the closed gate physically blocking my way, I know that the transition I'm facing — assuming? accepting? — isn't going to be as easy as me just driving up to the main house.

Is my aunt's body somewhere on the property, waiting

for me to stumble upon it? Or has she just ... disintegrated into the aether? More specifically, is she now my so-called sister in the transition to the *After*, snipping the threads of fate that now flow through me? And if so, what does that mean exactly? Does she still exist beyond this plane? If I hire the services of a mage with an affinity for the dead, will I be able to hunt down traces of —

I scrub a hand across my face. I'm still too near death myself. One foot dangling over the edge. Sections of my soul are still tangled in the aether. And I'm wallowing in it.

Instead of unlatching the gate, I climb it. The fencing is about six feet high on this edge of the property. Grasslands allowed to go wild stretch from here up to the house, which is set back from the bluff. A long, sandy beach stretches out as far as the eye can see — with enhanced or normal sight — from either side of that jagged, rocky outcropping. A low-lying beach punctuated by massive rock formations jutting out of the surf runs to the right. To the far south, near the very edge of the property, dunes begin to rise.

Except 'property' really isn't the right word to encompass the mass of land that the Conduit and the Gage family occupy along the coast of Oregon. It's a territory, really. Hectares upon hectares of land and beach. Even the foreshore is protected from public access, with both legal and essence-enforced boundaries. There's a no-fly zone above, and a no-boating zone set between us and international waters. No entry without permission.

I can't currently see that much of the property, of course. Not even while balanced on top of the gate. I can, however, see the conical roof of the turret tower on the main house, offset to the left on the asymmetrical structure. None of the usually ever-present soft glow emanates from its windows.

"Zaya?" Cayley asks. She's out of the car now, moving toward me.

I don't look back. I can't feel anything yet except for a shiver of chilly wind coming up the long, gently curved driveway. I climb down the other side of the gate, hesitating a beat longer before setting my feet on the pavement. The driveway and all the paths will need to be power washed in the spring.

Nothing happens.

I pivot in place.

Winter-dead grass stretches out before me on either side of the driveway, the edging neatly trimmed. The grass gives way to forested sections that have been left to go wild for centuries, since the first Conduit claimed the land. Not the actual first Conduit, of course. I don't think any of our personal records stretch back that far.

The world, with the gods no longer among us, is far older than centuries inked on paper, or even carved on tablet, can count.

Wildflowers grow in these front fields from spring through fall. But right now, the deciduous trees interspersed among the evergreens are still winter bare.

I take another step, then another.

Nothing happens.

Feeling like an idiot, I stride forward.

"Zaya?" Cayley calls. "Can I open the gate?"

She can try. But I don't say anything, because I don't know how to explain this part.

Once I get this process over with, I can invite Cayley onto the property. And she doesn't ever need to know that some inexplicable, universe-driven force ever impeded her entry. The natural boundary wards, the protection wards, that encase this territory aren't mage wrought. Nor can they be manipulated or altered by any mage, no matter the amount of essence that mage holds or the skill with which they wield it.

I'm a few steps from the top of a low rise when the house begins to come into view again. Still no light in any of the windows. No smoke curls from any of the four chimneys. Set just right of center on the wide-skirted front patio, the front door is closed.

I try to take another step, but stop suddenly in the middle of that movement with my right leg raised.

I'm frozen in place. It doesn't hurt. Nothing presses against or around me. No energy churns in the earth. No threads envelop me.

But I can't move.

I can't tilt my head, not even a dip of my chin, but I can see an ever-brightening halo emanating from the gold-caged, rough-cut pink diamond strung around my neck as it begins to glow under my sweater. Brighter and brighter until its light is literally burning through the thin knit barrier, sending pink-hued beams streaking out from me in all directions. I can't verify the feeling without actually being able to look, but I don't think the light slices through me.

My head slowly, almost imperceptibly falls back, so that I'm gazing up into the cloudy gray sky. I'm aware that all the light stretching out from me is now feeding back into the pink diamond, then into me. I swear I can also see the purple-hued blaze of my own eyes lighting the underside of the clouds.

I watch as the world slowly moves around me, over me ... sound filtering in, though I'm still caught in that mostly frozen state. Then I can hear actual voices, questioning and stressed behind me. I can see birds, seagulls, then something smaller, flying in flocks. Juncos? Then finally, turkey vultures swooping and spiraling overhead. Looking for carrion?

I haven't died.

But I am being remade ... or perhaps realigned is more accurate. My senses are being retuned to the energy, the essence, anchored in the property as well as in the rough-cut gemstone bequeathed to me by destiny.

The wind picks up, followed by rain. I can feel both stirring my hair, caressing my skin.

My still-suspended right foot falls forward onto the drive. Then my left foot rises. My head snaps down, and the house comes into view again. My arms swing forward, one and then the other.

I'm once again walking along the driveway toward the house, as if I never stopped in the first place. Except the afternoon has darkened into evening, and my clothing is damp, though not soaked through. The rain has picked up again.

I hear the gate being shoved open on creaky hinges behind me, then the sound of multiple engines. Cayley has called in reinforcements.

I don't look back.

I *need* to know now.

I already knew. But now ...

I walked these lands as a child with my mother, then with my aunt, and then alone. The estate has always accepted my inherent right to be here. But now ... now we are somehow bound?

I've been taught that this property protects one of the world's *intersection* points. I am the anchor, or rather the Conduit is the anchor, for all essence. But then that essence threads through the secondary anchors of the intersection points. Besides the one I've just claimed, there are six other intersections arrayed across the globe. Though centuries ago, maybe even a millennia, there used to be nine in total.

Until this moment, I hadn't realized what the intersection point on the estate meant for the Conduit. For me.

It is possible that I'm a goddess when I walk these lands.

I will be lesser when I step away, but never again the person I was before the necklace settled around my neck.

But ... if I am actually a goddess, or at least am now carrying some aspect of a divine immortal being, how and why is my aunt — the goddess before me — dead decades before her time?

Aware of the quiet purr of the Corvette and a rumble of three motorcycles following me to the house, I jog up the five wooden front steps, noting that the decking also needs to be power washed and revarnished. The house needs a coat of paint too. Has that much time passed since my aunt last had the property maintained?

A three-foot-tall stone gargoyle stands sentry by the front door, a key tucked within its clasped forepaw. Not just anyone can pull the key from that spot, though. Not without permission from my aunt —

No. Not without permission from me now.

Some of this sort of thing, the sorts of things scattered around the property, could be classified as essence-wrought or crafted. But I can only wield and feel intent, not specifically crafted and cast spells or charms or wards. I've inadvertently walked through protections or foiled essence-based attacks without even knowing it, numerous times.

But the key is mage wrought. My aunt, perched in her high tower and endlessly working, at least from my perspective as a child, always hated being interrupted to answer the door. The locks are automatic, and not via tech.

I unlock the door as the engines of the vehicles shut off behind me. I don't have to look back to know that Cayley is climbing out of the car, or that Grinder has returned with Doc Z and Presh's brother, Rath. Their life force is so robust, I don't need eyes with which to see them.

But I feel drawn, even momentarily compelled, to look back. Just once.

At Rath.

He's so huge, easily six and a half feet, that his large bike looks regular-sized as he swings his leg off it. His hair is brown, chopped short. As he removes his helmet, he favors his left shoulder, almost imperceptibly. I can't see the color of his eyes from this distance, but his features are broad, arresting.

I don't look closely, not even at the vibrant threads of fate that entwine them all — and which tie two of the three to me, loosely, but in a way I can't even begin to fathom. Because they aren't the mystery I'm here to unravel.

Moreover, it's possible I'm not entirely in control of my own actions yet. Not that I'm being puppeted or piloted, but just that my body remembers the last intention I gave to it — go to the house, look for my aunt — and is following through. But at the same time, my mind is shutting down to navigate whatever cosmic and otherworldly event just occurred, binding me even tighter to the woven fabric of existence.

Voices rise in argument behind me as I turn away again — Rath is questioning Cayley. Or ordering her around. I don't wait to see what conclusion they come to, striding into and through the dark-wood-paneled front entrance. I flick on the overhead light, and doing so triggers the lights along the hall leading all the way back through the house to the kitchen.

I glance into the sitting room on my left. A silver tea service is set on the antique coffee table. Three teacups, all mostly full, are set about the room. A large section has been cut out of a bright-yellow lemon cake with thick white frosting. I don't have to step any closer to confirm that the cake is starting to mold.

No bodies.

No sign of a struggle.

But I know …

I *know*.

The only life forces I can feel on the entire property are arrayed behind me on the front patio. Even if my aunt had just gone for —

No. My aunt is obviously dead.

Why do I keep questioning that?

But Aunt Disa also wasn't the only person who lived on the property. At least three others should also be here. Her chosen, though none of them were her soul-bonded as far as I know. She had never created, or rather found, a connection on that level. Honestly, I think that sort of universe-bequeathed connection is garbage anyway. Simply wishful or fanciful —

"Zaya," Rath says behind me. I've left the door open, but he hasn't stepped into the house. It isn't the first time he's said my name. Or asked me a question.

I ignore him, crossing the few steps to the main stairs. No matter what rights he thinks he can claim over me because of my abrupt rescue of Presh, I have no answers to any of his questions. I'm aware that I could kick him, all of them, entirely off the property. But I feel … oddly fragile, unsettled. And despite his pushy behavior, verging on inappropriately possessive, his presence is not … unwelcome. Yet.

Rath swears quietly behind me, possibly in Spanish. Then he starts issuing orders. No one enters the house. It's possible they can't without my explicit consent.

Instead of cutting into the dining room or continuing along the hall to the kitchen, I traverse the stairs to the second floor. The banister is dusty.

My aunt's house is never dusty.

Hundreds of years old, yes. But meticulously maintained.

"Grinder," Rath says behind me, "head over to the barn and check on the caretaker. It's still Mack, right? Cayley, check the greenhouse and the gardens for Ingrid, Disa's mage. I'll check the exterior of the house, then the beach house. And there was a third in the last few years, wasn't there?"

"Combat mage. Devlin. Never caught his last name," Grinder says. "He's been with Disa for about ten years."

Those names knock around in my mind as I slowly climb the stairs. My head feels hollow, but my limbs are heavy. Mack, the shifter caretaker. Ingrid ... and Devlin? Yes. They all lived here with my aunt.

Shouldn't they have contacted me?

Shouldn't I have contacted them? But I ... I haven't called anyone, reached out to anyone ... I'm not ...

Three weeks is a long time for my aunt and me to be completely out of contact. Not unprecedented, but —

"There's no one else on the property, Rath," Doc murmurs. "No one ... alive."

"It's a big fucking property, Zephyr," Rath snarls. "With a fuck-ton of essence-wrought shit that even your senses can't necessarily penetrate. Stay here, and get your hands on Zaya the moment she lets you —"

I turn left down the second-floor corridor, leaving their

conversation behind. I've never thought of the house as particularly dark before. But I haven't turned on any more lights, and the dark-wood wall paneling over aged-oak flooring is ... almost claustrophobic. Oppressive, even.

I cross by four closed doors — more dark wood. Then I'm hovering outside the open door to my aunt's bedroom. The extra-large, overwrought, curtained and canopied four-poster bed is perfectly made. The fireplace is empty and cold. The room is tidy. Not a thing seemingly out of place. I don't step in.

I continue to the final door set near the end of the hall. The door leading to the turret. A door that I never noticed as a child, maybe never even saw, until my aunt first invited me into her office, her inner sanctum. As with the key in the gargoyle's hand, more of my aunt's directed *intention* obscured it from casual sight.

But I can see the carved, heavy door and its ornate brass handle clearly now.

That handle yields to my touch, turning easily for me though it never has before, not without an invitation. Beyond, an intricately carved staircase spirals up the turret's outer walls. Creatures of mythology — or of a world long past, as some would claim — form the posts and rails, rendered in more dark wood. Walnut, I think. Running alongside the stairs, the entire space is lined with book-shelves. Thousands of books stretch up around me, easily eighteen or even twenty feet, not including the conical roof. Fiction, nonfiction, manuals, spellbooks, plus journals and keepsakes collected by my ancestors, fill the shelves.

I don't bother with the lights. Even though my mind is alternating between numb and whirling, my body knows these rooms, these halls, these stairs. The memory is buried at a subconscious level, but I don't falter, don't question.

I take the steps, ascending into the turret. Into my aunt's sacrosanct office. Though I really have no idea what she did up here every day. We had always trained in the ground floor multipurpose room, which the original builder had likely called a ballroom, or in the expansive workshop in the barn, or on the bluff, or on the beach, or in the grass fields.

Maybe it's the disconnect I'm still navigating, have been navigating since the last time I died. Maybe since even the time before. Because even though my body knows where to step, the house feels foreign around me, not just the turret. I haven't returned since the summer of my seventeenth year, but I've spent months of my life, adding up to years of my life, between these walls.

Shouldn't it feel different?

Shouldn't it feel like ... coming home?

Something itches at the back of my mind, almost like a touch of intuition or even the touch of a skilled telepath. But nothing comes from it. Just that itch telling me that more isn't right here, possibly even more than my aunt's abrupt demise. Her transition beyond this plane of existence.

Maybe I am still re-forming, still becoming, but my aunt always indicated that she could feel the one who came before her when she became the Conduit. I thought she meant her ancestor, her mentor. But I feel no connection to the *After*. Or to the *Before*, for that matter.

I shove the unhelpful thought away — the thought of being alone and suddenly not understanding my purpose as well as I thought I did.

A small circular room opens up at the top of the spiral staircase, the domed cupola ceiling in shadow above. A massive dark-wood desk sits at the very center. The desk has cabinets on one side and three slim drawers with ornate keyholes on the other.

I become aware that I'm still clutching the key to the house in my hand. And that I have no other keys with which to open other locks. I tuck the house key in my back pocket.

A matching wooden chair on rollers sits on the far side of the desk. The bulk of the walls are lined with books, though the shelves near one side of the desk are slightly less full.

A massive, curve-fronted armoire fills a rounded section of the room between two of the windows. It's constructed out of a lighter golden wood. Maple, maybe? But not so darkened with age. The armoire's double doors are inlaid with symbols or glyphs cut out of mahogany and rosewood, at best guess. The bulk of the glyphs surround the armoire's two wooden handles.

No keyholes.

No keys.

I'm drawn to the armoire, though seeking it wasn't my original purpose. But the doors don't yield to my touch.

Abandoning it somewhat unwillingly, as if there might actually be something beckoning me from within, I cross around the desk. A notebook sits open on a forest-green blotter. A half-finished entry in my aunt's handwriting covers three-quarters of one page.

The ambient light is too low to read it, but before I can reach for the desk lamp, a *tug* pulls my attention in another direction. I look toward, then cross to the window instead.

Outside the window, the sky is still darkening into evening. Across the expansive backyard, the craggy bluff juts into the open ocean, barren of trees and grass. From this higher vantage point, I have a clear view of the coastline, stretching out seemingly endlessly from either side of that bluff. The tide is halfway up the beach, with roiling, white-capped waves pummeling the gray sand.

To the right of the bluff, at the edge of the beach, Rath is hovering in the dark, open doorway of the beach house. He's already turned on some of the exterior property lights, so the stone pathway between the main house and the beach house is sporadically and softly lit.

Without moving, he reaches inside the beach house and flips on the light, just staring but not stepping within. He's so large that he fills the doorway.

As if feeling my gaze on him, he pivots and looks up, all the way up to the turret window. He looks right at me.

And grimaces, shoulders slumping.

Fuck.

I LEAVE THE HOUSE THROUGH THE MUDROOM, adjacent to the laundry just off the kitchen, stepping down the three wooden steps of the back patio onto the lit stone path. Neatly carved through the winter-dead grass, that path leads me forward a few steps before branching off in two directions. I take the right fork, toward the beach house.

It's still raining. It's chilly now that the sun has set behind a thick layer of cloud.

Rath is still waiting for me on the front porch of the grayed-cedar-sided beach house, his phone in his hand but not currently texting. I swear I could feel him watching me even as I moved through the main house, and he's certainly tracking my every step now. It's a disconcerting but not wholly uncomfortable feeling.

And yeah, for someone seriously allergic to drawing too much attention — attention that is in actual fact occasionally very bad for my physical and mental health — I get that my calm reaction to the shifter's intense regard, my willingness to allow him to explore the property, and even to follow the nonverbal cue he gave me to join him at the beach house is ... out of character.

Way, way out of character.

The path curves for a bit, then branches a second time, leading farther right to the beach or cutting directly toward the beach house.

I get two steps onto the beach house path, look over at Rath, and feel ... something. Not a *knowing* ... not a warning ... not a wrongness, but something is off. I stop walking, just staring at him.

He glowers at me, more upset than angry, though I really shouldn't be able to read him that well. I haven't even taken a glimpse at his threads. As if doing so would be too ... intimate?

Which is a weird reaction. Honestly, I'm not overly ... moral in how I use my sight, my powers. So why? What is this feeling?

I try to take another step forward. I manage it, but it feels like walking through ... nothing. Emptiness. Which makes no sense, because simply walking doesn't generally come with a huge amount of sensation. Right?

I eye the path between Rath and me. He's up on the porch but still directly across from me.

I step to the side easily. Just a normal step, with none of that weird empty feeling. But when I step forward, that nothingness returns.

"Zaya," Rath grumbles, crossing his arms.

He talks to me as if he knows me. All edged with intent, yes. But also with a kind of low-key chiding that only someone who knows you well uses when ...

I shake off the thought.

I don't know him.

I take another step to the side. I'm well onto the grass now and no longer lined up in a direct route to Rath on the steps.

I start forward again, without any weirdness dogging me this time.

What the fuck is going on?

I really don't have the headspace to sort it out right now, but why the fuck would moving along a path directly toward Rath be any sort of issue?

I make it to the steps, mounting them on the opposite side of where Rath is standing. He doesn't move back or give me space. I don't remember him being quite so massive last night — ridiculously broad shoulders and chest, tapering down into long legs. But then, I don't remember much of last night in the first place.

The Asian cast to his features is a subtle, intriguing flavoring. He's easily one of the tallest people I've ever seen in person. Heat radiates off him, but that might just be because I'm still seriously cold, still mostly soaked through from standing for who knows how long in the rain.

"Problem with the path?" he grumbles.

I step around him without answering, because I don't answer to him. Dealing with dominant shifters isn't usually a problem for me, but apparently Rath's ego outweighs any instinctual disconcertion that is the usual response to my awry nature. But also, I don't actually know what the hell just went on with the empty path.

The empty space between Rath and me.

He huffs at my dismissal, muttering under his breath, "Typical."

I cross to the wide-open front door of the beach house. Inside, the front room is brightly lit, backed by a small U-shaped kitchen. Rustic wood furniture, worn hardwood flooring. A scattering of rugs throughout.

It's been redecorated since I last set foot within. As far as I remember.

A red-haired older woman is sprawled on the floor. Clearly dead, but not showing any signs of decay. She lies as though she's fallen while crawling … toward the door or …

A puddle of dried liquid and broken glass spreads about a foot beyond her fingertips.

"Mage brew." Rath steps up right behind me, easily looking over my head.

"She was carrying it." I carefully step farther into the room. Giving the broken glass — some sort of carafe? — and the fallen mage a wide berth, I get a better look at the interior of the beach house. A scrying bowl has fallen to the side in the middle of the front room, as if it was hovering over the coffee table? No liquid remains on any of the furniture, but three weeks would have given any residual plenty of time to dry.

I cross through to the kitchen, not yet looking directly at the body. The kitchen is messy, strewn with pots and pans, dried herbs and other ingredients scattered everywhere. Including some slowly rotting animal remains that should stink but don't. Yet.

It takes time for residual to wear off after the mage who cast that essence dies. Such as the stasis spells on the animal remains. I step to check the pots on the stove —

"No, Zaya!" Rath barks, still hovering in the doorway.

I chafe at the command, but he's not wrong. Most essence-wrought spells can't really touch me, affect me. But I'm not at full strength. Nowhere near full strength.

"We're going to need a mage," I say, in that mildly disembodied, disengaged way that I'm still navigating. "Do you have a ... trustworthy contact?"

"And if I didn't?" He sneers, challenging me.

Over what, I have no idea. "Then I'd make a call."

"Of course you would."

I raise my hands slightly to the sides, in a mild 'what's your issue?' gesture.

He grimaces and pulls out his phone, texting.

I move to examine the fallen mage, but not before I glance into the nearest bedroom. The open doorway is just up the hall from the kitchen. The bed is a mess. Both pillows are indented. Two people slept there, possibly regularly. It's a complete contrast to my aunt's tidy bedroom in the main house.

A room that maybe my aunt never actually slept in?

I crouch by the mage, not wanting to touch her but needing to brush her red hair from her face. I force myself to do so. I'm fairly certain that if the timeline in the back of my mind is correct, a regular human would be showing advanced signs of decay by now. But she is ... was a powerful mage.

And more than just a mage, if I'm right about what has occurred here ... what happened to the mage at the exact same time I also dropped dead three weeks ago.

I brush back her hair to expose her face. Even without touching her skin, she feels utterly inert to me. A disconcerting nothingness. I've been around the dead before, but usually before all the life force has completely drained from them. Honestly, I occasionally feel more energy from an inanimate essence-wrought object or artifact than this ... nothingness.

A nothingness ...

I glance up at Rath, thinking of the feeling on the path, that nothingness, that emptiness. Was it this ... death? Was that what it feels like when a thread is snipped? Not a main one — not enough to kill, obviously. But ...

No. Who would be able to do that? Trim or snip a single thread, a possible destiny, from an awry as powerful as I am? And even if it was possible, why would I have felt that between Rath and myself?

"You don't recognize her?" Rath asks.

I've just been staring down at the mage, thinking, but Rath has misread me. And there's something else layered in his question.

Has he noticed me not recognizing someone else? Maybe Cayley said something about the owner of the diner, Tasmin?

Wait ... I'm not certain the kitsune shifter was around for that part of the —

"She was Disa's witch, Ingrid," Rath says.

"I know," I say stiffly, shaking my head — at myself. Because I hadn't actually recognized her before Rath named her. My mind really isn't back online yet. "She was scrying and making some sort of brew to facilitate or access whatever she was looking for ..."

"And then? Just dropped dead?"

"Apparently." And with the circumstantial evidence piling up, I'm almost certain that her death occurred at the same time the amulet settled around my neck and I suffered my own heart attack. When my aunt died.

I don't say that part out loud. I have no proof, and I'm a little shocked that my aunt would have tied her mage to her so tightly. Even chosen mates shouldn't die when their crux passes into the After. Except ... maybe a stronger binding would have been to the benefit of the mage? Lending her a longer-than-normal life span and maybe even a power boost?

"They were ... lovers, then," I murmur. "Essence bound."

Something oddly charged fills the space between Rath and me — as if I'm again picking up his emotions, though I'm definitely not empathetic. He rumbles doubtfully, "You didn't know?"

"Why would I be surprised if I knew?"

Rath narrows his eyes at me, his gaze burning with distrust. And something else I still can't figure out.

Doc Z steps around Rath in the doorway and hustles into the room, some kind of diagnostic device already in hand. I shuffle to the side, but don't straighten from my crouch. I trace my gaze over the room again, willing the threads to weave together. Only in my mind, though. I don't have the power to manipulate the past in such a fashion.

The scrying, the brew, the ... timing?

"She's been gone for a while," Doc says quietly, her head bowed as she deciphers the readings she's captured with her device. "Longer than it looks."

"Three weeks," I say.

She looks at me sharply. "Yes."

"How do you know?" Rath asks.

I ignore him, continuing to question Doc. "Heart attack?"

She nods. "Followed by a system-wide shutdown. I would have thought a stroke ..." She deliberately runs her gaze across the body, calling attention to the way the witch is sprawled on the floor.

I understand. A stroke would have dropped her in place, but she should have ... might have ... struggled more ... while suffering a heart attack.

I just nod, absorbing the confirmation and keeping my mouth shut.

"If it looks like a fucking stroke," Rath growls, "then why did you think it was a heart attack, Zaya?"

I don't answer, but I do straighten and cross back toward the door. And him. "Is your mage on the way? Leaving essence brew to puddle and mix while the mage's wards degrade after her death is —"

"I know," he snaps, clearly paying my intransigence back with sulky sullenness.

I level my gaze at him. And impressively, he doesn't wilt under it. Though he doesn't push me any further either, so he is capable of reading and correctly interpreting warning signs.

"Harlee is on her way," he says begrudgingly.

"Cayley's mage?"

He snorts. "Not anymore."

I just hum.

That gets me a raised eyebrow and a quirk of a lip from Rath.

And suddenly he's ... he feels like ... mine. As if we really do know each other ...

"You know differently?" he asks quietly, his voice a playful purr like we're sharing a secret. A secret we've shared before. Or a type of secret we've shared before. About the things I sometimes just *know*?

I swear to the universe that I actually sway into him for a moment. Enough so that concern crinkles the edges of his amber-flecked eyes, and he catches my hip, barely touching me.

"Zaya?" he asks, not even a hint of the playful purr or his former supreme pissiness in the question.

"Tired," I murmur.

"Doc?" Rath prompts. "You got another one of those energy brews?"

"Sleep would be better," Doc says, all firm about it as she stands and tucks her device away.

Cayley stomps up onto the patio behind Rath, then steps through the doorway with a growl. "Harls is on her way."

Before any of us can respond, if any of us were inclined to respond, she sees the mage's sprawled body and all but shouts, "Shit! Oh, shit, shit. That's Ingrid."

"Yes," Rath says. He's still barely touching me, but he hasn't taken his hand off my hip. He gestures promptingly and firmly to Doc even as he answers Cayley. Doc huffs and starts digging through her med kit.

"Ingrid is a Wisdom," Cayley says. "The fucking head of the West Coast Coterie. She occupies a seat on the mages' Coalition."

"Not anymore," I murmur.

"I mean, how the fuck has she just been ... how has no one checked on any of this? The Coterie is going to miss their head Wisdom."

I sigh, but it's Rath who answers. "No one can access any part of the property without an invitation. And after Disa died ..." He glances at me, but I don't fill the space, so he continues, "It was probably inaccessible to anyone but Zaya, yes?"

Again not answering, mostly because the fact that I needed to claim the property and intersection point makes everything he's saying completely logical, I step slightly away from him. Rath's hand falls back to his side.

Cayley, still staring down at Ingrid's body, purses her lips tightly. "Fuck. Harls is ... not going to take it well."

Rath frowns at her. "Do you care?"

"Yes, I fucking care, you big doofus," she snarls. "You don't just stop loving someone when they hurt you. You ... I ..."

"Did you just call me a doofus?"

Cayley pauses, mouth open and everything. She blinks and says, "Of course not."

Beyond the still-open door, Grinder stomps up the exterior stairs, giving Cayley a moment to duck out of Rath's line of sight and save face.

"We've got a problem ..." The older biker's gaze falls on Ingrid's body, and he clears his throat. "Well, a second problem, apparently."

"Mack?" Rath asks.

"Dead. In the graveyard."

"Like ... buried?"

"Nope. Appears to have dropped dead while digging up something."

"Fuck."

Doc hands the mage brew she's pulled out of her bag to me.

"Third," I murmur, accepting the swirling pink energy elixir. "Third problem."

I down the elixir as all eyes turn to me.

"Where is your aunt, Zaya?" Rath asks almost gently. "Dead."

He gestures impatiently toward the corpse of the witch. "I got that much. Where is Aunt Disa's body? Did you ... were you with her when she died? Were you coming back here to ... bury her or check on the others? Are all these deaths connected? Do we have some sort of serial killer in Outcast territory? Or a dire-wrought epidemic?"

Doc's elixir slides down my throat and radiates through my chest with a hint of warmth, a touch of energy. Despite my increasingly numb brain, I don't miss Rath calling my aunt 'Aunt Disa.' With a sense of familiarity. Ignoring that because I don't have the headspace for it, I turn to Grinder. "Which graveyard?"

His eyebrows rise. "There's more than one?"

I sigh. "Yes. There is more than one."

"The ... marble mausoleum?"

I nod. Then I step back out into the rain.

"Zaya?" Rath snarls again.

I glance at him over my shoulder. "Why do you think I owe you answers, Rath?"

It's a genuine question, without any heat, but it literally stops him in his tracks. His fists clench, and his nostrils flare as I wait for his answer.

"You're in Outcast territory," he finally says.

"I am my own territory," I say, and now I'm the one trying to be gentle. "Wherever I am, but most definitely here, on this land, I am my own ... domain." If he knew my aunt as he claims, then he already knows that. I wait for him to try again, to offer up another reason.

He doesn't.

As I walk back to the path, nothing impedes me, nothing feels off this time. I take the right fork, leading across the width of the property. Well, the width of the habituated, cultivated section of the property.

"I'll meet Harls at the gate," Cayley says behind me. "Might take her a bit to get here ... she sold the Corvette."

"Sold? To you?" Grinder asks, confused.

"Zaya," Cayley says with a sigh, sad and frustrated.

I'm too far away to hear the rest of the conversation, and too numb to worry about any of it. For now. Rath has overcome his sudden reticence and is on my heels again, his strides long enough that he catches up without effort.

I don't look back. Not at him, or in general.

I never do.

I am only the Now.

Even if deep down, buried under a lifetime of conditioning and understanding, I ache to be more than simply the Now and to have some say in what more I could be. A future that could be woven in the moment, instead of me being born into a tapestry already constructed for me.

But there are no subtle shifts in my destiny, no choices to be made, forks in the path, or threads to be followed. Not anymore.

THE SALTY WIND AND RAIN INCREASES AS FULL dark blankets the estate. The family plot, the mausoleum that Grinder mentioned, can't be seen from the house or the beach. Behind its wrought-iron fence, that area spreads beyond the grayed-cedar-sided barn, beyond the overgrown orchard, set on a slight rise edged by the forest.

We don't bury our dead in the family plot. We inter ashes. Though I was raised to understand that our physical bodies are simply vessels for the power, the essence, the abilities that flow through our immediate family, generation upon generation of Gages have been cremated — often wherever they'd died, all over the world — then interred in this plot. When I was younger, I witnessed my mother, two uncles, and a cousin I'd never met being set within the marble niches of the mausoleum. All but my mother arrived by courier, already collected within urns.

During my core training, my aunt insisted that no power, no energy, remained in a vessel beyond death. Now that I knew more about the other powers that exist in our universe, and specifically the power wielded by a mage with an affinity for the essences of death and the dead, I suspect that was a half-truth.

I suspect that we Gages are cremated for a fundamental reason. We are already terrifying to most when we walk the earth under our own power. But piloted by a death mage or dire mage with no moral compass, no allegiance to maintaining the delicate balance of the universe? We Gages — dead or alive — could be wanton devastation incarnate.

The remains, cremated or otherwise, of the Conduits who came before my aunt are not interred within the family plot, however. Because when the universe is done with a Conduit, nothing remains. Or so I've been told.

Still, that supposed fact isn't currently stopping me from looking for my aunt.

I step through the already-open iron gate, vaguely noting Rath's hesitancy to enter the fenced grounds behind me as I wander over to the main white marble mausoleum. Stark against the rain-clouded night sky, the structure is arched and open on two sides, just tall enough to walk within. For me, at least. Rath would practically need to bend in half and walk sideways.

Every space of the mortuary walls is filled with small niches, some open, some sealed. As I pass, I run my fingertips over the names carved in the exterior niches at shoulder height. Various pieces of white marble statuary are also collected within the plot, set against the wrought-iron fence, and mostly ornamental in nature. Angel and demon motifs dominate.

I don't have to look at the names etched in the marble to read them. And at the far end of the mausoleum, the farthest exterior corner, I linger. As I always linger. My fingers, feeling just as cold as the stone, press to my mother's name.

From this viewpoint, I can see legs sprawled across the ground just around the side of the mausoleum, clad in work pants.

Mack.

I look up at the sky instead of stepping forward to investigate. Just for a moment. The rain is so heavy that it runs down my face. I'm so cold that I'm beyond shivering.

I still feel half dead myself.

I trace my mother's name, top to bottom, immortalized in stone until the time when that too crumbles under the weight of existence. M ... E ... R ... R ... I ... C ... K ...

Rath steps around me from behind, glancing my way for only a moment, then crossing to crouch by Mack's body. He heaves a heavy sigh, then scrubs his face. He's soaked through now as well.

How stupid is it to not have at least grabbed a coat and an umbrella?

I skip the dates of birth and death etched below my mother's name. No last names are carved on any of the niches. Even if we didn't use the name in our lifetime, we are all Gages in death. I run my fingers over the ornate script that I know reads 'Mother,' though it's harder to distinguish those curves and curls with just my fingertips. My numb fingertips.

My mother, Merrick, was more than just a mother. And

I often wondered — out loud, once — why that was all that is carved on her epitaph.

It was because of me, my aunt informed me brusquely. My mother's entire life, all her talent and fierceness and love, had been distilled into one title, one purpose. Because she gave birth to the next Conduit. Me.

Rath, still crouched, shifts back on his heels, his amber-flecked gaze on me. There's no moon or starlight through the clouds, so he's just a dark shape. But I can see his eyes. I catch a hint of his *intent* even though I'm still deliberately not looking beyond the surface.

He scrubs his hand over his face a second time. I don't bother, just letting the rain have its way with me.

"I always hated it in here," he finally confesses ruefully.

"The graveyard?" I hear myself asking, even though I already know what he means. It feels similar to when the universe speaks through me, but more ... more as if I'm being forced to acknowledge the connection between us? Or his ... claim on me?

"Yeah." He shakes his head, turning his attention back to the fallen shifter. "No wounds, no signs of a fight ... no ... decay ... no signs of scavengers ..." He clears his throat. "Looks like he just dropped, like Ingrid."

"Heart attack," I murmur. "And ... there's no decay or scavenging because ... well, I suspect that the property has ... had locked down somehow after ... after ..."

Rath hears something he doesn't like in my tone, because he glances at me sharply, opens his mouth to say something, but then pauses instead. He inhales deeply, maybe scenting the air? Then says, "I'll get Doc to confirm."

"They were lovers, then," I say, speaking the thoughts out loud as they form. I feel utterly disconnected now. My dying, and then the transference of the estate — for lack of a better way to encompass what's happened — has left me ... hollow. "All of them."

"All three?"

Devlin, my aunt's combat mage, is unaccounted for. But he is the barest of memories to me, so I don't mention him or confirm Rath's count one way or the other.

"Essence bound," I say, rambling more than answering him. "And the connection could only have been this strong if ... reinforced. Continually. Sex, the ... physical and emotional connection, but also the transference of bodily fluids, tends to do that ... with one of the awry at least."

"I know," he says gruffly. But then he sets aside whatever renewed pissiness he really wants to level at me and adds, "You knew Ingrid and Mack. You knew that they were Disa's lovers." That isn't a question. Or an assumption. It's a statement of fact.

"I must have. But I ..." I don't manage to articulate that sense of loss yet. I'm somehow missing pieces of my past — more than just the hazy moments that occur each time I die and reset — and I had no idea. Mack was at my mother's interment. Ingrid's residual essence is all over the estate, in the gargoyle at the front door, in the ...

"You need sleep," Rath says.

I just stare at him, swaying slightly. Am I somehow anchoring myself through him into this moment? If so, the connection is tenuous, malleable.

"Don't make me carry you."

I think he intends it as a threat. Low grade, yes, but it came out with warmth. A warm promise.

I catch the sound of a muted car engine. On the driveway, I assume, as the road is too far away for me to pick up such sounds. I should articulate what I need from the mage.

From Harlee, I remind myself. I should make it clear I'm hiring her, that she reports to me, not to the Outcast MC.

"The bodies should be cremated," I say instead.

"Always." Rath's voice is a much gentler rasp as he straightens from his crouch. He carefully steps around Mack's prone body.

"And … interred here if they don't have family."

"I'll make sure everyone knows. There might be … some sort of investigation requested."

I laugh. The sound is hollow, thin. "No. There won't be."

He just nods at that, stepping close enough that the rain running off him is dripping onto me. I allow my head to fall back again, but I'm not looking at the sky this time. I'm looking at him.

Rath.

Do I know him? Have I forgotten him as well?

He feels … he feels as if he's … mine.

No. No one belongs to me.

While I belong to everyone and to no one person.

I open my mouth to ask him what beast he shifts into, because he's freaking huge in human form. I open my mouth to … flirt? To tease? To invite him to carry me back to the house, strip off my wet clothing, and fill me up in a hot shower? Make me less … hollow.

Make me … whole?

I close my mouth.

"At least try to get some sleep, Zaya," he says, still all gentle.

I nod, giving in. I'm maybe functioning enough for the walk to the house, but I'm not strong enough — nor am I equipped — to deal with the bodies and the implications of their deaths.

I move to step away. Then I remember what Grinder said. "Mack was digging? With his hands?"

Rath points toward the fence. "Shovel."

It's too dark for me to distinguish the tool from the wrought iron I presume it's leaning against.

"I should know … I should know what he was looking for."

"Or burying," Rath mutters. "Do you … do you want me to keep digging?"

"No," I say, abruptly blunt and harsh, even though I have no idea what secret I'm trying to protect. What could be buried in the graveyard at all?

I catch the tension that runs through Rath. It scrubs away that gentleness I felt from him.

I turn away, reminding myself it's better this way. I'm only reacting oddly — in my head at least — because I'm cold and tired and vulnerable. Rath Guerra is not the right partner to add to my revolving roster of hookups. Assuming he's even interested. For one thing, I'm planning to stay. I'm not actually certain how long I can be off the property now. With everything changed. And I never live anywhere near my occasional lovers.

Yeah, 'lovers' isn't the correct term. That implies … more. And I don't have more to give, not on such a personal level. I don't really like being skin-to-skin with many people, not for extended periods. Most people find my energy off-putting. And I'm just not equipped to … be intimate, body or soul.

Still, I occasionally give it a try.

I make it to the gate before an echo of the conversation comes back to me. I turn around, noting that Rath is following but keeping back from me, perhaps making certain that I'm staying on my feet. "What did you mean, 'I always hated it in here'?"

"Seems obvious," he says, all stiff-voiced again.

"You've been here before, then?" I ask. "When?"

He doesn't respond.

"Is ... one of your ancestors interred here? Are we ... related somehow?"

The related thing would explain a lot of what —

"No," Rath says sharply, as if I've forced him to speak.

I wait a moment, allowing him space to elaborate. He's more than hinted that he knows me, or knows of me, hasn't he? And he certainly acts like it. His anger and frustration with me feels ... intimate.

His fingers curl into fists, but he doesn't offer any explanation.

I walk away.

Even though I'm out of his direct line of sight beyond the barn and orchard, I can feel him watching me, tracking me all the way to the house.

I CROSS DRIPPING WET INTO THE MUDROOM AND almost continue through into the kitchen before some part of my brain clicks on for a moment. I duck into the laundry instead, stripping out of my wet clothing and wringing it all out as best I can in the laundry sink. Then I pull the clothesline out from the wall and string all my wet things up so they hang over the washer and dryer. I note that the power coursing through the pink diamond when the estate accepted me burned a hole through the center of my only remaining favorite sweater. If I ignore it, it will go away, right?

I blink at the wet clothing for a bit, absently wondering why I can remember that the laundry room has an interior clothesline, but not … not the diner or … other … people.

Am I supposed to remember Rath?

If so, why hasn't he said anything?

No. I don't know Rath. I can't know him, because no memories of him have filtered back to me, as they've done for Ingrid and Mack.

There are towels for the dogs in the cupboard, though I can't remember the last time my aunt had a pet. I use one. It's frayed at the edges and a little crusty. I should put them all through the wash.

As for the dogs, I wouldn't know, would I? I haven't been to the estate since the summer of my seventeenth year. Maybe that's what Mack was doing in the cemetery? Digging a grave for a recently lost pet, not looking for something.

A little bit drier, I cross naked into the kitchen. I make sure I have my phone. No tech programmed by Coda is going to have any issue with getting wet, but I still ignore the text messages swamping the lock screen.

Muta is still in his dormant form, ringing my forearm in gold and topaz. I'm surprised he didn't leave me to go hunting the moment we arrived on the estate. But then, he does hate the rain.

The kitchen has been more recently renovated than the rest of the house, the stainless steel appliances looking practically pristine. And seriously expensive. The cupboards are also newly stained, in contrast to the house's overall rundown appearance.

And that's a little odd, isn't it?

Especially because I got the impression, blurry brain or not, that the beach house looked more lived in ...

As I head to the kitchen's farm-style sink, I note a large box sitting on the back counter. I wouldn't have seen it while coming through in the other direction. I pour myself a glass of water, then flick on the overhead light to eye the box.

It's an ice cream maker. With a built-in compressor. A note is taped to it.

> *I'm sorry for everything you are about to discover*
> *and that I wasn't the one to tell you.*
> *The armoire will open when you're ready.*

It's my aunt's handwriting, but I'm really too numb to process much else. I take the note with me, though, not wanting anyone else to see and try to interpret it while I'm sleeping.

A *knowing*.

That's what this note, and the purchase of the ice cream maker, represents.

Just not a *knowing* of my own.

I write notes too, as I did for Doc in the motel. I send letters and emails, make connections between people, and fix situations without ever discerning the fine details. Because the details aren't for me to understand. They just flow through me.

So this note of my aunt's ... it has to be a *knowing*, right?

Her knowing.

Because I have to believe. I have to hang onto the belief that if she had any inkling that it was all about to pass to me, that she was about to shift into the *After*, that my aunt would have warned me, warned her lovers.

Wouldn't she?

Time enough to buy an ice cream maker. To have it delivered. To write the note. All that would have been more than enough time to reach out to me ...

I realize that I've moved through the house and up the stairs without thought. My mind is whirling, but the rest of me is on the verge of collapse. I need to dry my hair, to put on some sort of clothing.

Instead, I open the door to my old bedroom, cross to the bed, and climb under the covers, still clutching the note in my hand.

I ignore that the bed is made with fresh sheets, and that there's an oncidium orchid on the bureau gently scenting the air.

My aunt's last words to me tumble around in my head, following me into an exhausted sleep.

VITKOVSKAYA_ART

SEVEN

I WAKE TO A BRIGHT MOON OUTSIDE, ITS LIGHT pouring through the bedroom windows and streaming across the bed. I've slept two, maybe two and a half hours given the position of the moon, and that's not nearly long enough. Though apparently, it has stopped raining.

I roll out of bed, noting that my wrist and forearm is bare. Muta must be hunting down a meal. Otherwise, he'd never swap the warmth of me curled in a bed for the possibility of getting at all damp. Rats are plentiful on the property, and I hope that if any bunnies are slipping out of their burrows in between rainstorms this early in the season, they sense the danger long before Muta scents them.

And yes, I'm aware that bunnies shouldn't be ranked above rats in any sort of 'okay to kill' category. It's just that the larger the prey, the longer Muta takes to digest, which makes him all bloated and extra heavy. Either way, though, he'll enjoy being on the property for a while. He doesn't feel the need to stick with me quite as closely here.

Nothing can bring harm to the Conduit while this near to the intersection point. The universe will literally rise up to thwart any and all threats. So ... it was utterly stupid of me to expect to find my Aunt's body on the estate.

Because she would have been killed somewhere else entirely.

Did whomever she served cake and tea to lure her from the estate?

What was Ingrid scrying for before she too dropped dead? Did she lose contact with my aunt? Or get some sort of other warning through their bond?

And ... where is my aunt's third bond mate, Devlin? I would have to go to the forest cottage in the morning ... I couldn't just rely on the shifters to investigate. For a multitude of reasons. Technically, we aren't even affiliated, and with no contract between us ...

Shoving away thoughts of all the problems I couldn't actually solve while lying in bed in the early-morning hours, I blink up at the ceiling for a while longer. Totally wide awake. I'm going to have to close the curtains to get back to sleep.

I manage to all but cocoon myself in the eiderdown duvet as I roll off the bed, dragging the long tail in my wake as I cross to and reach out to pull the heavy fabric curtains. Through the sash window, I have a moonlit view of the jutting craggy bluff, the raging ocean, and the still-well-lit beach house. But that's not what makes me pause.

No. It's the items arrayed on the deep dark-wood windowsill that have somehow stopped up my brain. A collection of seashells, ocean-smoothed quartz stones, and sea glass ...

And in the far right corner of the sill sits an antique mason jar filled with what appears to be ... handwritten notes?

I swear ... I catch glimpses of my own handwriting on

the tightly folded bits of paper, including the extensively practiced curly *Z* of my name. I don't sign my name quite the same way now ... but I also can't actually remember the last time I did sign my name at all. I can't remember the last time I jotted down a note to anyone. Well, a note from me specifically, not just passing on a hint of a *knowing* as I'd done for Doc.

My heart is suddenly thumping, my mind ... straining ...

I don't ... I don't really remember ...

Has someone else been using my room?

I glance around, realizing that even by moonlight, the room feels uninhabited, undisturbed ... but also not wholly familiar to me.

I reach for the mason jar of notes and find myself stretching my fingers into an odd emptiness ... that same unexplained feeling I stepped within when approaching Rath earlier.

My hand hovers only inches away from the jar. There's nothing logical stopping me, but my fingers, then my lower arm start to tremble as though I'm holding something heavy.

I withdraw my hand. Panic starts to curl through me, through my nervous system. I can actually feel the slow creep of it, surrounding my heart, filling my belly.

What the fuck is going on?

Not enough sleep, I tell myself. Again.

But I can't bring myself to step back, to step away.

If I angle my head just right, focusing where the moonlight illuminates the glass jar and its notes, I can see other writing ... another signature?

No.

I tilt my head further. Not letters ... symbols. Three

triangles, two branched off the larger central symbol, which is topped with a small circle and a larger oval ...

It's a rough, basic sketch. It's an ... angel?

Pain streaking through my head at the effort of focusing through the emptiness, I force my gaze away, down to the neat line of seashells and stones and sea glass. I hover my fingers over each in turn, and they don't tremble. No emptiness encases my hand.

Then I spot the tiny wooden box at the opposite corner of the windowsill. My name is carved across the top. The shaking starts again as I reach for it. I push through, flipping the lid up. Only the lid isn't hinged, so I inadvertently throw it to the side. There's a strung piece of jewelry in the box — a bracelet constructed from polished semiprecious stones? But when I force my arm through the pocket of emptiness that's somehow trying to impede my reach, when I try to pick the bracelet up, I realize it's broken. The rounded stones fly everywhere, and I ...

I stupidly cry out.

Like I've lost something precious to me.

Even though it's not mine. Is it?

Dropping the comforter, I scramble around, trying to collect the scattered bouncing rounds, tucking each within my palm. And in doing so, I somehow reclaim them for myself. The empty feeling eases, though it doesn't disperse. I lay the broken bracelet back into the box, hoping I've found all the missing beads.

Only then do I notice the black velvet pouch also tucked within.

I pull the pouch out by one tiny drawstring. The velvet is cheap, but the black, rough-cut stone that spills out of it and into my palm is anything but. Obsidian? Or tourmaline?

I can feel the potential energy contained within the precious stone.

A protection spell, maybe?

Or a spent protection spell?

I flip it over, noting the tiny gold loop adhered to the back. A charm? For the broken bracelet?

I set the charm back in its pouch, then back in the box, and replace the lid. I run my fingers over my name carved into the wood — ZAYA. The woodwork isn't exactly rudimentary, but this box definitely wasn't made by an artisan.

A personal gift.

I have no idea why I know this, but the box, the folded notes in the jar, and the bracelet were given by three different people.

Given to me?

Three gifts I can't remember.

Three people I don't remember.

A collection of touchstones arrayed on my windowsill that I don't remember.

I shove myself away from the window. Just a step or two back — and I can suddenly breathe again. I didn't push through that odd emptiness, that weird void, at all. I just got used to it.

And I swear ... I swear it was slowly suffocating me.

Distant movement out the window draws my attention. Cayley steps onto the front porch of the beach house and stretches her neck, then shoulders.

I should go down and check on the mage, Harlee. I haven't given her any guidelines, haven't even officially asked her to investigate, to look at everything she can. And I need her to prepare the bodies, either for cremation or to be returned to their families.

Yes, that's actionable.

And actionable should be the opposite of this numbing emptiness, right?

I abandon the objects on the windowsill, including the collection of notes — even though they might actually serve to illuminate me. Because the idea that there's a truth to be uncovered here disconcerts me enough that I desperately need to avoid it for a little longer. I cross to my built-in wardrobe and yank out underwear, socks, a tank top, jeans, and an oversized hand-knit cardigan.

All of it feels and smells as if it's been recently laundered, not musty at all. Like the sheets on the bed.

The well-worn clothing fits only because I've lost too much weight. Each piece feels ... wrong. As if I shouldn't be wearing it. I have no idea who hand-knit the cardigan, with its antique brass buttons and soft, soft fabric — qiviut, maybe? But it looks like something I should remember.

Fuck, it's just clothing. I need to stop reading into everything. I'm feeling fucked up because I've died twice in the last three weeks, taken on a literal universe of power, and claimed one of only seven intersection points in the world.

I just need to deal with all that.

Because there's nothing I can do about whatever lies in that empty void I keep coming up against.

So I ignore the mounting evidence that someone has done what I would have thought impossible — stolen time, or memories, or something even worse from me.

I tug on thick wool socks and march downstairs. I shove my feet into gumboots that are slightly too large for me, and put on a puffy waterproof jacket that is most definitely too big.

Then I head out back toward the beach house to check on the mage and the shifter.

I was planning to go to Harlee and Cayley immediately. But at the junction along the moonlit path, I continue forward across the damp, winter-dead grass rather than veering right.

I feel drawn toward the bluff. The gumboots are tall enough to protect my jeans from the damp grass, but the closer I get to the ocean's edge and the raging surf, the more the mist-filled wind has its way with me. My hair, specifically. Then the grass abruptly gives way to craggy rock, and I continue forward until I'm hovering over the sheer drop and looking into the whitecapped surf crashing against the cliff. My hair and face, my lips, are beaded with salty water.

I ... I must have jumped from this cliff a dozen times or more. Always during the day when the tide was high, and into the more sheltered cove on the north side. Yet I can't distinctly remember a single instance of doing so. As if the understanding or knowledge of the act is there, but the memory is muted or shadowed from my sight somehow.

The face and top of the craggy bluff are all rough rock above the high-tide mark. It looks almost black in the moonlight, as does the tumultuous sea below. An intense energy spreads around me, not just under my feet but radiating from this point — radiating from here throughout the world as it connects to the other intersection points. I instinctively skirted what I identified as the intersection's primary anchor point as I traversed the bluff.

I know, I've been taught, that others of the awry hold five of those intersections, only two of which I've visited.

Both of those points are held by awry with vast powers that are utterly unlike my own.

I step back from the edge. Something, some feeling or impulse that isn't a *knowing* — at least not a future or even present knowing — tugs me a few more steps back. I keep moving blindly backward, unsure of my course but taking the steps nonetheless.

The feeling intensifies ... the pressure. Then, after a couple more steps, it eases. I pause, eyeing the ground for a moment, seeing nothing unusual.

Maybe I'm simply sensing the apex of the anchor point acutely? Except it feels as if I've been drawn here, am drawn to this particular spot for a reason.

I step forward again. Then I find myself lying down on the uncomfortable rock before I'm even aware of deciding to do so. The hood of the puffy jacket creates a bit of a pillow for my head, but my shoulder blades and pelvic bones don't like my sudden urge to lounge back on rough stone.

I stare up at the starlit sky for a moment, blinking as I try to absorb the sensations that have drawn me to this exact spot, that are continuing to hold me here. They aren't all ... external — not all a result of my nascent binding to the intersection point. There's something else too. More of that emptiness. But it's not an external pressure or a void like before.

It feels like ... like ... I'm missing something inside me.

I press my bare hands to the rock. Then I bend one leg outward and crank my head in the opposite direction, so that I'm staring toward the sheer drop a few feet away.

Arrayed as such, I'm somehow echoing the sensation that has brought me to this spot, that continues to hold me here somehow.

As if I'm a puzzle piece that has suddenly been notched into a larger background. Part of an image set down on a bigger canvas.

Except as the Conduit, I'm no longer a simple, multi-edged piece. As the Conduit, I am the canvas. Or maybe the spool that holds and feeds the threads that create a tapestry — to belabor the metaphor and for lack of a better way to define the place I now hold on a universal level.

Is this feeling, this sense, connected to my recent ascension? Perhaps I'm still absorbing, still *becoming*. I mean, I know I am. Logically, I know it will take decades to wield even half of what my aunt wielded.

Except this isn't about logic right now. I'm not sure I've taken any logic-based steps since I left Vancouver, since I laid eyes on Presh.

I try to narrow my focus, to home in on the sensations in the hopes of finding clarity.

I can feel the pounding of the surf echoing through the rocky ground underneath me. Clouds are starting to edge the night-shrouded sky again. The break in the rain won't hold through dawn.

My nose and cheeks are cold. My hands start to ache from that same misty chill.

Yet I stay.

I close my eyes and open myself up to whatever is trying to make itself clear to me. I hold myself in place. My breathing slows.

And then I feel it ...

The echo of a memory? But it's more than that ... it's somehow visceral.

My neck ... hurts. Or am I remembering my neck hurting?

Then, all but hidden under the pounding surf, I hear

the sound of cartilage shattering or ... vertebrae being snapped?

Someone is shouting ... multiple someones. And ... so much essence ... so much essence flooding through me, from me ...

But ... that's just an echo of earlier today, isn't it? Just me recalling the feeling of claiming the intersection point along with the property.

I suddenly feel Rath hovering over me. His breathing is ragged, pained. His hands land on either side of my head.

I'm back in the *Now*.

Aren't I?

Before I can get my eyes open to confirm — I might have been on the edge of falling into a deep sleep, or at least a deep meditative state — Rath groans in utter agony. "Zaya! Fuck! Zaya!"

I blink, straightening my head enough to meet his wild, amber-ringed eyes.

He's ... utterly ... terrified?

"What?" I mutter. I'm still deeply mired, almost buried, within the sensations I've been chasing, even if only in my own mind.

Rath grabs my upper arms, yanking me into a sitting position so quickly that it hurts. I feel it in my neck and all my joints, which have gone cold and stiff. I cry out in pain.

He doesn't loosen his grip, shaking me. A snarl from deep within his chest, deep within his being, emanates from him. "What the fuck are you doing?!"

I get my hands wrapped around his wrists. His skin is searingly hot. I gasp, almost letting go.

He's still shaking me.

"Stop it!" I snap.

He doesn't. I'm actually not sure he sees me at all. I'm

not sure he's even reacting to this moment. He looks crazed, unhinged, and utterly devastated.

"You're hurting me!" I cry.

He releases me so abruptly that I fall back, just managing to catch myself on my elbows and not smack my head on the stone.

"What the fuck, Zaya?!" Rath shouts.

Even crouched before me, he's huge. And for the first time I can honestly remember, as an adult, at least, I feel truly frightened — tiny, weak, and overwhelmed.

He inhales deeply as if he's trying to calm himself, then he flinches. Catching the scent of my fear? His trembling hands slowly come up between us, either in surprise or surrender ...

Or he's going to try to grab me again.

I scramble back, still on my ass. My heart is pounding in my chest. I feel like screaming and sobbing. And even though some part of my mind understands that I'm overreacting, I can't seem to stop, to quell that reaction.

"Zaya ..." Rath says. His voice is shaking as he tries to soften it. He reaches for me.

And completely irrationally, I scream. I scream as if my voice were a weapon. I scream and scramble back farther, still crouched. I try to make it to my feet, but my limbs won't work, and I fall hard on my knees and elbows, scraping my chin on the rocky ground.

It feels possible, according to my rational mind, that I'm still mired in the sensations I've been chasing. The memory I've been trying to recall? And with that comes this weakness. This limb-weakening fear.

I curl in on myself protectively. I can't take my eyes off Rath, though. I can't look away.

If I look away, he'll be able to grab me and ...

"Oh, Tempest, no," Rath whispers. "Oh, my Tempest, no, no. I didn't mean ... I would never ... you scared me. You ... you ... you looked like you were dead —"

Energy finally floods through me — but I can't tell whether it's my own or is coming from the intersection point. Utterly livid, I surge to my feet, so that I'm now the one looming over the crouching Rath. "You don't touch me without permission," I snarl viciously.

"I know," he whispers. "I'm sorry. I wasn't —"

"There is no excuse. Get off my property."

He slowly straightens, hands held slightly forward as if I'm a rabid animal. As if I'm the problem.

I already know I'll have bruises on my arms from his grip. I've never had someone — someone who knows me, at least — touch me with violent intent. Even most strangers fear the color of my eyes, fear even drawing my attention.

And those who know me? They know what I can do.

Rath's chest is still heaving. Not as much as before, but he's clearly only just hanging on to his control. "Zaya ... please, just listen."

My clenched hands, my clenched jaw, all ache. "Get the fuck off my property. Don't come back without an invitation." I can feel the energy embedded in the craggy rock under my feet stir, then rise at my words. It doesn't do anything as dramatic as physically eject the biker shifter from the estate, but it's there. As if it's waiting to be utilized.

I glare at Rath.

The weird anguish drains from his expression, from his hunched shoulders. His eyes narrow in anger. His jaw looks as clenched as mine as he curls his hands into fists. His back stiffens and straightens until he's once again looming over me, not curling forward ... protectively?

I'm not interested in whatever his damage is. Not interested in learning what him seeing me on the ground triggered for him. This is my property. I follow my own path, and I don't owe him an explanation.

He also doesn't deserve my fear.

He has no right to lay hands on me. Not in anger. Not even for the sake of his own fear.

Shoving away as much of the residual terror that overwrote all my senses as I can, I raise my hands in response to his own aggressive posturing, fingers splayed.

I reach for his life force, for the threads of his destiny. He's now forcing me to look for what I instinctively did not want to know before.

Rath's nostrils flare, as if maybe he can smell my power. His chest starts to heave again. In disbelief?

He knows what I can do.

"Don't make me," I say. His life force is robust. Without looking at all closely, I can already feel the fierceness of it, the intertwined layers. "You might be able to hurt me physically —"

He makes a noise of protest, trying to cut me off or counter me.

I ignore it. "But I can ruin your life."

Rage, still mixed with that odd aching anguish, suddenly radiates from him. I swear I can feel it, experience it, even though I'm not empathic in the least. All of that emotion is etched across his face as he speaks.

"Not any more than you already have."

Then he turns and walks away.

The energy I've called forth in my pathetic attempt to bar him from the property ghosts his footprints in an odd way, as if it can't actually grab hold of him. As if he has permission to walk here that I can't revoke. That doesn't make sense, though, because I am the Conduit. I am the intersection point now. My will — all the energy of which I'm composed, and by which I'm fueled — is the preemptive power here.

He also shouldn't have been able to grab me so harshly ... though perhaps his intent was key in that moment.

Confused, I call out, "Don't come back without an invitation," to his retreating back. Repeating myself, utterly childishly.

He half-turns to look at me, snorting derisively. "I never want to set eyes on you again, Zaya Gage. Unfortunately, I also never get what I truly want in this world."

I can feel the falseness in his words as they thread between us. Perhaps because I deliberately reached for his essence, perhaps because we're somehow connected through the energy of the intersection point. But one of his two statements is a lie.

"Don't worry," I say, speaking without conscious thought ... or maybe that's what the universe feels like when it speaks through me now. "You'll get what you deserve."

"Fuck you."

"No."

Silence falls between us as we just stare at each other. His hands are still clenched, moonlight masking most of his expression. I've told him to go, then stopped him from leaving. Twice. I don't understand my own actions. I don't understand my extreme reaction to him grabbing me. I could feel his concern, his fear.

Why would that have terrified me?

"I would never hurt you." His whisper is so low that I barely catch it against the wind.

But something about his insistence on that point after clearly hurting me — I don't doubt that despite the padding of the puffy jacket, I'll have bruises on my upper arms tomorrow — breaks me free from the moment.

I head back toward the path to the beach house, my initial destination. As I pass Rath, I speak without looking at him. "You already have hurt me. So don't linger. Don't come back."

He makes a noise in the back of his throat. The beginning of another protest, maybe, but it sounds more like ... a swallowed expulsion of pain.

I walk away.

By the time I check in briefly with Harlee and Cayley, then make my way back to the house, the sound of a motorcycle tearing away down the drive filters through to me. Then I can no longer feel Rath on the property, and a sliver of that emptiness, a sliver of that void from before has lodged itself in my chest. The tiniest of aches. In the vicinity of my heart.

DAWN IS ENCROACHING BY THE TIME I'VE READ through the instruction manual for the new ice cream maker and mixed a base for chocolate-coconut ice cream. The kitchen cupboards yielded chocolate, cocoa, and sugar, but the milk and cream in the fridge are weeks past their expiry dates. Thankfully, there's an entire flat of coconut cream in the pantry. I have no doubt it's been placed there just for me, next to a flat of coconut milk, because my aunt wasn't a fan of many ethnic foods. Not like I am. If I could eat nothing but any kind of Asian or South Asian or Mediterranean food for the rest of my life, I'd feel blessed.

Unfortunately, I'm not actually capable of cooking any of it myself.

When the ice cream base has been poured into the maker to churn, I check the time and deem it not too early to reach out to Coda. My walk in the mist and fight with Rath has actually cleared my head. And though I rarely follow up on knowings — whether I've forced the manifestation as I'd done with Precious or not — I have questions. I have no idea what hours Coda keeps, or where the awry hacker is currently residing, of course. But dawn on the West Coast feels like an okay time to reach out.

If I am going to tangle myself in Precious's life, train her, deal with her overbearing brothers, I need to know more. For her safety. My little trick of rising from the dead is as rare as all the other power I wield. Now that my aunt is truly dead, I might be the only one in the world with that particular ability. Precious is awry, but not Everlasting. She's not immortal.

I ... I want to train her. I feel a distinct need to take her in, shelter her through the next few years of her life. But I'm also not ... I don't take apprentices. Honestly, an apprenticeship with me is a little ... much. Even unnecessary. For most.

Though I already know that Presh is different.

If I'm going to take her on, focus on one person instead of just allowing my actions to be guided by my power, by my own so-called destiny, then I need to know I can also protect her. Because even though all the awry need to be protected in some fashion, I already know that Presh will need it more than most.

I call Coda on my phone. I don't have a phone number for the awry hacker — or an email or any other sort of other traditional contact info. Rather, some software or programming I don't even bother trying to grasp is triggered by pressing a prearranged sequence on the screen of the phone. It's a great security measure — no one can get anything off my phone that easily leads back to Coda — but it's a bitch to learn the sequence every time the hacker insists on changing it.

It takes forever for them to verify that it's me calling and that they want to answer, giving me time to double-check all the dials and settings on the ice cream maker ... things like level of hardness and churning time. If I were big on crushed-iced drinks, slushies or whatever they're called, the machine can apparently be programmed to make those as well.

"A phone call?" Coda's mocking tone emanates over the speakers of the phone. Which wouldn't be as startling if I had, you know, actually activated the speakers. "Now I'm the one who should feel blessed."

Before I can reply with some sort of sarcastic comeback that I don't have the energy for, Coda adds, "Where the hell are you? Your phone is pinging out of the middle of ... nothing."

"My aunt's property on the West Coast," I say. And then I hear what I've said. "My ... my property. The ... intersection point." I hesitate only a little on that last bit of info. I try to not keep secrets from Coda because the hacker is way more effective when they've got all the facts at hand. But intersection points are ... well, not one of those verifiable-by-science things. More of an underground understanding among a certain subsection of the essence-wielding community. And some religious zealots, of course.

Coda thinks about the bit of information I've just dropped in their lap. Like, with actual quiet contemplation.

No keyboard tapping or clicks across a trackpad or a mouse accompany this silence.

"When?" Coda finally asks, as muted as I've ever heard them. Almost ... reverent. "When did you ... did you? I mean ... you said your aunt, then corrected yourself."

I inhale, wondering if this is the moment I lose one of my only friends, one of the only support systems I still have, whether or not we spend much time together. I breathe out, splaying my hands across the cool marble counter. "Three weeks ago."

For the briefest of moments, dead air emanates over the phone speaker. Then Coda's fingers are flying over their many keyboards again.

Stress, that I didn't really understand I was holding, eases from my shoulders.

"How am I supposed to keep track of shit-all if you don't keep me informed?" Coda grouses. Except their tone still holds that softer, considerate resonance.

"There was nothing for you to cover up," I say, swiping my finger along the edge of the now-empty bowl and sucking off traces of the ice cream base. It's heavy on the cocoa and a little bitter. Hopefully, the churn smooths the flavor.

"You were in Vancouver?"

"Yes. But I need your focus elsewhere right now."

"On the cadre of himbos following you around?"

"Cadre of himbos?"

Coda snorts. "I mean, I'm all over it. Why the fuck shouldn't you construct your harem on the base of the three prettiest half-brothers I've ever had the pleasure of cyberstalking?"

"Three?" I'm not completely following the conversation. Which isn't unusual with Coda and is why I keep most of our contact on a text message level. Their texts are a little clearer, more streamlined.

"Rought, Rath, and Reck," Coda purrs, then cackles. With enough edge that it practically radiates through the phone, causing me to actually flinch.

"I'd drop by for a visit, except Gigi is practically drooling over all that Adonis dick you're collecting, and I don't think I can keep her focused if she has an opportunity to sample it in the flesh."

Gigi pipes up from somewhere deep in the background, "Fuck off, you fucking asshole."

Coda cackles again, except neither Gigi nor the hacker sound at all amused. And I don't think it's himbos or beguiling dicks that has them on edge.

It's me.

It's who I am among the awry. Well, among anyone with even a hint of an understanding of the function I perform for the universe.

I don't realize I've gone silent, then have let that silence stretch as I watch the countdown on the quietly churning ice cream maker, until Coda pipes up again.

"So ... it's not the dick you want me to look into?"

"I'm thinking of taking on an apprentice."

Coda clicks a few buttons, presumably calling something up on one of their screens. "You know who her old man is, right?"

I don't answer right away because I'm thinking through why Coda would bother asking me — asking me if I'm aware of the danger of taking on Precious Guerra — when I've just told them that I'm an immortal who is also considered a divinity, or an aspect of the divine, by many factions.

I mean, I am. There really is no point in couching it,

not even in my own head, any longer. I'm just not sure I've absorbed it.

When my aunt was the Conduit, she was also just my mentor. A person who laughed at the strangest things and collected pretty cards that she never actually used, and lost her cool when even a hint of spice made it onto her plate. Our three months of training and being tugged around by one knowing after another in India were torture for her stomach. For her ... the divine ...

A terrible sob tears free from my chest, from my throat. Hot tears spike at the edges of my eyes. Grief ... pure, unfettered grief pouring from me, as some rational part of my mind informs me. I press my hand over my mouth as if I can hold it back. Except I can't.

I can't.

I can't stop sobbing, so hard that I'm practically shouting, screaming. I can barely gasp for air through the onslaught, and my sight hazes at the edges. I brace myself on the counter, vaguely aware that Coda is actually panicking on the other end of the line.

Then Gigi's voice filters through to me. Far sweeter and softer than I've ever heard her. "Breathe, Zaya. It's okay to cry. It's just, you have to breathe as well. Long inhale ... one ... two ... three ... four ..."

I held myself together enough to get from Vancouver down to the property. I distracted myself with rescuing Presh — being utterly reckless when there were so many other things I could have done in that moment ... things that would have extracted the girl without fucking traumatizing her further.

"Exhale. Four ... three ... two ... one ..."

My aunt is dead. At least a century before her time.

Making me the Conduit with minimal training and only an inkling of what it all means ... and I can't do anything about it. I can't even ... I don't even have a support system. I should have had decades to build up my own family, whether blood related or not ... more siblings, partners, even children ...

I honestly hadn't even thought about it.

I had just been drifting through life, playing at being a fucking fixer when it suited me, when the universe shoved what needed fixing in my face.

The next time Gigi does her inhale count, I manage to follow along. Three more sequences of deep breathing and I've managed to calm the sobbing, and to stumble, phone in hand, to the powder room off the main hall to blow my nose and splash water on my face.

I don't turn on the light. I just perch sideways like a gargoyle on the toilet seat with my back pressed against the velvet-embossed wallpaper, pulling tissue after tissue out of the ornate silver tissue-box holder.

"Tell me what you need," Coda croaks through the speakers. If I didn't know any better, I might think the hacker was trying to not cry along with me.

I breathe through another well of painful emotion, my face heating with it and eyes filling as I struggle to suppress it. I dash a few tears from my cheeks. But before I can articulate even a smidgen of what I intended to request from the hacker, Gigi interrupts.

"Us, you neanderthal," she spits. "She needs us. Zaya, it's going to take us at least thirty-six hours —"

"That's okay," I protest weakly. "I'm not —"

"But," Coda moans, "my tech and —"

"I'll help you pack," Gigi spits again. "We'll ship it. Zaya, we're on the other side of the fucking globe, sorry."

"This isn't necessary," I choke out. "I just haven't had much sleep."

"We're coming," Gigi says. "End of discussion." Then I can literally hear her stomping off, doors opening, then slamming shut.

A long pause follows, in which I unfold myself from the pretzel shape I've twisted myself into and cross back to the sink to splash more water on my face.

"I'm sorry," I murmur. "I'll talk her out of —"

"We're coming," Coda says tersely. "What Gigi wants, she gets."

"But ... you —"

"I'll be fine. We'll spend some favors and get a private plane. No shipping, and minimal time outdoors needed."

I huff, trying to wrap my mind around the monumental offer that Coda and Gigi have just made to me. It's possible that Coda is actually agoraphobic, among other things. The hacker could and would compensate with multiple travel routes and methods to move through the world — and multiple escape routes to back those up.

I should protest more, except I just ... I just don't want to.

"There's a beach house ..." I say lamely. "And a cottage deeper in the south woods. Plus, here in the main house, lots of places to tuck yourself away."

"It'll be fine," Coda snaps, getting testy now.

"At least use some of my favors," I say, getting a bit pissy back.

The hacker ignores me. "Tell me what you need."

I sigh, forcing myself to leave the comforting closeness of hiding — from no one — in the tiny bathroom and to wander back into the kitchen to check on my ice cream.

"Your aunt?" Coda asks.

"I don't have enough info about that yet," I say, scrubbing my hand over my face. According to the timer on the machine, the ice cream still needs another ten minutes to churn.

"I need photos to track her movements," Coda says, the tapping of their fingers heard in the background once again as they fly over keyboards. "That is … if she left the property? Because that's just one big … void … even for me. Maybe when I'm actually on site, I'll be able to see it all better on a digital level?"

"I think …" I still haven't managed to piece much of the puzzle of the last few hours of my aunt's life together. The cake I still need to clean up left to grow moldy in the front room, afternoon tea interrupted. Or a visitor? The mage in the beach house scrying before dropping dead, and the shifter digging something up in the family graveyard. The third bond mate … missing? Or maybe they, Devlin, dropped dead somewhere off the property? That could be something for Coda to track.

"She … Disa … would have to leave the property to be killed. Not that I even thought that possible, at all. There must be some photos on my phone …" Except I can't think of a single recent shot that would have included my aunt, not even on her last birthday. Lots of shots of the food we ate that day, though. "And her combat mage, Devlin, is unaccounted for." I haven't been out to the cottage, didn't even know if Devlin used it as a base, but the shifters have presumably checked it by now. That assumes they know the cottage exists, of course. But Rath seems to know the property. Too well.

"I'll start working with what you have," Coda says, having obviously already checked my phone for photos.

"But if you can find something originally captured on film, it would be better."

Essence didn't generally unintentionally affect technology, but digital selfies with the Conduit were a completely different thing.

"They can be older, but a solid shot of her face is best," Coda adds. "I can feed in the other details, height, weight, you know."

"Well, she never looks ... looked ... much older than her midtwenties, so ..." I struggle, suddenly breathless again, through another staggering well of grief.

Another pause, then Coda speaks carefully. "Same as you."

I don't answer.

"You didn't call about your aunt. Didn't ask me to help."

"No. I ... couldn't."

Coda lets it go, but I get an inkling they aren't that happy that I've been keeping secrets. "I've sent you everything I have on Precious. Her father is a fucking piece of shit, and he pretty much runs the Federation. The government there are just pretty puppets. Shifters, sex, drugs, he traffics in all of it. Weapons, money laundering. Mercenaries. You want someone killed in the nastiest of ways? You hire through Cataclysm MC."

Fuck. And yeah, I would have already known that if I'd bothered to take the time to think about it. The awry avoided traveling through that section of North America. As did most other people, for that matter.

Chains and Breaker waited to run us off the road in neutral territory for multiple reasons.

"How the hell did the club princess give them the slip?" Coda says, talking more out loud than to me.

I blow out a long breath. "I gather it involved hopping on a random train and slipping through at least two borders undetected."

"Yeah, I doubt she has a passport."

"And getting it scanned? Would have put her right back on their radar."

"Wily kid."

"She's awry," I say. "We learn fast."

"Or we die even quicker."

Yeah, that. "It's not Precious I'm concerned about. I'll move her onto the property if I have to." Despite the evidence of the two bodies and my recently dead aunt, the property — powered by the intersection point — offers a certain layer of protection to those invited onto it. And while there are obvious exceptions to that rule, none of those exceptions should affect my ability to keep Precious safe from her father.

"I'll get the paperwork going," Coda says. "Just in case."

The awry have certain legal protections that can also be triggered, in some countries at least. Such as levels of diplomatic immunity and the ability to request protection from local law enforcement. Problem is, most local law isn't up for fighting the forces that actively hunt and kill the awry.

"Guardianship?" Coda asks. "Or do you want adoption papers?"

With my level of diplomatic immunity, backed by my clout in the overall community of essence-wielders, I can simply take Precious as my mentee and expect most others to be ... well ... wary of what it might mean to cross me. But such paperwork and legalities mean nothing to the Cataclysm or within the Federation.

"Get it all ready," I whisper. Then I strengthen my

voice. "There are a few conversations I'm going to need to have before we're signing anything."

I honestly don't know what the fuck I'm doing. I'm way, way out of my depth, and there are no shallows nearby. I just need to tread water. Until ... until ...

Maybe for the rest of my long existence ...

I squeeze my eyes shut, achingly aware that I'm muddling things up in my head. I'm confusing my unleashed grief with my disconcertion over my abrupt ascension. I've latched onto this ... I've latched onto Precious as if she's some sort of life raft I can cling to while I get my bearings.

"It might not be ... fair," I murmur. "To drag Precious into all ... of this ..."

Coda scoffs on the other end of the line. "Where would she be right now if you hadn't snatched her? Where will she be in a month, in six months, if you don't take her in and train her?"

I press the heels of my hands over my eyes, massaging lightly.

"You don't actually need me to paint you a picture, do you?" Coda asks, all snark fully back in play.

The reverent tone took a little longer to wear off than I'd hoped, but I find myself smiling sadly in response. "No."

Precious isn't my first rescue, and she isn't going to be my last. Same with Coda. We've worked together for years now. I doubt the hacker could walk away any more than I could — and Coda hasn't even been in the same room as Presh yet. Hasn't felt the life-affirming energy radiating from her.

"Are you ... are you really coming?" I ask, like an utterly needy bitch.

"Apparently." Coda sniffs. "Gigi's already sending me

to-do lists. I'll start digging on your aunt and the combat mage. And keep digging on the kid and her family. But give me something juicier to focus on. I know you're holding back."

"The berserker," I say, as if the thought has just been fed through me even though my mind is scattered. "I was a little busy at the time, but I'm not certain I was facing off with a normal berserker."

"Normal." Coda snorts. "How would you know with a berserker?"

"Well, he ... talked. And, like, remained somewhat ... rational ..." I can't really believe I'm using that word in connection to what happened on the beach. "What are the chances that the Outcast cleanup crew took blood samples? And their medic —"

"Zephyr Rae. Club name Doc or Doc Z," Coda interrupts, fingers once again flying over keyboards. "Not just a medic, she's got her doctorate in emergency medicine and kinesiology. Not registered ... but ... let me take a peek ... she's a fucking pegasus. A pegasus! Brilliant, eh?"

"Right." Doc probably isn't going to be a fan of Coda going around crowing about her being an exceedingly rare type of shifter. But she wouldn't have identified as mixed clan or joined up with Outcast MC if she were average. If any shifter could ever be considered only average. I wonder if Coda could call up Rath's shifter designation as easily as

—

I shut that thought down fast. Not certain where it came from, to be honest. I was pissed ... am pissed at Presh's pushy brother. I don't care what creature resides only skin-deep within him.

I'll just keep reminding myself of that.

"Doc Z has this device ... a medical scanner ..." I say,

getting my beleaguered brain back on track. "And if someone on the cleanup crew used that type of thing on the berserker corpse —"

"You don't have to spell it out, Zaya," Coda grouses. "I'm already digging. I relish going up against AD again." Referring to the Outcast's personal hacker, Rought.

"I thought there were three ADs now?" I tease.

Coda grunts, then just says, "I'm still putting together my reports, sadly currently without dick pics so far. What dudes grow up with a camera phone practically surgically attached to their hands and don't take any pictures of their cocks? You might need to reassess your harem building."

"I'm not —"

The line goes dead. Not nefariously, but just Coda being done with the in-person conversation. I know because my screen — which remained black through that conversation — now flashes with a series of incoming messages. Five of which are from Coda.

Thankfully, the ice cream maker beeps. Because I need to taste-test the recipe and decide if it needs five or ten minutes more to churn, letting me ignore my new reality a moment longer.

EIGHT

ROUGHT

THREE OF MY CODE-BREAKING ALGOS SCROLL across the monitor on my left. I'm five layers into the stupid levels of protection Reck has on his personal device — which is way, way more than just a phone. And yeah, I lifted it out of his suit jacket pocket before he shoved his way past me into the interrogation room. A room that he had no invitation to enter, and within which he has no authorization and no jurisdiction.

Reck — or rather, Sergeant Carlos Guerra of the Authority — shouldn't even be on club property while wielding his badge, let alone pummeling answers out of the unaffiliated bikers Grinder escorted in before racing off hours ago. Not that the bikers were willing participants during that escorting. And no shifters are truly unaffiliated. That status just means they haven't proven their worth to the club they're pledging, or they don't have a blood tie to the current leadership.

It's Reck's blood ties that allow him to blur lines. Like continually, in all aspects of his life. And it's going to bite him in the ass. Real, real soon.

My workstation stands at the center of a concrete bunker under an outbuilding on the edge of the main pack property. Wires and cables thread down from the ceiling, with other connections running under the slightly raised dais the station sits on. The bunker is directly connected to the main house by a tunnel, and to the upper floors by an elevator. Both are accessed through a door to my far right.

I hate all of it.

We're completely underground here, hidden from casual view. And I've got access to the three satellite dishes on the roof of the main house, and two more on the above-ground garage that look perfectly legit. The garage is used mostly as covered parking with access to the elevator. There's also an equipment room, a weapons room, and a medical suite one floor above. But I fucking loathe spending any more time here than absolutely necessary, and I've been trapped in this space since I left Zaya still sleeping in the motel.

After cracking the third level of encryption on Reck's device with minimal effort, I easily identified — and disabled — the monitoring our older brother was running on Rath's personal device. I also easily uncovered and disabled the bugs Reck had embedded in various places around the main clubhouse and the main pack estate.

Rath is going to be pissed — at both of us.

The physical tech, likely Authority issued, hasn't been detected in any of my biweekly sweeps — but there's no way that Reck has Authority-issued requisitions for those taps. And illegal taps against a club like the Outcast are practically a declaration of war. The Authority definitely doesn't want to come at us all messy like that. We make better allies, even if the relationship is seriously strained. Plus, even if Reck somehow swung the okay to place taps with his superiors, there's no way he should be running any of it from his personal device.

Even more interestingly, though, after cracking that third layer of encryption, I bumped up against a fourth. Having no idea what Reck would want hidden that badly, I had to keep digging, obviously.

What could be more important to conceal than illegal wiretaps on his own family?

It has to be something tiny to be so well hidden. And it's years old, possibly a decade. Literally before my time as the pack's primary hacker. Or should I say primary tech. The age of the deeper layers of encryption meant that I needed to hardwire the device so that if my algos don't make a dent in those layers quickly, Reck is going to wander out of the interrogation he's unlawfully commandeered and find me fucking with his shit.

While I keep plugging in scripts to counter Reck's ancient encryption, I've got multiple facial recognition programs running over a dozen vid feeds on the monitor to my right. I'm pretty certain I've scraped it for all it's worth, achieving frustratingly little for all the hours I've put in.

I've finally got eyes on Chains, though — including the little meet-up he had with one of the three assholes Grinder picked up nosing around the motel after he and Zaya had left — and who are currently getting beaten down by Reck in interrogation.

The irony being? Reck doesn't need to beat the truth out of his suspects. Shifters with heightened senses are pretty hard to lie to outright, but actual truth seeking — through utter terror, to be specific — is one of the aspects of Reck's beast that carries over into his human form.

Finding and containing Chains might appear to be my current main focus — with my info-gathering efforts liberally spread across three of my five active screens. But that focus has been forced upon me by Rath and my undying commitment to the club.

Because as for me? All my focus is on trying to retrace the last thirteen years of Zaya's life. Her life without me. And I've not found nearly enough to remotely satisfy the seething but empty vortex that occupies the core of my very being.

I'm always happy running algos and scripts — fixing anything and everything is my thing — but I don't want to be confined to this room, for more than all the regular reasons I hate being here.

Zaya is so near, but still so untouchable.

Despite the distance that remains between us, something has settled within me since I held Zaya again. Perhaps it's my beast, which is more active, more present than it's ever been before. So even despite itching to be at her side, I feel more myself, more in my own skin, more ... actively participating in my own life than I have for thirteen years.

I glance at the clock. It's near dawn. I resolve to not spend another day away from Zaya Gage. Then I focus back on what I need to do to make that happen.

While I run various scripts on the other monitors, I'm adding to my report on the main monitor before me. I've broken down the key points in the timeline of Presh's attempt to flee our sperm donor, right up to the moment she enters the Choices Cafe with Breaker and Chains. I've got them arriving, and then Breaker and Chains tearing out of the parking lot.

Vid of Presh in the cafe, though? Nothing. Zaya doesn't appear on any of the feeds either. And it's not that the footage has been destroyed or cut. In fact, the only way I know it's been tampered with is Presh's accounting. Someone extremely skilled has simply wiped Presh and Zaya from the footage I've managed to gather. I even found some random vidTuber's feed that matches the timeline, but in which neither Presh nor Zaya appears.

That level of video manipulation, leaving no traces that I've been able to spot, is beyond me. I would have said it was beyond current technology. Except I've had my hands on Zaya's personal device. Her phone is a pretty, shiny thing, all titanium and shatterproof glass wrapping around internals that don't exist. Not for open purchase, anyway.

A shuffle of noise beyond the code-sealed door in the corner to my far right draws my attention.

No matter the acuteness of my shifter hearing, even in human form, I can hear nothing beyond the steel doorway in the wall directly in front of me, beyond which stand the interrogation room and three holding cells. I can only hope Reck isn't actually murdering the bikers Grinder dropped off earlier. But I can easily hear the person slinking in from the main house. The fact that she didn't use the elevator, coming instead through the tunnel to sneak past all the extra enforcers Rath has monitoring the house and grounds, gives her completely away.

She isn't nearly as sneaky as she thinks, though.

But then, she isn't a shifter.

I haven't really absorbed that yet.

The keypad on the door in the right corner flashes. The door opens just a crack, and a small hand curls around the edge. One purple-blue eye fills the slit of the opening, blinking rapidly. Though the light is low in my secondary lair, it's pitch black in the hallway beyond.

"It's just me," I murmur, shifting my attention back to my monitors. Okay, shifting my attention back to one of the three pictures I'm using for the facial recognition algos.

It's a shot of Zaya. Asleep.

Yes, I snapped a picture of Zaya Gage curled up in bed yesterday morning. Like a complete creeper. I took multiple pictures, in fact, though only one of them came out with minimal blur. It was either that or crawl into the bed with her. That, or I wouldn't have been able to force myself to leave the motel room, even though the club needed me, Presh needed me —

"I can't sleep anymore," my baby sister whispers. Presh slips into the room, carefully shutting, then locking the door behind her. She steps past a well-worn brown leather couch set against the wall, which along with the coffee table and two stools at my workstation are the room's only furnishings. The half-eaten pizza I had dropped off for dinner sits abandoned on the coffee table.

How the fuck Presh knows the access codes into and through the tunnel from the main house, I have no idea. Just like I have no idea what those purple eyes manifesting for my sister mean. What kind of awry power will she wield? It's a huge and possibly explosive unknown.

I know that's part of what's fueling Reck's current rage. It's not just his utterly irrational response to Zaya's reappearance in our lives.

Presh shuffles over to me. I wrap her in a one-arm hug, and she leans into me, head on my shoulder, blinking at my screens.

"That's ... footage of me at the train station. In Dallas?"

She swallows hard. "I was trying to figure out what train would get me over the border into California."

"Yes." I've run the footage I've illegally accessed from the station spanning twenty-four hours before and twenty-four hours beyond Presh's slipping out of the shadows and purchasing a ticket three nights ago. As far as I've been able to track, she made a clean getaway. No Chains or Breaker on her tail.

"How did you get it?"

I shrug. Cracking Federation code is fucking child's play, even that of the Transportation Bureau. The Federation government is a sham, meaning personal protections aren't regulated. Nor are personal freedoms, for that matter. The entire country is as lawless as it can get within its own borders. Borders that many residents of the Federation are careful to not cross, because the countries surrounding them take strong exception to the violation of any and all fundamental rights.

That makes Chains and Breaker's movements through Cascadia, even prior to snatching Presh, exceedingly suspect. Because they weren't just in-country to grab my little sister back. The timeline doesn't match up. The train is way faster than a couple of shifters on bikes. They had to be in or around Tacoma already, near where Presh disembarked and tried to purchase a ticket back to Portland. I'm still piecing their movements —

"What the fuck, Rought?" Presh suddenly jabs her finger toward the picture of Zaya on my lower screen. "Is she asleep?"

Before her death thirteen years ago, I had easily lost count of how many times I'd watched Zaya sleep. Dozing in the shade on the beach after a summer swim. Or curled in a nest of blankets in the tree house I built in one of the massive firs overlooking that same beach. Or ... as the years progressed and we grew from childhood friends to something much, much more, cradled in my arms, deliciously spent after coming multiple times on my fingers or my tongue —

"Rought!" Presh snaps.

"I'm running facial recognition, Presh," I say, glad my voice sounds normal, not husky or broken.

"Doesn't make it any less creepy," she mutters under her breath as she shuffles over to the couch. She pulls the pizza box off the coffee table and cuddles up with it as she sits. "You need a blanket down here."

"You need to be in bed."

The thought of sleeping down here is horrifying. I would so much prefer to be working out of the loft over my garage at the far edge of the main pack property, but this site is more secure. My other tech lair, sectioned off from my apartment, is smaller and has only three satellite feeds. But it's not underground. My skin crawls every second I spend surrounded by this much concrete.

Also, my place is closer to the outskirts of Newport. And so is closer to the estate that Zaya has inherited.

Another thing I haven't completely wrapped my head around.

Another of the things currently enraging Reck. I don't have to be in his head to know that much about my older brother.

Zaya is back, but Reck can't touch her. No matter what badge or rank he's achieved by devoting the last decade of his life to it — or, to my mind, by throwing away his life, his beliefs, and his family — Zaya Gage is literally and figuratively untouchable. Her inheriting her aunt's property and position makes that doubly so. Not that any of us have a great sense of what that 'position' is, exactly. Just that it comes with a monsoon of power.

To make all of it worse for him, Reck's latent lie-detecting ability doesn't work on any of the awry. Not that he'd ever admit it.

My baby sister still carries Zaya's scent. It's faded, but she transferred a brush of it to me when she laid her head on my shoulder. My beast, quelled by my current surroundings — sulking at being underground, really — shifts under my skin, stretching toward that scent, inhaling it through my currently wholly human lungs.

I try to settle the beast by looking at the picture of Zaya again. I don't tap it so that it fills the screen, because Presh will notice, but my eyesight is sharp enough to take in every detail.

The creature who tore free from my skin to stop me from killing myself eleven years ago doesn't speak directly to me — though I understand that some shifters do communicate with their other selves. No, since saving my life, my beast has been silent, docile even, for years. Even when I call it fully forth. Until it set eyes on Zaya yesterday ...

I glance at the clock. Again. Thirty-six hours ago now.

Thirty-six hours since I finally understood *why* — why my beast saved me when most shifters willingly follow their mates into death.

I hoped, of course. When the bite mark on the meat of my thumb healed over but never faded completely, I clung to that hope. But I didn't know for certain until thirty-six hours ago.

The beast has just been biding its time.

The keypad on the door to the tunnel and elevator lights up again, drawing my and Presh's attention. I catch the sound of the elevator doors, but unlike our baby sister, the person beyond moves silently. He also hates being underground as much as I do.

The door opens with a sharp movement, and Rath crosses out of the darkness beyond. My half-brother is huge enough to fill the doorway. He's also sopping wet.

"Keep your dripping the fuck away from my tech," I snarl.

Rath huffs and runs a hand through his brown hair, which goes darker when wet, as if he might be able to press it dry. Now that Rath is here, he'll want to dig into the report I'm trying to finish up. But I catch his distraction the moment he smells Presh.

He goes utterly still, pupils dilating and tension edging his jaw. It's a complete overreaction.

Because Precious still smells like Zaya.

Rath swivels his head with such intent and malice that our baby sister actually squeaks and drops her gaze.

That rare display of anger, of any intense emotion really, falls instantly away as Rath growls, almost playfully. "What are you doing in here, precious girl?"

Before Presh can respond, the elevator beyond the still-ajar door slides open, and Doc marches into the room, looking seriously pissed. She's got her med kit and isn't sopping wet. Apparently, she's not an idiot and either pulled on rain gear for the trip in, or she left her bike and got a ride.

"This isn't the medical suite," she snaps at Rath.

He ignores her, zeroing in on and squinting at my monitors as if he can actually understand any of what's on screen.

"I'm treating that bullet wound now," Doc continues, trying for a cooler, more professional tone.

Rath's gaze fixes to the picture of Zaya sleeping, but he

simply grumbles under his breath and starts peeling off layers. First his jacket, then cut, then T-shirt. Each item is soaked through and summarily tossed into a pile next to the couch. He must have actually stood out in the rain for a significant amount of time without the jacket at some point.

Doc blinks at my brother, first at his casual disregard for his patched jacket and cut — items normally sacred to club members — and second at the blood-soaked healing patch on his left shoulder.

I wait for Rath to chew me out about the picture of Zaya.

He doesn't.

Doc lays a hand on his shoulder, gently coaxing him to sit on the empty stool next to me.

But my brother doesn't do or accept gentle. With only one exception. He hasn't since we were children. Reck might be older, but it was Rath who was always the steady, reliable one. Reck was wild and fierce and just a little terrifying, even back then.

Rath tears his gaze away from Zaya's picture, twists away from Doc's touch, and sits down on the stool. His focus fixes on me and what I've compiled on the central monitor. Doc hovers behind him for a moment, as if uncertain what to do with herself.

Rath and Doc Z have been fucking on and off for the last three years. I've gotten the sense that Zephyr chose to patch into the club about five years ago — medics are highly sought after — partly because she met Rath at university. But as best I know, she's never tried to formalize their relationship.

Smart of her, because Rath can't give her more. I'm honestly surprised he can even fuck her regularly in the first place. But then, he never got his teeth on Zaya, or hers on him. Not in the most significant way.

That's all done now, though.

Even if Doc doesn't know it yet.

No matter how deep Rath's denial might run, no matter how much the human side of him might fight it, the creature that resides within his skin won't allow him to bond with anyone but Zaya.

"Report," Rath says. Weariness pours off him, though his back is straight and his shoulders squared. Nothing shakes the Outcast lieutenant that Rath has become, that he strives to be. I've seen him go a week on protein shakes and barely any sleep. I've seen him beaten and bleeding. I've seen him stabbed and shot. Nothing rattles him.

Except Zaya.

Zaya is always the exception.

For all three of us.

"Zaya?" I ask, disobeying the direct order implied in his demand.

Rath's gaze flicks in Presh's direction, though it's unlikely he can see her all that well without turning his head. He doesn't even acknowledge Doc peeling off the blood-crusted patch, then covering the weeping wound in his shoulder with some of that foam antiseptic cleanser that stings like fuck.

"Safe," Rath says. "On Disa's ... on the ocean estate property. Cayley is still with her. Harlee as well. Grinder is tracking down Mack's extended family, but we're not sure anyone is still alive to give notice to. Not anyone who knew him well enough to worry about what to do with the body. Zaya wants him cremated and interred on the property. Ingrid as well. The combat mage is missing. He was a new addition since ..." He trails off.

I finish the thought but don't speak it. Since Zaya was murdered.

"Devlin," I say. "I'll add him to my searches, though I'll have to dig up something more than just a first name."

Rath nods stiffly. "Chains?"

"Got him. Hunkered down for the night just over the California border." I gesture toward a live feed in the upper right of my screen. The vid rotates through a few different camera angles, all of which show sections of the exterior of a motel. "Other than a brief meet with one of the assholes Grinder brought in, he rode like hell to get out of Cascadia before nightfall."

Out of our territory. Out of our reach.

"Fucker," Rath snarls. "Who have you got on him?"

"Pepper and Piston are on their way." The Outcast have certain privileges within our neighboring countries, California included. But those privileges are limited, and they certainly don't include outright kidnapping Chains and hauling him back across the border. Pepper and Piston are fraternal twins, plus dual citizens.

"Why the fuck aren't they there already?"

I don't answer the asshole because the answer is obvious. First, I had to find Chains, then track him. Once I realized he'd made it over the California border, I had to track down the twins and get them moving. "About three hours out. What should be concerning you is why Chains and Breaker were in Cascadia in the first place."

Rath snarls, seemingly at me — but Doc is also now actively poking around in his shoulder with tweezers of some sort. Black veins run out from the wound, etching through Rath's tattoos. He was shot with an essence-imbued silver bullet. And it's still embedded in him thirty-six hours later.

Fucking Rath. Everything else is always more important than him, right up to the moment he drops. And when he does, very few of us are strong enough to pick him up.

"They were tracking Presh," Rath says, trying to keep us focused on the conversation.

Yeah, my brother is a fan of embracing denial until it becomes his truth. "Nope. She got away clean."

Rath frowns.

I give him a moment. It's always best to let my brother come to his own conclusions, or at least it's less of an effort. But he's tired, fighting off silver poisoning, and both Zaya's return and Presh's kidnapping — along with our baby sister's purple eyes — have him rattled. Whether or not he'll ever admit it.

Unaffiliated bikers don't dump money or resources into essence-imbued silver bullets, black market or otherwise. Not unless someone is backing them, formal contract or not. "What are the chances you get silver-shot right around the time that Chains and Breaker lose Presh to Zaya?" I ask, as if I'm just casually posing a question.

Rath scrubs a hand over his face. "Did Grinder get anything out of the unaffiliated he brought in before I called him back out?"

"Reck interrupted."

"What?" Rath snaps.

"He's in there with them right —"

Rath tries to stand up. Doc — in a show of impressive strength — manages to pin him on the stool with her free hand on his unwounded shoulder. Then, before he can knock her off him, she yanks the bullet out.

He roars in pain, clenching his hands into fists and pressing them to his knees. Instead of punching her, I assume.

Doc presses a wad of gauze over the now-bleeding bullet wound.

Then Presh is off the couch and shoving Doc back a few steps, to step between her and Rath with a shout. "What is wrong with you?!"

Doc, still holding the bloody bullet in tweezers in one hand and the bloody gauze in the other, blinks down at Presh. "He's had that bullet in him for over a day! He'd begun healing around it —"

"So?!" Presh fiercely snatches the wad of gauze from Doc, then gently presses it against Rath's shoulder. She doesn't take her gaze off the medic, keeping her body between Doc and Rath. The purple underlying her blue eyes brightens. "He deserves any extra pain you can dish out while pretending to help heal him?"

Doc pales, glancing between all three of us before dropping her gaze to Rath's shoulder.

"It's okay, Precious," Rath says, smoothing a hand down Presh's spine, then pulling her into a loose hug against his undamaged shoulder. She dabs at his wound with the gauze. The bleeding has stopped. "Doc knows I'm resistant to painkillers. Or ... local anesthetic."

"Did you use any?" Presh demands of Doc. "Did you even try?"

Doc swallows, then stiffly steps over to her med kit and pulls out a small plastic bag. She drops the bullet in the bag and seals it, setting it next to my main keyboard so I can scan it before handing it over to be processed for evidence. Or rather, to gather dust on a shelf somewhere because we've already got the shooter, and there's no reason to involve the local police. They keep their jurisdiction tightly focused in club territory — as in, focused away from club business as much as possible.

Doc's hand is shaking almost imperceptibly. "You're right, Presh. Though I know the levels ..." She clears her throat. I see her glance over at the picture of Zaya. She glances away just as quickly.

Doc isn't an idiot. Rath has pissed her off more than once — mostly with his utter indifference and after she's had a few essence-laced drinks. But I've never seen her less than professional when acting as club medic. So today is different somehow.

Because Rath has actually hurt her? Or, more likely, is in the continual process of hurting her?

Maybe promises I don't know about have been made between them, and are in the process of being broken?

Doc reaches for the items she's already set out on the edge of my workstation. More gauze and butterfly sutures. She doesn't look up as she speaks. "I can give you some —"

"I'm fine," Rath says, his tone even as he continues to rub Presh's back gently. "I'm fine," he repeats to our little sister.

Presh doesn't take her gaze off Doc. Her purple-tinted, deep-blue, narrow-eyed gaze. And I wonder whether the purple is what's causing Doc's hand to shake, rather than any remorse.

We three brothers are used to gazing into purple eyes with awe rather than fear. But the awry — even one just slowly awakening — scare most people, even rare shifters like Doc. Most people can go an entire lifetime without meeting a purple-eyed essence-wielder, with only stories — fantastical, miraculous, or terrifying — on which to form their opinions.

"Why aren't we seeing a feed to the interrogation room?" Rath asks, scanning all my monitors. He ignores Doc as she crosses around — skirting the opposite side from Presh — to clean the wound and bandage his shoulder. Presh begrudgingly allows the medic to tend to our brother, though she doesn't step out of Rath's loose embrace. The slow creep of the black veins radiating from the bullet wound has lessened already.

I tap a couple of keys, opening the fuzzed-out feed to the interrogation room on my left monitor.

"What the fuck?" Rath snarls quietly.

"He's got a black box."

More Authority tech being used for non-Authority business. Reck is walking a very fine line — or rather, stumbling all over a very fine line — even when factored against the Authority's usual morally ambiguous standards. A black box is a generic term for an essence-wired device that can be used for ... well, less-than-legal things. It does everything Reck's personal device can't, including knocking out all vid feeds and comms lines in a localized area.

I have a feeling that the box wouldn't do a thing against Zaya's brilliant bit of essence-wrought tech masquerading as a regular high-tech phone. But I know that the only reason Reck's box isn't currently fucking with my own tech is because that tech is in a room I personally shielded with enough iron and steel to put a bank vault to shame.

"He has no fucking jurisdiction here," Rath says.

"Everyone knows it but him."

"And you. You fucking let him in there."

"How would you have kept him out?"

Rath's nostrils flare. Yeah, he's got no answer to that quandary. The same as I hadn't when Reck stormed in after Grinder got called away.

The timing was too perfect. Reck was obviously tailing Grinder, had seen him bring in the unaffiliated bikers, then waited. But now that I had all of Reck's bugs identified, he wouldn't be able to gain such easy access to any club-related business.

I need to check all the club members' phones, at least those of the inner circle. And vehicles. That would take days. More days away from Zaya. Because she's secure on the oceanside property, and my eldest brother is a fucking asshole.

Rath and I are both staring at the fuzzed-out vid feed to the interrogation room, in which Reck might be slowly and methodically beating our prisoners to death, as if something might miraculously appear on it.

A notification flashes at the top corner of the monitor, informing me that my script has finally broken through the last layer of encryption on Reck's phone.

A picture fills the screen.

The item that Reck deemed so valuable that he hid it under at least ten years' worth of encryption is ... a single picture.

No. Not just valuable.

Cherished.

Doc clears her throat.

"Um ..." Presh says, her voice suddenly far away because every atom in my body, every sense, is trained on the photo stretched across my monitor. "Is that ... Zaya?"

Zaya Gage, age seventeen, her skin as sun kissed as it ever got, her light-brown hair streaked blond — she'd tied lemons in it that early summer — is sprawled out on a towel ... on the beach. Sunlight catches in the dusting of sand that is the only thing covering her. No tan lines. Nothing but miles of smooth skin, punctuated by small fucking perfect breasts tipped by dark, tight nipples.

I'm instantly and inappropriately hard, straining against my suddenly way-too-fucking-tight pants.

Just staring.

Because Zaya is gazing up at whoever is taking the picture — Reck, obviously — a vibrant purple ringing her bluish-purple eyes, lush lips slightly parted on a moaning smile. And that flush across her cheeks ... that look in her eye ... she's either just orgasmed or is in the fucking process of coming.

I tear my gaze off Zaya's face — before I fucking come in my own pants. Because apparently, her orgasming in a fucking picture can trigger me almost as much as it can in person. My gaze traces down past the nipple that Zaya is pinching, to ... the picture doesn't show anything much lower than her belly button, but she has her other hand pressed there ... pressed over someone else's hand ... long fingers, slightly darker, suntanned skin splayed across her stomach ... holding her in place ...

And the angle is wrong for it to be the hand of the person taking the picture ...

"What the fuck!" Rath snarls, lunging forward, his hands on my desk as if he'll be able to refute what he's seeing if he gets closer to the monitor.

He put it together quicker than I did.

In my defense, Zaya is fucking stunning when she orgasms.

It's the three red-jade rings, worn on the first three fingers of the hand partially hidden under Zaya's hand, that click the image together with the act that's been immortalized and hidden on Reck's phone. Rath's rings. A gift from Zaya that summer, from a trip to Hong Kong with Disa the winter before.

Those rings shattered, I believe, that night when we fought for Zaya's life and lost ... lost everything. At least I've never seen Rath wear them after.

"I'm going to fucking murder him!" Rath shoves back from the workstation, knocking the stool aside and almost clipping Presh with it.

In the days leading up to the day that Zaya died — was murdered right in front of us — Reck somehow snapped a picture without Rath knowing, while Rath was eating Zaya out. Likely the three of them had been fooling around together, totally consensually. And Zaya could have easily stopped Reck from taking the picture ...

"Whose picture is that?" Presh asks, getting pissed now. "That's private. You shouldn't be looking at it. You shouldn't have been looking for it in the first place." She leans around me, reaching for my keyboard as if she can somehow delete the picture.

There is no fucking way I'm deleting that fucking picture.

"It's not ours," Rath says. "Leave it, Presh."

Precious rounds on our brother as if she wasn't just totally babying his wound a moment before. She's tiny against his huge bulk, but she glares up at him defiantly. "She saved me! She's my friend ... my mentor."

"She is not your mentor. Or your friend."

Presh pokes him in the chest. "Leave her alone. Rought only does this creepy shit because you order him to do it."

Rath snorts, but he's struggling to take his eyes off the picture just as much as I am.

"It is creepy," Doc says. "That picture looks ... private, and ..."

"Take it up with Reck," Rath snaps. "He took the fucking picture in the first place." Then he clamps his mouth shut, shaking his head just once, angrily. Yeah, he's said way more than he intended.

Because Rath is still in denial about Zaya. Past and present.

"Oh ..." Doc looks at the picture, then scans over my desk to the phone plugged into the hard drive. "Oh ..." she breathes, as if she thinks she's put something together. She hasn't, though. Not completely.

"Check on the Outcast," Rath says sharply. Not 'our uncle.' Rath is attempting to cover his blunder with formality. "Take Presh with you."

"But ..." Presh protests.

Before Doc even gets her bag zipped, her back stiff and movements jerky — a response to Rath's orders, I assume — the door to the interrogation room slams open.

Reck strolls out, grinning like a total fucking madman and casually tossing the tiny black box — hopefully disabled now — in his hand. His knuckles are bloodied.

We all stare at him for long enough that the heavy steel door swings shut. His gaze falls on his phone, still tethered to my setup, and his smile fades.

Rath is fucking growling. The voice of his beast is actually rattling through his chest.

Reck's gaze snaps to our brother, then quickly takes in Doc and Presh, who's now frowning again.

Doc grabs her bag, then tries to snag Presh's shoulder. But our sister snaps her arm to the side, pointing at my screen with a single finger. "Why do you have that photo of Zaya, Reck?!" she screeches. Loudly.

Reck barely gets a chance to glance at the photo I've stolen off his phone before Rath's fist is slamming into his jaw and he's stumbling back.

Doc grabs Presh — who shrieks in vehement protest at being safely removed from the room — and darts toward the door to the hall.

Rath gets Reck in the gut with another juggernaut of a punch before Reck manages to lunge forward and wrap both arms around our brother, pinning Rath's arms to his sides. They wrestle upright for a bit. Then they drop onto the coffee table, smashing it to pieces — Rath on top of Reck.

"Rath!" Presh cries.

I'm fairly certain Rath is mindlessly considering choking Reck out, but Presh's shout pulls him back into his own head. He gains his feet, wiping some blood off his lip. I missed the hit Reck must have gotten on him, maybe while checking on Presh and Doc. Shifters of our power level move stupidly fast.

Rath shakes his head as if clearing it, stepping away from Reck and the splintered ruin of the table. He points down at our brother. "You fucking prick."

"What else is new?" Reck says, exhaustion heavy in his words. He just lies on the ground, chest heaving.

"At least the pizza made it through unscathed," I say. The box is upside down on the floor, but managed to stay closed.

Reck snorts at me, dropping his head back to blink up at the ceiling.

"Back up to the house, please, Presh," Rath says, all gentle now.

Presh looks between us, still partially tucked behind Doc protectively. She chews on her lip. I can't imagine how many questions she must have.

"You can help me check on the Outcast," Doc says.
Shit.

Three weeks ago, the Outcast — our uncle — suffered a massive heart attack. He's up and moving around now, but it's possible that only his tie to the pack kept him in the land of the living. The club is keeping the info that its leader was ever anything but hale and hearty as 'need-to-know.' Meaning Reck doesn't know it, because we're never certain he can be trusted not to blab to the Authority.

Confirming that we've managed to keep that info from him despite his surveillance, Reck's head snaps to the side, eyes narrowing on Doc. "Why would that be necessary?"

Doc opens her mouth, then looks to Rath, her eyes widening almost comically.

Presh's cellphone pings. Squealing again, but happily this time, she tugs it out of her hoodie pocket. "It's Zaya! She says I can come by this afternoon!"

Rath mutters under his breath, reaching for his discarded T-shirt, then realizing it's still soaking wet.

"Under no fucking circumstances," Reck snaps, "will you —"

"I'll drive you," I say, cutting off my bossy fucking brother's rant.

"Absolutely fucking not," Reck snarls. "Even if she's who she says she is —"

"She is," Rath says wearily.

"She's fucking poison —"

"That's why you were hiding the photo?" I ask, being a complete asshole about it.

Reck snaps his mouth shut, eyeing Doc and Presh. Taking the hint, Doc tugs Presh with her through the door. Presh is still grinning at her phone, texting back to Zaya. She glances up at me after hitting send. "You'll drive?"

I nod. "I'll come up to the house for breakfast and sort out the timing. Then I'll grab a couple of hours of sleep."

"You don't leave the property, the main house, Presh," Rath says wearily. "Again. Not without a guard."

Presh juts her chin out, but then smartly takes her win and keeps her mouth shut.

We all wait until the door closes behind Presh and Doc. Then Rath very deliberately leans over to my keyboard and sends the picture of Zaya to his phone. It pings, and he accepts it. I had no idea he knew my systems well enough to do such a thing. But the picture is pretty fucking motivating.

Reck appears to be imagining what it would be like to murder the both of us. "Start talking," he snarls.

Rath just looks back at him, all detached and in control again. "It's you who has things to tell us."

"It's just a fucking memento," Reck spits. "It means nothing."

Rath folds his arms across his bare chest, ignoring that the bullet wound has got to hurt when pulled like that. He leans back against my workstation. It groans under his weight. "The unaffiliated bikers you just illegally interrogated? Start talking."

Lip curled in a vicious snarl, Reck makes it up onto his feet, then leans over to open the upended pizza box and swipe a slice. He mows through it, speaking around bites. "The Cataclysm is making all sorts of promises to locals, most of whom have recently relocated, and who've either been rejected by the Outcast or are still pending review."

"To what end?" Rath asks.

Reck sneers at our brother, always so fucking superior. "Looking for a foothold in Cascadia, of course."

"That's obvious," Rath says coolly. "To what end."

"Why don't you ask your little Tempest?" Reck mocks.

I snort. "There is no way Zaya is involved with the Cataclysm."

Reck shrugs, snagging the last piece of pizza. "Lots of movement on the board."

"The Conduit is above the game," I say.

Reck shakes his head at me. "You're as deluded as ever."

"I don't think he is." Rath's tone is still cool. But much deadlier. "I expect your full report on your conversation in an hour. Did you leave them alive?"

"I don't fucking answer to you."

"It's either me or the Outcast. You pick." Rath turns his back on Reck, picking up the overturned stool and settling down beside me. "Now get the fuck out. Because we certainly don't owe you anything." He runs a hand over his face and speaks to me, all even-keeled again. "Run me through what happened to Presh, Rought. All of it, in order."

Behind Rath's back, Reck's face falls. And just for a moment, his gaze flicks to the picture of Zaya on the screen. He lunges forward to snatch his phone off my workstation, fucking ruining the cord I've got it tethered to at the same time. Then he slams his way out of the room.

NINE

ZAYA

I'm finishing my second bowl of ice cream of the morning when Harlee and Cayley wander in through the mudroom. Not that I need to justify that consumption, but the earthenware bowls are the size of my palm. So it's actually more like just one regular-sized bowl. Also, I tried to nap for about fifteen minutes in between the comforting consumption of creaminess. And of course, I was dead less than forty-eight hours ago.

Thick threads of Harlee's essence are twined all around her hands, but I blink a few times and clear them from my vision. The mage has been casting for hours, but normally I don't see residual like that. Hopefully, it's just because I haven't slept properly, because if that's suddenly a new thing I do, it's going to be an ongoing annoyance.

Cayley spins right, flinging herself on the couch in the large open family room just off the kitchen, close to the TV niche. She closes her eyes and lets her head fall backward with a sigh.

Harlee hovers in the doorway to the mudroom, hands folded in front of her, gazing toward me but slightly downcast, not meeting my eyes.

I rinse the ice cream bowl, then put it and my spoon in the dishwasher. "Cause of death confirmed?" I ask.

Cayley scrubs her hand across her face, leaning forward with her elbows on her knees. "Doc confirmed before she left. Both Ingrid and Mack dropped at the exact damn same time. Massive coronaries. Harlee got the bodies ... tidied —"

"Preservation spells laid," Harlee says quietly. "I also scoured the beach house after I moved the bodies to an empty section of the barn. Or maybe it's a workshop? That was ... it's a simpler space for the spell work and for ... viewings ..."

I narrow my eyes at the suggestion that anyone else is going to be coming onto the property for a look around. Harlee swallows, twisting her fingers together.

"Right." Cayley eyes the rambling mage for a moment, then looks to me. "The mages' Coterie has been informed. As has the Outcast MC. Well, officially now. There will be ... questions."

"There won't be any questions," I say.

Harlee looks up at that. Looks at me. "Ingrid Belke was a Wisdom."

"I know."

"There was residual essence on the bodies ... that ..." Harlee swallows, then glances at Cayley. "That ... suggests ..."

The kitsune shifter huffs. "Now? Now you're scared of Zaya? You couldn't have been a bit more cautious before you sold my fucking car?"

Cayley's tone is mild, but Harlee bristles. "It was my car. You gave it to me. And then ... you just took off, who the fuck knows where, and ... you came back different!"

"Actually, I've always been bisexual," Cayley says in the same deceptively neutral tone. "It's never been just a phase, as you like to insist."

I don't even have to know the shifter to understand that tone means 'back away slowly and don't return without some sort of tribute.' With her other half being kitsune, no one should really expect anything less.

Though it's pretty apparent that Harlee doesn't understand that part of Cayley at all.

"That's not ..." The mage casts a look at me. "What I ... meant ..."

I raise an eyebrow, too tired to leave my own kitchen and let them have at it with their argument.

Harlee inhales deeply, squaring her shoulders. "Those weren't natural deaths —"

"*The thread is woven alongside choice and misdeeds,*" I say. That bit of litany likely sounds far too flippant, but my point is valid. All death is naturally occurring, especially under the guiding hand of fate.

And yes, I'm still blithely ignoring all the wrongness that I'm also sensing in my Aunt's seemingly untimely demise. Well, I'm trying to ignore it. But beyond that, it isn't any business of Harlee or the local pack or even the mages' Coterie. The bonds between my aunt and her chosen weren't lightly undertaken by any of them. No matter the ramifications of my aunt's abrupt death.

Harlee eyes me while attempting to not actually meet my gaze. "If you wanted me to cover it up, you should have —"

"Who said anything about a cover up?" Cayley snaps.

"Well, no one. But —"

I interrupt before they can clash words again. "Did you get any sense of what Ingrid was scrying for? She was attempting to scry, yes?"

Harlee inhales deeply. "As best I can tell, it was a combination of a seek and a find spell, and what looked like a modified ..." She shakes her head. "A teleportation spell? I'm honestly not ... if it worked, I assume it's because Ingrid was essence bound to whoever she was looking for. Because even with a visual lock through the scrying, I can't see how she thought ... she was powerful but ... maybe it's beyond me. I'm not a Wisdom."

"Currently," Cayley mutters under her breath.

For once, Harlee ignores her.

"Any evidence that Ingrid found the person she was scrying, or had tracked them previously?"

Harlee shakes her head. "No. Just evidence of multiple attempts to refine the casting over a few days."

So my aunt had been missing, or at least out of contact, for a few days before she died. Died and took her bond mates with her.

Harlee clears her throat. "I left the personal effects, of course."

"Thank you. Please send me your bill."

Harlee opens and closes her mouth, then glances between me and Cayley, then back to me. "That's it?"

"Do you have more to tell me?"

"Yes, of course. There are intricacies to the essence —"

"Do you want more than just the broad details?" Cayley asks, a little mockingly. And not toward me.

"No." I turn back toward the freezer while Harlee quietly sputters. "Does anyone want some ice cream? I just made it, so it's still soft serve."

Cayley practically launches herself off the couch as I pull the tub of ice cream out of the freezer and set it on the counter between us. The shifter has the top off the container by the time I pull three spoons out of the drawer. I pass a spoon to Cayley, keep one for myself, and set one of the spoons on the counter, close to the disgruntled mage.

Cayley doesn't question the lack of bowls, simply running her spoon through the ice cream to create a perfect small scoop of chocolate creaminess. She pops the scoop into her mouth and moans.

Harlee's gaze snaps to the shifter. She looks away just as quickly.

"Oh, fuck me, yes. So, so good."

Harlee slowly crosses to the counter, finally untwisting her fingers and letting her hands fall to the marble. "I'm ... I don't do well with dairy."

Cayley snorts. "For this, you don't worry about a little farting."

Harlee throws her a dark look. "You know it's more than —"

"No dairy," I say around my own mouthful. "Coconut cream." Then I find myself wondering whether spending time with the two of them is always going to be an exercise in thrusting myself between them to keep the conversation on track. If I loved drama, that might not be overly taxing. But I control too little of my own life to truly embrace that level of chaos. Not that I generally have chances to cultivate friendships ...

Harlee nods, picking up her spoon and taking the tiniest of scoops.

Cayley side-eyes her. Then, smirking, she takes another huge bite, groaning enthusiastically.

Ah. The shifter noted the mage's reaction to her first — more genuine — moan.

Harlee squirms, almost imperceptibly, keeping her gaze off the shifter.

"Are you guarding Harlee?" I ask Cayley. "Or me?"

"You," Cayley says without hesitation.

I hum doubtfully. "And are you guarding me or guarding others from me?" I ask, my tone even.

Cayley doesn't have an immediate answer.

Harlee snorts, then takes a larger scoop of the ice cream. "I'd like to act as your liaison with the West Coast Coterie. And be your local contact in general. If you're staying?"

Out of the corner of my eye, I catch sight of a text message as it appears on my phone, still on the counter.

"This isn't some advancement opportunity," Cayley sneers at Harlee.

The mage squares her shoulders and raises her chin, eyeing the shifter. "Isn't it? You find yourself sidelined, your club questioning your —"

"My club never questions my loyalties!"

"Right. That's why this 'guard duty' is the first thing they've tasked you with in eighteen months." The mage puts actual air quotes around guard duty, though she doesn't put down her spoon to do so. The ice cream is too good to ignore even while in the midst of a pissing contest with your ex-lover.

For a second, I'm pretty certain Cayley is considering tearing out Harlee's throat. Then she smiles viciously. "The first task ... that you know of."

That wipes the smirk from Harlee's face. It takes her a moment to come back. "It's a fine line between secrets and lies, Cayley."

I reach for my phone. Presh has texted back, enthusiastically accepting the invitation I sent her while waiting for the ice cream to finish its second churn. And I realize that I've somehow managed to quell the argument between mage and shifter by turning my attention elsewhere. Good to know.

I meet Cayley's eyes, holding her gaze for long enough that she shifts on her feet almost imperceptibly. "I don't need a guard," I say evenly. "Nor can you actually guard others from me if I choose to involve myself in their lives."

Cayley swallows. "As I well know."

Harlee is glancing between us, wide-eyed.

"But ..." Cayley adds in a rush, "I'm ... my not being here, not trying to at least act as your guard, would put me in bad standing with the club."

"This is my territory." I take another bite of the ice cream, allowing it to melt across my tongue. "The Outcast MC's territory might border it, but they have no dominion here. I'll thank Grinder for his consideration, make sure he ... understands."

Cayley nods stiffly but doesn't counter me, confirming that no matter his more laidback attitude, Grinder ranks higher than Rath in the club.

I offer her a smile, not certain why I feel the need to do so. "Take the Corvette. Unless Harlee can give you a ride home?"

I already know the answer, of course, but I have to suppress a smirk at Harlee's response.

"It's in the opposite direction," the mage says stiffly. Then she flushes as she realizes she probably should have protested the transfer of custodianship over the Corvette instead. "And are you staying in the area, Zaya?" She digs her phone out of her pocket. "Would you consider ..."

I reach for her phone. She unlocks it and swipes open

her contacts app before handing it to me. I add my name and phone number. "If you're inclined to write up your observations —"

"Yes!" Harlee snatches the phone back from me — careful to not actually touch me — and glances down at the screen, practically glowing with glee now. "I'll text you. And I'll let the Coterie know that any questions can be forwarded through me."

"And your invoice."

She bobs her head in a way that lets me know I probably won't see an invoice from her. I'm not a fan of incurring favors. I narrow my eyes at her.

Her smile widens, more emboldened now for some reason. Because I gave her my contact info?

Cayley shakes her head, taking another large scoop of ice cream and stuffing it into her mouth as if doing so will stop her from caustically commenting.

I can't blame Harlee for her reaction. She's known me for less than two days and has already gotten a clear view of the unusual magical events — and of the death — that are my day-to-day experience. She's intrigued. And sure, a relationship with me? The other Wisdoms who head the local Coterie are going to be incensed. And begrudgingly impressed.

"Are you okay to drive?" I'm not accustomed to having so many people near me when I'm not fully functional.

"Yes. I took an energy brew. I won't sleep for hours yet." Harlee steps back from the counter, not looking at Cayley. "If you need anything ... if I can do anything ..."

"Anything mage-related and you'll be my first call."

She backs out of the kitchen as if I'm royalty ... or maybe as if I'm a dangerous creature, which isn't all that much of an overreaction. I don't miss the smugly satisfied look she throws Cayley before she pivots to cross steadily down the hall and eventually out the front door.

The shifter sighs, though only after the mage is well out of hearing range. "I can't take the Corvette."

I ignore that for a moment, saying first, "There's a cottage deeper into the southern woods."

She nods. "Empty. But recently lived in." She eyes me for a moment. "You're still missing someone."

"Not me. But yes, my aunt's ... combat mage isn't on site."

Cayley smirks, not missing my hesitation. I'm still not certain whether there was a third bond in my aunt's life. Or if there was, whether it was still active. It's been years since Devlin and I crossed paths ... which makes less sense the more I think about it. Because the more I think about my life, the more the summers spent with my aunt come back to me ...

There were three half-full teacups in the front sitting room. Two side by side and one across. It could have been Ingrid or Mack sitting there with whoever came to the property, bearing information that drew my aunt away so quickly that no one took the time to put the cake away ...

I shake my head, trying to ease my beleaguered brain. I'm getting fixated on the past. And I have no ... influence over the past. I deal only in the Now. But ... I mean, I know ... I knew the transition between me and my aunt, my *becoming*, wasn't going to be peaceful. I didn't expect it to be any less ... abrupt than it has been. The Conduit power isn't something my aunt could have just given to me ...

"Zaya?" Cayley asks gently. Then, inexplicably, she reaches across the counter and lays her hand over mine.

I realize that I'm still holding my phone in that hand. That I'm frozen with my spoon in the other, hovering above the ice cream. My empty spoon. I gently slide my hand away from Cayley, filling my spoon at the same time.

"Thank you for your concern," I say stiffly.

It's a weird feeling, having anyone concerned for me. But shifters are territorial, and they take protection duty seriously.

Cayley casts her gaze down, nodding uncomfortably. Or maybe ... disappointed?

"There should be other vehicles in the barn, if you don't want to take the Corvette," I say. "The keys are in there ... somewhere ... likely in the cars themselves. I mean, who would try to steal them?" My attempt at humor falls flat.

"There's just a truck. A pretty F-100 classic that Grinder instantly salivated over. It's probably worth more than the Corvette ..."

I don't bother adding to my argument. I'll just let her talk herself into going home in what is pretty clearly her own car, loaned to Harlee. It was the 'for insurance purposes only' comment back at the diner that had made that pretty clear.

"I'll pay you back for it," she says, quietly insistent.

I shrug. "The club is probably going to make you tail me whenever I leave the property, right?"

She glances away from me, then mumbles, "For a few days."

"Consider it hazard pay."

She snorts with half-hearted amusement. "If hazard pay is needed just to track you around town, then the club should pay it."

"Well, consider it a preemptive apology, then."

"Because you aren't going to make guarding you an easy task."

"Not deliberately. But *life unspools as it wills*."

She meets my gaze steadily. Then she says, hushed, "I'm pretty certain life does as you will it, Zaya."

I laugh. It comes out a little bitter, but I can't seem to soften it. I don't want to soften it.

Cayley takes another bite of the ice cream. "Sorry, I've almost finished this. Harlee has that effect on me."

"I'll make more."

"Yeah? Maybe ... you can invite me over then, too?" She takes her phone out of her pocket, unlocks it, and slides it over to me.

I've never given my phone number out to so many relative strangers in my life. But my life isn't my own anymore. And being the Conduit, holding the intersection point is ... it means I must be more than just myself now. I understand that. On a rational, logical level at least.

Cayley does a bad attempt at quashing a smirk at whatever she sees written across my face.

I plug my info into the phone. The shifter quickly takes it back from me, as if worried that I might change my mind.

"Drive safely," I say, again all stiff and dismissive. I need to be alone. Well, I need to sleep, and I'm hoping that being alone on the property helps me sleep.

Cayley nods, then leaves. I can feel her life force all the way to the Corvette and then along the driveway. As she turns onto the road, I have an inkling that I could trace her thread even farther if I wished, but I pull back into myself, because that reach is overwhelming right now. On the property? I can justify it to myself. Off? That's too much.

I've held the essence of the Conduit for only three weeks, and the anchor of the intersection point for just over twelve hours. It's all too much if I stop and think about it.

I finish the dregs of the melting ice cream, not really

tasting it. Then I rinse the tub and put it in the upper rack of the dishwasher, even though I know it should be hand washed.

I rebel in my own little ways.

As I make my way through the dark house and up to my bed, I text Presh back.

I'll see you this afternoon, Precious.

In the bedroom, I pull the heavy curtains against the early dawn, ignoring the items on the windowsill. Somewhat inexplicably, I take my phone to bed with me. Normally, I just leave it wherever I last used it.

Is it the connections I've just inadvertently forged that make it more comforting to keep it with me?

I stare up at the dark ceiling. My aunt and I never spoke about the others in her life ... her chosen. But why didn't we speak about them? Why weren't they part of my life as well? Why was I all but banished from the estate, without actually realizing that was what was going on?

And why, when we traveled together, trained together, followed knowings together — why didn't my aunt's fucking combat mage come with us?

My phone buzzes in my hand, the screen lighting up the room as a text message comes in. From Precious.

>Rought is making me hash browns and scrambled eggs. With cheese! Yum! Then he needs a nap before he drives me over.

I wouldn't mind someone cooking breakfast at dawn for me, but I'm not jealous. Rather, I'm oddly pleased. Comforted?

I'm moody as fuck. I seriously need to sleep.

I send a drooling emoji back to Presh. Then a yawning face. She instantly texts back a series of symbols that my blurry mind can't handle trying to translate. I set the phone on my bedside table, then curl on my side to fall asleep, thinking of cheesy scrambled eggs and potatoes. And wondering whether Rought, the hacker who messed with my phone, was the brother who slept in the second bed in the motel.

Sleeping isn't conducive to guard duty, though. So why? Why sleep next to me? To an awry of my power?

And ... is this something else — someone else — I forgot?

TEN

I'm up again after only two hours of sleep, dragging my feet even while still feeling like I'm not wholly occupying my own body yet. If it's possible to be anchored firmly yet still feel a breath away from floating away, then that's what I am.

I ignore it as I head back to the family plot in the daylight.

I'm only steps away from the house when I realize I can suddenly sense the far borders of the property, the presence of what feels like every animal on it, and Muta's exact location. I try to smother that impression, to focus on the immediate, but I'm only partially successful.

Mysteries abound on the estate, and I'm not certain I have enough information to even hazard a guess at solving them. But when I reach the mausoleum, I can see by the light of day what I couldn't last night.

I can see what Mack was digging up when he dropped dead.

My aunt's chosen has been removed from the area, but the site where he fell looks otherwise undisturbed. That makes it clear where the shifter was working around the back of the marble mausoleum. A large marble urn has been shifted out of place to make room for his excavation.

After retrieving the shovel where Rath left it against the fence, it takes only a few minutes of additional digging to reveal a sealed niche set into the far bottom corner of the mausoleum foundation. Formerly hidden just beneath the ground.

Nothing is carved into the stone, but the idea that I'm about to disturb an interment bothers me. I'm glad that a bit of sunlight is filtering in through the partial cloud, warming my face a little as I stand there indecisively.

Then I remember my aunt's note with the ice cream machine, and the preemptive apology about everything I'm about to find out. So I scrape along all four edges of the sealed niche, digging out dirt and whatever mortar was originally used to seal the front-facing piece, until I can shove the tip of the shovel firmly into the space I've created.

I put a bit of weight onto the handle of the shovel, for leverage.

The front of the niche pops open a few inches, detaching cleanly from the marble on either side. No cracks or crumbling. That feels fortunate to the point of being just short of miraculous.

Or it might mean that I'm meant to access whatever is hidden here.

I drop the shovel, not wanting to press my luck and end up damaging the mausoleum. Then I hunker down to get my fingers into the gap I've created. Another firm yank gets it open enough to peer inside with the help of the light on my phone.

A simple metal urn and a narrow wooden box occupy the space within the foundation stones. I retrieve the latched box. An inlay of various woods, reminiscent of the armoire in my aunt's turret office, decorates its top. The box opens without resistance, to reveal a knife set on a black velvet lining. It's double edged and wickedly pointed, with a wood-inlay handle that matches the top of the box.

I don't have to touch it to know that it's filthy with dire-wrought essence. It shimmers with that essence, though it should have dulled and corroded with age.

The blade is also stained. With old blood.

The implications of it not being wiped clean and interred with the ashes in the urn are instantly clear to me. I lean forward to try to get a better look at the urn, without touching it. But its slightly tarnished metal has no design or name carved into it.

Who would be interred in the Gage family plot, but also hidden away like this? And with the knife that was likely used to murder them?

I have even less idea why Mack would have been digging up this interment. Unless he was trying to get the knife. Because it killed whoever's ashes are in the urn, and the evidence of a decades-old murder needed to be ... what? Hidden somewhere else? Destroyed? Who would ever have found it here?

The knife, even after decades, still seethes with twisted essence. So perhaps Mack needed a dire-wrought blade for some reason? Paired with the idea that Ingrid was likely trying to scry for my aunt, that made more sense. Harlee had said something about a teleportation spell ... making it an easy guess that Ingrid was trying to teleport to my aunt. And did she need this knife to do so? For what? Perhaps the spell kept failing ... or ...

Was the knife meant to be used against whoever was powerful enough to hold my aunt?

I've been awake for less than an hour, and my head is already aching. I'm trying to put mismatched pieces of a puzzle together.

Maybe Mack murdered someone years ago, then hid the evidence and just randomly decided to destroy it. The timing might mean nothing.

Except ... the design of the knife hilt, matching that of the top of the box, seems at utter odds with the malignant intent I can feel from the blade itself.

I've uncovered another fucking mystery that might be completely irrelevant. As all mysteries truly are to me — because the past doesn't matter.

My aunt is dead. I am the Conduit. The *why* doesn't really factor in. The *why* is a petty human concern. Selfish, really. Because I have other responsibilities in the Now. To the fucking universe.

Wanting to put everything back the way I found it, though a bit better hidden, I grab the lid of the box. And a piece of the velvet lining the inside flaps forward, revealing the edge of a black-and-white photograph.

I tug it free, staring down at a photo of my aunt surrounded by three huge shifters. Their size gives that away. They're on the beach, the craggy bluff and roaring surf occupying the distant background. The photo is aged, but not otherwise damaged. If it's been protected by any magecraft, I can't feel it. Though that isn't unusual.

My aunt looks to be in her midtwenties, as always. The casual clothing in the photo — her plain sundress, the shifters' sweaters and jeans — are difficult to date accurately.

My hand is trembling as I flip the photo over. My aunt's distinctive handwriting fills the back:

Oso, Ward, Disa, and Ari. Summer 1989.

The photo was taken thirty-four years ago. Almost five years before I was born. I don't know any of these men or what they meant to my aunt. Except that the ashes of one of them has been interred with the knife likely used to kill him.

I put the top on the box and tuck it into the niche. Then I close it all back up, dirt included. I nearly hurt myself shoving the marble urn back into place.

I keep the photo, even though it isn't mine to collect.

I DECIDE TO MAKE A TREK DOWN THE DRIVEWAY before heading back into the house. I've already walked as much of the property as I can manage in a couple of hours, including checking out the cottage in the south woods — empty as reported — and the two other gravesites where those not of the immediate Gage bloodline are buried.

I've found no fresh graves or other recently disturbed interments at the other sites. But a trickle of memories is now filtering back to me of the combat mage missing from the property. I remember a male with light-blond hair and tanned skin. Laugh lines radiating from light-brown eyes.

It bothers me that it's taken walking through the cottage — Devlin's claimed space — for those memories to surface. And I'm left wondering why that is, alongside still wondering why he didn't accompany my aunt and me on our trips. My 'training' often involved situations that my aunt's combat mage should have ... would have wanted to ... shield her from.

I shove the thoughts away. Because again, the past is not my domain. But I'm aware that I'm going to be forced to fully examine those thoughts, and likely soon.

For me, I don't think ignorance is going to be bliss.

As I near the end of the drive, I see the two vehicles parked on the grassy edge of the road on either side of the gate. Despite the chill of the intermittent mist between sunny breaks, Cayley is leaning against the back of the Corvette, watching as I approach. She's got two insulated mugs in her hands. Waiting for me to appear.

The second vehicle is a massive beast of an SUV. Black on black, with deeply tinted windows. For anyone else, those windows would be a fineable offense. In Cascadia, at least.

But not for the Authority.

I can't see through the windshield, but I can feel two people within. A mage and a shifter. So even as they attempt to be all sorts of creepy and stalkerish, they can't negate my senses or the impressions the property has been feeding me since I woke for the second time today.

Those continued impressions are annoying when my head already aches. Despite having trained my whole life to surf the threads of essence when I choose to do so — and only when I choose — I've had to practice intense mindfulness three times since I woke up, just to focus.

The Authority really shouldn't be wasting their time staking me out. My aunt will have an open file somewhere, deep in their archives. Therefore, whether or not they know I've taken on the Conduit mantle, they should already know they have no jurisdiction over me or anyone on the property.

Though I would have to double-check the fine print with one of the Gage uncles or aunts who handle those sorts of legalities, the entire property is actually ceded land. As in, technically its own country. Hence me having to negotiate new treaties with the local club. And the Coterie. And the government.

Ugh. I'm not looking forward to any of it. But there must be another uncle or two I can fob most of it off on.

Neither of the Authority goons' essence signatures feels familiar. I ignore them.

Grinning, Cayley closes the space between us as I near the end of the drive, setting her elbows on the top of the still-closed gate. She's wearing jeans and her jealousy-inducing custom-patched leather jacket. Her dark hair is clipped back into a high ponytail, which somehow brings her cheekbones into even sharper relief than normal. I imagine she's intentionally giving the Authority goons something pretty to obsess over.

I hope she's got some sort of water-repelling spell or charm on her jacket.

Still grinning at me, Cayley takes a long sip from her coffee. As I draw near, the steam coming off the insulated cup and the scent both confirm the contents. But she wags the second mug in my direction. It has a straw.

Smiling back at her — because she already knows me well enough to know that I don't drink coffee or tea unless necessary — I take the mug. Then I take a long, chilly slurp of a vanilla milkshake. Despite the insulated cup, it's mostly melted, but I don't mind one bit.

Cayley tilts her head, smirking at me. "Tastes like your essence."

I'm not particularly skilled at flirting, but even I know a come-on when I hear one. I smirk back, and with my lips still partially around the straw, I say, "It's too sweet for that."

She throws her head back and laughs. Then the doors opening on the SUV draw her attention. And a deep frown.

The two Authority agents step out, booted feet crunching in the loose gravel that collects at the edges of the road. The shifter is male, bulky and red haired with ruddy skin. The female mage wears her blond hair swept back in a smooth twist. What I can see of her skin is lightly tanned.

Both are outfitted in dark-colored suits with lighter shirts, underneath layers of essence-wrought protections.

I don't have to look at them with my other senses to know that the mage is the more powerful of the two. Combat grade, perhaps. Or she has a rare affinity that aids her team in capturing powerful essence-wielders.

Cayley casually leans her hip against the gatepost, half facing the approaching agents. "Way to ruin the moment, assholes," she says, her tone almost playful.

She knows them, but doesn't like them either?

The mage ignores the kitsune shifter, removing her sunglasses to get a better look at me. The other shifter curls his lip.

They manage another two steps in my general direction before Muta suddenly appears, curled around the top of the opposite gatepost.

"What the fuck!" Cayley almost drops her mug.

The two agents stop midstep.

Muta has some sort of short-jump teleportation ability. As far as I've been able to figure out, he can only move toward me, not away. Though it's always possible he hides the full extent of his power. Even a cantankerous death god trapped in the body of a snake has to have his amusements.

He stretches the first three feet of his body upward,

then begins bobbing and weaving his head. Slowly. As if trying to mesmerize the Authority interlopers.

Cayley relaxes with a slight smirk. She's figured out Muta's game before the agents.

The shifter bares his teeth — likely a wolf, then — at the death god incarnate taunting him. Though it's unlikely he's figured out the taunting or the death god part.

The mage doesn't flinch, nor does she react to Muta at all. I expected as much. Even the hints of essence — and of life force — I feel from her are darkly tainted. She's either become numb to what she does for the Authority, or was emotionally and mentally dampened to begin with.

"If you bite them," I say casually to Muta, "it's your responsibility to clean up the mess."

If he were capable of feeling anything as mundane as joy, I would say that Muta's bobbing takes on a playful bounce. Dancing for his targets.

Cayley represses a laugh.

"Thanks for the milkshake," I say, turning away as I take another long, fortifying sip of vanilla creaminess.

I don't invite her to join me, and she doesn't ask to.

"Ma'am?" the shifter calls after me. "I'm Brett Shaw, and this is my partner, Clara Wilson. We'd like to ask you a few questions about the events of the last few days."

I ignore the agents. It's an appropriate response just for them calling me 'ma'am,' but they also know I have diplomatic immunity. I could have them run off, even from the edge of my property, if I felt like making a couple of calls. Unfortunately, those calls would also require me to build relationships — with the local police, the Outcast Motorcycle Club, or both — and I don't have the energy or inclination to do so. Not right now.

Cayley calls, "You've got text messages."

I still don't look back as I head up the drive. "I know."

She snorts, then adds, "Will you at least let me know if you want to leave the property?"

"Doubtful." I flash her a grin over my shoulder.

She swears under her breath.

Then I give her a bit of a break. "I don't have any plans to go anywhere today or tonight or for the next few days."

The shifter offers me a little salute.

By the time I'm at the top of the rise in the drive, with a view of the house in front of me and the road behind, Cayley has driven off in the Corvette. The Authority agents, ignoring the mist, are still watching me. The mage has her phone to her ear.

I continue on to the house, for some food to top off the milkshake. And to tackle the last task I want to be tackling — my aunt's office at the top of the turret, and all the secrets I now know it holds. Even without the missing or muted memories filtering back to me, her note on the new ice cream machine and the interred knife have already made that clear.

I'm actually scared of what I'm about to uncover. I'm not sure anyone of my blood, no matter how distant our relationships, has ever outright betrayed me before. Why would they take the risk? My aunt, though, is the most powerful of the epically powerful elite who make up the Gage-blooded awry —

No. She was the most powerful.

I'm the Conduit now.

THE ARMOIRE IN MY AUNT'S OFFICE STILL WON'T open for me, and I still haven't found the keys to the three drawers in the desk. A quick scan of the last few entries in my aunt's notebook, before setting it on the shelves next to the others to be further explored, offers no illumination to her last days. I struggle to be patient as I smooth my hands over the varnished wood of the massive cabinet, trying to get it to accept my essence, to accept my right to look within. But as more time passes, and as each measured breath I take seems wasted, I become more and more aware of the necklace. The obscenely expensive, epically powerful amulet hanging around my neck.

Despite all the entwined threads of gold and the size of the rough-cut diamond, when the necklace settled around my neck three weeks ago, it didn't come with any real weight. Or at least what weight it had was negligible. I was born to wear it, created by the fucking universe to wear it. Or, more accurately, imbued by that universe with the necessary essence to eventually become the Conduit.

But ... as I continue to shift through the bits of my aunt's life, trying to piece together what's happened to her, or to find something to help Coda track her — and as I try to open the armoire that draws me, draws me and repels me, I know that something within that seemingly simple piece of furniture is going to ... break me. I know it in my hindbrain, not as an actual knowing. I know there are multiple somethings behind that locked door.

Those things will break me. And I'll have to put the pieces of myself back together. And then I'll never quite fit again.

Those shattered pieces ...

Even worse than the last time ...

Just like when I woke that first time at age seventeen

and I'd lost so much of myself. I had lost ... chunks of myself ... of my soul ... ripped away from me ... by ... by ...

I stumble back from the armoire, sliding down the side of the nearest bookshelf and tucking my knees into my chest. That sense ... that visceral sense of my first awakening isn't an actual memory. Or at least it wasn't, even a few days ago. My aunt told me ... I woke up in bed, and my aunt already had me packed to leave the estate ...

I can't ...

I can't ... pain streaks through my head, and I'm panting, fucking panting ...

What is wrong with me?

I'm unraveling.

Why is the necklace so fucking heavy? And growing heavier and heavier still.

I shove farther back from the armoire ... sliding my ass across the wood floor ... my palms are slick with sweat ... my heart is racing so fast, and I'm breathing ... breathing ...

Am I breathing properly?

I can't get air into my lungs ...

I'm ... I've forgotten how to breathe?

How can I forget how to ...

I force myself to lie on my back, knees still bent, bare feet pressed to the wood and my hands settled on my lower ribs. Gasping like a fish as I try to anchor myself and regulate my breathing. I inhale and exhale, ribs rising and falling under my hands, as I stare without seeing up at the dark wood of the cupola ceiling.

I haven't suffered a panic attack in years, not since my awry power started to assert itself in my early teens. Even then, my recall of having such attacks is more a familiarity of the sensations and not actual memory.

It feels as though my body isn't large enough to contain

all that flows through me, whether or not I'm living, breathing ...

I'm ... nothing ...

Nothing but an empty vessel at the command of the universe ... of those who came before me in this endless thread of ...

I function, but ... I have no ability to affect the course of my own life ... I'm not a person ... I ... I ...

Pure panic streaks through me.

I need to run.

But I can't move.

I'm frozen in place.

I'm trapped here.

I'm being strangled by the fucking necklace, no matter how benignly it seems to rest along my collarbone.

I had more time.

Didn't I?

I had more time.

I was supposed to have —

Tears stream from the corners of my eyes, across my cheeks, and into my ears, but I make no sound.

The sensation of tears pooling in my ears is off-putting. And that's enough ... that's enough to free my limbs. I roll to my side, knees tucking up to my chest, forehead to the hardwood.

I manage a deep breath.

Then another.

I manage to get my eyes closed.

I manage a third breath.

And just for a moment, tightly curled on the quickly warming wood, I remember a warm hand running gently down my spine, and a soft murmur in my ear. Then arms banding around me and tucking me against ... sun-warmed skin?

I spread my hand on the hardwood floor. But for a moment, I swear I can feel sand under my palm, and a strong, steady heartbeat under my ear.

A breeze stirs my hair ...

The hands tighten their grip.

I tilt my chin ... up ... up ...

As if ... as if ... reaching ... wanting ...

A kiss?

The lightest brush of lips against mine.

And the panic recedes, as if retreating from the sunlight and warmth and ... love?

I open my eyes.

I'm still on the floor of my aunt's office, but I'm ... relaxed. My limbs are heavy, languid, as if I've slept ...

No, not slept.

A different warmth, the embers of a lingering curl of desire, has settled under my skin.

The panic attack has eased. I'm still overwhelmed, but not consumed by it.

What the fuck was that?

An echo of the past? A moment to come?

My gaze settles on the armoire, drawn to it as I am every moment I'm in this fucking turret. I sit up, crossing my legs.

"I need to know," I say, speaking to myself.

I don't know why the last moments of my aunt's life matter so much when in the grand scheme of the universe, I understand they truly don't matter. But they do.

"I have to know," I say, speaking to the armoire. I can't walk into this new existence without understanding. What is missing? What am I missing?

"I must know," I say, speaking to the energy flowing through me. If I'm to fully function, to be what the world, the universe, needs me to be, I need some ... understanding. Some self-determination?

The armoire doesn't open.

Nothing stirs within the essence that underpins the property.

No clarity blooms within my mind.

I make it to my feet. I cross back to the armoire, resting my hand upon it.

I can feel it.

The energy drawing and holding me here.

I slide my hand higher ... trying to remember if I've ever seen the armoire standing open before.

Yes ... yes ... the middle section held books, more note-books? And some heirlooms? But there's also a shelf, isn't there? Right at this level.

And there, under my palm, I can feel it. Intensely.

It's not essence. It's not a sense.

It's an emptiness.

An echo of the emptiness I felt on the path leading up to Rath. An emptiness I grew numb within, picking over the keepsakes on my windowsill that I have no memory of.

Something that once belonged to me resides in this cabinet.

I know it. I just know.

Something terrible enough to be locked away.

I have no idea if what's here is tied to the bloody knife or to my aunt's death. All I know is it's been locked away until I'm ready to see it, according to my aunt's note.

"I'm ready," I whisper — ignoring that the panic attack I just navigated is evidence to the contrary.

I close my eyes, pressing my forehead to the armoire. Then I deliberately recall the recent memory.

The feel of those lips against mine.

No one has ever kissed me like that. With reverence, mingled with love and desire. No hands have ever held me so firmly, as if I'm neither breakable nor dangerous.

I drop my hand from the armoire, taking a step back.

It wasn't a memory.

Not a glimpse of the future either.

Just my brain, my mind, trying to calm me, feeding me sensations I never knew I wanted, never knew I needed.

But that kiss, that strong yet gentle embrace shielding me from the panic building within my own mind, is something I know I will never have.

I take another step away, then another, until I'm heading down the stairs and carefully closing the door at the end of the upper hall behind me.

I'm alone in the house. By my own design. But also because anything else would just be a temporary illusion.

I will always know.

I will always know now that I'm only the Conduit.

No person will ever want to kiss me so gently or help soothe a panic attack when the universe feels like it's too big to hold within my only-mortal form. Too big to channel. Any bonds I take — as with the bonds my aunt took — will just be an extension of my function as the Conduit.

I just ...

I thought I had more time.

I feel Precious's approaching presence just as I finish setting a batch of caramel ice cream to churn in the ice cream machine. With a coconut-cream-and-white-chocolate base. Because rather than embracing my destiny, I'm apparently being ridiculous.

However, it's someone else who steps over the property boundary to open the gate. Someone else who climbs back into the vehicle and brings it up the drive, leaving the gate open.

I'm practically running for the front door, still drying my hands with a tea towel, when I hear the rumble of the high-powered gas-guzzling motor.

I get the door open, my gaze already turned toward the winter-bare fruit orchard to the right and the weathered, cedar-sided workshop-barn beside it — as a pristinely restored 1967 gold Camaro coupe pulls up in front of the wide front door.

The engine hasn't even died before the driver's-side door is opening, and a male steps out — dark-blond hair, naturally tanned skin, and shoulders so broad I'm surprised that he slips out of the car so agilely. Though he is clearly a shifter.

The moment his booted feet hit the ground and the energy underpinning the property rises to ghost his footsteps, I know that he is a ... *presence*, a power. He's in black jeans and a light-gray henley. He lays his hand on top of the Camaro, pivoting toward me — not bothering to look at the barn or the property or anything else as he reaches to shut the car door with his other hand.

He meets my gaze. His eyes are light colored, either blue or green, but I can't tell which at this distance.

He's still moving, hand running across the top of the

car, then down the back window, then fingers only along the trunk.

He fucking caresses the fucking car as he crosses alongside it, then continues steadily toward me. And for a moment of utter insanity, I want it to be my curves under those fingertips.

The passenger-side door thunks closed. I feel Presh's presence as well. But I can't tear my gaze away from the golden god in worn black jeans taking long, steady strides toward me. I'm locked in his gaze.

The nearer he gets, the more I see ... in his expression, in his body language, in the way his essence entwines with that of the property.

More specifically — with the intersection point.

I'm not lightheaded.

I'm not beguiled or enchanted.

The nearer he gets, the more anchored I feel.

Not frozen. Not overwhelmed.

I'm in this moment. Breathing it. Savoring it. As if ... as if ... my very soul has been starved? And he is ... he is ...

A slow smile spreads across his face.

His eyes are both green and blue at once.

Tattoos twine around his forearms, decorating the backs of his hands and up his fingers. More black ink teases the edge of his collar, as if trying to creep up his neck.

He doesn't pause at the base of the front patio steps.

He climbs. One step. Two steps. And now we're the same height. Then he takes that third step, and he's slightly taller than me. Then one more, still a step lower but towering over me now.

Still holding my gaze, his hand lifts, reaching for me, for my face ...

I'm not wearing my sunglasses. I'm the Conduit,

standing on a claimed intersection point. I must be radiating power, my eyes glowing purple. Yet he doesn't hesitate for a moment.

I tip my chin up.

Am I going to let him kiss me? A total stranger?

His hair is long enough that it curls at the ends. It's tousled as if he's been running his fingers through it, not crisp and perfect as if he's styled it that way.

"Rought!" Presh cries from somewhere near his elbow. "You said you'd behave!"

Rought's grin widens, but he keeps leaning over me despite his sister's admonishment. His hand is poised to cup my face, though he doesn't touch me. He leans close enough that he brushes his cheek along mine, inhaling deeply as he does so.

Scenting me.

Scent-marking me?

Presh shoves at his shoulder. He doesn't move an inch, but he chuckles — deep and husky — as he shifts back enough to meet my gaze again.

I realize I was wrong about his eyes. Both are an even mixture of green and blue, yes. But both are now also thickly rimmed in burnished gold.

"Zaya Gage," he says, pure joy laced through his words. As if it delights him to say my name.

I don't scare him in the least. My violet eyes don't bother him at all.

"Rought Guerra," I say, my tone smooth ... too smooth? Am I ... flirting? "Your reputation precedes you."

He laughs.

My chest warms, as if he's the fucking sun and I'm a beleaguered flower.

I've never had such a visceral reaction to anyone, no matter how much of a presence or charisma they exude.

He glances down, between us.

I've raised my hand to him, to his chest. As if to caress, not to push him away. He cups the back of that hand and presses it ever so lightly against him.

His heartbeat pounds under that connection — steady and sure.

And in that moment, I'm sure I know him.

I know him.

Under my skin, embedded in my bones, deep in my soul —

Except I've never met him before.

I drop my hand, and he lets me go easily. I angle my body toward Presh, who's grinning up at me. Meeting her gaze seems to be all the acknowledgement she needs before she flings herself at me. I tuck her against my side without even questioning the impulse.

Rought finally looks away from me, grinning down at Presh instead.

She doesn't loosen her grip on me as she narrows her eyes on him. "You said you'd be on your best behavior."

Rought rocks back on his heels, raising both hands placatingly. Then he transfers that grin to me again. And again, I feel the heat of it, as if I'm somehow greedily lapping up energy from him, from his mere presence.

"Where will you practice?" he says. "In the ballroom?"

"I think we'll take a walk," I say, not bothering to question how he knows that the former ballroom of the main house is used for training. I feel no need to question him, to question my odd reaction to him.

Rought is the source of the *presence* I felt in the motel. He slept in the second bed. It was he who put all the tracking software on my phone. He was the one, according to Coda, who wanted to know where I've been and where I'm going to be.

He sent me to Cayley, to rescue Kiki.

And I don't feel the need to interrogate him about any of it.

"I know you had Cayley take the Corvette, so while you work with Precious, I'm going to make sure you've got a working vehicle." He nods toward the garage alongside the barn.

Having no intention of leaving the property, especially not while still suffering jagged crying spells and seemingly random panic attacks, I haven't even bothered to think about a vehicle.

"I want to check what equipment Mack has here before having the BMW towed to you. I'll work on it during your training sessions with Presh."

I know I should question that. Shouldn't I?

Yes, I should. But I don't want to.

I understand that Presh's brothers are likely to feel uneasy leaving her here on her own, but it's not that understanding that has me just smiling at Rought, all soft and sweet.

Getting hold of myself, I flick my gaze over his shoulder. "The Chevy is a beauty. At least two of my uncles would make you an offer for it on the spot."

Still grinning, Rought runs a hand through his hair and throws a look behind him. I try to ignore the way his bicep flexes, threatening to tear through his henley, but I fail miserably.

I fail ... delightfully? Delectably?

"I finally got the Outcast to completely sign her over to me," Rought says, smirking as if he knows I'm panting after him. "After I got caught one too many times taking her out." He levels his gaze on me, and I see that the gold rimming his eyes has disappeared. He arches an eyebrow — again, knowingly.

As if we share a secret. About the car?

I look at the Camaro again, frowning slightly.

"What?" Presh asks. "I thought it was your car?"

Rought clears his throat, dropping his gaze, his focus, from me. For the first time. A hint of that emptiness presses against me. From the inside this time.

Rought shakes his head at Presh. "Took me three years to fully restore her. The Outcast gifted her to me for my twenty-first, along with the promotion to lieutenant. Youngest ever in the club."

Rought glances at me out of the corner of his eye, stepping back and down the patio stairs, completely surefooted without looking. His grin is somehow quieter now.

I've said something wrong. Or missed something.

"I'll let you work," he says. Then he turns and walks away.

The hollow feeling inside me expands. The feeling I didn't truly acknowledge before, always just pushing it away to be examined later. But I refuse to stand there like an idiot, watching him leave while I dissect every moment of our brief interaction.

Presh is here.

And I'm here for Presh.

I squeeze her shoulder slightly, then drop my arm.

She hikes her backpack up on her shoulder a little higher, smiling up at me tentatively. She's also in black jeans and thick-soled boots, but she's wearing a black puffy coat over a thicker, multicolored patterned sweater. "We're walking?"

"We're going to investigate the flow of essence and see what you can sense. There are various points on the property that are perfect for that kind of work."

She bobs her head, not quite hiding her trepidation.

Presh has spent the fifteen years of her life thinking she was going to be a shifter. I don't want her to be afraid of the purple taking over her eyes.

"But first we've got freshly churned ice cream to taste-test." I nod her toward the house. I've left the door open, and Presh steps past me eagerly.

I pause in the doorway. Presh is already wandering up the hall, looking eagerly around as she heads toward the kitchen. And I glance back toward the barn, toward the shifter who feels as if ...

Who feels as if he belongs. On the property, yes. But also to me?

Rought has opened the rolling door that leads to the garage section of the barn. The large multipurpose space has always been called that, though my aunt never kept any livestock. Beyond the garage and workshop are the two floors of the caretaker's suite that was Mack's. The classic black pickup that Cayley had seen sits alone in the garage, and Rought has crossed back to the Chevy to pull it inside one of the two empty spots.

Except he's looking at me. Again.

I don't know why I do it, but I raise my hand and smile.

A grin swamps the shifter's face. And even at this distance, he looks relieved.

As if he has some sort of hollowness inside himself as well.

As if my smile, my presence, fills him as well.

I shake my head, my smile twisting at the stupidity of my thoughts.

Rought Guerra has a powerful charisma. A *presence* potent enough that the energy anchored in the property is simply reacting to his proximity. He doesn't belong to me.

Still, I'm grinning like an idiot as I cross into the house and close the door behind me.

It's drizzling rain as Precious and I walk the grounds of the estate, but it isn't the weather that inspires me to direct us back toward the barn after only a few hours. Rather, it's because she's starting to flag.

When she showed up, I was pleased with how well rested Presh looked — and far healthier than when I'd dragged her from the grasp of the Cataclysm shifters. Okay, I didn't so much drag her as bumble about, get her even more hurt, then get both of us to relative safety.

But the property is that. Safety.

Presh is quiet about what she's picking up with her embryonic awry senses, but I can feel her essence shift slightly when I direct her attention or have her focus on specific things. We avoided the intersection point during our walk. It's my intention to have her spend some concentrated time on the bluff, but even before she starts tripping on her own feet, I know she's not ready for that yet.

The bodies in the barn provide a different opportunity — as morbid as it might be — because they're without essence. Even amid the abundant energy of the property, they're inert. And sometimes understanding the opposite of a lesson is a path to grasping the fundamentals of the main objective.

No matter how anyone might want to shield her — myself included — Presh is awry. She will be no stranger to death. And possible mass destruction, depending on where her powers lie. The point is to help her understand how to not get overwhelmed by the energy, the essence, that wants to eagerly flow through her. She's an awry among generations of shifters. It's as if the universe reached out and decided that she's the vessel it wants, the vessel it needs in the Now ... or at least the near present.

The why isn't for me to know. At least not at the moment.

I try to ignore that sense — that little bit of insight — as it filters into my consciousness, instantly deciding that it's just a logical observation and not a hint of a knowing. Because surviving as an awry is firstly and mostly about surviving yourself, and only then about navigating what others will want from you, demand of you. Awry who abruptly manifest have the shortest life spans, if not also the briefest ... freedom. Presh's liberty will literally be tested every day, until the day she's too strong to be shoved in a cage.

Under the right circumstances? Even I'm not so strong that I couldn't be caged. If only for a moment.

Rought has all the lights on in the garage and workshop areas of the barn. I've been feeling the shifter's energy the entire time we've wandered the property, even while actively focusing on Presh. It should be easier to tune him out, though it's already obvious that my tie to the intersection point comes with a heightened sense of its boundaries and inhabitants.

I choose to actively ignore that multiple essence-wielders were on the property for a large portion of yesterday, and I wasn't as continually aware of them as I am of Rought. As achingly aware.

On the far side of the garage as we enter, Rought is working on the pristinely restored, high-gloss black 1956 Ford F-100 pickup. But his gaze is already trained on us as I step over the threshold. The garage section of the building is divided from the workshop by a set of now-open doors. The floor is well-worn shiplap in the workshop, but concrete in the garage. The trestle ceiling is far above us in the central section of the barn.

The workshop is tidier than I've ever seen it. Power tools are boxed and organized on shelving units, with hand tools hung along the wall that separates the workshop from Mack's suite. The workbenches are all bare, scoured clean.

Harlee's work maybe? The mage might have cleaned the space out of deference to the two bodies currently set in the cleared central area of the workshop. Mack and Ingrid are each intricately wrapped in plain off-white sheeting, and set side by side on two antique-looking wood-topped folding tables. They're surrounded by fresh herbs and flowers, though whether Harlee found those in the greenhouse or went off the property for them, I don't know.

Presh stumbles over the threshold after me, and I reach back to tuck my hand under her elbow. I catch Rought straightening from the engine of the truck in my peripheral vision. He tugs the rag he's stuffed in his back pocket out and starts cleaning his hands.

"I'm fine," Presh murmurs quietly, her gaze on the bodies. She glances toward her half-brother with a slight smile, reassuring him, though he hasn't said anything.

I start to ask her if her brother's essence feels as intense to her as it does to me. If she is as continually aware of him as I apparently am. Then I shut my mouth on the question, which feels both too personal — and too revealing on my part.

"I've seen bodies before," Presh says, as if that should reassure her brother, reassure me.

It doesn't.

"And they weren't ..." She approaches the smaller of the two, the dead mage. "They weren't treated so well."

Even though this is my skewed idea of a valuable primary lesson, I suddenly want to pull Presh away, bundle her back through the mist-drenched late afternoon into the house. I can ply her with ice cream, and we can watch a movie by the fireplace in the family room. But instead, I keep my distance, as does Rought, so that my energy doesn't permeate the space and muddy the essence-sensing lesson. Well, not any more than it likely already does.

The idea of curling up next to a fire has never seemed so comforting to me before ... before this moment. I don't glance over at Rought, though I can feel his gaze every time it touches on me.

Presh hovers her hand over the wrapped forehead of the mage. "They were your aunt's chosen mates?" she asks.

"I believe so," I say.

"You couldn't feel that connection?"

"Not after ... not once they were dead. And I ... I didn't really know them ... before ..."

But I should have. I spent summers on the property for years. And rationally, I understand that my aunt had other companions. But I'm becoming more and more achingly aware that I'm missing something ... something fundamental —

Rought steps closer. His gaze is on his sister, but he moves near enough that I swear I can now feel heat radiating off him. Either I'm colder than I thought from our walk through the drizzling rain, or it's his essence that warms me.

Both possibilities are unsettling.

So I ignore them and stay focused on Presh.

She brushes her fingers across the flora tucked around Ingrid, murmuring, "Mage."

"Are you sensing that from the preservation spell or the body?" I ask.

Presh shrugs, tired but offering me a slight smile. "The other person is a shifter. His size gives that away."

She plucks up some thyme and tucks the woody stems under one of the folds across Ingrid's chest. I don't caution her, don't tell her that she might be messing with Harlee's casting, because I can already sense that she isn't. Her quiet, barely-there essence doesn't stir or interrupt what has already been laid across the bodies.

Instead, I eye the thyme she's shifted and wonder at the connection. Why she felt the need to move it, the impulse to set it in a specific location. Over the mage's heart.

The difficulty with trying to train another of the awry is that there are so few of us, we are all essentially unique. I can only guide Presh to find her own way, or until she manifests enough ability that I can find her a mentor better suited for her.

Of course, finding a mentor who I would trust with Presh's life is a completely different issue.

She crosses toward the second body, hovering her hand over the wrapped forehead of the shifter as she did with the mage.

"It's all gone, then," Presh says quietly. "When we die? The energy that makes us who we are ... our souls ... does it ... does it just dissipate?"

I open my mouth to answer, then realize that the question is rather complicated, so I backtrack a bit. "Some of it depends on your belief system."

Presh nods, toying with some of the leafy oregano and flowering lavender tucked under the shifter's arms as she watches me steadily. "Like ... that our souls travel into the After, and that we cycle back into the Now. Is that what you believe?"

I nod. "I can't say I ... I can't confirm reincarnation as a fact. But energy, essence, continually flows through the universe, changing shape and tenor but never truly being destroyed." Energy flows from the universe to the world through me, more specifically. But I leave that potentially belief-shaking bit of info for later. Or for never.

Presh nods again, thoughtfully. "These are ... were your aunt's mates. And they died when she did?"

A wash of cold shivers down my spine when I nod my own acknowledgment. I know my aunt is dead. But apparently, I'm still caught up in the how and why and nowhere near acceptance.

"So does that mean they were soul bound? Shifters believe in that sort of thing. In fated or destined mates."

Hyperaware of the silent male at my side and all the warmth, all the presence, radiating from him, I attempt to skirt the question without completely destroying or attacking Presh's belief system. "I believe, as does Harlee, that my aunt and her companions must have been essence bound."

"Your aunt shared essence ... they shared essence."

"Yes."

"Through sex?"

I inhale deeply. I'm not a prude. At least I don't think I am. But I haven't ... I've never been with more than one person at a time. "It's not necessarily a single action, or a switch, or a lock that can just be triggered. The essence bond, that level of connection, can take years to fully develop.”

Presh smirks at me, a little too knowingly. “Shifters bite their chosen mates.”

Rought chooses this moment to enter the conversation — just as he tucks his right hand in the front pocket of his jeans. “And their soul-bonded.”

I valiantly try to keep the essence-sensing lesson on track. “Not all bonds are sexual in nature, but sex, and biting, can be a way to anchor and reinforce a chosen bond.”

“So you don’t believe they were soul bound to your aunt,” Presh says.

“I don’t know.”

“What about you? Do you have soul bonds?”

“No.”

Rought stiffens beside me, but I keep my attention on Presh as her interrogation continues.

“Do you have essence bonds?”

“No.”

“Chosen bonds?”

I shake my head, smiling at her as gently as possible. “That isn’t my path.”

“But it was Aunt Disa’s?” Rought’s question is a harsh rumble that seems to emanate from the depths of his chest.

I get another of those pained pings, through my chest. “I can’t speak for my aunt. I’m ... I apparently didn’t know her as well as I thought.”

“But you spent your childhood here?” Presh asks.

I know she’s talking to me, but her gaze strays to Rought. “Portions of it,” I say.

“And?”

"And?" I smile, not quite certain I'm following how her train of thought has stretched from soul-bound mates to my childhood.

Presh looks at her brother steadily.

I glance his way as well.

He offers me a toothless smile, sweet but not as sunny as before. He's got both hands stuffed in his front pockets now, shoulders slightly curved forward. And his energy has contracted.

I frown, glance to Presh, then back to Rought, then back to Presh. I've missed some subtlety underlying the conversation. About mates?

"Are you soul bound?" I ask Presh.

She snorts. "Nope. Don't believe in them either."

I glance at Rought. "But you do?"

His smile widens as I once more feel its warmth spreading through my chest. "I believe in my soul-bonded mate, yeah."

My stomach drops. I'm not certain I've ever felt that particular sensation before, but all the warmth that was building in my chest somehow falls into a deadened weight inside me. Heavy with disappointment and ... grief? Or heartache?

The smile slips from Rought's face. His concerned gaze flicks between my eyes.

I misunderstood his ...

I misunderstood.

I swallow, deliberately trying to blank my face as I say, weirdly brightly, "Well, there you go! I think a nap would be ... restorative."

"Here?" Presh asks hopefully.

"How about the house?" I turn back toward the exterior door, not looking Rought's way.

"Zaya ..." he murmurs.

"Does the truck need more work?" I ask him, keeping my gaze on Presh as she crosses to join me.

"No ..." He clears his throat, also looking at Presh, then back at me. "I just checked it over. It's not fuel converted, but I started it up, and the tank is full."

"Thank you." I push open the door for Presh to go ahead of me.

"I'd like to show you something," Rought says.

"Me?" Presh asks.

"Zaya." He gestures toward the closed door that leads into the caretaker's quarters. "And there's a couch in the other room for a nap."

I really just want more ice cream. Pure want, not need this time. And it's a completely impractical desire. I can't just drink milkshakes all day, every day.

Presh changes directions without protest. Exhaustion is dragging at her heels. "Less rain in this direction," she murmurs.

I have had her out for hours. She can certainly nap here, especially if Rought is still checking the truck over.

Presh pushes open the door to the suite. But before I can follow or beg off and return to the house on my own, she turns back and blinks at me solemnly.

"You died, Zaya."

"Yes."

"But you never felt truly inert. Not like these bodies do."

That's news to me. But then, I've never died around one of the awry before. Even when in my aunt's company, she always made sure I never took on that level of debt.

I'm reckless only with my own mortality — testing my own mortality? — when I'm ... alone ...

I'm really not a fan of the personal revelations that keep piling up. Perhaps it's all just part of the transition between who I was and who I must now become.

"And ... your aunt?" Presh asks. "Will she wake up like you did and find all her essence-bound mates dead?"

The question hangs between us, and for a brief moment, it feels too complicated to answer. It's not that any of it, any of this, is a secret. Not from Presh, at least.

But when the silence sits unanswered for long enough that it gains weight, I answer simply, "No."

Presh opens her mouth, as if to press me. But then she just offers me a sad sort of smile and steps through into the living space beyond the door.

"Zaya?" Rought murmurs so quietly that my name is more a brush of air across my forehead than a vocalization. He's hovering his hand at the small of my back, not touching me.

I step to the side, not forward or back, leaving his hand hanging in the air. I turn away, intent on heading back to the house. I'm not interested in what someone who claims he has a soul-bonded mate wants to show me. I feel weirdly raw and vulnerable, even though it's obviously my misunderstanding of his attention. Of the way he interacted with me like I was a ... person.

Yes. That's all it is.

My hand closes around the latch to the exterior door before I remember I should probably try to act as though I have some manners. I glance back over my shoulder in Rought's general direction, though not truly looking at him. "Thank you for tuning up the truck."

"It barely needed anything."

I just nod and open the door, instantly buffeted by a

misty breeze across my face and neck. The wind has shifted. "Will you tell Presh I've gone for a nap myself?"

I have no intention of napping. For someone who feels so empty, still so heavy with that emptiness in my guts, my insides, I'm weirdly keyed up. I'm not sure I'm capable of napping now even if I try. "I'll text her to set up another time."

"Tomorrow, same time?"

"I'll text."

I step through the door into the grayed-over sky of the late afternoon, bow my head to avoid the mist — even though I'm usually perfectly happy to walk through it — and trudge back to the house.

"Zaya!" Rought calls after me. I don't look back, but I can sense he's hovering in the doorway. "I won't push. But I think you might like Mack's photographs. He's got a gallery of them in the loft of the suite."

I wave over my shoulder but don't look back. Rought watches me the entire way to the house.

I should do all sorts of things. Specifically, I should continue my haphazard investigation of my aunt's last days, or follow up on any of the messages beginning to pile up in my inbox from family members who have all felt the reverberations of the intersection point transferring to me. The energy tied into the intersection sustains us all. It's the reason the Gage bloodline burns so bright.

But I don't do that.

Instead, I strip off my wet clothing in the laundry room, put yet another load through the laundry or to hang to dry, and cross through the house in a tank top and underwear.

I crawl into my bed.

I stare up at the ceiling.

Maybe thirty minutes later, I track Rought's and Presh's energy as they leave the property.

Even when Muta joins me, sliding under the duvet to line up along my leg and torso and rest his head on my clavicle, I still feel empty.

Lost.

I know this feeling. Though I usually don't let it get so intense. It's the feeling that usually propels me into another country, into seeking out things that need to be fixed. Into testing myself.

But I'm the Conduit now.

How can I be the anchor when I'm so unmoored?

ELEVEN

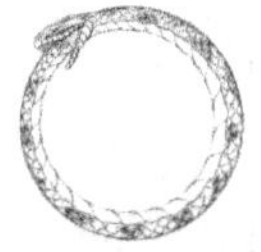

I REALIZE THAT I MUST HAVE FALLEN ASLEEP WHEN I wake suddenly to see that the dark of the night has fully encroached on my bedroom. I'm not certain what's woken me, except that I'm ravenously hungry. Grocery shopping, or at least getting food delivered, would have been a great idea.

Then something buzzes against my leg, and it takes my blurry brain a moment to recognize that I've uncharacteristically crawled into bed with my phone, which is now sandwiched between the bed and my thigh. Also, I'm certain that I had it on silent, not whatever the current buzz alert is. Though I wouldn't put it past Coda to change it in an attempt to screw with me. Or even just to get my attention.

I haul the offending device up to my face, ignoring all the text notifications scattered across the screen except for the most recent. They're all from Presh. And I instantly know that it isn't Coda who made my phone buzz — it's the universe giving my shoulder a little tap. A tap that will likely turn into a shove if I continue to wallow in bed and hide from my present. And my past?

>*Can you pick me up?*
>*Yes, I snuck out.*
>*Again.*
>*And yes, it's late.*
>*Will you come?*

I slide out of bed, crossing through the dark to the shallow walk-in closet that I haven't so much as looked in since my arrival. I score some skinny-legged jodhpur-style pants that haven't been in style since I likely wore them last, so about thirteen years ago. I'm lucky the pants are stretchy — and black — because even with my current death-warmed-over physique, I'm definitely not seventeen anymore. I find surprisingly lacy panties and a camisole in the top drawer of the bureau. Also black, and rather sexy for teenage me. Rather sexy for adult me, honestly.

As I exit the closet, I spot an adorable vegan-leather minibackpack that looks brand new. And I certainly don't remember it, so maybe I never used it.

I text Presh back as I head downstairs.

Address?

In the laundry room, I retrieve my oversized charcoal cashmere sweater — thankfully now dry — and my second-favorite pair of ankle boots. Apparently, I'm ignoring the hole that's been burned through the sweater just a little while longer. Thankfully, the edges are seared, so it's not unraveling.

Presh gets back to me, and I instantly click open the map app on the phone because I don't recognize where she is. Even with the route mapped out, I have no idea where I'm heading, except it's about fifteen minutes away.

On my way.

In the barn, I slide into the pickup, with its pristinely restored dual-tone interior and its red steering wheel just as glossy as its black finish. I remember that the key is tucked into the sun shield — before remembering that I have to get out again to manually open the garage doors. Then I need to remind myself how to drive a truck. It might all be set up the same, but it certainly doesn't operate like a luxury car, even if both are equally classic.

I drive right past the Authority agents in their mammoth SUV. And that's all the evidence I need that I'm on an errand for the universe, despite not feeling the tug of a full-blown knowing. The gate is already open, presumably left that way by Rought when he and Presh left the property. The agents have presumably both *accidentally* fallen asleep while on duty, and I just go with it. As I usually do.

The map leads me south along the edge of the Gage estate for about seven minutes, then cuts abruptly east toward the outskirts of the nearest township. Newport, I think. The streets are wet, but it isn't currently raining. It's dark enough that I don't need my sunglasses, though my face feels bare, exposed without them.

The map app takes me on a weirdly winding route that I figure out the reason for only when I'm a block away from the destination. We're deep into a warehouse district I honestly didn't know existed. I can hear music pouring out from a derelict-looking three-storey building before I even shut off the truck.

It's some kind of underground club or rave. With the truck window open, the sweet, metallic-tasting air that surrounds the building hints at the rampant use of essence-imbued drugs — the definitely illegal kind. The concrete or pavement or whatever it is underfoot is cracked and crumbled at the edges.

I feel more like myself the moment I step out of the truck, which lets me know exactly how overwhelming being on the property is right now. It's swamped my senses so much that I'm not even aware of being suffocated by it.

The front doors of the building are shut behind thick metal bars. The windows are boarded over, even on the top floor. I slip around the building, easily following the thick trail of accumulated essence that leads down the side and around the back. Dozens of essence-wielders have come and gone from this location tonight. I normally don't feel such things without actually looking for them — notwithstanding that there's never really been anything normal about me. And there certainly won't be now that I'm the Conduit.

I sense Presh's quiet essence ahead, almost completely subsumed by what feels like shifter energy. But her pastel rainbow-colored hair is unmistakable even in the moonlit alley. She's clinging to the edge of a metal barrel of some sort and heaving out her guts.

I'm only a few steps from her side when her two companions jolt upon seeing me. They're both shifters, so I know that the universe is definitely doing that thing where it randomly chooses to mask my presence. In this particular case, I figure it's some sort of lesson in humility. Not for me.

A lanky male in his late teens starts to shove himself between me and Presh, face shrouded by artfully mussed, chin-length hair that I'm pretty certain is an odd dark gray. His eyes are gold-flecked green, his skin a medium brown. But he loses his ready sneer when he truly takes me in. Noting my eyes, I presume, because the rest of me isn't remarkable enough to stop a young male shifter with something to prove in his tracks.

"It's fine," Presh gasps between heaves over the barrel.

Nothing is coming up, but her system isn't convinced that it's purged her stomach yet. "Zaya. That's Zaya."

I recognize the second shifter from the Tasty Tart diner — the server, Kris. She's doing a terrible job of holding Presh's hair back, and not because of my sudden appearance. She can't keep her gaze off the dark-gray-haired male. Kris's dirty-blond hair is randomly braided in a few places, and dusted with the same glitter that highlights her cheekbones.

Both girls are dressed to party in short skirts, heeled boots, and lace tank tops. Presh's skirt is swishy, and Kris's had better be stretchy, or I'm not sure how she can move in it.

They both have to be freezing even though it's not raining. Except I presume they're also both juiced up enough to not feel the cold.

I keep walking, and the protective shifter is forced to cede way to me. A completely disgruntled look takes over for his seemingly permanent sneer as he realizes what he's done.

Presh spits into the barrel a few more times. Then, still clinging to the edge of it, she straightens enough to peer at me over her shoulder through watery eyes. "Don't be mad?"

She and Kris have taken some sort of essence enhancer. I can feel the unnatural energy sparking off them, discordant with their own. The male is either sober or has stuck to alcohol.

Kris steps away from Presh, tucking herself slightly behind the male shifter. Her wide-eyed gaze flicks between him and me. His shoulders are tense, hands fisted at his sides.

"You look familiar," I say, not looking at him as I run a hand down Presh's back.

Presh sucks in a deep breath and then gags, likely getting a hit off the contents of the barrel. She steps back, closer to me, shuddering in relief as I run my hand down her spine a second time. "Andy is Rought's half-brother," she says. "Same mom."

"DeVille," he corrects.

Presh ignores him, her gaze on me. "That's Kris. She's Doc Z's kid sister. All three of us are going to be in shit if our elders find us here."

I just hum under my breath and do a third pass down Presh's back. The false tenor to her essence eases under my touch. I'm not a healer, but I can manipulate essence.

"Oh," she sighs, swaying into me. "That's nice. I thought ... maybe ... I thought we could hang at your place tonight? If you aren't too mad?"

"I told you I can drive," DeVille snaps.

"And take us where?" Presh finally deigns to address DeVille. "You live with your parents."

"I have access to Rought's place."

She snorts. "Where Rought always is, glued to his computers."

"Yeah, and he's currently seriously distracted. Not that anyone will tell me why." He narrows his eyes on Presh, sneer firmly back in place, as if he knows that she has the answers he seeks.

He's not wrong. Because I suspect that most of Outcast MC is firmly focused on making sure Presh is safe, if not actively seeking retaliation for her kidnapping in the first place.

It's not really my business. Except for the keeping Presh

safe part. Which is apparently why I'm hanging out at the site of an illegal rave in the early-morning hours.

"I'm starving," I say. "Is there a drive-thru near here? Some place that serves milkshakes?"

Presh presses a hand to her stomach at the mention of food, but then seems fairly perky when she says, "Dairy Queen is still open, isn't it?"

"Ice cream?" DeVille sneers under his breath. "Seriously? Gross."

Kris slips her hand into DeVille's, and he frowns down at her as if he's just noticed her presence. "You can drive me home, DeVille. We can sneak into my bedroom from the backyard window."

He grunts noncommittally, training his attention on Presh again. "They do onion rings at that location, don't they? I'll follow you in my 'Stang."

"Whatever," Presh says, curling her hand around my arm. "I didn't ask for a babysitter."

"And I didn't want you ruining my chances of getting laid when you wandered into a fucking illegal rave without a bodyguard."

"What do you know about it?" Presh sniffs offishly.

He grunts, seriously pissed. "I know you aren't to set foot anywhere without a senior club member with you at all times. I know you are a fucking attention-seeking brat —"

"Nobody asked you!" Presh shouts. Then she sways on her feet and holds her stomach. "You wanna get fucked so bad?" She gestures sharply toward the building's badly lit exterior. "Go ahead!"

"Um ..." Kris attempts to interject. She's transferred her hold to DeVille's forearm because he's clenching his fists.

Again. "Presh and I just wanted to dance. We weren't following you or anything."

Presh narrows her eyes on Kris. "Why would we have followed him? When you snuck into my room, you said —"

Kris interrupts Presh in a rush. "You don't have to go back in, DeVille. Like I said, you can come —"

With his sneer still firmly in place, DeVille keeps his attention trained on Presh. "Maybe I'll make a few calls."

"I already made a call. I called Zaya."

DeVille glances my way, sneering doubtfully now. It's the double raised, arched eyebrows that really sell it.

I wonder if he practices in the mirror.

"And who the fuck is she?"

"My mentor," Presh snaps. "And she isn't going to sell me out just to get ahead with my brothers."

"Our brothers," he snaps back.

"We only share one! And you'd do anything to get your patch!"

"I watched your ass all night, didn't I? I protected you, kept those guys away."

Kris is chewing her lip, glancing between the other two as if she's desperate to redirect the conversation.

I'm getting more than a little antsy myself. It could just be the pungent scent of drugs, vomit, and urine getting to me ... but it might also be the beginning of a knowing.

"I don't need your pathetic protection," Presh says. "You haven't even transformed yet. I have Zaya."

DeVille actually takes a step forward before he gets hold of himself. Taunting shifters who haven't manifested their beast yet is never a good idea.

Presh just raises her chin defiantly.

It's freaking adorable, and maybe it's the almost perfect

mundanity of the moment that keeps me from forcing us all to move on, to move forward.

"Zaya looks like a gentle fucking breeze could knock her over." DeVille's condescending tone as he says my name is spectacular, but the rest of the comeback likely sounds as weak to his own ears as it does to the rest of us. Because his perpetual sneer transforms into a grimace for the briefest of moments.

"Try using all your senses, Andy." Presh draws his name out tauntingly. "Let me help. The moment Zaya stepped into the alley, the entire area got a whole lot more dangerous and a whole lot safer."

"Fine." He settles back on his heels with a belligerent shrug. "Let's see what your brothers have to say about it."

Presh folds her arms, smiling smugly. "Yeah, let's see."

"Okay, onion rings." I finally interject because for some reason, the mention of Presh's brothers rubs at me weirdly. I turn back toward where I parked the truck. Presh instantly follows, only slightly unsteady on her feet. "What else? Fries?"

"Mmm," she says, "they do this double-beef-patty cheeseburger that's great."

I don't eat red meat, but this isn't the time for exchanging personal details.

DeVille, with Kris practically skipping alongside him, dogs our heels. "Then what?" he asks. "The drive-thru and then?"

Presh opens her mouth, but I get there first.

"And then ..." — the universe speaks through me — "... we go to the Outcast main clubhouse."

Presh groans dramatically. "What?! No, Zaya! Everyone we're trying to avoid will be there on a Saturday night!"

I shrug. "That's just how life goes sometimes." Then I

keep walking, because I ignore a nudge from the universe only to my own detriment. And I'm most certainly not going to ignore one when I've got Precious at my side.

"Oh, I can't go to the clubhouse!" Kris cries. "My sister will be there. Plus we're, like, all underage. They won't even let us in."

I stop walking, abruptly and oddly enough that the teens all fall silent around me. The music from the rave is loud, but it doesn't drown out the sound of approaching motorcycles.

"Zaya?" Presh asks quietly. "Your ... um ... your ..."

DeVille interjects, "Your eyes are fucking glowing. It's fucking creepy."

"Stay with me," I murmur. Then, keeping Presh tucked to my side, I pick up my pace until we're back at my truck.

DeVille whistles appreciatively at the restored classic F-100 under his breath, as I practically shove Presh and Kris into the cab. He climbs into the bed of the truck, abandoning his car without prompting from me.

I'm climbing into the driver's seat when three bikers blow by us, then execute a wide U-turn at the next intersection. They pull up in front of the warehouse.

I reach over and press my hand to Presh's head. She curls down in Kris's lap without further prompting. DeVille is casually slumped in the truck bed, but he watches the bikers from the corner of his eye as they stomp off around the warehouse toward the back entrance.

"Unaffiliated," he mutters under his breath, tugging his phone out of his pocket and taking a picture of the motorcycles. That's safer than trying to snap pictures of the bikers themselves.

I close the door and start the engine, then get us back on the road.

"Can we still go to the Dairy Queen?" Presh peers up at me from Kris's lap, seemingly not remotely fussed about being shoved there. And with the way Kris is finger-combing her hair, I can see why.

"Yes," I say.

Presh hums happily.

"I could sit on DeVille's lap," Kris says as she glances over her shoulder to get a glimpse of the shifter in the back of the truck.

All three of them have crushes on the wrong people. Yes, I haven't missed the underlying denial punctuating every sneering word leveled on Presh by DeVille.

It's so ... refreshing.

I would live in this moment with Presh if I could.

That isn't possible for me, I know. I've experienced the life my Aunt Disa led, and she didn't get this. She didn't get to be ... regular.

That doesn't stop me from wishing for it, though, and letting their snarky conversation wash over me for the time it takes to drive to the Dairy Queen.

PRESH, TUCKED NEXT TO ME IN THE MIDDLE SEAT, rests her head on my shoulder. We're waiting for our order in the small parking lot adjacent to the Dairy Queen drive-thru lane. On her right, Kris's attention is trained through the front windshield on DeVille, who's leaning against the front bumper of the truck and smoking. An actual cigarette, which I honestly wasn't certain were even manu-factured anymore. Maybe he has access to a stash.

"Can I ask you something?" Kris murmurs quietly to Presh.

"Anything," Presh says, not sounding at all sleepy. There's a lot of nuance packed into that word, but Kris only reacts to the most surface permission.

"The Outcast and DeVille's mom. They're chosen mates, right?"

"Yeah." Presh straightens, turning toward Kris. "For, like, almost twelve years?"

I keep my gaze on my phone. I've been half-heartedly responding to text messages, but not really wanting to dig into any of the deluge of info Coda has filled my inbox with in the last twenty-four hours. In other words, I'm shamelessly eavesdropping. Because apparently, twenty-nine-year-old me suddenly lives for teenage gossip and intrigue.

"They bonded to strengthen the pack." Kris's gaze hasn't wavered from DeVille's back. "Like, a bitten bond with a ceremony and everything." Her tone is wistful.

Even I can see where this is going.

DeVille, the object of Kris's wistfulness, is gazing off across the parking lot into the nearby closed businesses, all shrouded in moonlight. Presumably watching for any potential attacks coming at us from the main road or the neighboring buildings. He hasn't pulled his phone back out once. At his age, that would usually point to psychopathic leanings — except I suspect he just doesn't want Presh to think he's narcing on her.

Plus, true psychopaths have wonky essence. And yes, I use the term 'wonky' in a purely scientific manner.

"After they had the twins," Presh says with a shrug. "Makes sense."

"But ... they believe in mates," Kris says, with just a hint of it being a question. "Your family, I mean. Like, even essence-bound or soul-bound mates? Zephyr scoffs at all that."

Presh makes a noncommittal noise in the back of her throat, but when Kris leans into her conspiratorially, her lashes flutter and her breathing hitches. Just for a moment.

Again, Kris doesn't notice. Or maybe she doesn't care.

Maybe Presh has something she wants? Maybe being friends with Presh comes with benefits.

I frown internally at the wanderings of my own mind.

"I heard," Kris murmurs, "that DeVille's brother, that your brother Rought, found his soul-bound mate, like, when they were still kids."

Presh stiffens but doesn't answer.

"I heard ... that they bonded, and then she died." Kris, her gaze on DeVille, actually lays a hand on her chest, as if Rought losing his soul-bonded is romantic, not an utter tragedy. "That's why he doesn't date or even fuck anyone. He's still in love with his mate."

"Where did you hear this from?" Presh asks with a bit of a growl.

"Does it matter? The point is ..." Kris tilts her chin pointedly toward DeVille. "None of us are too young to find our soul-bonded mate." She threads her fingers through Presh's, clasping their hands together with a quiet squee.

Presh starts to pull away, but Kris turns her big, guileless, hazel-green eyes on her. "What if it's all three of us?"

Presh scoffs, but her protest comes out a little hollow. "We're way too young to tie ourselves to anyone, even if soul-bonded mates actually exist. Plus, I'm not interested in DeVille."

Kris laughs doubtfully under her breath.

"Kris," Presh says, her tone low and intense, "this is really bad gossip. You shouldn't be repeating it. Rought is an Outcast lieutenant."

Kris shrugs. "I heard Zephyr and Cayley discussing it tonight before they headed out. My sister isn't a gossip."

"But you are."

She giggles. "I so am!"

Presh snort-laughs, seemingly involuntarily. Silence falls between the two, with Kris gazing at DeVille and Presh trying to not stare at Kris. They're still holding hands.

"Why did you want to go dancing tonight?" Presh asks quietly, as if she doesn't actually want the answer. "Because you knew DeVille was going to be at the rave?"

Kris tries to shrug, but Presh gives their clasped hands a little tug, and she sighs instead. "You're going to be mad."

"Why would I get mad?"

"Because the first thing I do when you get back into town is use you to get into a rave. Even though I knew you were on lockdown for some reason."

Kris pauses to give Presh time to offer up clarification. She doesn't. The teen shifter peers at her a bit more closely. "Are you mad?"

"No. I like ... dancing."

Kris grins. "Plus ..."

"Plus what?" Presh sounds preemptively grumpy about whatever secret Kris is about to unload.

"I had a reading."

Presh groans. "Not another one. You're wasting your money!"

"No. She had purple eyes and —"

"Like Zaya's?"

"No, but —"

"You can get purple contact lenses, you know."

Kris groans. "Presh!"

Presh giggles, smirking. "What was your reading?"

"That I would meet my mate while dancing!" Kris squeals quietly.

"So we went dancing," Presh grumbles.

"And met up with DeVille!"

"There were hundreds of people there ..."

"Yes, but ... the psychic also said a bunch of specific things."

"Like?"

"Like ... I would be with a friend with multicolored hair, that we'd have to defy the odds to get where we needed to be. And like, you know, sneaking off the pack property wasn't easy. Also, it had to be the night of the last quarter moon! That's tonight! Well ... almost."

I stop pretending to answer text messages, turning to the girls. "Someone told you to bring Presh to that rave tonight?" I ask.

Both of them turn to look at me, wide-eyed and blinking.

It's possible my tone is a little harsh.

Kris starts shaking her head in a way that reminds me she's still stoned. "No ... no ... no ... not like that. It's just for fun ..."

Presh touches my hand. "It's nothing, Zaya. You know it's a sham, and the so-called psychic just asked some questions and then twisted the things she got off Kris into a fake reading."

Right. Sixteen-year-old girl. What else would she be interested in but mates and raves? "The multicolored hair ..."

"Oh ..." Kris says quietly, as if coming to a realization.

"We ... we were at the Nail Bar ... Cayley was doing Zephyr's nails." She glances over at me. "Cayley's family owns all the Nail Bars along the coast. And she can fix your hair for you too."

Apparently, my hair and nails look so hideous that a sixteen-year-old has managed to shake off her terror of my eyes for at least long enough to offer me personal advice. Great.

Kris continues rambling. "I asked to tag along ... and I ... I might have mentioned Presh's hair, from our last chat, you know ..." She looks at Presh, emanating utter despair. "You think the psychic ripped me off?"

Presh snort-laughs again. "Yeah, she totally played you."

Outside, DeVille snuffs out his smoke, crossing to intercept the guy carrying takeout bags toward us.

"Like there's dangerous goods in Dairy Queen take-out," Presh mumbles. "And the guy is clearly a null."

"It's adorable," Kris says, rolling down the window. "The way he wants to take care of us. Protect us. Plus, nulls can take down shifters. Ever heard of poison?!"

Presh shakes her head at her friend. "Wait! Were Doc and Cay gossiping about Rought in the fucking Nail Bar?"

Kris actually flinches, completely called out.

Presh sighs affectedly.

Outside, DeVille is actually sorting through the bags. The delivery guy looks an instant away from bolting.

"He'd better keep his lips off my shakes," I say. Yes, I ordered two.

Presh laughs, calling through the now-open window, "Don't be a dork, Andy. We're hungry!"

Then, as the three sort through the food, all I can think about is that Rought doesn't have a mate.

His childhood love is dead. So I might not have misread the situation between us at all.

And suddenly, I'm flushing with ... hope? Anticipation? Just like the teenagers fighting over the onion rings.

TWELVE

RECK

Zaya fucking Gage wanders into the fucking clubhouse, sipping from a fucking milkshake, with my little sister in tow. They're trailed by Rought's brother DeVille and Doc Z's little sister, Kris. The teens aren't old enough to have gotten past the bouncers, yet here they are.

Because no one says no to Zaya fucking Gage.

I feel the moment that Rath, situated across from me with Doc perched in his lap, notices the intruder. He's been lounging all insolent and half stoned, barely paying attention to the piece of ass who's been wiggling against his groin for the last fifteen minutes as she chats up Cayley across the table. My brother stiffens, and all his energy zeroes in on Zaya as she saunters over to the bar, barely giving the rest of the biker-crowded room a glance, sucking on that fucking straw.

I must react outwardly as well, though I'm trying not to, because Cay's hand on my thigh drifts higher, and she slants an intrigued look at me. She sat down maybe ten minutes ago. I've barely been paying attention to anything but the trickle of reports coming in on my phone all night. My beer is probably warm, and my suit wrinkled from slouching.

Zaya must have driven right past the Authority agents I've got assigned to her, because I hardly have to glance at the live feed on the top corner of my screen to see that they're still sitting at the edge of the fucking Gage property.

The urge to go on a killing spree floods through my limbs. I keep really, really still. Not ignoring it, but not allowing it to overflow either.

But it's Zaya who notices, not my brother or Cay. Zaya who turns and looks right in my direction, drilling straight through my nonexistent soul with those fucking purple starlit eyes.

The beast pressing rage and heat and burning fucking desire against the inside of my skin — a beast who's been so dormant for the last thirteen fucking years that I've lost access to most of my secondary gifts — writhes under her gaze. Panting with fucking glee.

I refuse to look away.

Zaya smirks in my direction.

Fucking smirks, like I'm nothing. Like I'm nobody.

And the beast quiets.

Just like fucking that.

Because I remember those fucking lips wrapped around more than just a straw. I remember when it was my fucking come she eagerly worked for, that she swallowed with an actual smile.

Cay nestles her hand right up to my groin. I break my staring contest with Zaya and almost shove Cay away, viciously, before I catch myself. And yeah, I'm rock fucking hard. At the simple sight of Zaya Gage drinking a fucking milkshake.

Under the table, Cay tightens her grip on my stiff cock, which is in the process of threatening to burst through the suddenly chafing zipper of my pants, abandoning her conversation with Doc to lean into me and murmur, "You wanna take a trip to the bathroom? I can take care of —"

"No," I snarl. The idea of her lips wrapped around me, of pumping into the heat of her mouth instead of the mouth I want, is abhorrent enough that I instantly soften under her grip.

Cay frowns, then shrugs it off. She doesn't remove her hand from my still-softening cock, though. And the urge to remove it myself itches at me. Yeah, seemingly random erections are unusual for me, sprung forth without pharmaceutical help, or a hell of a lot of effort on Cay's part. Or an even more generalized biological need to simply get off — usually in a room dark enough that I can't see who I'm fucking, and any pussy will do.

I'm an asshole.

I've always been an asshole.

I'm just more vicious about it now.

And Cayley is the one who consistently comes back for me. So I let her, knowing the entire time that I'll fuck up any good thing in my life. And I'll be gleeful about doing so, over and over.

Because I don't deserve good things.

My gaze strays back to Zaya chatting with the kids all perched in a line at the bar and drawing way too much grinning attention from the fucking bartender, who's stupid enough to flirt with fucking danger.

Because I can't take care of good things.

Rath rumbles out something, but before I can piece

together the words, Doc and Cay get in on the conversation.

"Better they're here than at that rave you supposedly aren't sponsoring tonight," Doc says, more playful than judgemental.

Rath grunts, unconvinced. He hasn't taken his eyes off Zaya. Though from this distance, it probably looks like he's eyeing the teens accompanying our wayward, deceitful bond. We're slumped around a table on the far side of the small, currently empty area of the club reserved for dancing. Or, let's be honest — reserved for fucking while removing as little clothing as possible. Bikers, as well as their so-called dates, have to be fucked out of their minds to even plug cash into the jukebox, let alone dance.

A motorcycle club's main clubhouse, especially one filled with mixed-clan shifters, is not the place for our baby sister, Precious, to hang out. I'm surprised that Doc isn't more concerned about her own sister. Everyone is pissed out of their minds or high as fuck, and there are at least three blow jobs in progress in the immediate vicinity. I'm also fairly certain a trio is fucking at the table in the far corner. They're shadowed enough to be discreet, yeah. But the woman is clearly bouncing in one fucking lap while bent over another fucking lap.

Incensed all over again, though it's not that rush of pure killing rage, I'm knocking Cay's hand off me and halfway out of my chair, ready to march over, confront Zaya, and drag Presh back home. A vicious shouting match with Zaya would be almost as good as bending her over the fucking bar and reaming her until she howls my name. But before I can take a step, the front door slams open, hard enough to bang against the wall and rattle the pictures of the club founders hung on it.

Then fucking Rought is striding through into the clubhouse as if he owns the place, as if he shows up every late Saturday night, with his patched leather jacket slung on over a henley and jeans. Dark-gold hair tousled. An easy, wide grin on his golden fucking tanned face.

But none of those things are the norm. Not the smile. Not the easy demeanor. And certainly not him showing up at the clubhouse. Not at night, anyway.

Because everyone wants a piece of Rought.

And Rought wants no one except for his dead soul-bonded fucking mate.

He makes a beeline for Zaya. She's perched on a stool, suckling her fucking milkshake, with the three teens still bunched around her as if they know they're about to get kicked out.

Rought walks right up to her, still grinning like a fucking idiot. He claps DeVille on the shoulder, actually getting a grin in return out of the sullen kid. He presses a kiss to Precious's temple, and she leans into him, smiling softly.

But he doesn't look away from Zaya the entire time.

And she's eyeing him back, face tilted up as he looms over her. He leans around Presh, moving slowly, deliberately, as if he's worried about spooking Zaya. He places a single finger under the milkshake she's holding loosely. He presses upward, raising the shake inch by inch.

They are still fucking staring at each other, deep into each other's eyes. A hum of energy brushes against me. I see Rath twitch when he feels it as well. Cayley and Doc are glancing between our brother and Zaya, leaning across the table with their heads bent together and practically giggling. They don't react to the brush of essence.

Because even a hint of that combination — Zaya with

her golden Angel — is as familiar to me and Rath as the fucking air we're forced to breathe just to fucking survive this shitshow of a life.

Rought twists farther around Presh as he wraps his lips around the straw and takes a long fucking slurp of Zaya's fucking milkshake.

Laughing when she should be nutting him — because no one steals any sort of ice cream from Zaya fucking Gage — she presses her hand against his face, shoving him to the side. He resists, cheeks hollowing as he clearly takes another long drag of the milkshake through the straw.

I can remember what it felt like to be skin-to-skin with Zaya. Even when she was too young for us to be lusting after each other, even before the energy that shifted between us grew in intensity. I remember it so acutely that I can practically feel it dancing across my cheek where she's now touching Rought.

My beast shifts suddenly, as if lunging forward to look out of my eyes. But it's eager, not jealous, radiating a contented fucking warmth that is completely contrary to everything else I struggle to hold at bay inside me.

Fuck me.

Rought allows Zaya to push him off the milkshake, straightening as he smacks his lips, all fucking playful and full of innuendo.

And all the while, I'm hovering half out of my chair, lost in the fucking moment like a completely different kind of asshole. The soul I don't profess to even have aches, all lovelorn. And still viciously angry about it all.

I sit down. I try and fail to tear my gaze away from my brother and the woman who was supposed to be ... supposed to be our crux, our reason. Our existence.

Doc, who always sees too much — and who heard way

too much in the motel room that night — is glancing between Rath, me, and Rought now. Rath is watching our younger brother flirt with our soul-bonded at the bar, a twitch of a smile at the edges of his lips.

I bet he doesn't even know he's fucking smiling. Does his beast purr in satisfaction at the sight? I've never asked either of my brothers if the creatures that make up half their being have been as dormant as mine since Zaya was murdered before our eyes.

Maybe it's just me, and all the guilt I harbor — deservedly — for that day. That dark night of our souls.

Cay, still leaning over the table to gossip with Doc, throws me a knowing smile over her shoulder, settling her hand back on my upper thigh. "I didn't know that Rought and Zaya knew each other. That's so ..." Nose flaring, she trails off before finishing the thought. Probably because she can't figure out my expression, my reaction.

Kitsune shifters are supposed to have other powers. It's not particularly well documented, because like all shifters who transform into unusual creatures — myself and my brothers included — they're careful about what they share of themselves. But I'm fairly certain that some sort of future sense or backsight is one of those abilities.

Which makes the why of 'why did Cayley ever offer to suck my dick in the first place?' a real mystery. Likely because of my position. In the Authority, and unofficially in the club. I didn't question it then, and it doesn't matter now.

Because I can drown myself in alcohol. I can get off in bar bathrooms, I can hunt down essence-twisted criminals and execute them on the spot. And there will still be something wrong with me. Perhaps it's my missing soul, but the silence is never filled, and I've been hearing it for way too long.

And I know.

I know that not even Zaya's return can fill it.

She won't forgive me, won't accept me a second time.

And I'll never ask for that forgiveness, because I fucking loathe her for leaving in the first place. For ruining everything, destroying our futures. Leaving only this rage and silence to fill all the places she's touched.

Presh grabs Rought's phone out of his back pocket and skips off to the jukebox with Kris in tow. DeVille has gotten his hands on some beer. He probably told the bartender it was for Rought, but the teen is the one sipping it straight from the bottle as he leans back against the bar to casually keep watch on Presh.

I finally give in to the impulse to actually push Cay's hand away — she's been teasing up against my still-semi-hard cock again. Because it's Zaya and her stupid milkshake that has me in that state, it's fucking sickening to have Cay's hand on me.

She frowns at me. But this, whatever it even is, is over between us. It's never even really started.

Because I already know that Presh is going to find a song she likes on that fucking jukebox, use Rought's cash app to pay for it because she's a fucking brat, and Zaya is going to dance.

I'm not going to sit here and watch Zaya dance. Watch as the others flock to her, fawn over her, bask in her presence.

I'm going to berate the agents who should be parked outside the clubhouse, not idiotically hovering around a property that no longer contains their target. Then, though my hands have barely healed from this morning's beatdowns, I'm going to see if I can't find a few more assholes to beat near to death.

I shove out of my chair as the first strains of music emanate from the speakers. Doc Z has slid out of Rath's lap at some point while I was fixated on our deceitful bond. I doubt he noticed either.

I also know Rath isn't going anywhere. He'll watch Zaya dance all night. Fuck, he'll watch Rought fuck her in the middle of the dance floor without asking for anything himself. Without even fucking expecting anything. Because as darkly tainted as I am by our childhood, somehow Rath and Rought made it through just slightly less scathed.

But then, they didn't betray our love. Our future.

They didn't conspire, however inadvertently, to murder our soul-bonded. The one person we were created, were literally put on this earth, to protect.

I turn my back and walk away, brushing off whatever Cay calls after me. I pass the bathrooms, heading through the back of the clubhouse to the rear exit, because I can't be in the same room with Zaya Gage one moment longer.

Not without hating her.

Not without wanting to kill her. Because I can't exist, can't function, in the same world as her, and I'm not going to kill myself.

Not without falling to my fucking knees and begging her just to look at me. Look at me and remember.

She could at least remember my fucking name.

I walk away.

I leave my brothers, and I walk away.

I'm good at that.

THIRTEEN

ZAYA

PRESH COAXES MUSIC OUT OF THE JUKEBOX THAT I don't recognize. It's danceable though, and I tell myself that it's a good teachable moment — as I force myself to walk away from Rought, who's grinning at me again like he is the sun and I'm a planet he wants to warm. Presh is relaxed, still slightly stoned, but just enough to get her out of her own way.

I savor the last few sips of my milkshake as I wander into the center of the cleared space that's something like a dance floor. The shake is my second one — Rought wouldn't have gotten his lips anywhere near it otherwise.

The clubhouse is situated on the southern edge of Newport, another of those small townships that pop up all along the coast, about a fifteen-minute drive from the Dairy Queen. The interior space is large and dimly lit, which pleases me, of course. Dingy around the edges, but not dirty.

The decor is worn wood, tarnished brass fixtures, and pockmarked tables, all seeming like a deliberate choice. Comfortable for the club members, and just slightly off-putting to anyone who might accidentally wander in. Not that the two massive shifter bouncers outside double steel-strapped front doors, each with the club patch tattooed on their cheek, wouldn't be deterrent enough.

The thruple who I'm fairly certain I saw fucking in the back corner, as well as the few open blowjobs that were going on under the shadowed tables when we walked in, have either finished up or taken off for more semiprivate spaces. Catching sight of the three teenagers — and recognizing that Presh, the Outcast's niece, was one of them — might have had something to do with that.

Rought doesn't follow me onto the dance floor, but he's still a presence behind me. A lingering warmth at my back that I inexplicably want to cuddle into. I've never felt so instantly comfortable, so hyperaware, with another person. Not even after years of knowing them. Presh's other brother Rath is a silent, mountainous presence at one of the tables, set with a clear view of both the front door, the room in general, and I presume the back door.

Reck, the ridiculously pretty, dark-haired, olive-skinned brother who I vaguely remember confronting me outside the motel, is in the process of shoving his way through the tightly clustered tables, either to take a piss or leave out the back way.

The essence that surrounds Reck is discordant. Volatile. He doesn't feel like a berserker, but he doesn't feel like a normal shifter either. It's not really my business, of course, but I hope someone has him tightly leashed. Because when he cracks, he's going to take a whole lot of people with him.

I don't have to look any closer to know that.

I also … he resembles someone I've recently crossed paths with. Or saw a picture of in the news. Or perhaps he's connected to something I've fixed? It's a more immediate and substantial sense than that hint of familiarity, the otherness, I feel from all the Guerra siblings.

Presh bounces on her heels when I catch her gaze and gesture her toward me. She comes without question. Kris lingers at the jukebox, her gaze over my shoulder on DeVille. Or maybe on Rought. He drew the attention of everyone in the bar when he entered, and most have barely managed to glance away.

I mean, I most definitely see the appeal. But people are gawking as if they've never seen him before, and I would have assumed he's been a fixture in the club for years. A lieutenant by his twenty-first birthday, he said.

Presh, still bouncing gently to the music, hovers a couple of feet away from me. I lean over to say, "Shall we play a game?"

She smirks, nodding eagerly.

"Close your eyes."

She does.

I take a final sip of my milkshake as I step around her slowly. One of the waitstaff turns from bussing a nearby table, and I pop my empty drink container on her tray with a murmured thank you. She nods at me distractedly, heading back to the bar to pick up another round of drinks.

Stepping in time with the music, I complete my circle around Presh, speaking next to her ear again. "The game's called 'stay with me.'"

"Okay," she gushes excitedly.

I allow myself to move to the music a bit more, letting it tug at me, direct me, while I open my senses to take a peek at the vibrant coil of essence, of life force, that surrounds Presh.

We are clearly connected now. The thread between us glimmers, vibrant and full. I allow my focus to fall on that connection, then I tease my fingers across it.

I've never had a person so tied to me before — by pure intent, that is, rather than by blood. So perhaps this is a lesson for me as well as for Presh.

Her mouth falls open a little, and she sways into me, but she keeps her eyes closed.

"Stay with me," I murmur as I move, twisting and bopping to the music myself, slowly twirling around Presh but not quite close enough to touch her.

She's hesitant at first, as expected. But then she falls into dancing. And it's mostly that, just dancing. But once she relaxes, I stay in one place. Mostly. Shifting my hips and shuffling my feet to the music, and every so often giving my connection to Presh a slight tug or tweak.

Still dancing, she moves with those tweaks, guided slightly to the left or directed to the right.

Under the right circumstances, I can move most anyone in a similar fashion by grabbing one of their threads, whether they're connected to me or not. But this is different because of the connection between Presh and me. Once I show her, whether or not she fully understands what she's feeling, I let the thread between us do as it wills.

Then I move.

Presh stays with me, ghosting my footsteps, following my lead. It's subtle. It will look to outsiders as if we're simply dancing together. It might even feel that way to Presh, but subconsciously, she's reacting to the shifts in my essence, in my energy now.

Grinning, I turn my attention to the side of the dance

floor, reaching out and giving the vibrant energy that surrounds Cayley and Doc Z the slightest of tugs toward us. A bare whisper of *intent* because I want to complicate the lesson but not disrupt it. I then glance at Kris and beckon her in the same way.

All three come to us willingly, already dancing, then surrounding Presh and me.

"Stay with me," I murmur to Presh a third time. My words, my command, strengthens the connection between us. Presh gasps.

I step back, then start to slowly weave my way around Cayley, Doc, and Kris. Eyes still closed, Presh follows me. Some of it is pure instinct, and some of it is feeling the energy that crackles around us — and being able to distinguish the tenor of my essence among it.

The song changes. The tempo becomes more upbeat.

Cayley's eyes widen. She glances over my shoulder a moment before a warm body ghosts against my back. He's suddenly close enough to share the energy we both emanate, though not actually touching me.

Rought has joined us.

Presh's eyes snap open to take in her brother with a grin. I don't miss the surprise that flickers over the faces of the others.

More people pile onto the tiny dance floor, forcing us all closer together.

Forgetting the lesson, Presh turns and starts dancing with Kris. Cayley and Doc dance solo near us.

Rought's hand ghosts my hip as I sway and move to the music. Words, lyrics, filter in, the beat moving me. But nothing matters — just for that breath — except the energy shifting between us.

He moves with me like our souls have danced in the

aether before, as if they will dance again and again. And I don't bother questioning that sense. I don't bother analyzing it.

Maybe this moment — though moments are always doomed to end — is a gift from the universe.

Who am I to deny such a thing?

Rought's breath stirs the hair on my neck, and I suddenly wish I'd worn it up. His hand closes gently on my hip. But it's me who takes that step back, closing the space between us.

My heart is pounding, skin prickling. The energy that usually disconcerts … well, everyone … must be pouring off me, but Rought doesn't pull away. His hand tightens on my hip as he runs his fingers down my other arm. I helpfully stretch that arm out to the side, then up around his head. I thread my own fingers through his hair and brush my ass against his groin, barely managing to hold in a groan when I feel his hard, ready cock against my lower back.

No one pays any attention to the two of us, as if all the essence entwining us has created a shield of sorts. Everyone is dancing and laughing. Nobody gives a shit that I'm actually considering twisting around in Rought's arms, somehow getting out of my pants while simultaneously releasing his woefully compressed cock from his own, then climbing him like he's a tree.

My nipples harden, almost painfully.

I've never been so turned on in my life.

The dancers part around us for a moment, and I catch sight of Rath. He's still seated at the table, and his gaze on me, on us, is intensely focused. I can practically see steam rising off him. He deliberately slides one hand off the table, reaches underneath it, and adjusts himself. Leaving his hand out of sight, seemingly on his cock. His other hand is fisted tightly on the table.

Rought laughs. I can see the grin he levels at his brother from the corner of my eye. The rumble of that deep, husky chuckle emanates from his chest across my back.

Heat blooms between my legs. And muscles I'm not sure I've ever properly used clench. Clench! I'm aware that I've been slowly and steadily getting wet, even slick, but this is … I've never felt —

The front doors — both of them — crash open, hard enough that the crack of the hinges, maybe even the door jambs, can be heard over the music.

Chains, backed by two enforcers who are bigger than Rath, maybe even as big as Breaker was, strides into the clubhouse as if he owns it. I see no sign of the two bouncers who were posted at the doors. The interlopers are wearing Cataclysm leathers and literally bristling with weapons.

The kinds of weapons that writhe with dark-tinted essence. Energy presumably designed to take down other shifters.

I know not because I'm usually sensitive to such things, but because I'm supposed to *know*.

Someone pulls the plug on the jukebox.

For a brief moment, as a manically grinning Chains surveys the room with deliberate intent, silence reigns. He has the attention of every shifter in the clubhouse, including Doc and Cayley flanking me, and Rought at my back.

It takes me only a moment to understand that no matter the dark miasma surrounding their weapons, there is no way Chains has stepped so boldly into the literal heart of Outcast territory with only two shifters to back him.

Rath is up from the table and moving past our

grouping before I've even sensed him standing. Maybe he doesn't tweak my senses because he means me no harm. Maybe he can just move that quickly.

The moment Rath's broad back blocks Presh from Chains's view, Rought reaches around and tugs her behind me, placing his baby sister between me and him. Doc does the same with Kris. DeVille is statue-still by the bar. But then there's a ripple of movement through every single other biker shifter in the bar, and he moves through them all to get to us, tucked up against Presh and Rought.

"Chains." Rath's voice rumbles out of the depths of his chest. "You better have a good reason for showing up here."

"Don't worry, junior," Chains says. His Southern-tinted accent is thicker than I remember, likely deliberately so. "I'm not here for baby sis. Though she'd be a bonus." Chains shifts deliberately to his right so he can look around Rath. A wide grin swamps his face as he makes eye contact with me. "Hello, twist." He uses the derogatory term like it's actually an endearment.

Rath briefly glances over his shoulder, eyeing me. Then he flicks his gaze to the side and over my shoulder, taking in the guard now surrounding me. Me and Presh.

"Come with us, and we'll be all gentle-like," Chains continues coaxingly. "The Cataclysm is a little pissed at me, you see, for what you did to Breaker. But we can make it up to him. Together."

Rath chuckles. "I'm tempted to let you have Zaya, just to watch her utterly annihilate you and your ... friends." He sniffs the air, then exhales harshly as if he's smelled something disgusting.

I presume it's the weapons or the dire-wrought essence that I'm certain is what fuels those weapons. But maybe it's the two shifters backing Chains. Now that I've spent some up-close and personal time with a berserker, I'm absolutely sure Chains has gone and collected two more before wandering into the club.

"Ah," Chains croons. "Don't worry about us, junior. We're warded for awry." He shoves back one side of his jacket, displaying a cracked black stone set in a metal brooch pinned to his belt or through one of his belt loops. Pewter, maybe?

It's a dire-wrought construct. More specifically — because dire mages manipulate or destroy everything they touch themselves — it's a protection artifact crafted by a fabricator, then infected with dire essence. The blackened, cracked gemstone makes that obvious.

I don't know exactly what it does. But what it doesn't do is ward anyone against the likes of me. Because despite how many lives would have been sacrificed to darkly twist that artifact, whatever dire mage the Cataclysm Motorcycle Club has in its ranks can't possibly contend with the Conduit for all life force, all essence. Even if she — me — hasn't fully settled into that position yet.

Before more words can be bandied about, a *knowing* seizes me. I actually freeze in place, the sensation wiping out my regular senses long enough that I miss a few bits of the mounting aggression between Chains and Rath.

I open my eyes, not realizing I've closed them. Lines of essence are now suddenly woven through the room. In the second it takes me to get my bearings, I see a slow creep of black along the threads emanating from Chains and his two berserkers.

Well, that's uncomfortably new.

But the slow creep of those pending deaths makes one thing immediately clear.

I can stop this.

"Zaya," Rought murmurs from behind me, concerned.

The *knowing* tugs on me, gently but in three separate directions — Presh, DeVille, and Kris. I need to get them out of the building.

Presh curls her fingers around mine, and I spare a moment to offer her what I hope is a comforting smile. "Stay with me," I whisper.

She nods tentatively. "Do I need to close my eyes?"

The *knowing* shoves at me, pushing me in the direction of the bathrooms and presumably the rear exit beyond. "Grab DeVille."

Presh instantly wraps her hand around DeVille's.

Without looking at her, I grab Kris and attempt to tug her away from Doc Z and toward DeVille. Even after desperately flirting with him all evening, the teen shifter resists me, yanking her arm free from me with a short, terrified scream.

She stumbles to the side, instantly snagging Chains's and the berserkers' attention. But they quickly look to me.

"Already, twist?" Chains laughs, leering. "Practically begging for it, ain't she?"

Doc lunges for Kris, grabbing her arm and snarling under her breath, "Go with —"

It's too late.

The *knowing* slams into me, and all I can do is move with it, taking Presh and DeVille with me. I turn and walk off the dance floor, cutting back through the tables. Not running, but moving at a steady pace. The bikers close ranks around us as we go. Rought and Cayley shift forward to back Rath.

We're at the start of the hall when Chains smashes a potion vial on the floor at Rath's feet. He must have had it tucked in his hand. Black shadowy essence pours from the vial, instantly flooding the floor.

Presh screams a warning and tries to tug away from me. I keep moving. The *knowing* has me in its grasp, and I'm not foolhardy enough to try to manipulate or even bend it to my will. Not yet.

Two more vials crack on the floor behind us. Presh is thrashing against my hold. DeVille, surprisingly focused, flips her up over his shoulder and grabs my hand instead.

She shrieks again.

DeVille snarls. "Keep your fucking mouth shut and hold your fucking breath, princess."

I don't glance back. I already know what's happening behind us. It's the sharp cries of pain that really sell it. Shifters typically have a high tolerance for pain, likely because they start transforming in their late teens. Even though they harness their internal essence to do so, rearranging your entire physical being into a completely different form hurts.

But I don't turn back, because the *knowing* — thick threads of it still wrapped around Presh and DeVille, even while the tie to Kris thins with every step — pushes me, pushes me, pushes me all the way to the club's back door.

The universe wants, maybe even needs, Presh and DeVille to survive whatever is about to happen. But fate and destiny are always somewhat malleable — free will and all that — and Kris clearly made a different choice in the moment.

I get a flash of memory, of a note I recently jotted on a piece of motel stationery. For Doc. At the behest of the universe.

Choice, not fate, not love or devotion, twists the path.

And not always in the way intended.

I shove the unhelpful recollection away.

Behind us, the hallway lights start to wink out, though from the blackened essence swelling behind us, not any sort of electrical issue. DeVille is squeezing my hand so hard that he's grinding my bones together. Presh has gone quiet.

The miasma of dire magic keeps filling, keeps flooding into the hall behind us. We pass the bathrooms and a couple of offices on our left. I can see the glow of the emergency exit sign just ahead.

Quiet falls behind us — except for the crunching of bones. Then pounding footfalls follow in our wake. We're about to be chased. Which means that Chains and his enforcers are immune to or protected from whatever they hit the rest of the club with.

I run now, not having to encourage DeVille in the least. Practically side by side, we blow through the rear entrance and into the mist-shrouded night. There's an overhead light above the door, a composter to our right, and a large fenced parking lot filled with motorcycles between us and the neighboring building.

Reck and the two Authority agents, the mage Clara and the shifter Brett, spin toward us as we tumble through the door. They've clearly been arguing, and clearly haven't heard or felt any of what's occurred in the club. At a quick glance, the rest of the immediate area is quiet, practically silent. Windows in the apartments tucked behind and over the closest storefronts are all dark.

The mage and the other shifter instantly train weapons on us.

The *knowing* snaps out ahead in a pulsating pattern,

toward them, presumably because they're attempting to block our way to the side street.

I realize that it must look as though we're trying to kidnap Presh.

But before I can offer any explanation, time slows. Literally.

The agents fire their weapons.

"Stay with me," I whisper, shoving my shoulder against DeVille's side and forcing him two steps to the right as we continue to run directly at the agents.

A projectile wings past my cheek, cutting through my hair. Another skims DeVille's shoulder, creasing his leather jacket.

"No!" Reck screams.

I let go of DeVille's hand, stepping fully in front of him. And because the universe has a strange sense of humor, that *knowing*-prompted maneuver puts me directly into the path of the third bullet. Apparently, the shifter has already pulled a second weapon.

Purple eyes really do freak the Authority out, even more than for most other people. Through hard-earned experience, no doubt.

Reck grabs for the extended arm of the mage — she's pulled a wand — even as the shifter gets off a third shot.

The fourth bullet — because I'm apparently counting while still trying to run — abruptly veers to the right, taking a chunk out of the brick back wall of the clubhouse instead of embedding itself in my forehead.

The fifth bullet explodes just as it's exiting the chamber of the gun. It takes the gun, and possibly the shifter's finger, with it.

"Holy fuck!" DeVille shouts, tight at my back.

Still running, I weave between the now-screaming

shifter clutching his hand and the mage who's wrestling with Reck.

The rear door to the clubhouse slams open a second time. Surrounded by that darkly tinted miasma of corrupted essence, Chains strides through, swiftly followed by his two berserker buddies. The berserkers haven't transformed. Yet.

Reck and the mage instantly turn to confront this new threat. But whatever was contained in those dire potion vials gets to them first. It twists up around their feet and legs. The last licks of it grab the wounded shifter as well. He screams, as does the mage. But even as the darkness is twisting around Reck's neck, he somehow manages to look to us and shout, "Run!"

We're already running.

We are not, however, faster than a shifter and two berserkers.

Presh screams once more as her brother goes down. I veer around the corner out onto the street, DeVille keeping pace with me.

The *knowing* holds me tightly in its grasp, forcing me to run down the middle of the street, toward the beach — I can hear crashing waves in the near distance. A few resorts and motels speckle the coastline to the north, but that all ends abruptly at the forested border to my dominion. A residential area spreads out on the other side of the main road behind us. All the other shops and restaurants around us are closed. I'm hoping that means few innocent bystanders will be caught up in what's happening — in what's still about to happen, given the strength of the *knowing* dragging me forward.

Chains and his buddies are on the street behind us, closing in quickly, when something explodes. Something massive. Debris is suddenly pelting the pavement all around us — metal roofing, hunks of two-by-four, plywood, drywall, and copper piping.

None of it touches me or DeVille or Presh. A clearly delineated path stretches out before us.

Chains and the berserkers shout behind us. Splitting up, they dart to the sidewalks and under the cover of storefront awnings and covered doorways to avoid the rain of debris.

An earth-shattering roar follows the explosion.

The *knowing* hiccups oddly, releasing me for a moment.

I stumble to a halt, glancing back.

A massive creature has burst through the roof of the clubhouse. It claws itself partially upright, even as the walls crumble under its weight. Then it perches for a moment, gaze trained on the road.

On us.

Iridescent scaled skin. A massive sharp-toothed maw. Razor-sharp hooked claws. Wicked white bone antlers. A wild mane flickering with energy ...

The creature's head is larger than what I can see of its serpentine body.

It's a ... it's a fucking dragon.

A celestial dragon?

"Put me down," Presh says. And when DeVille just stares up at the fucking dragon that's taken out the entire roof of the clubhouse, she pummels his back. "Put me down, asshole. It's Rath!"

I blink.

It's Rath?

Chains dashes back into the middle of the street, staring back at the dragon as well.

Rath — who is apparently also a celestial dragon, an

actual mythical creature — opens his maw and emits a roaring challenge.

I clamp my hands over my ears.

The sound wave rolls up and over us as windows explode all along the street. DeVille wraps himself around Presh, hunkering down, but not a single shard hits us.

I'm honestly not certain if it's the universe intervening, or if there's something more going on. Something with all three of the brothers and me.

Chains snarls viciously, shielding his face.

The two berserkers drop hard, slamming into the pavement and confusing me for a moment. Darkly tainted essence roils around each of them as they start to transform. They tear through their leathers as they manifest shaggy fur, rounded snouts edged with jagged teeth, and claws longer and thicker than my fingers. Both of them are larger by far than Breaker was on the beach — whose own transformation was perhaps impeded by Muta's venom?

Yeah, if I had a secondary form that was nearly impossible to kill, I'd make use of it the moment the dragon showed up as well. I'm guessing that the dire potions Chains used on the Outcast shifters had an unintentional side effect. Because Rath presumably wouldn't have chosen to transform while inside the clubhouse if he'd had the option.

The *knowing* snaps sharply into place, yanking me ever forward.

"Stay with me," I say, tucking Presh's hand in mine. I start running again, but manage only four or five strides before over a dozen bikers overrun the street ahead of us. Unaffiliated bikers as far as I can tell — maybe even including the three that we last saw outside the rave.

The fact that they're all pointing primed weapons our way makes it clear whose side they're on.

I keep running.

"What the fuck, Zaya?!" DeVille shouts from Presh's other side.

"Stay with me," I say, not giving myself a chance to question the *knowing* as it directs us straight through the center of the biker mob. Because questioning it might unintentionally affect it to some extent. And Chains is right behind us.

Farther back, Rath roars again. Then, punctuated by the sound of the remainder of the back wall of the clubhouse crumbling, he launches himself into the sky.

He can fly. Without fucking wings.

Though it's almost sleek in comparison to his head, his serpentine body is easily the length of two city buses. Maybe three.

The sky abruptly opens up, torrential rain suddenly pounding us, flooding the street.

I keep running, puddles splashing underfoot now.

We're only a dozen feet away from the wall of shifters.

I can literally feel Chains at my back. The berserkers have to be near as well.

Then the entire area is suddenly alive with transformed shifters. They swarm in on silent paws, hooves, and wings from the direction of the clubhouse. They gallop, leap, and wing their way past us, attacking the unaffiliated bikers. A creature in the form of a red fox with multiple tails leads the charge, so large that she easily comes up to my shoulder. Shrieking as if she's exalting death and all it entails.

Kitsune. Cayley.

The bikers discharge their dire-fueled weapons. Pained

snarls and sharper shrieks fill the air. The rain obscures my vision.

Still running, I follow the *knowing* as it guides me through the shifter war zone.

DeVille and Presh stay with me.

A fucking glowing satin-white pegasus lands in front of us, right in the path of the *knowing* and forcing us to stumble to a halt. Kris is sliding off the mythical creature's back and flinging herself into DeVille's arms before I even fully recognize her through the rain.

Chains grabs for my shoulder from behind, but his fingers slip off my soaked-through sweater.

The pegasus — Doc Z — rears up and slams both her front hooves into Chains's chest.

I grab the teens and spin us all, twisting us around the pegasus as she pummels Chains.

More dire energy explodes between them. The pegasus shrieks in pain.

"No!" Kris cries, trying to yank free of me and DeVille.

But I keep hold. I keep running.

A thick fog is rolling toward us from the beach. The *knowing* guides us within it. The fog muffles sight as well as sound — making it clear that there's nothing natural about it. The rain continues to assault us. But I don't take the time to ponder what the *knowing* shields us from and what it doesn't.

Unable to see or sense more than a couple of feet ahead, I slow my pace.

Kris is sobbing, pressing herself to DeVille's chest enough to impede his stride. Likely noting my look, Presh tries to console her friend quietly, though her own deep-purple eyes are wide with terror. Shimmering with whatever power is in the slow process of manifesting within the emerging awry.

Seeing that purple hue in Presh's eyes, I realize that my own eyes are glowing so strongly that they reflect back against the thick, light-gray fog as it begins to slowly part before us. The *knowing* has quieted, as if we're momentarily shielded from whatever destiny is coming for the three teens at my side.

One of the berserkers — easily seven and a half feet tall, with the bulk of a grizzly and a much longer reach — suddenly appears out of the fog. It pivots, snarling, as if it's just sensed us as well. The berserker's head is set slightly forward, shoulders rounded. Jagged sharp teeth bristle in its wide mouth, dripping with blood-tinged saliva.

And it's not slowly dying from Muta's venom, as Breaker did.

Fucking Kris shrieks and literally drops in place.

I have no idea if she's fainted or simply lost her mind.

DeVille manages to keep Presh on her feet, though Kris almost takes her down as well.

The berserker's attention snaps to the prey so willingly making itself available for consumption.

DeVille shoves Presh behind him.

The *knowing* is still inexplicably tugging us gently forward. Right into the claws of the berserker.

I might be a believer, but even that gives me pause.

Kris twines herself around DeVille's leg in utter stupidity. So she hasn't fainted. She's just a fucking moron.

My right arm goes heavy as Muta takes on his bushmaster form, slithering up my arm under my sweater and out the collar to curl over my shoulders. He's going to be seriously pissy about getting so wet, though getting his fangs into another berserker might mollify him some.

The berserker stalks toward us, chuckling and darkly gleeful.

DeVille presses Presh up against my back, sandwiching her between us even as he reaches down and tries to drag Kris to her feet.

Anchored on my shoulder, Muta rears up, hissing at the berserker, who is about to attempt to eat us.

"When Muta strikes," I murmur, "we run. Forward."

"Forward ... ?" DeVille asks doubtfully.

"We'll stay with you, Zaya." Presh presses her face against my back, between my shoulder blades, almost as if she's gaining strength from the connection.

The fog suddenly presses down around us, a swirling vortex encasing us and the berserker. Then it parts overhead. I blink up through the torrential rain as a huge shadow sweeps past, then spins back. Sharply taloned legs drop into strike position.

The creature's body composition is ... odd ...

The winged form emits an ear-shattering shriek.

I clap my hands over my ears, noting the teens all doing the same, though they're ducking down even as I stand upright like an enchanted idiot.

The berserker has a moment to look up and get an arm over its head before the creature slams into it from above.

I catch sight of gold-edged wings, a sharp yellow beak the length of my forearm, the wicked talons of an enormous bird of prey, and the muscled, golden-furred body of a huge lion — then the creature and the berserker are in an all-out brawl of tooth and claw, literally tearing into each other as they roll off into the thick fog.

I instantly break into a run. Muta cinches just a little too tightly around my neck, which is his oh-so-subtle way of letting me know he doesn't enjoy being jostled. Drawing the teens with me, I race for the beach — I can hear the surf clearly now. But I can't help but gasp, "Was that a fucking gryphon?"

"Rought!" Presh announces proudly, tucking her hand back into mine.

Fuck me. A celestial dragon and a gryphon in the same familial line? I know they're half-brothers, but ... mythical creatures no longer walk the earth. At least not to my knowledge.

The universe — or maybe the sleeping gods — is having a colossal laugh today.

As I let the steady tug of the *knowing* draw me on, I glance briefly back. I've got Presh's hand in mine, but taking off again without warning DeVille has left him a few steps behind. Sneer firmly in place, he's got Kris clinging to his upper front body like a cuddly bear — and looks pissed as hell about it. Understandably so, since having her over his shoulder or on her own feet would make it easier to fight if he needs to.

Whatever kind of shifter Kris will eventually transform into, she's definitely prey. Though understanding that the pegasus is her sister, Doc Z, I'm reminded that not being a predator doesn't necessarily make her any less fierce.

The *knowing* snaps back to me, almost as if the thread has been snipped ...

I stumble to a stop, the fog thickening again.

Something has shifted.

Something powerful enough to momentarily stymie the fucking universe.

A sharp curl of fear runs through me. I tuck the three teens behind me as best I can while I slowly pivot. DeVille gets Kris on her own feet finally, then sandwiches her and Presh between us as he turns to face the other way.

The *knowing* roils in place under my feet, as if waiting ... waiting ... to send me off in the correct direction.

The fog slowly thins in a circle around us, as if pushed back by a force I can't feel. The rain eases to a light shower. We're soaked and panting, but too pumped from running to be cold yet.

The fog clears even more. And I finally see that we're surrounded.

A dozen or more shifters are arrayed at our backs, bloodied and bleeding. I can see the kitsune and the pegasus — who's favoring a broken leg. The Outcast shifters stand grouped together, holding but wary.

The group blocking our way to the beach includes Chains and one severely mauled and panting berserker. Chains holds a weapon the size of a small cannon, and he points it at me the moment he catches sight of us in the thinning fog. He's scratched and battered, but clearly hasn't been injured enough that he's been forced to transform to help himself heal.

Needing to heal might explain why the Outcast have all taken their beast forms, even when some of them, including Doc Z, might be more effective retaining human form. Rath would definitely have preferred to not destroy the clubhouse if he could help it.

Silence hangs, disrupted only by the steady sprinkle of rain on the metal rooftops of a restaurant to our left and an antique shop to the right, both closed.

The berserker trembles, vibrating. In anger, not fear. Its mouth is still dripping a steady stream of blood-laced saliva.

A huge form pads out of the fog to our left, past the restaurant and directly in between the two groups. It heads in our direction even as its broad head swings side to side. Though shaped vaguely like a huge hound, it's as large as the largest bull I've ever laid eyes on. Its soft-footed paws are the size of dinner plates. It's covered in thick and shaggy green hair, and its glowing gaze, its energy, is utterly malevolent.

I have no idea what sort of creature this is, but each group of shifters, friends and foes, collectively takes a step back as it reveals itself.

That malignant energy — death incarnate? — emanates from it, causing a ripple of fear, of terror, to run through everyone gathered around me. Including the teens pressed against my back.

Chains aims the small cannon, and the dire charge loaded within it, at the hound creature.

Well, that clears up the loyalties. The creature might not be on our side, but it isn't on Chains's payroll either.

Presh tries to shift around me. I catch her with one arm stretched to the side, but she resists being pushed back. "Reck," she murmurs in my ear.

She knows the shaggy bull-hound creature. Which flashes a wickedly sharp set of teeth in our direction, showing off long canines. The split of the gigantic maw is too large even for the wide head. The creature chuckles darkly.

So ... that's a smile?

Behind me, Kris vibrates with pure terror but is otherwise frozen in place. And she's not the only one. At least a half-dozen shifters on both sides of the fray stumble back in sheer terror.

"Cu-sith," I say — pronouncing it 'coo-shee,' from the old Gaelic. The universe voices the knowledge of what we're all facing through me. And my naming the creature, acknowledging Reck's beast form, pulls his attention firmly to me.

With wisps of the fog clinging to him, the cu-sith pads across the wet pavement, closer and closer to me. I'm caught in his gaze, also frozen in place.

And I know what I'm looking at now.

Another creature of pure myth — this one occasionally called the grim reaper.

Looking into his glowing green eyes, I'm completely certain that Reck isn't in control of his beast right now.

And with that assessment made, I finally see the energy streaming from the cu-sith in all directions. Those thick ropes of essence tangle with and through the weave of all the life force — all the life-fueling essence within every being — in the immediate area.

As I watch, it all blackens. Not simply the creeping blackness — the pending promise of death — that I saw radiating briefly from Chains and the berserkers in the club.

No.

Every single thread.

Of every single being in the immediate area.

Withers.

Dying.

Presh inhales shakily, pressing her face against my back.

She can sense it as well.

A *knowing* snaps into place, wrapping around the trio of teens and yanking me so harshly to the right and away from the cu-sith that I nearly stumble. A desperate tenor I've never felt from a *knowing* now runs through that energy.

But instead of following blindly, I try to ignore it. Just for one more moment.

The silent hunter steadily approaching me will chase us if given the opportunity. If we run, not all of us are going to make it.

The universe never minds playing with steep odds, but I occasionally do. Especially because the radiating lines of life force woven through and around both foe and friend are continuing to wither. Some are starting to flake away.

I've never seen such a thing, not unless the person in front of me is actually in the process of dying. And even that process is different. More of a fading.

The *knowing* might save me, might save Presh.

But everyone else is going to die.

"Shut your eyes, Presh," I order, not taking my gaze off the cu-sith.

"What?"

"Shut your eyes."

"But —"

I press her hand into DeVille's. And I know he understands, because he heaves the utterly terrified Kris up over his shoulder.

The cu-sith hasn't barked yet. Hasn't made any noise other than that earlier chuckle.

What was the myth? The fable?

Three barks, and anyone within hearing distance will die of sheer terror?

"I can't do it without you," Presh cries.

"Then just run, Precious. Just run. Hold onto DeVille." I press their clasped hands between mine, not dropping the cu-sith's glowing gaze as I silently wish them safe passage. "The path leads directly to the beach. Don't stop!"

She hesitates.

"Now!" I bark.

Everything happens all at once.

The cu-sith gathers himself to leap the last few steps to me. The fucking dragon that is Rath swoops out of the sky and snatches the last berserker in his front set of claws.

Chains pivots and discharges his hand cannon at the dragon — only to get attacked from behind by the gryphon that is Rought.

DeVille, dragging Presh and carrying Kris, takes off toward the beach, following the beckoning path of the *knowing* whether he's aware of it or not.

And I step away from the path the universe wants me to take, trusting that it will guide Presh. Instead, I stupidly step into the path of the cu-sith.

The shaggy bull-hound nearly barrels into me. But he manages to check his forward momentum, ending up with his nose practically pressed to my neck.

He inhales deeply.

Still otherwise silent.

So silent.

A vibration runs through Muta, still curled up my arm and over my shoulder. But instead of biting the cu-sith, the death-god bushmaster simply turns his head away dismissively. Then he re-forms into a bracelet around my bicep, as if he couldn't be bothered to slither all the way down my arm. Muta really does hate the rain that much.

Also ... it's possible that he's ceding to the cu-sith because they are ... alike, somehow? One god of death acknowledging another?

I can't think about that. I can't worry about anything else — not the battle that's resumed around us, not Presh fleeing unguided behind me, and not even the knowledge that ignoring a *knowing* comes with consequences. Always.

Instead, I reach up and gently rub the tip of one of the cu-sith's shaggy-furred pointed ears. The bull-hound huffs a breath against my neck, and I feel the slight scrape of teeth as he angles his head into my hand.

"That's enough for tonight," I say, continuing to scratch behind an ear larger than my hand.

The cu-sith chuffs again, clearly disagreeing.

"Precious needs us," I say, hoping Reck is aware and functional within his beast. "Let's go make sure she's okay."

The cu-sith nudges me — likely trying to be gentle, but strong enough that I stumble back, tightening my hold in his thick fur to keep my footing. He doesn't appear to mind me clinging to him.

A residual sliver of the *knowing* still stretches toward the beach. As I blink a few times, I see that the promised death and destruction that blackened all the life force surrounding us has eased.

Chaos reigns around us, but with the cu-sith prowling silently at my side — so large I can't actually see over him — I begin to run again.

More malignant essence explodes behind us. Chains and the Cataclysm Motorcycle Club came ready for this fight, and they don't seem to care how many people get caught between me and them. With Presh as Chains's 'bonus.'

Apparently going back to the Cataclysm empty-handed isn't an option.

THE BEACH IS EMPTY.

No Presh, DeVille, or Kris.

No footprints.

The surf is raging halfway up the shore. Long stretches

of rain-soaked empty beach stretch to either side. The *knowing* has completely dissipated.

I've fucked up.

I'm certain I saved a lot of lives, but now I'm going to have to navigate the aftermath on my own. While keeping the murderous cu-sith placated as he stands sentry at my side.

I hear Presh shout, "No! Kris!" from somewhere behind us.

The shaggy green monster stays with me as I pivot and run from the beach, back the way we've come. Which is good, I suppose, because he's not the benevolent sort. And although rushing ahead of me to his sister's rescue might be ideal, I don't want him accidentally killing her in the process.

The road that runs along the beach is empty. The *knowing* doesn't kick in, though, no matter how hard I strain all my senses in search of Precious.

"Which way, cu-sith?" I ask coaxingly. Struggling to keep calm as I slow my pace at the first cross street. A closed bakery occupies one corner with a dress shop on the other. The glass in both sets of darkened windows has survived the roar of the celestial dragon.

The cu-sith huffs — just a breath of air, no actual sound — but otherwise doesn't offer an opinion. I choose to believe it's because he can't pick up his sister's presence and not because he doesn't care.

I pause and strain some more — my ears, my eyes, and my other senses. I just need to be patient for a moment more. Some of that dire-wrought magecraft seeps toward us, most likely residual from all the battles that have been waged in the last few minutes on the streets of this small township. But it's coming at us from three directions, so it's no help.

How many malignant potions and spells could Chains have possibly been carrying? One of the reasons dire mages are held in natural check is that they burn themselves out, usually fairly quickly after they've gone dark. Moderation is fundamentally contrary to what fuels a dire essence-wielder.

Though I once would have thought the same of berserkers, and I've recently been given a painful lesson in my own ignorance.

What I do know for certain is that dire-wrought spells and potions have a shelf life. A short one. Otherwise, a single dark-essence-wielder could spend a half-dozen years building an arsenal — then wipe a fortified city from the face of the planet before anyone strong enough to stand against them could even be notified.

"The dire mage is here," I whisper to the grim reaper at my side the moment I realize it. "Can you track her?"

Has Chains brought the mage for backup? Or has she decided to join the raiding party on a whim?

The battle has quieted up ahead, and despite the dark night and continual rain, I see a winged form and a large serpentine creature take flight, swiftly gain altitude, then sweep around. Toward us.

I continue walking, still reaching outward with all my senses.

"Oooo, aren't you a pretty monster?" The voice emanates from the center of the street to my left.

A street that appears empty.

Cloaking spell. A casting strong enough to obscure my sight despite the amulet hanging around my neck.

The universe's sense of humor is more twisted than I could have guessed. Or I'm way, way off the path.

"We have the princess," Chains says. His voice is clear,

echoing lightly against the low buildings around us. He's pissed. But not at us. "Teleport us the fuck out of here."

"Not yet," the other person says. "You brought me here to play and look at the pretty puppy!" Her voice is pitched high and playful. And terrifyingly familiar.

All the hair on the back of my neck prickles.

"That is not a fucking dog!" Chains snarls.

Energy buffets me from behind, stirring my sopping-wet hair. Then the ground rumbles under my feet. Literally. Twice.

Two more massive presences, both even larger than the cu-sith at my side, now occupy the entire width of the block behind me. But I don't look back.

At any moment, the cloaking spell shielding Chains and the others from view is going to part — to my sight at least — and I need to be ready.

The celestial dragon and the gryphon tuck up around the cu-sith and me, as much as the narrow street allows. At least one parked vehicle gets crushed in the process.

Rought, the gryphon, rears up on his lion's hind legs and strikes at the seemingly empty air before us with his taloned front feet.

He tears through the dire-wrought cloaking spell. Literally.

Perfect. And much better than waiting for my own sight to compensate.

The cloaking spell hangs in pieces, revealing Chains with DeVille prone at his feet. I can't tell if the young shifter is breathing.

The Cataclysm biker's clothing is shredded, and he's covered in blood, though I can't make out any open wounds against the black of his leathers. He must have gotten away from Rought and the main battle, maybe transforming at some point to help heal himself. Though I'm not sure enough time has passed for that.

Presh stands on the sidewalk, well out of Chains's reach, with the darkened windows of a used bookstore at her back.

She's pointing a large weapon, looking like some oversized gun, at Kris's chest.

Only a couple of feet away from Chains, Kris shimmies her hips affectedly, grinning manically at us.

Precious's arms shake from holding the dire-wrought gun. She's gotten it off Chains somehow? Maybe when DeVille attacked him? It teems with more of that malignant essence.

Kris shifts her feet and sways her hips even more, stretching her arms to the sides. As if mimicking dancing, but there's no joy in the movement. Her hazel eyes no longer sparkle with mischief. And she's ignoring DeVille for the first time all night.

Even in the minimal light from the streetlamps, I can see that her eyes are now edged in darkness ... black bleeding through the whites.

Possessed.

"Zaya?" Presh asks fearfully. "Can you ... can you ..."

I know what she's asking.

I also know there's a really good chance that Kris is already dead.

Because the dire mage is, in fact, not here. But either through previous contact with Kris or something Chains triggered when he realized he wasn't just walking away from this fight, the mage has gained access to Kris's consciousness. To her body and voice. Enough to either channel essence through her — and Chains's demanding to be teleported backs that supposition — or to utilize the last of Chains's arsenal.

Except for the gun now in Presh's hands.

Kris's gossip session at the nail salon takes on an entirely new tenor. Chains couldn't get to Presh on my property — assuming he could even determine its location — or on the main pack property. So the mage stepped in to lure Presh to the rave, using Kris.

"Come to me, Presh," I say, trying to sound calm and completely failing. I've never gone up against a dire mage, not one-on-one. But I've seen the devastation they can unleash. Multiple times.

"Yes," the mage piloting Kris says sweetly. "Run over to your ... Zaya, was it? Is there a last name to go with the first?"

"Playtime is over, Bellamy," Chains snaps. "We've lost. Use your fucking eyes. Grab the princess, bring us home."

Kris whirls around and slaps Chains across the face. He actually staggers back from the blow.

She giggles. "Nasty, nasty shifter. You know what you were supposed to do!" Then she twirls in place as if testing out the body she's wearing.

Rage is bristling off the cu-sith at my side. The energy emanating from the gryphon and the dragon is oddly staticky. They've both taken a beating, including whatever Chains originally hit them with in the clubhouse.

More problematically, anything any of the fucking mythical creatures at my side attempt to do in the next few moments is liable to get Presh hurt. Or dead. They're too large for this space, too much. Overkill.

"Come to me, Presh," I say again.

"And you'll save Kris?"

"Yes," I lie. "I'll save Kris."

Precious finally relents. Arms now shaking with the effort of holding the weapon aloft, she skirts the front of the bookstore, heading in our direction.

Kris watches her, pouting.

Chains flicks his gaze between me and the dire mage inhabiting the sixteen-year-old walking dead.

"Now, Zaya," Kris says, "lying doesn't become you."

Presh stiffens, stumbling to a stop. Then she levels a look of disbelief on me.

Kris throws her head back and laughs. Malignant, stomach-roiling energy floods from her.

Then she drops to the pavement like a rag doll, head thunking hard.

Drained of essence, dead.

Presh cries out. The sound slices through my very being like an empathic knife. I almost stagger under an onslaught of grief that isn't my own — even as that grief tangles with my own recent pain and loss, amplifying it twofold.

Chains stares down at Kris, utter disbelief etched across his face. Then he looks up at me, at the monsters standing with me.

His energy shifts. His essence is twisting, but he's not ... dying ... he's ...

"No!" I cry, not even certain what I'm trying to stop. And it's just me, my voice. Because the universe has abandoned me to my fate, to live through the ramifications of what I've caused by ignoring an ongoing knowing.

Chains lunges forward, snatches Kris off the ground. His teeth lengthen as I watch in horror.

Then he rips out her throat. Drinking Kris's blood even as it goes cold.

Oh, Precious.

She screams. More pain rolls off her, lashing against me as she drops the gun and runs to her dead friend.

DeVille suddenly moves, not dead after all. Brought back to consciousness by Precious's scream? He tries to surge to his feet, grabbing for Presh as she passes, but he manages only to slow her for a moment.

Chains is still gulping down Kris's blood, though most of it appears to have soaked her limp body and the pavement around his feet. He slams a kick to DeVille's ribs, the blow so forceful that DeVille loses hold of Presh as he tumbles across the street.

The young shifter slams into a streetlight. Something snaps — possibly his spine. He falls flat, face down, and doesn't move.

I'm already running. But then Chains, moving too fast for me to track, drops Kris and grabs Presh. He pulls the little awry against his chest, wrapping a bloody, clawed hand around her throat.

And I stop.

I stop, still too far away, with my hands held forward, pleading.

The shifters surrounding me halt their forward lunges as well, brushing up against my shoulders before an intense energy swamps over both Rought and Rath. They're trying to trigger their transformations, but can't. Maybe whatever dire-mage potion they inhaled back in the clubhouse has a hold on them still?

All my focus is on Chains's claws slowly pushing into the tender skin of Presh's neck.

"Please," I whisper to Chains. "You can walk away."

"Trade yourself for the little twisted cunt and I will," Chains says. His voice is a pained growl. The bones in his face shift.

The blood drinking ... he is trying to go berserker. But it shouldn't happen that quickly, should it? It shouldn't be something that can just be triggered.

"I will," I say, keeping calm. My gaze is steady on Presh. Her face is turning purple. "But not if you kill her. You're killing her."

Chains still has enough presence of mind that he loosens his grip on Precious's neck.

She gasps, "No, Zaya!"

Chains shakes her so hard that I'm afraid he's going to snap her neck.

"I'll come with you!" I shout. "I'll come with you."

Chains stills, narrowing his eyes on me.

I step forward.

"No, Zaya ..." Presh sobs, her voice strangled and bruised. Broken.

The cu-sith reaches a huge paw around me, claws slicing through my clothing from my lower ribs to my upper thigh. The grim reaper holds me to his chest.

Chains laughs mirthlessly. "Apparently, we're at a stand-off. Fine. The littlest twist will do. He never has to know you even fucking exist. But you better fucking believe he's going to be very interested to discover that the rumors are true. Your mystical fucking pets will be in cages next."

I'm certain that the 'he' Chains refers to is the Cataclysm. I have no idea how the three brothers have managed to keep the nature of their beasts from their own father. Not that it's important in the Now.

And the Now is where I exist.

"I can ... smooth all of this, Chains," I say. "I can give as much as I take, if not more."

Chains scoffs. But he is listening.

"You want to be rich? Powerful? I can fix it all."

"You can't beat the Cataclysm, twist. You've only had a tiny taste of what he can do." He starts dragging Presh back. One step, then another.

Rought and Rath are still caught up in their transformations. Reck in his cu-sith form won't loosen his hold on me.

"No!" Presh kicks uselessly at Chains's legs. "No, I'm not going back!" Her essence curls all around her as usual. But as I watch, all that vibrant energy, all those threads that lead to so many futures, deepen in color.

Not black, but red.

"I won't go back." Presh sobs. "I'd rather die. I'd rather die!"

My heart starts pounding. I've seen this before.

I've seen an untrained awry manifest under duress. And Presh won't survive it.

It's also possible that she could take Chains and her brothers with her. Maybe even the entire township.

"Don't, sweet girl," I plead. My hands fall to the massive claws hooked gently into my clothing, trying to wrestle out of the cu-sith's grasp. "I'll fix it, Precious. I'll fix it."

"He killed Kris!" Presh sobs. Her essence is now condensing, threads weaving tightly together and cocooning her in energy. "He killed DeVille!!"

"What the fuck are you doing?!" Chains snarls — at me. So he can feel the energy about to explode, but he can't see it or reckon its source.

"He wants to cage me. To cage you, Zaya!"

Presh is completely irrational. She has been from the moment she dropped the gun and charged Chains instead of shooting him.

I raise my hands. I reach for all the energy surrounding her. If I can just soothe her ...

The universe nudges me.

Hard.

And I *know* this is my punishment.

I know, and I still follow.

The *knowing* nudges me toward Chains's life force, not Presh's.

I grab hold of it.

Every single thread, and there are more than three. Chains is meant to walk away from this, maybe even with Presh in tow.

He was always supposed to take her back to her father, but then I intervened in the cafe.

And I'm going to do it again.

The moment before I decide to tear every single one of those threads of destiny away from Chains, they blacken under my hands.

I rip away.

I strain with the effort, though essence, life force, weighs nothing. I don't stumble, but only because the cusith holds me in place.

I do what no Conduit should be able to do.

I snip Chains's threads. No. I shred them. Completely. Utterly.

I murder him without laying a hand on him, without a weapon. I hold Presh's future in the forefront of my mind, and I allow the universe to force me to do something I would never have thought myself capable of doing.

I end the very energy that I'm in this world to conduct, to feed, to fuel.

Chains totters on his feet — not knowing he's already dead. He locks eyes with me. His grasp on Presh loosens, and she tumbles to the ground before him. Next to where Kris lies.

The blackened threads of Chains's life, of his fate, of his destiny, jump back to me, elastic and snapping harshly. Those snipped threads twine around my forearms. They bite into my flesh, slicing into my bones.

It hurts.

Enough that I struggle not to scream, not to pass out.

Chains keels over, falling face first onto the pavement.

The threads attempting to etch into my skin and bones disintegrate.

Presh looks up at me. Holding herself over Kris and soaked in the blood of her friend, her crush, she gazes at me in utter terror. The red eases from her life force. That energy begins to settle into a multithreaded spiral around her again.

Rath and Rought finally achieve their human forms, rising naked to their feet behind me. Rath lunges past me to scoop Presh up in his arms. Rought goes to DeVille, hastily but carefully checking his neck and back. Then he lifts him gently, confirming that the young shifter is alive.

They both turn to gaze at me with wide eyes, awed more than terrified. Perhaps.

The cu-sith chuckles darkly — emitting an actual sound this time — and pure terror traces up my spine.

Then, pain still streaking through my forearms and radiating up my arms, shoulders, and neck to drill into my brain, I see, feel, nothing more.

FOURTEEN

I FIND MYSELF STARING AT A WOOD-PANELED coved ceiling. Realizing suddenly that I'm awake and in my childhood bedroom — with no memory of how I got here.

I can feel the shifters nearby without even reaching for them. I can feel Presh. But my room is empty when I finally turn my head to look. Daylight filters around the edges of the drawn curtains. Muta is curled alongside me, between me and the open door to the hall. I'm still wearing the clothing I left the house in last night, minus the boots and my now sure-to-be-ruined cashmere sweater.

Was it last night? I have no idea how much time has passed.

Have I died? Again?

I do feel ... hollow. But it's different than how I feel when the universe resets me.

It's ... wrong. Something has twisted inside me.

My forearms ache, though my skin is unblemished. I look toward the window and the sill covered in what I logically understand are collected memories — the jar of notes, the seashells, the carved wooden box and the broken bracelet. Though I still have no memory of collecting them. The odd hollowness that has settled in the bones of my hands and forearms is a sharper, more painful echo of the emptiness I felt when touching those items.

I've done something I shouldn't be able to do.

I tore the life force from another person.

I cut Chains's life short — literally snipped his threads — by tearing his fate, his destiny, away from him.

I ignored a *knowing*, allowing Presh to fall into the trap that Chains — and the dire mage, I assume — set for her. Another of their traps. It was clear to me that I was meant to protect Precious and DeVille and Kris. And instead, I paused and saved dozens of lives from the cu-sith.

It wasn't even five minutes. Not even five minutes off the path of the *knowing*.

And then ...

I sit up. I force myself upright.

My head swims.

Hunched, I gaze down at my unmarked forearms settled limply across my lap.

I am the Conduit for all the life force — all the fate and destiny that flows through the world — yet I snipped threads last night. I remember the nudge from the universe, yes. But I still chose to do it, with only the barest hope that it would stop Presh from imploding as her awry power manifested under extreme distress.

Had it truly been a personal choice?

I swing my legs off the bed, stand, and slowly cross to the walk-in closet, catching sight of myself in the full-length mirror before I can look away. I look the same, but with a little bit of the weight gained back from dying on the beach. And I can see the bruises on my upper arms from when Rath grabbed me.

So I definitely didn't die last night.

I strip off what I'm wearing and tug on the only other thing that's likely to fit me among my old clothing. A calf-length dark-purple silk skirt, though it might have been longer on me in my midteens. The elastic waist is snug when tugged down to my hipbones.

I find a hand-knit sweater carefully folded in tissue paper. The ribbed collar is a silvery white, and large-petaled flowers of the same color flow down from the collar across the chest, back and shoulders, stopping midway. The rest of the sweater is a gradient of blues. A deep blue, almost purple, starts as a backdrop to the flowers, transitioning to indigo, then to a slightly lighter blue. Then the gradient reverses, so that the bottom hem is edged in that deep purple-blue again.

The knit fabric feels like cashmere, but paired with something sturdier. Merino, maybe?

I have no idea why I'm standing in the closet of my childhood bedroom obsessing over a hand-knit sweater. Except it's a work of art and ... and ... I don't remember who gave it to me. Who knit it? Who thought me precious enough to let me wear it?

I tug the sweater on over another lacy camisole. It's perfectly slouchy. Though it's slightly cropped and boxy, it will keep me warm.

I go barefoot because I'm not planning on leaving the house. I need ... information. I need to know what I did last night, how it was even possible that I did it ... and why ...

Why didn't my aunt tell me such things were within her power as the Conduit? Why didn't she better prepare me? Explain the ramifications?

Except ... maybe she never ... maybe she never corrupted the power of the Conduit? Maybe she didn't know?

And there is no one else to ask. No other expert. Not among the living.

I need to get into the locked drawers and the sealed armoire in the turret office. I step away from the closet to do just that, padding barefoot toward the hall.

Muta hisses after me pissily from the bed, but I ignore him.

A golden-haired, golden-skinned shifter is sprawled across the hall opposite my door. He's found himself a pillow and thankfully some black sweatpants, but the rest of him is gloriously naked.

The sight actually stops me in my tracks. Stops my brain up.

Rought.

Is he guarding me?

There's a chaise in the corner of my room. My bed is big enough for three people, even those of his size, but maybe he didn't want to be in my space ... uninvited?

An uncluttered web of tattoos — all black ink — spills over his shoulders, his collarbone, and what I can see of his back ... feathers and claw marks and other things. But it's the tattoo that sits over his heart that draws all my attention.

I lean closer, close enough to feel the heat of him against my chilly toes. The ink etching over his heart is a rough rendering of an anatomical heart in which flowers and leaves spring forth from severed arteries and veins. It's harsh, but beautiful.

A word that I assume is a name because it's capitalized — a nickname, perhaps — is etched along the inside curve of the heart. 'Marrow.' It's a memorial tattoo? What kind of name is Marrow?

Then the possible meaning hits me — innermost or essential part or core.

I actually jerk away. A hot wash of shame floods through my chest and up my neck and face as I realize I'm standing in the hall ogling a man who lost his soul-bound mate.

Pressing my cold hands to my shame-hot face, I slip down the hall and peer into the next bedroom. Presh is curled under a small hill of blankets, but she looks peaceful. Her life force is once again a vibrant multitude of glowing entwined threads.

DeVille is in the next room, closest to the stairs. He's sprawled across the bed, quite literally, and snoring quietly. Healing patches are plastered to his chest, arms, and face. The one leg hanging out from under the bunched and crumpled bedding is fully wrapped and splinted. Because his beast hasn't manifested yet, he can't simply transform to help speed his healing. But just as a shifter, he'll heal quickly enough.

I'm pleased he's alive.

Even as I understand how truly I failed Kris.

With the way the knowing seemed ... ambivalent about me dragging her with me, it's doubly clear that the dire mage had already gotten hold of her. That sort of possession is tricky. It requires a massive amount of power, enough so that I presume an animal or human sacrifice was involved in the initial implanting. Then another sacrifice to power the takeover of Kris's mind and body.

I close my eyes for a moment, forcing myself to just breathe. Gently and steadily.

I've never felt this uneducated, this ignorant in my life.

Coda can help with the dire mage. She'll be easy to

track with a name — Bellamy — and the knowledge that she has ties to the Cataclysm MC.

I ignore the two other bedrooms, fairly certain that Doc Z and Cayley are sleeping within. The conversation with Doc can wait. I presume she's in the house to watch over DeVille, and maybe Cayley, Rought, and the others I can feel spread around the property.

My stomach growls. And it's just easier for now to let that pure need-based activity — feeding myself — overtake all other lingering and pending concerns.

I turn back to the stairs — then narrow my eyes at Muta. The death god bushmaster has slithered into the hall behind me and is now intently studying Rought's face, watching him sleep. From far too close.

I don't speak because I'm concerned about waking the shifter. I am not up for any sort of exchange of words, let alone the multiple full conversations or possible arguments that are no doubt about to be foisted on me. Instead, I reach along the thread that binds Muta and me — a bond of choice, the energy flowing both ways, initiated by Muta in the moments before my mother's death — and I give it a slight tug.

Ignoring me, he flicks his tongue at Rought's nose, smelling him. Then he rears back and eyes the shifter's neck and chest, as if actually considering curling up on him. I'm surprised. I can also imagine the wanton destruction that might occur should the shifter be suddenly woken by a massive snake looking to share body heat.

I tug the thread that binds me to Muta, then head down the stairs.

Muta slithers after me without further reticence, catching up quickly. Someone has helpfully laid logs in the fireplace in the open family room off the kitchen. I light the fire. Then I pull a large, low-lying velvet cushion out of the built-in cupboard beside the TV niche so Muta can curl up beside it.

I'm all the way into the kitchen, noting bananas in a bowl on the counter that I definitely didn't buy, when I realize I have no idea how I knew that velvet cushion even existed, let alone where to retrieve it from.

My already hollow stomach grows leaden.

I FLIP THE LAST BATCH OF OAT-BRAN BANANA breakfast muffins out of the tin onto the cooling rack, wishing I had some fresh blueberries. I have no idea where the eggs, milk, or butter I found in the fridge came from, but I've put them to good use this morning. And yes, apparently it is morning, and I've slept only a few hours.

People have invaded my house — though for some reason, I don't remotely mind. But they're all going to wake hungry. I've already eaten three muffins from the first two batches myself.

I also have scalloped potatoes in the warming oven already. And I'm capable of scrambling eggs. That's my cooking arsenal, though. When you live mostly in Vancouver, cooking isn't a required skill. There's literally a sushi place or an Indian diner or a Greek restaurant on every corner, each just as good as the next. So I do one kind of muffins, with or without blueberries. Anything to do with potatoes — because forget ambrosia, potatoes are the actual food of life. And scrambled eggs. Not boiled eggs, not fried, and certainly nothing resembling an omelet.

Oh, and ice cream.

Not content with a flickering fire and a velvet cushion, Muta is now lounging across the top of the stove, enjoying the heat radiating up from the oven. I quickly flip all the muffins upright on the cooling rack, singeing my fingers in the process — even as a quiet musical trill draws my attention to a small desk built into the dark-wood wall unit that runs from the kitchen eating area into the family room. A landline used to be plugged into the wall on that desk, but now it holds only my phone and an empty antique vase.

I'm not certain when I last saw my phone. Presumably, I left it in the truck, and someone plugged it in for me. The screen flashes with a text message, and for once, I don't immediately decide to ignore it. Because only Coda and Gigi can make my perpetually silenced phone trill or flash.

I cross to pick up the phone. Beyond the kitchen window, the remnants of a morning fog — natural, thankfully — has mostly dissipated under a partially cloudy sky, but it still clings lightly to the trunks of the few winter-bare trees nearest the house, including a massive, thick-limbed oak.

The text reads:

>*We're an hour out. We need somewhere to hook up the trailer, but unlike the technocrat, I'd appreciate an actual bedroom and a hot shower.*

Gigi. And if she's calling Coda 'technocrat,' I gather the trip has been tense.

I make sure the main oven is off, double-checking all the gas burners even though I didn't use any. Not only is Muta not to be trusted around appliances, but I'm still feeling hollow, especially in my head. Then I pull on a jacket and brave the misty morning to inspect the caretaker's suite.

I haven't set foot in there yet, so I'm not sure it's the

right place for Coda and Gigi. But outside the workshop-barn is definitely the best place to hook up a trailer. Because I have no doubt that any trailer Coda has bought to travel in, and to carry as much equipment as they have brought with them, isn't going to be a small tow-behind model.

I know the beach house is also an option, though I suspect it's a fair bit smaller than Mack's former suite. Also, I can already feel that it's currently occupied by another shifter. A shifter who I kicked off the property. But I don't feel up for a fight with Rath.

The cu-sith, or at least the man who transforms into a cu-sith, isn't anywhere within reach of my other senses. Reck's Authority agents in their huge SUV are parked again on the road, though, just beyond the property boundaries.

A quick glance into the garage reveals it filled with vehicles. My truck is back, along with DeVille's Mustang, which is definitely a work in progress. A motorcycle is strapped into the back bed of my truck, and two more bikes that have been seriously trashed, presumably during the battle with Chains and his berserkers, are propped next to the Mustang.

The battle with Chains, his berserkers, and a dire mage. Not that I really need to remind myself of the mage.

I slip through the door off the still-tidy workshop, passing Ingrid and Mack — and making a mental note to arrange their transportation to and from a crematorium. Then I flick on the lights to reveal the lower main living space of the caretaker's suite.

I have a vague memory that the loft contains two bedrooms and a full bathroom. The lower level has a small open kitchen, another bathroom, and the large living area I stand in now. Everything is tidy, almost sparsely so. A wool blanket is folded neatly over the back of the sectional couch where Presh napped.

I head up to the loft. But I don't manage more than a cursory look into the main bedroom and bathroom — because my attention is instantly ensnared by the gallery-sized photographs lining the wood-planked walls of the second bedroom.

Large black-and-white framed photos spread out from either side of the door, encircling the entire room. There must be twenty of them at a quick glance.

I remember Rought mentioning them. Telling me I might like them ...

The photo to my immediate right, next to the door, is a shot of a woman in a windswept, rain-soaked dress standing on the bluff. It takes me a moment to recognize my aunt. Not that she looks any younger or older. Just that I've never seen her so ... at peace. Her face is raised to the sky, arms seeming to float at her sides, feet bare on the rock.

Entranced, I move to the next photo. Every inch of the shot is filled with wildflowers — purple larkspurs? — that grow along the edge of the beach. Compared to the majesty of the first photograph, I feel physically let down as I gaze at it. Then I see him peering out from among the tall stems, practically hidden with his color and essence muted within the medium of black-and-white.

Muta. All narrow-eyed and suspicious.

I laugh, quietly but involuntarily. Then I eagerly step to my left again, in the hopes of seeing my mother within one of the other frames. It's difficult to capture one of the awry in a photo or video, but since the photographer managed to get a shot of my aunt and Muta, then ...

It isn't a picture of my mother.

No.

A young girl perches on the bough of an oak tree. The tree trunk and multiple branches fill the bulk of the photo, the child looks almost doll-like framed within.

I know it's an oak. And I know which tree it is. Because it's a photo of me.

Muta is twined around a narrower branch, resting his head on my shoulder. And I'm looking at something. Not the photographer. My gaze is tilted up, riveted upward. Am I looking up at my aunt's turret?

My arm is in a cast.

My gaze, my demeanor, is heavy with sadness.

I peer closer at the penciled note in the bottom corner. 'Zaya. May 1, 2003.'

This photo was taken only a month after I lost my mother. I heal like a regular human, but my aunt had access to healing mages. Yet my arm is still in a cast.

My heart hurts.

I move to the next picture and then the next, all just landscapes. But my mind is still caught back with the first three photos, so I barely see them.

Then I see another of me. I'm barely older than the first photo, but the cast is gone. I've got my back to the photographer, and I'm perched on a weathered log, the ocean and two other blurred figures in the deep background, farther out on the beach. But a boy around my age sits next to me, close enough to touch. He's looking at me, grinning, and I'm smiling back though it's a restrained expression. We're in summer clothing.

I can practically feel the warm sand under my feet. The photo is black-and-white and blurred around the edges, but I know the boy's hair goes golden in the sun, and his already tan skin deepens in color as well.

I move to the next picture and the next, barely glancing

at them once I see they don't show what I'm looking for. Not acknowledging what that is even as I search for it.

Because I know the boy in the picture. Even in profile, he looks a little like DeVille. But only because DeVille looks like a younger version of him.

I stop at another image of me on the beach, but this time, a group of us are roasting marshmallows at a small campfire. I'm a couple of years older — eleven or twelve — and I'm leaning against the boy's shoulder and laughing. Muta is twined around both of our ankles in the sand. A slightly older, darker-haired teen with broad shoulders is seated to my other side, grinning quietly and directly at the photographer.

I move to the next photo, then the next. The group is older in this shot. We're in our midteens now and seemingly caught unaware by the photographer. I'm up to my ankles in a long run of the surf, wearing a short-sleeved wetsuit with my hair slick wet. My fingers are tangled with the teen, the golden-haired boy who is the same age as me. My left hand holds his right. We're carrying bodyboards under our other arms. The top of his wetsuit is unzipped, hanging down around his waist and exposing his long, slim back. No tattoos.

The broad-shouldered teen — now even taller and wider — wears his wetsuit unzipped but folded down more deliberately. As if the freezing open ocean is too warm for him, for any of them, to wear their suits zipped up. He's on my other side, only a couple of steps away, carrying a surfboard and gazing over at me. I'm looking ahead and slightly to the left, mostly in profile.

Another figure stands ahead of us, much deeper into the surf already. He has unruly dark hair, a wicked smirk of anticipation, and a surfboard poised to catch the next wave.

I don't look at any other photos closely. Just enough to glance at the dates in the corners and to understand that they're arranged in chronological order. There are wildlife shots and a picture of the main house, and a few others of my aunt and her chosen.

A couple of pictures away from the opposite side of the door to the hall, I find what I'm searching for even though I didn't really know it — another group photo. A picture we definitely didn't pose for.

Rendered in shades of gray, the sky is dark, speckled with stars. Firelight plays across all the skin on display. I'm wearing a modest bikini, and my hair is damp. The three males, ranging from my age — which I know without looking at the date noted at the corner of the photo is seventeen — to a few years older.

Though they're more than thirteen years older now, I know each of the three in the photo with me. Without question.

I'm leaning back against the bare chest of the teen closest to me in age. He's got his fingers tangled in my hair, hand resting at the back of my neck. But my legs are spread across the lap of the teen with the almost ridiculously broad shoulders, and it's him I have my eyes narrowed on. Playfully, I think. As if he's just said something funny and the others are laughing, but I'm pretending to be mad.

The third teen, possibly in his early twenties, is the one I've only seen in the background of the other photos I've paused to study. He's set slightly to the side, not cuddled up with me like the other two. But I've stretched my foot out to him, resting it on his upper thigh, and he's covered it with his hand.

I'm not feeling hollow now.

I'm feeling frozen in time and space. But also like if I

take another breath, I'll start trembling and won't ever be able to stop.

I force myself to look away from the last photo, from the people I know now as adults. The three men who my memory tells me I first met only days ago. I look for their names, and to confirm the date, in the penciled note in the bottom right corner.

The caption simply reads 'Zaya and her boys. 2011.'

Zaya and her boys.

Zaya and *her* boys.

My gaze catches on the teen who I know to be Rought. The firelight plays on his chest just enough for me to see the outline of a tattoo over his heart. It's the only one he has.

I glance at Rath in the middle of the shot. He has more tats, mostly on his forearms, but the one near the center of his chest looks similar to Rought's heart tattoo.

I'm even more lightheaded as I try to focus on Reck. He has more tattoos across his arms and upper chest. But he's partially in shadow, and I ... I can't be sure, but I think he has the anatomical floral heart tattoo as well.

I press my hand against my own chest, fingers splayed over the same spot above my heart.

Behind me, he steps into the room, long strides consuming the space between us until he pauses a few steps away, just outside my peripheral vision.

Zaya and her boys.

Zaya and *her* boys.

I recognize the girl, the young woman, in the picture as me. But I haven't lived that life ... that life filled with laughter and ... love.

Emotion clogs my throat.

I don't know what's going on.

But I don't feel hollow anymore.

I feel ... too much ... I'm too much.

Too much energy trapped ... trapped in a mostly mortal body.

No one loves me like these three boys, these three young men, loved me in these pictures.

"Zaya?" Rought asks in a soft, gentle whisper. He doesn't reach out to me.

I don't have to look back at him to know that no threads bind us.

We don't share a bond.

We don't share the friendship, the love, that is so clearly captured in these photographs.

I reach out and touch the edge of the picture frame. And for a stifling moment, pure rage streaks through me.

I want to yank the picture off the wall.

I want to smash it all over the floor.

I want to reach through the shards of broken glass and tear the photo asunder with bloodied fingers.

Because not only is it not a photo of my life, not my past — it won't be my future either.

Because the Conduit doesn't have a future filled with love and family.

The rage leaves me so suddenly that I sway, exhausted all at once. I drop my hand from the picture frame, my fingertips from the caption.

"Did I get a tattoo as well?" I ask.

Rought exhales heavily. "Yes. All four of us. About a week before ... this ... I think. At the time, I didn't know Mack ..." I feel more than see him glance around at the gallery's worth of photos.

"You didn't know Mack was taking sneaky pictures?"

"No."

I turn to him, numb but no longer hollow. I'm filled with grief. I'm filled with loss. And hopelessness.

Rought has pulled on a plain black T-shirt over his black sweatpants. He still looks as though he could sleep for another twelve hours. His hair is tousled, and a thick ring of gold edges his blue-green eyes. His gryphon is present, watching.

"I have no tattoo."

Rought slowly reaches toward me — his right hand, palm up. An almost-faded scar — teeth marks — mars the fleshy pad under his thumb. "No mating bite either."

I raise my left hand. My skin is unmarred. But somehow ... somehow I know it was my left thumb pad that he bit. "So that when we held hands ..." I trail off because I just can't continue.

"Yes," he says simply.

"We know each other."

"Yes."

"We loved each other."

"Yes."

"But ... I ... I can't remember any of that!" I stumble over the words, but I'm shouting at the end.

Rought's tone stays even, calm. "I know."

"How? How?!"

"I know because you never would have left us otherwise."

My heart stops for one terrible moment, lungs constricting breathlessly, as visceral pain shoots through my chest. I want to sob, to scream, in agreement with that utter truth.

He's right.

He's right. I never could have left him, left them ... I ...

But I can't breathe. I can't find my voice.

I never would have left ...

Rought still has his hand out to me, but I can't close the distance to him.

I never would have left voluntarily. I know that even when I know nothing else.

I know that to be true.

"That doesn't explain ..." I gasp, my mind on overload. My chest aches. "Who could have done this to me? ... I'm ... I'm ... I should be immune to any essence manipulation. I should have been immune even then, even at seventeen!"

I press my hands to my face, and for yet another terrible moment, I think I might be going insane. "What if ... am I me? What if I'm not her?!"

"You are."

"How do you know!?" I cry.

Rought reaches for me. And as gently as he can while I'm fighting him, he pulls my hands away from my face. "I know you, Zaya. You are part of me, part of my soul. My Marrow."

And I know it's true.

I'm his fucking soul-bonded mate, tattooed across his heart, my teeth marks on his flesh.

And I remember nothing.

Nothing of that love, of that connection, of that life.

"No threads connect us," I murmur.

Except I'm not sure who I'm speaking to.

Possibly the universe.

Because what else could take so much from me but the universe itself?

ACKNOWLEDGMENTS

With thanks to:
<u>My story & line editor</u>
Scott Fitzgerald Gray

<u>My proofreader</u>
Pauline Nolet

<u>My beta readers</u>
Anteia Consorto, Terry Daigle, and Gael Fleming.

<u>For their continual encouragement, feedback, & general advice</u>
SFWA (esp. the Discord crew)
FAROFEB (esp. the Discord crew)
Hailey Edwards
Carrie Ann Ryan

<u>For 'buying MCD a hot chocolate' and supporting the serialization of the first draft</u>
Edie Kidd
Elizabeth Gigliotti
Gail Barker
Jennifer Fraser
Jennifer Hoh
Jennifer Scully
Kathleen Wilkinson

Kelly Sarmiento
Margaret Murray
Margo Knight
Mary Gillis
Melinda Harvey
Melinda Johnson
Nina Straatmann
Patricia Ernst
Rebecca Suter
Rosemary Roe
Sharnee Chalmers
Sherri Anderson
Silvia Urizar
Susan Sander

And a very special thank you to all my lovely readers who supported the Tenth Anniversary Dowser Series Kickstarter (in Jan 2023)! Including:
Tasmin Baker — for Tasmin
Jordon Charles — for Zaya's boys
Pamela Coleman — for Zephyr (aka Doc Z)
Elizabeth Dicken — for Kris
Melinda Harvey — for Cayley
Kim Larson — for Harlee
Heather Marsh — for DeVille

ABOUT THE AUTHOR

Meghan Ciana Doidge is an award-winning writer based out of Vancouver, British Columbia, Canada. She has a penchant for bloody love stories, superheroes, and the supernatural. She also has a thing for chocolate, potatoes, and cashmere.

For recipes, giveaways, news, and glimpses of upcoming stories, please connect with Meghan via:
www.madebymeghan.ca
info@madebymeghan.ca

facebook.com/MeghanCianaDoidge
instagram.com/meghancianadoidge
tiktok.com/@meghancianadoidge

ALSO BY MEGHAN CIANA DOIDGE

<u>Novels</u>

After the Virus

Spirit Binder

Time Walker

Cupcakes, Trinkets, and Other Deadly Magic (Dowser 1)

Trinkets, Treasures, and Other Bloody Magic (Dowser 2)

Treasures, Demons, and Other Black Magic (Dowser 3)

I See Me (Oracle 1)

Shadows, Maps, and Other Ancient Magic (Dowser 4)

Maps, Artifacts, and Other Arcane Magic (Dowser 5)

I See You (Oracle 2)

Artifacts, Dragons, and Other Lethal Magic (Dowser 6)

I See Us (Oracle 3)

Catching Echoes (Reconstructionist 1)

Tangled Echoes (Reconstructionist 2)

Unleashing Echoes (Reconstructionist 3)

Champagne, Misfits, and Other Shady Magic (Dowser 7)

Misfits, Gemstones, and Other Shattered Magic (Dowser 8)

Gemstones, Elves, and Other Insidious Magic (Dowser 9)

Demons and DNA (Amplifier 1)

Bonds and Broken Dreams (Amplifier 2)

Mystics and Mental Blocks (Amplifier 3)

Idols and Enemies (Amplifier 4)

Instincts and Impostors (Amplifier 5)

Endings and Empathy (Amplifier 6)

Misplaced Souls (Misfits 1)

Awakening Infinity (Archivist 0)

Invoking Infinity (Archivist 1)

Compelling Infinity (Archivist 2)

Awry (Conduit 1)

Grand Romantic Delusions & the Madness of Mirth (Part 1 & 2)

<u>Novellas/Shorts</u>

Love Lies Bleeding

The Graveyard Kiss (Reconstructionist 0.5)

Dawn Bytes (Reconstructionist 1.5)

An Uncut Key (Reconstructionist 2.5)

Graveyards, Visions, and Other Things that Byte (Dowser 8.5)

The Amplifier Protocol (Amplifier 0)

Close to Home (Amplifier 0.5)

The Music Box (Amplifier 4.5)

Moments of the Adept Universe 1

Misson Recon: Bee (Amplifier 5.5)

Soulmates, Doorways, and Other Unruly Magic (Dowser 9.5)

www.ingramcontent.com/pod-product-compliance
Lightning Source LLC
Chambersburg PA
CBHW070305310726
48976CB00005B/1578